The Shenandoah Road

A Novel of the Great Awakening

LYNNE BASHAM TAGAWA

THE SHENANDOAH ROAD

A NOVEL OF THE GREAT AWAKENING

LYNNE BASHAM TAGAWA

Blue Rock Press

To my father

Robert Russell Basham

descendant of an Edinburgh cabinetmaker

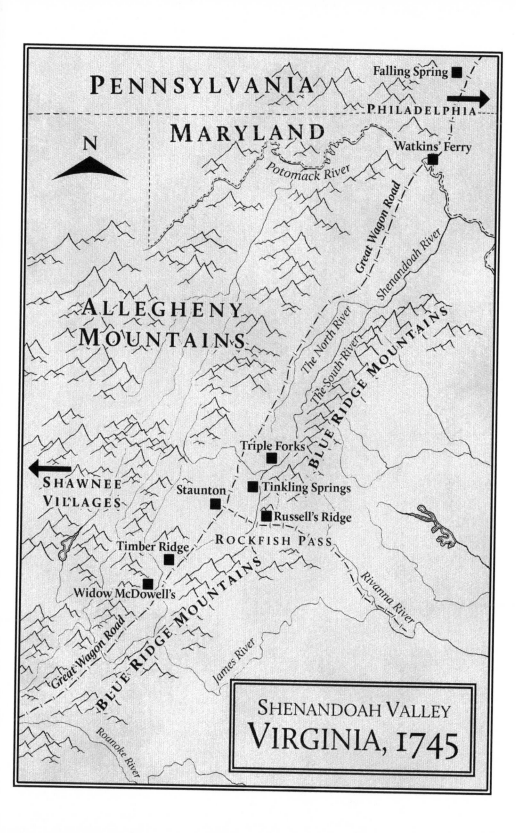

PENNSYLVANIA

Falling Spring ■

PHILADELPHIA →

MARYLAND

N

Watkins' Ferry ■

Potomack River

Great Wagon Road

Shenandoah River

ALLEGHENY
MOUNTAINS

The North River

The South River

BLUE RIDGE MOUNTAINS

Triple Forks ■

SHAWNEE
VIL'LAGES ←

Staunton ■

Tinkling Springs ■

Russell's Ridge ■

ROCKFISH PASS

Rivanna River

Timber Ridge ■

BLUE RIDGE MOUNTAINS

Widow McDowell's ■

Great Wagon Road

James River

Roanoke River

SHENANDOAH VALLEY
VIRGINIA, 1745

1

The Lord's my shepherd, I'll not want;
He makes me down to lie
In pastures green; He leadeth me
The quiet waters by.

—Psalm 23:1, *The Scottish Psalter*, 1650

May 1744

John Russell knelt on the grass growing over the grave. The small hickory cross had survived the winter. And so had her name.

His wife's name.

Janet Russell (1719-1742)

He had spent hours on the little cross, finding the best wood, hand carving it, engraving it, and rubbing linseed oil into it again and again.

Still, it would not endure the elements forever. Wood never did.

But her soul was safe with God, and though he had grieved long and hard, his peace was real, too. The peace that went beyond all understanding.

He stood.

"She was a good wife," Sarah murmured behind him. "And she willna mind you marrying again."

"I know." John turned to look at his sister. She meant well, though words couldn't lessen the ache. Still, death was a constant in the wilderness. Fever, accident, Indians. He had thought them relatively safe from Indian attack in this place, but he had been wrong.

He corralled his thoughts. God was in control of all things and would bring good out of evil. The truths he found in his worn Bible had kept him sane in the dark places.

John couldn't help a wry smile. His sister was right. His daughter did need a mother.

"Susanna will be well looked after with us," his sister said. "Do not look at me like that. I will teach her the Catechism."

"I ken that all the Bashams are good Presbyterians, aye." Sarah could be so serious. He would miss her. Most of the Basham family lived well to the east of the Blue Ridge, and after the deadly skirmish with the Indians, his brother-in-law James Basham had lost his taste for the rich soil of the Shenandoah Valley. Their wagons were packed.

"Have ye written Da? Does he ken ye're coming?"

"Aye, a month past." He frowned. "He's no' a matchmaker, now, is he?" Not that he minded all that much—he didn't know how to look for a new wife and had not the heart for it.

Sarah's features relaxed, and a merry glint shone in her eyes. "Ye ken how he is. He will have something to say. And Philadelphia's a big place, with young ladies arriving from Ulster every day, if what I hear is true." Her expression changed, and she reached into a pocket. "Here, Johnny. For a pony."

A wisp of Sarah's auburn hair escaped its braid in the gentle spring breeze as she handed him a small leather pouch.

He hefted it. Heavy. Loosening the drawstring, he slid the contents into his palm. Gold Dutch ducats winked up at him, nestled among silver Spanish dollars.

He blinked. "Sarah." Money was scarce in the backcountry. "A pony?"

His sister smiled and cocked her head. "Aye, here's what James is asking. Buy an Irish Connemara mare, bred, and he wants the get. Filly or colt."

"I see. That makes better sense. Not a hunter or quarter mile horse?"

"No, he would look to Williamsburg or Richmond for those. But he trusts you to be a good judge of a sturdy pony. And Susanna can ride it eventually."

She turned and looked over the landscape, bright with the green of new leaves, the creek peeking through birch and tulipwood trees beyond the tiny cemetery. Even the rough-hewn logs of the meeting-house failed to interrupt the gentle beauty of the valley.

Was she trying to memorize it?

"I will miss this place," Sarah said finally. Turning back to face him, she studied his face. "Send word when you return and get settled. You'll see your daughter again soon."

Then she departed, striding quickly down the slope to the path that wound its way along the creek. Soon her indigo skirts merged with the foliage and she was gone from sight. Gone to join her husband and his servants.

And his four-year-old daughter was going with them.

Until he could find a wife.

JOHN DIRECTED his mare through a stand of oak and hickory, his cousin's wagon rattling behind him. His sister and her family had left a week ago, and the swollen Shenandoah had begun to subside. A ferry crossed the larger Potomac, but the current could get treacherous in the spring. No sense inviting trouble.

The McClures' place appeared through the foliage, the pearly light of dawn casting uncertain shadows in the open space before the cabin.

"Ho, there you are, John." Samuel McClure stood in front of his cabin, rubbing his grizzled jaw.

"McClure." John dismounted from his prized Rhode Island pacer. "What do you have for me?"

Tying his horse's reins to a nearby sapling, he turned his attention to the wagon. The mules snuffed as his cousin Roy circled them to the front of the large, two-room structure that not only housed the McClures but also served as general store for the families nearby.

"The Cunninghams heard you were taking a wagon north. They brought a keg of whiskey from their still for you to sell. I have four from mine."

"Going to Philadelphia?" Maggie McClure's solid form burst from the cabin. "Needles! I need needles—and fennel, ye mind it?"

"Fennel. No ribbon or lace?"

She shook her head. "Did Samuel tell ye we needed wool?"

"Aye, Mistress, fifty pounds, dyed and carded." John smiled at the midwife. Few women could face the wilderness with such resilience of spirit. Maggie was one such woman.

Janet, too.

His smile faded. Janet had been a treasure among women.

John climbed into the wagon bed and loaded McClure's whiskey alongside his goods and Roy's leatherwork. He laid the fruits of his hunting and trapping, including a bearskin, on top of the barrels and secured everything under oilcloth. He'd sell the goods in Philadelphia and shop for supplies. And he hoped to visit Ben Franklin's print shop—the man always stocked sermons as well as newspapers and books.

Finally, they were ready. Roy clucked to the mules, which swung their long ears for a moment, as if considering all options, before shifting their weight against the harness. The wagon creaked, and they were on their way.

～

JOHN STUDIED the trail over his horse's chestnut neck. For the first time in six years the familiar valley road seemed drab and lonely.

A gentle breeze cooled the back of his neck. Which meant that they'd catch no doe unaware just ahead, even if that were possible, with the ruckus the mules and wagon were making behind him. He shook his head to stay alert. There was still danger—from man.

Seeing nothing, he turned his mount and circled back behind the wagon, scanning the trees. It would be impossible to prevent a well-aimed Indian arrow or musket ball from harming them, but it was foolish to plod ahead blindly. Especially after the skirmish just over a year ago, which was more the result of misunderstood intentions than anything.

John fingered the stock of his musket lying across his lap, loaded but not primed. Roy sat on the wagon seat ahead, hair ruffled by the breeze. His cousin appeared relaxed, the mules' reins held loosely in his hand. But the dark stock of Roy's Brown Bess rested ready on his left forearm, and his gunpowder horn nestled under his right arm, strapped to his side, like his own. Priming their firearms would require mere seconds.

Bandits were his main concern, though few would be found here. His sister's gold ducats made themselves known now and again as he shifted in the saddle; he'd sewn them into the seam of his buckskin breeches for safety. The silver, still in the leather bag, kept company with his rock collection safe inside his linen shirt. Rocks of all shapes and colors, pleasing to the eye. Who would know what the stones were? A goldsmith?

A good beaver pelt yielded about eight shillings, but his entire winter's hunting and trapping would only pay for supplies and taxes. He had walnut burl in the wagon, always a good find, but if he wanted one of Jake Deckard's long rifles he'd need more funds. It was too much to hope that one of the stones would be worth something. Maybe next year he'd have enough.

If he'd had a Deckard rifle that day... If only.

Ahead, trees crowded the track, their slender branches reaching overhead, while sumac and rhododendron swelled underneath, spilling into the path. John slowed his nimble mare, watching her ears. She'd catch the acrid odor of bear or the faint musk of a painter before he'd know of their presence. All he could smell was the honey-suckle vine wound around the pin oak to his left. And a hint of pennyroyal from the goose grease salve on his neck.

No, nothing alarmed the horse, and no wonder. Bears tended to avoid people, and the great cats only hunted at twilight. He urged her forward, glancing behind. The wagon was doing well, the trail having widened over the years since they'd settled here.

Unwelcome thoughts invaded his mind. He was going to Phil-adelphia for a wife, but could he love another? It certainly did not seem possible. Janet's sunny smile had begun to fade from memory, and the knife-edged stab of grief was lessening, but she would never be replaced. Only Susanna's need of a mother drove him.

Duty was the foundation of all good choices, his father had said once. John remembered laboring over the foundation of his cabin. Some settlers used logs. He'd chosen stone for the base, digging into the ground, laying stone and gravel, mixing a crude mortar from a slurry of clay and ground limestone. His neighbors had then raised the logs he'd accumulated on top of the base.

Aye, stone was a good foundation. As was duty—and duty meant faithfulness. He purposed to be faithful and honorable. He hoped the young lady in question would understand he was a man only partially healed of his wounds.

The trees thinned. He slowed his horse until he rode beside his cousin's seat on the wagon. Nearby, to their right, the Shenandoah River sparkled in the sun.

Roy caught his glance. "Ye expect trouble from the Indians?"

"No." They both knew Governor Gooch of Virginia had paid the Iroquois a hundred pounds immediately after the recent conflict. In return the Indians had relinquished their rights to hunt along the Shenandoah, which lay on the fringes of their territory anyway.

Such an agreement would help to keep them away from the new settlers, minimizing the chances of further skirmishes. Some had misnamed this latest a "massacre." Foolishness on the part of the militia, in John's opinion, but then, he knew he was biased. He had struggled so long to keep his heart from bitterness that verses on forgiveness would come to mind every time he thought about that dark day. No, it didn't matter what the clash was called.

"Not from the Indians," John said. "McClure says there is a final treaty in the making. With gold to secure it."

"Glad to hear that." Roy smiled. "I'd like to bring a wee wifie down here too."

John raised an eyebrow. "I dinna suppose any place is totally safe. And I'm not just speaking of Indians, mind ye."

"There's plenty of rabble in all colors," his cousin agreed. "Especially in the Cumberland."

"Aye, I dinna want to stop there. Not at Magraw's place. Not with all this whiskey."

Roy nodded in agreement. "We can camp in the woods."

"We'll trust in God—"

"—and keep our powder dry."

Their grandfather's favorite saying seemed especially appropriate out here.

2

_____

O blessed man, that in th'advice
Of wicked doeth not walk;
Nor stand in sinners way, nor sit
In chayre of scornful folk

—Psalme I, *Bay Psalme Book*, 1640

June 1744

*A*bigail Williams bent over the large leather-bound volume. Absently, she pressed her spectacles more firmly onto her nose.

Milk thistle. Also known as Mary Thistle or Sow Thistle. That was a new one. She reached for a humbler volume, her own sketchbook, a bit dog-eared in places, full of the discoveries she'd made over the years.

Abigail flipped through the first pages containing simple drawings of the plants found around Philadelphia. Midway, specimens she'd seen only in books graced the pages, their drawings augmented by alternate names, medicinal value, and even the new Latin name when she could find it.

Scooting closer to the glass-paned window of their "keeping room," as Mother insisted on calling it, Abigail grabbed her charcoal. She copied the image of the plant from the borrowed volume with care, not wanting to smudge the pages. Generous with his books, Mr. Logan viewed his personal collection as a lending library; she wanted to honor that trust. They were expensive, unlike her ragtag collection of soiled or water-spotted castoffs sea captains sometimes sold to her father for a pittance.

Only rarely did books on botany or herbals come her way. Several weeks ago, Father had presented her with a novel. *Robinson Crusoe.* She'd scooted the stained book underneath her knitting. Mother would not approve of something frivolous.

Now that she was almost three and twenty, she desired something on midwifery, if there were such a thing. Such a book would be practical if she married. She bit her lip as she finished the sketch. Her sister Hannah had married at two and twenty, and her sister Mary ...

Mary. She frowned, knowing she would not make the mistake her oldest sister had.

Movement caught her eye.

"Papa!" In her surprise, Abigail had slipped. Mother insisted she call him "Father." She glanced toward the kitchen. No, Mother hadn't heard.

His old-fashioned bottle-green coat swinging almost to his knees, her father must have come from the ship's chandlery. He was still neatly attired for business.

"Abigail." He greeted her with the smile fathers reserved for daughters, eyes twinkling. Then his lined face slipped into a new expression. One she could not read.

"Father? You are come home early. 'Tis only the nooning."

He stepped to the faded settee near the hearth and sat gingerly.

Was something wrong? Abigail adjusted her skirts.

"I'll be returning to the shop presently." His gaze flickered around the room. "We will have company tonight for supper."

She blinked. "Anyone special?" Father knew many people. Maybe it was someone important.

"You know Mr. Russell." Finally his eyes met hers.

"Your bookkeeper." He had visited before. She remembered a lively smile and spectacles like her own.

"His son is in town." He cleared his throat and studied his hands. "He needs a wife." He explained that the man was a widower with a young daughter.

Abigail looked at the floor. A widower? She didn't know what to say or think. She hadn't had many suitors. Only Josiah Mather had taken an interest in her, and that had not lasted long. He'd made fun of her botany book.

"Just meet him."

She nodded and forced a smile.

Her father headed for the door, and the smile left her face.

PHILADELPHIA STANK.

John was accustomed to the stench permeating the area near the docks: the oily miasma of the waterfront, mixed with the bit of salt from the brackish river water; the middle note of horse manure everywhere; the occasional addition of metallic odors from the butchers' lane; and the rank, eye-watering blast of sewage that made trips to Dock Street well nigh unbearable.

But catching a whiff of the odious mixture this far from the docks surprised him. He'd paid the ferryman a tuppence for seeing him and his horse across the Schuylkill, and he hadn't made it very far when a stray bit of breeze brought the familiar smell to his nose. Philadelphia was growing.

To his left, a new home was rising from a pile of lumber and brick. He nudged Perseverance forward, and soon the chestnut mare was trotting down Walnut Street, the mud underfoot making popping sounds as it sucked on her hooves.

"Good girl, Percy. Long journey, this."

Yesterday he'd received a good price for the whiskey and pelts. After all the transactions were finished, his cousin Roy had departed for New Londonderry and his family's farm not far to the south.

Just west of the Schuylkill River lay the little plot of land his father had purchased when they'd come from Ireland. The fertile soil near the river brought forth plentifully, enough for his father, his brother and his wife, and the indentured servants. He remembered walking behind the plow in his youth, hauling water and chopping wood, familiar tasks still, but his father had always made him study first.

"Time enough for labor," he'd say. "Your mind must be prepared. And your soul."

John had walked from the farm into town many times as a lad, but Philadelphia had seemed far away then.

Now the town sat nearly at their doorstep. Limestone and lime for mortar poured out of the Fitzwaters' quarry nearby, and buildings sprouted up all over William Penn's grid of streets. And land prices were going up, too, his father had commented, just last evening. But that wasn't all they'd talked about.

John rolled his shoulders underneath his coat. It didn't fit anymore; he'd grown an inch or two since he'd acquired it at seventeen, and he was heavier, too. But the twelve-year-old coat was all he had, and buckskin gear was not appropriate for supper at the chandler's home, which was where he was headed after his errands. He'd never thought of his father as a matchmaker before. But he'd agreed. If his father liked the lass, well ... he could at least eat supper with the family.

He placed a finger underneath his stock. Simple in style, it had still taken him a quarter-hour to tie it just right, standing in front of Da's mirror. It wasn't really tight, but still he felt like choking.

As he approached the shops, the smell grew more intense. He

directed his mare to Front Street and the goldsmith, having heard Mr. Dutens dealt with precious stones. Maybe the man could identify them as well.

John spotted the goldsmith's sign and tied up his horse in front of the unassuming shop. Entering, he addressed the wiry man behind the counter.

"Mr. Dutens?"

"Oh no, I'm Miller, the journeyman. What can I do for you?"

"I have some rocks."

The man's eyebrows shot up. "Rocks?"

John opened the pouch and spilled out the little stones. Many were smooth, rounded by the water in the streambeds where he'd found them. A few were not. One, in particular, a clear sky blue, possessed the crystalline structure of an obelisk.

"Ahhh." He smiled. "Just let me pull out a few tools."

Soon the journeyman was inspecting the stones one by one.

He held up the blue prism. "This is quartz. No value at all. But the color is unusual. Very nice specimen." He squinted at it. "In fact, you could make it into a simple pendant."

"Hmph." Well, he was here for a wife. Maybe he would. "It would have to be a strong chain. Sturdy enough for everyday."

The journeyman nodded. "Can do."

"What have we here?" A gravelly voice cut through the air.

John hadn't noticed the older man emerge from the back room. Wearing a powdered wig and tailored coat, he appeared to be the proprietor.

"Sir, I'm John Russell. I've brought my rock collection from the mountains."

Mr. Dutens nodded and fished a file from the tools on the counter. John winced as the man attacked each stone with it. The journeyman peered over the goldsmith's shoulder, clearly interested.

"Fear not, valuable stones will not be injured by steel. And there is little chance they are worth anything. I've seen garnet a few times, but ..." His voice trailed off as his fingers sorted the stones into groups.

Then the wigged man pulled out a little drawer and selected a few more items. Soon, a chunk of purple rock had his full attention; he examined it under a jeweler's eyepiece, quiet for a long moment.

"Where did you say you found this?"

"Rockfish Gap, near my home in the Shenandoah Valley." Since the goldsmith looked puzzled, he added, "In the mountains of Virginia."

Mr. Dutens snorted. "Well. 'Tis amethyst. Nice size and color. What do you want to do? 'Tis uncut, and I do not cut gemstones. No one in Philadelphia does."

"Might I sell it?" John frowned. How valuable was amethyst?

"I can take it down to the exchange for you. Get a good price, for a commission."

"Thank ye kindly."

Soon the details were arranged. John pushed open the door, his eyes adjusting to the late afternoon sunlight. Time to meet his father at the chandlery.

ABIGAIL STARED at the man in the doorway.

Blue eyes. Tall—taller than her father. Standing next to the familiar bookkeeper, he looked at her for a long moment, face expressionless, then made a slight movement, as if adjusting his shoulders under his blue coat.

The coat was too short.

She froze, suddenly conscious of the ordinary linsey skirt she was wearing, covered with a tired apron. She hadn't thought to change. She looked down at the dish in her hands and moved off to help her mother and Gretchen in the kitchen. Behind her, she could hear the murmur of men's voices. One was her father's. Then she heard the bookkeeper's friendly voice, with its strange rolling r's. Then, briefly, another man's.

Abigail looked about the steamy kitchen, searching for something to do.

Her mother eyed her curiously. "Gretchen will help me. You go out and put on the tablecloth, then have a seat."

Out of long habit, she obeyed her mother, carrying the cloth into the keeping room, where a long board table nestled against one wall. Stomach tight with tension, she gave great attention to the texture of the rather ordinary weave of the unbleached linen tablecloth as she spread it out over the oak surface. Abigail took a long time smoothing it over the length of the table, listening to the men as they lingered near the doorway. They would come into the room at any moment.

Suddenly the men seemed to fill the space, her father directing the others to the settee near the hearth. She sidled toward the window and perched on her stool in the corner, then reached up to her coif, making sure it was secure, fully covering her hair.

"My daughter Abigail." Her father made the introductions. "Mr. John Russell."

The man stood and nodded his head. "I'm verra pleased to meet ye." He resumed his seat.

Her mouth went dry. "I am pleased to meet you as well," she managed.

The younger Russell's hair was dark and pulled back into a neat tail; neither he nor his father wore a wig, unlike her father, who had retained his for the evening. She rubbed the hem of her apron between her fingers, not knowing what to do with her hands.

"My son arrived in town several days past." The bookkeeper's blue eyes sparkled behind his spectacles.

Unlike the older men, John did not wear a waistcoat, but his linen shirt glowed white. A fine weave, no doubt. Several inches of linen protruded past his too-short coat sleeves, ending at large, well-made wrists the color of honey oak.

Then a strange bulge near his knee caught her attention.

"That's my skinning knife."

Mortified that he'd followed her gaze, she watched as he pulled it out of his stocking and held it up.

"Verra useful." The young man's mouth twitched.

"It's a Scottish knife." The elder Mr. Russell smiled. "Highlanders hide it in their sleeves as a secret weapon."

Abigail returned the smile. According to her father, his book-keeper was a former schoolteacher.

"Highlanders?" she asked.

"Aye. Scots in the north of Scotland are called Highlanders because much of their land is hilly and rough."

"What are you?" she asked, fascinated. "Irish?" Her father had mentioned a large number of ships coming from Ireland.

Just then Gretchen bustled in with several platters balanced on her generous forearms. "Boiled ham and my very own schnitzels."

JOHN SETTLED on the bench and surveyed the table. Ordinary but abundant savory-smelling food spilled over the sides of pewter platters. His stomach growled in anticipation.

Silver cutlery gleamed on the tablecloth, the only sign of Mr. Williams's prosperity. Da had said they were from Boston, and certainly their speech sounded strange, as though they spoke through their noses. The stone house was a sturdy Quaker design, common to Philadelphia; their furnishings reflected simple but sturdy craftsmanship. Their faded padded settee, the seat of honor, seemed old but clean. Everything was clean, even the floors. Was this how all New Englanders lived?

He lifted his eyes. Abigail sat across from him, suggestions of blond hair peeking out around her forehead from under her head-gear. His sister would never wear such a tightly fitted cap. Only a mobcap or straw hat, and sometimes nothing at all.

The spectacles were a surprise. Behind them, keen blue eyes focused on his father, who had begun to answer her question.

"Do ye ken why your ancestors made the trip to the New World?"

John smiled around his bite of boiled ham. His father loved to teach.

"Oh, yes. They were harried for their faith in England."

"Our forefathers were Presbyterians, very like to your Puritan ancestors, living in the Lowlands of Scotland. They were harried, as you say. Sometimes killed."

Chewing on the tough meat, John glanced at the girl again. She was comely enough. Not overly thin, like many of the newest immigrants. His innards warmed unexpectedly.

"So you came here?" she asked.

"A few, over the years. Most went to Ulster, a sparsely inhabited region in the north of Ireland. Ye ken, the king thought it would be better for everyone if he could get rid of religious troublemakers that way."

Mr. Williams cleared his throat. "He shipped the Quakers here for that very reason."

John's father nodded. "The king did well by the Quakers. They have been allowed to govern their own affairs here. Ulster isna quite the same."

Still hungry after forcing down the ham, John speared a slab of breaded meat he supposed was the schnitzel. German food was generally good—and German butter. Their housekeeper obviously spent time in the kitchen. Glancing up, he noticed the merchant's wife's gaze upon him. Might as well be a colt paraded at auction. Listening with half an ear to his father explain the political upheavals in Ireland over the past century, he took a bite of the tender, warm meat.

"My father fought at the siege of Londonderry as a lad. And he kent things would not improve. Others told him he was foolish to go to the colonies, that it was dangerous. Indians and such."

His stomach clenched. *Indians.* Did Abigail know about his wife?

He glanced at her surreptitiously. She was leaning forward a bit, intent on his father's explanation. She did not seem fearful or concerned.

"So he waited. Worked hard. We all did. Saved our money until we could afford both passage and land."

"So the folks coming off the ships from Ireland aren't really Irish?" Abigail had followed every word.

"Depends what ye mean. Do ye hail from Philadelphia or Boston?" his father asked, rhetorically. "Some call themselves Irish, but most are good Scottish Presbyterians."

"Pumpkin pie," Mistress Williams announced, as Gretchen entered the room.

John smelled warm nutmeg and crisp pastry. Anything sweet would be a treat.

ABIGAIL'S SHOULDERS RELAXED A BIT. The bookkeeper's presence was a godsend. She could ask questions and not have to look at the man's son. Well, she did steal a few glances.

He had clearly enjoyed Gretchen's schnitzel. *I should learn how to make that.* She dismissed the alarming thought.

"So you are Presbyterian?" she asked the bookkeeper.

"Aye. We are members of Mr. Tennent's assembly right here in town."

"Gilbert Tennent?" asked her mother. "Isn't he the minister who encourages the enthusiasts?"

As John turned to look at her mother, Abigail noticed a white scar interrupting one of his eyebrows. What had happened to him?

John's father eased the awkward moment. "Aye, if ye are referring to Mr. Whitefield. Interesting, that. Mr. Whitefield is an Anglican, and if ye mind it, it was the very same Church of England whose worship the king had sought to impose on the Scots. And Scots have long memories," he added with a smile. "But it soon became evident that Mr. Whitefield was a faithful preacher of the gospel, despite his origins. Many have supported him, and not only Presbyterians. Congregationalists and Baptists as well."

"What does Mr. Tennent say about the hysteria in Connecticut?" her mother asked.

Abigail sighed inwardly, thinking of the letters she received periodically from her sister who now lived near Northampton. She pursed her lips. Hannah's accounts conflicted with what her mother believed.

"Mr. Edwards, pastor of the church in Northampton, has been in communication with some of the most eminent divines here in the colonies, including those in Boston. Mr. Tennent has been favorably impressed, as have others. And it isna just Northampton. The Spirit of God seems to have done wonderful things in many towns."

"And in England, from what I hear."

She stared at her father in some surprise. Beyond a simple devotion in the evening, he wasn't much for religious conversation. But he tended to hear things in the course of his business. His bookkeeper was nodding in agreement.

"Hannah has many interesting things to say about Northampton," Abigail ventured.

Her mother narrowed her eyes. "Hannah is one of our married daughters. She has been influenced by the distemper there."

Abigail studied the crumbs on her pewter plate. Then she looked up and saw John's clear blue eyes focused on her. She couldn't read his expression.

Her mother recovered herself. "In any case, Abigail is a good girl. She is obedient and keeps the Commandments."

Heat crept up her cheeks. What was her mother doing?

3

...if God should let you go... your own care and prudence,
and best contrivance, and all your righteousness, would
have no more influence to uphold you and keep you out
of Hell, than a spider's web would have to stop a fallen
rock.

—Jonathan Edwards, _Sinners in the Hands of an Angry God,_ 1741

Sitting on her bed, Abigail fingered the edge of the quilt her
mother had helped her sew. The glow of a single sheep's
tallow candle warmed the colors of the embroidered border. Instead
of fanciful vines, she had stitched leaves and flowers, true to life,
mirroring her botany sketchbook.

Her finger traced a mint leaf. The bookkeeper's son had smelled
of mint when he'd approached her at their leave-taking. No, not mint
exactly. Stronger, a bit acrid, accompanied by a slight smell of grease.

A salve then. But made with which plant of the mint family? Not a kitchen herb. She knew those.

The Russells hadn't stayed late, saying they needed to catch the ferryman before he went to bed.

She recalled John's last glance upon her. His serious blue eyes. Strong frame. Lilting voice. He had seemed interested. Or was she imagining it?

There was no way she was going to fall asleep any time soon. Buttermilk sounded appealing. Gretchen had churned fresh butter yesterday; the crock was sure to be full of it. She opened her bedroom door as noiselessly as possible.

And froze. Her parents' voices echoed in the hallway. Perhaps the door to their room wasn't quite closed. Abigail could hear every word.

"He's a Presbyterian." Mother's voice, raspy with challenge.

"Our own Savoy Declaration is well nigh copied from their Westminster. He's a good and godly man." *Papa.*

There was a pause. But Mother regrouped. "He's in league with enthusiasts."

"He seems sober to me. And remember, I know his father quite well."

Abigail leaned against the doorjamb, not feeling guilty. After all, it was her future. Her parents would never force her to marry someone she couldn't love, but on the other hand …

"His first wife was killed by Indians," Mother stabbed.

Abigail gasped. She clutched at the doorjamb, willing herself to stay upright. Was this true? No one had mentioned it to her. She knew John's wife had died, but …

"That was an accident."

"A savage kills someone—a helpless woman—and it's an accident?"

"The Indians were only traveling through. Apparently they were hungry and killed some livestock. The settlers attacked them."

Abigail slid to the floor. This was too much.

"It was a stray musket ball." Her father seemed convinced everything was fine. But how could that be?

"It's dangerous in the wilderness."

Her stomach tightening, she pulled her knees to her chest and tugged the hem of her shift over her feet.

"It's dangerous in Philadelphia." Father's voice.

There was silence.

Then her father voice spoke again, but more quietly. "Look at your hands."

Abigail stared at the clean oaken floorboards. Her mother's hands were still reddened from scrubbing all the floors of the house with hot vinegar several weeks ago after a neighbor died of a strange fever. Gretchen had scrubbed everything in the kitchen, and Abigail had hauled tin pails of steaming vinegar up the stairs for her mother in the effort to ward off sickness.

"I thought living in this house, a good mile from the docks, we would be safe. But no. Philadelphia is a town of bad air and mysterious agues, and it's come here too." Her father's gentle tone made it clear who had won the argument.

Their voices dwindled. Abigail stood and gently closed the door to her room, no longer in the mood for buttermilk. Grabbing her comb, she sat on the bed and loosened her hair. Doing something mindless might help her to think.

Indians! She had assumed fever or childbirth. Mother described them as savages, although she had seen Delaware Indians in town who seemed calm enough. Some were even Christians, Papa had said once.

Pulling the comb through her thick hair calmed her. *An accident.*

The rest of her father's words made sense. Danger lurked everywhere. She hadn't imagined he worried about her. Then she thought about Hannah, marrying Amos. Mother had put up a fuss about another daughter moving away, but Papa had been taciturn. The country air was healthful, he'd said.

Her hair combed, she knelt by her bed. She wasn't sure if God heard her prayers, but Mother said it was a duty. And a privilege. She wasn't sure about a privilege. Especially in the winter, when her room was cold.

Tonight, though, her thoughts confused her. Thoughts of the bookkeeper's son made her stomach flip like a sixteen-year-old's. Thoughts of Indians frightened her. Her father could probably convince her mother to allow the suit, if John Russell desired to court her.

But if Papa did convince her mother, what then? What did she want? She didn't know.

Still on her knees, she mumbled her way through her nightly prayer and added, "Lord, show me if I should marry this man."

No answer. Only silence, and the flicker of the candle throwing dancing shadows on the wall.

She reached up and snuffed out the tiny light. Exhausted, she crawled under her quilt and fell asleep.

STRONG MORNING SUNLIGHT peeked through the gaps between the distant buildings of Philadelphia. Accompanying his father into town, John absorbed the beauty of the sunrise in silence. Gray gave way to pink, finally climaxing in the pure gold of the sun, a light so strong he couldn't stand to look directly at it. Like the light of God. Beautiful, but overwhelming.

Percy plodded faithfully beneath him, unmoved.

Abigail. John forgot the dawn, wondering what her hair looked like underneath the cap. *No.* That wasn't the most important thing in a wife.

"Da, I think she's too sheltered. Too spoilt, maybe."

"Hmph." His father pursed his lips. "No one can really be ready for the wilderness. I assume she can spin and sew?"

"I would think so, but I can ask."

"You did tell me what ye hoped for," his father reminded him. "A godly woman with some learning." He paused as they guided their horses around a huge muddy place in the road. "Did I tell you her father buys her books?" His father's gelding sidled closer.

"Novels?" John could smell a whiff of Dock Street. The ship's chandlery where his father worked was not far from the water. He supposed folks became used to the stench.

"No, botany is her favorite."

"Botany? That is interesting. Some women take interest in herbs. Still, it's hard to imagine her in the valley." The saddle leather creaked beneath him.

"They're New Englanders, ye ken," he said. "Some of their ways of doing things are a bit different. And she may find you strange, especially dressed as ye are." His father glanced at him pointedly.

John's mouth pursed. Da was undoubtedly right about that. The tomahawk at his side felt especially conspicuous now, not to mention the buckskin jacket. And what about her parents? "Her mother seems verra strict."

"Mr. Williams explained to me that they desire a godly man for their daughter. I think ye will pass that test. There are few Congregationalists in Philadelphia."

"Hmph." He was right. A Presbyterian was probably the next best thing.

"They willna mind ye spending time with her. In the parlor, ye ken. And in the end, it's her ye have to convince. For all their strictness, New Englanders believe in love matches." His father slowed his horse. "I'll see ye at supper, lad." He continued toward Dock Street and the chandlery.

John nodded and turned the mare onto Fourth, the breeze rippling through his horse's mane. Well, the Scriptures commanded that a man should love his wife. Whether it was this girl or some other, he would have to find a way to show her love. Even if he felt nothing.

~

ABIGAIL UNWRAPPED THE SMALL PACKAGE. A linen bag slipped out from between the pages of a letter. She recognized her sister Hannah's neat slanted penmanship, marred only by outrageous spelling.

" ... as you requested, I encloas Seeds of Wood Betony. The Good-Wives heer esteem it highly ..."

That's what this was. Frowning, she held it, touching the linen weave. So far, she had very little in the way of simples, only a very small collection of seeds and dried herbs. Mother kept herbs for common uses, and Gretchen had a few favorite remedies.

Perhaps she ought to enlarge her collection of medicinal herbs. She already helped Gretchen dry herbs for the kitchen. She could grow her own, harvest, dry ... perhaps trade for some she didn't have.

Abigail glanced at the cedar chest containing her trousseau. Bed linens, a tablecloth, an embroidered petticoat. Why shouldn't herbs be a part of it too?

Especially if she married John Russell and lived far from apothecaries and physicians.

She shook her head. A store of herbs would be useful no matter who she married. Grabbing the letter, she continued reading.

"Little Nathaniel grows quite Large. He darts about Swiftly, and in my Condition I can scarse keep Up. He can recite a few lines of the Catechism, tho of coarse he cannot Read. Remember when we minded Mistress Doyes's children? And you taught the Elder his Letters? I beleeve you would make a good Mother. Your children would all be Scolars."

John Russell had a daughter.

Abigail turned toward the tiny north-facing window that illuminated her bedroom with tepid sunlight. The bookkeeper's son haunted her mind's eye. How could he care for a daughter on his own? Still grasping Hannah's letter, she rubbed her thumb against the rough texture of the cheap paper. *Why do I keep thinking about him?*

A sharp rap at the door startled her.

"Yes?"

"Abigail, may I come in?" her mother asked.

"Of course."

A bundle in her arms, her mother took several steps inside and cleared her throat. Abigail laid the letter on her dressing table and rose to greet her.

"I have something for you." She stood awkwardly for a moment, as if not knowing what to do. Then she laid the bundle on the bed.

A bolt of fabric. Yellow, with blue swirls. Abigail sat next to it, brushing the surface of the fine weave with her fingertips. It was beautiful.

She looked up. "What is this?"

"Don't tell your father. I was supposed to make bed and window curtains with it. Can you imagine? Wasting that fabric on a window?"

"It looks expensive."

"He purchased it cheap because of water damage, and most of that was to the outermost turn of cloth, which he trimmed off." Sitting beside her, her mother pointed out a few tiny stains at the very edge of the bolt. "Other than that, 'tis perfect."

"Is it Holland linen?"

"No. Cotton all the way from India."

Abigail tilted her head. "What do you want to do with it?"

Mother blinked rapidly, then sighed. "It's for your trousseau," she said softly. "For a new Sabbath gown. And anything else you may need it for."

Abigail gaped at her. What was Mother thinking?

"I knew Josiah was unsuitable, despite his good family. Do you know who his great-uncle is? No, never mind. The young man is foolish."

"Do you think I should marry John Russell?"

Her mother picked at some lint on her apron. "I don't know." She took a deep breath. "I don't like sending you off to the wilderness. But he seems like a steady, good, and godly man." She turned and faced Abigail. "But 'tis your choice. He's coming here later today. Just spend time with him."

Then she stood and brushed off her skirts. "Gretchen and I will help you cut out the gown." She flashed a smile. "We'll make it in the new style. With an overskirt."

Abigail was speechless. The new style. "But Mother, you said Mrs. Noyes's Sabbath gown was extravagant."

"Making window curtains from that fabric would be extravagant," her mother huffed.

The door creaked as she departed. Abigail gazed at the fabric next to her, overwhelmed.

Maybe this was some sort of answer to her feeble prayer.

IN THE DIMNESS of the printer's shop, John spotted a figure behind the cluttered counter.

"Might Mr. Franklin be here?" he asked the man. Not someone he recognized. A journeyman? No, his dress was too fine, his waistcoat flashing maroon between dark lapels.

"Good day, Mr. Hall at your service. No, I fear Mr. Franklin is away. But he is in town. Not sure when he will return."

The other man answered calmly enough, but John felt his gaze flicker to the tomahawk suspended from his belt.

"John Russell. Pleased to meet ye. Do ye hail from London?"

The other man raised an eyebrow. "Is it so obvious? Is it my speech or my dress?"

John smiled. "Speech. And I suspect we all sound strange to you." The man's inflections gave him away, as well as his posture and carriage.

Mr. Hall harrumphed. "Quite. Some still seem to speak the King's English. You, I daresay, sound like a Scot but look like an Indian."

"Oh, we Ulster Scots are fairly common. As are the deer that have provided my clothing. Ye must have but recently arrived."

"Yes. I have come to serve as Franklin's assistant and agent for London booksellers."

"Interesting." John glanced about. Copies of the *Pennsylvania Gazette* lay piled to his right. Booklets and tracts to his left. "Books, ye say?"

"Yes. Mr. Franklin prints some books, as you must already know, but he has decided, wisely in my opinion, to develop contacts with British publishers. He believes the sale of books can only increase."

Turning, John spotted a few shelves laden with books. Not a large selection. "A good decision, I am sure."

The door creaked.

"John Russell?" A hearty voice split the air.

John recognized the man's form, backlit by the daylight outside. "Mr. Franklin! Good to see ye again."

"Has my friend Mr. Hall been able to assist you?" Dusty and disheveled, the printer filled the room with his presence.

"I just arrived."

John described what he needed, including sermons. Soon he had a stack of newspapers and booklets on the counter.

"Have you heard of this?" Franklin handed him a slim volume.

John read the title. *The Distinguishing Marks of a Work of the Spirit of God.* Jonathan Edwards. The preacher of Northampton.

"No, but it sounds fascinating. I'd like to purchase it." It joined the stack.

Hungrily, John scanned the shelves of books. He picked up a volume of hymns.

"I first published a book of Isaac Watts's hymns years ago," Franklin explained, noticing his selection. "No one bought it. But now, I can't seem to keep them in stock. Ever since Mr. Whitefield came through, folks love to sing. And not just from the Psalter on the Sabbath."

Carefully, John opened the volume.

Jesus shall reign where'er the sun
  Doth his successive journeys run;
  His kingdom stretch from shore to shore,

Till moons shall wax and wane no more.

"This is beautiful," he murmured. "I'd like this as well. And do ye still print that little New Testament?"

"Yes."

"I'll take one, then. Thank ye kindly." Even as he spoke the words, his eyes were drawn again to the books. "What is this?"

Picking up a leather volume, he traced the stamping with his fingers. *Pharmacopoeia extemporanea.* John's mind flickered back to Mr. Tennent's Latin instruction. A book of medicine. Or rather, how to make medicine. He opened it. Plants dominated the pages. And instructions.

"Ah." Mr. Franklin peered at it. "I acquired that when an apothecary passed away several years ago. You have an interest in such things?"

"I ken someone who does. I'll take this as well."

4

In 1739 arriv'd among us from England the Rev. Mr. White-field, who had made himself remarkable there as an itinerant Preacher. He was at first permitted to preach in some of our Churches; but the Clergy taking a Dislike to him, soon refus'd him their Pulpits and he was oblig'd to preach in the Fields.

—Benjamin Franklin, *Autobiography*, 1793

S he almost didn't recognize him. Blinking against the brightness of the sunlight, Abigail stood in the doorway, paralyzed.

An Indian. No, the face was wrong. Blue eyes gazed down at her under concerned brows. John's face, but he was wearing Indian clothes. A button-less buckskin jacket, belted in place, fell to mid-thigh, where long leggings covered his breeches.

"Abigail, you may sit in the keeping room." Her mother's voice seemed far away.

"Yes, Mother."

Stepping back, Abigail motioned for John to enter. The smell of herbal salve and new sweat accompanied his strong presence as she led him toward the hearth. An object hung from his belt. Some sort of axe?

She settled on her stool and found her voice. "Welcome."

Incongruous against the backdrop of buckskin and gleaming steel, a large book nestled easily in John's broad hand.

Noticing her gaze, he stood and stepped toward her, book in hand. "For you."

Abigail scanned the front of the leather-bound volume. The title was in Latin. *Pharmacopoeia extemporanea.* What did that mean?

"My father told me ye like botany. Plants and such."

She nodded, opening the beautifully embossed cover. "Oh," she murmured. This was wonderful. She turned a page, transfixed. Some plants she knew, but now she had instructions on their practical uses. *Grind finely, steep in hot water ...*

The sturdy pages crackled slightly as she turned them. *Sassafras. Jesuit's bark.* Finally she looked up. "Thank you. I don't know what happened to my manners."

"Ye like it?"

"Oh yes. What does the title mean?"

"How to make medicine."

"'Tis lovely. I've been trying to learn more about the medicinal properties of plants and the knack of using them, but it is an art, and usually passed down from someone. Like a midwife."

"Or apothecary."

Abigail nodded. The man sat calmly across from her, regarding her with steady, clear eyes. He didn't make light of her interests.

"Apothecaries are men," she said. How could she learn from one?

"Aye, they are," he agreed easily, lifting his scarred eyebrow. "This book once belonged to an apothecary." He leaned forward. "What is the difference, think ye, between an herb woman and an apothecary?"

Abigail pressed at her spectacles. "An apothecary has a shop."

"But a woman might have the same knowledge?"

"I suppose." What was he getting at?

"There are no apothecaries near my home."

His home, in the wilderness. Strange sensations fought for dominance inside her. Fear at the thought of Indians. But a surge of excitement accompanied it, startling her. She could use her knowledge. For her own family, and for others.

Her own family? Her own children? She forced away that thought.

Indians. And she'd almost mistaken him for one. She examined his clothing more closely. The buckskin jacket hung loosely, the familiar ecru of a homespun linen shirt peeping out from underneath. A shaft of afternoon sunlight penetrating the window glinted off the keen steel edge of the axe tied to his belt.

"Mr. Russell?"

"Please call me John, if ye will," he urged gently.

She nodded. "John, why do you wear an axe?"

He chuckled. "It's a tomahawk. An Indian invention, though aye, it does seem like to an axe. It's lighter, and meant for chopping or throwing."

He unloosed the ties and slipped it to her, handle first.

"The goal is to throw it so it lands blade first."

Abigail wrinkled her nose. She didn't touch the edge, which looked sharp. "Blade first?"

John tilted his head. "Aye. It is often used as a weapon. Ye can use it up close, like a sword, or from a longer distance, but then ye need to throw it. Many Indians do this quite well."

Her insides stirred. "Have you killed Indians with it?"

John shifted in his seat near the hearth. "No. I did kill a buffalo with it. The creature had gone down with several musket balls in the chest, but it wasna dead."

She pursed her lips. "How big is a buffalo?"

"Imagine a huge ox with a brown wooly coat. The skin of a buffalo is warm and verra useful come winter."

Abigail had never seen a buffalo skin but had seen plenty of other types at the dry goods merchant's shop. "Do you kill many animals?"

"My cousin and I go hunting when we are not occupied with planting and such. We are farmers, ye ken, but it is not enough to be farmers in the Shenandoah." He gazed out the window. "After harvest is a verra good time for hunting. The bear are fat, the turkeys plump with chestnuts. The women collect nuts and berries, and make preserves if they have the sugar. Few people have orchards yet; it takes more time to grow apple trees than barley or Indian corn."

"What else do the women do?"

John blinked. Was he surprised at the question? "Mind the house and the children. Spin and sew, much as ye would here." He tilted his head as if concentrating. "Sometimes they work in the fields helping the men. But more often they plant a kitchen garden. Some have chickens, but wild fowl are so plentiful that truly they raise them only for their eggs."

"I help Gretchen with our kitchen garden. And sometimes with the cow."

John glanced briefly out the window then met her gaze. "Most of the women in the valley have no servant to help them with such tasks. Ye enjoy certain comforts here that may not exist there. The deer and rabbits may harry your kitchen garden. Sometimes worse things happen." His expression altered. He looked older for a moment. *Sad.*

His wife.

Then a smile rippled across his face. "We think it's worth it. The land is beautiful." His shoulders shifted underneath his buckskin jacket. "But it's a challenging life."

He stood and seemed to fidget. Then he looked at her.

"I hope ye enjoy your book."

And then he was out the door. Abigail closed it and leaned against the comforting oak frame.

What had just happened?

Clearly, he didn't mock her interests. He had come with a gift. But he also seemed to warn her against the idea of marriage to him. Speaking of hardships, of challenge. And why had he worn his buckskin outfit—complete with tomahawk—when coming to court her? The bookkeeper's son knew Latin. He was no backwoods ruffian.

John Russell was a puzzle.

A challenging life. Did she want that?

THE LATE MORNING sunshine warmed the muggy air as John led Abigail to the wagon. He circled the mules, their skin shuddering, throwing off trespassing flies.

"What type of mare did you say?" Abigail's voice sounded small. Small, but not nervous.

John helped Abigail up onto the wagon seat before answering her. He was glad his visit two days before hadn't scared her. Not even the tomahawk, which he'd worn on purpose. If he would court her, she had to know who he really was, and what kind of life it would be. Thankfully, her father had intimated she'd be receptive to an outing.

"Irish. It's a small horse, a pony really, called the Connemara. My brother-in-law wants to breed them, and promised me the mare if he could have the get." She wasn't wearing her spectacles. Did she not need them?

His blue coat was too tight, but Thomas Fitzwater was the wealthy owner of a quarry north of Philadelphia, and he didn't want to look like a poor man when he wanted to buy something. Da had even loaned him his cocked hat, a three-cornered construction that folded easily under the arm.

John gathered the mules' reins. Roy had come up to town to place a few orders from the shops, and had loaned him the wagon. He helped the housekeeper onto the wagon seat.

"What is so special about these ponies?" Gretchen's eyes shone above her apple dumpling cheeks.

"These ponies are sweet things," he said to both of them, hopping on the seat. "But sturdy. You don't need to baby them or feed them oats. Sure-footed, too."

"For your daughter to ride?" Abigail asked.

"Partly." Turning to answer her, he noticed red marks on either side of her nose. The spectacles. Did they hurt her?

John clucked at the mules, and the animals eased the wagon away from the house. It wasn't far to Limekiln Road, the only paved road in Philadelphia, which ran directly to the Fitzwaters' property.

"These sturdy ponies can carry a man, but I prefer a pacer for myself. I'm a rather large man, and I prefer not to overburden any animal."

Under the summer sun, the horse droppings on the residential street filled the air with a pungent earthiness, much easier to bear than the effluvium near the docks. They rode in silence for a while, the creak of the wagon barely audible under the gentle hubbub of the street. The homes were set widely apart, but dogs barked, horses snorted, and occasionally, a housewife scolded a child.

"What is your daughter Susanna like?" Abigail asked suddenly.

John's grip on the reins tightened momentarily. Where did this come from? Abigail's mother dominated her, and her father, well ... Perhaps she had more spirit than he'd thought.

"She has dark eyes," he said. "Like her mother." His gut clenched and he swallowed. "She is sweet but also a bit impish." In the dark days following Janet's death his daughter would cling to him one day, and the next, she'd become irascible. Occasionally he would simply send her over to Sarah's, not able to deal with Susanna's changeable moods and his own crippling grief at the same time.

Later, she'd calmed down, but the dark-haired girl now went about her play and brief chores with a quietness that smote his heart. Sarah and Agnes filled the gaps in some ways; he was infinitely grateful to both women. But grief was not easy, not even for a child.

"Who cares for her now?" Abigail's blue eyes gazed up at him from under the brim of her straw hat.

"My sister Sarah. They moved back across the Blue Ridge and live on the other side. It's not verra far, maybe three days by wagon. Two by a good horse."

John guided the mules onto Limekiln Road. They were well into the country now. Stands of maple and birch alternated with small homesteads. Bobwhites chirped, lifting his spirits. His shoulders relaxed.

"Do your spectacles hurt ye?"

Abigail frowned. "A little. I don't have to wear them all the time, just for close work. And reading." She rubbed at the red marks briefly.

"So ye can see things far away without them?"

"Yes. All this is so beautiful. The country ... the trees. Sometimes I take the cow out for grazing, but otherwise ...is that it?" she asked, peering ahead.

Ahead, on the left, a cluster of trees partially concealed a large brick house; to the right, clouds of dust announced the path leading to the quarry.

"Aye."

The mules' ears perked up, and their pace increased perceptibly, as if they sensed the end of their travail.

"Gee," barked John to the mules, and soon they had pulled up at the stables. Hatless and wigless, Mr. Fitzwater appeared from the direction of the brick house, huffing. A groom led out a pony from one of the stalls.

"A handsome animal, Mr. Fitzwater." Praising a potential purchase went against all principles of horse-trading, but John couldn't help his response. With a finely made head well set on a beautifully arched neck, and gleaming gray coat, the mare was beautiful. He studied the pony's gait as the groom led her back and forth a few times.

"I acquired her a year ago, soon after her arrival from Ireland," Mr. Fitzwater explained. "Horses suffer on board ship, but she responded well to good pasture. I have another mare and a stud. Covered her a month ago."

John smiled. "And ye are willing to give her up?"

As they continued the conversation, discussing the price, John watched Abigail surreptitiously. She slowly drew near to the mare. Fitzwater noticed too.

"She's gentle," the older man said, motioning.

Soon she was stroking the pony's soft nose. The animal's large dark eyes regarded her calmly. "She isn't dapple gray."

"You're correct. She's a rose gray."

"Has she a name?" John asked.

"Something Gaelic," Fitzwater said. "I call her Rosy for her coat. But 'tis not truly rose or red, 'tis the way folks describe that kind of gray."

"She looks more like she emerged from the sea. Like a mist. A gray mist." Abigail always surprised him.

"Rosemary," John blurted. "It comes from the Latin. *Ros* for mist, *marinus* for sea."

Abigail stared at him, mouth slightly open. "It's perfect."

Silently, John blessed Mr. Tennent and the long hours in the classroom.

THE AFTERNOON SUN flickered through the trees flanking the road as they returned to Philadelphia, ruts in the road jarring them occasionally. Abigail glanced past John to the mare, which moved easily beside them. He'd chosen to wrap her lead rope around his arm instead of tying her to the wagon.

"Just in case she stumbles," he'd said.

John was so kind. Even with animals. Emboldened, she decided to ask something personal. "What is that salve you wear? What herb is in it?"

His head jerked around. "Oh, that. Agnes makes me a salve with pennyroyal in it. For the midges and mosquitoes and such."

"Pennyroyal. I've heard of it. A potent herb." Other mints repelled insects. "Does it work well?"

"Oh aye, but ye must put enough on. Enough to make you smell like it." He smiled at her.

"It doesn't smell bad. But 'tis stronger than mint."

"Aye."

On the other side of the wagon seat, Gretchen gave her a half smile, eyes twinkling. Abigail's brow lifted in embarrassment. Gretchen was not one to intrude, exactly. She knew her place. But clearly the woman liked John Russell.

"Abigail, how is a man made right before God?" John asked, gently.

"I'm not sure what you mean." Made right? Made righteous?

"How is a man justified? What is justification?"

The terminology triggered a memory. "Justification is an act of God's free grace ... wherein he pardons all our sins, and accepts us as righteous in his sight."

He glanced at her. "I see ye ken the Catechism."

"All children are taught it. I'm not sure I could recite it now, though." She straightened in her seat.

"How does the Spirit apply the redemption purchased by Christ?"

"I only remember parts of this," Abigail said. He was catechizing her.

Well, she didn't blame him. Recent doctrinal errors near Northampton had terrified many, according to Hannah. As a result, seriousness had gripped the local inhabitants and some had been converted.

She frowned, concentrating. "By working faith in us."

"So where does faith come from?" John clucked to the mules,

guiding them to the side; a large wagon approached going the opposite direction. Rosemary, the pony, kept her head high, ears alert, but did not flinch at the traffic.

Abigail rubbed her fingers together in her lap. If the Spirit worked faith—wasn't this the same question?

"From God." God was always the safe answer. And it seemed to fit with something she'd heard preached.

"Aye, Abigail. There is nothing good in us. And even the faith we exercise is the gift of God, that no man should boast."

Of course. Ephesians. Had she passed the test?

She hoped so.

5

Q. 33. What is justification?

A. Justification is an act of God's free grace, wherein he
pardoneth all our sins, and accepteth us as righteous in
his sight, only for the righteousness of Christ imputed to
us, and received by faith alone.

—The Westminster Shorter Catechism, 1647

*J*ohn smiled as he watched Roy emerge from the shop.
His cousin was only five years his junior but often
reminded him of a mere lad. Bouncing from the brick
sidewalk to the dusty street, Roy headed his way, copper hair glinting
in the sun.

John had already made his own purchases: needles, thread, and
other small items filled his saddlebags, both for himself and the
McClures. They had everything they'd come for on this trip ... except
for a bride.

"Do well, Roy?" John stroked the neck of his mare as she waited patiently. The breeze had strengthened. Out of the north, the gusts felt good on his sweaty neck.

"Aye. Besides the moccasins and a pair of leggings, I sold him a lad's coonskin cap and a lady's hat with feathers."

"Lady's hat?" John knew his cousin had a fair hand with a needle, but this sounded ridiculous. He scratched between his horse's ears and she leaned toward him as if she were a giant dog.

"Oh, aye. Ye ken the widow McDowell?"

How could he not? Her husband had led the militia that awful day a year and a half ago. And more than once he'd felt the woman's eyes on him during the aftermath, when the widows began to seek new husbands or to make other arrangements, a few leaving the valley entirely. She was older than he by ten years, at least. And dressed with feathers in her hat. He thought her eccentric.

"Aye, I mind her. Are you saying her feathers are the latest fashion?"

"John, I ken that ye are alert in the wilderness. But ye dinna always see other things." Roy grinned. "Even the Quakers here in town have begun wearing baubles and lace."

It was true. He'd noticed the lace of some men's cravats, mainly because his own neckwear choked him so. "But still, Robert Russell, a lady's hat?"

"Who else can sew up fox fur and swan feathers? Not every woman handles leather well. And besides, I dinna have your eye for tracking or your hands for fashioning wood. I have to find something to sell."

"Mr. Russell?" Both of their heads turned at the interruption. A lanky man approached, dusty from the streets.

"Aye?" John recognized him as the journeyman from the goldsmith's shop.

"Just delivering a message from Mr. Gutens. He says your item sold."

"Thank ye kindly," John replied. "I'll be along presently."

"What is that all about?" his cousin asked, after the man had left.

"Lancaster long rifles, is what." John laughed at his cousin's puzzled expression. "One of those stones turned out to be an amethyst."

He grinned at Roy's expression of surprise.

"Amethyst?" he sputtered.

"Come, lad, let's see what we netted from the sale."

"Twenty gold guineas. And the balance in script." Mr. Gutens presented a receipt for John to sign. "The total is less the amount for the pendant."

"Thank ye kindly." He picked up his pen and signed neatly, with a small flourish.

The goldsmith presented him with the necklace. "Thank you for your business."

John turned to leave, then stopped. "Mr. Gutens, might I trouble you with a question?"

"Of course."

"If a person's spectacles hurt him by pinching the nose ..." He rubbed his nose in demonstration.

"Oh yes, I understand the problem. It's not terribly uncommon." The goldsmith leaned on the counter.

"Is there a another way to support the lenses? With attachments around the head or ears?"

"Actually, yes." The man pulled out a page from his receipt book. "I saw this in a London paper." He sketched a pair of spectacles with extensions curved at the ends. "See here? These go around the ears. Haven't seen anyone wear them in Philadelphia, but they shouldn't be difficult to make." He paused. "Try Mr. Hawkins on Chestnut Street. He's a tinker and an inventive sort."

"I thank ye verra much."

Roy said nothing until they departed. "Och, that's grand. Cash money."

"Shush. Not here on the street. Let's go to the chandlery for dinner. I want to talk to Da."

Clouds overhead relieved the pressure of the midday sun as they urged their mounts along. John sensed the approach of rain, welcome after the heat of the past week.

"What was all that about spectacles? Is that for your da?"

"No, for the lass I am courting." John guided Percy around a lumbering wagon, Roy following on Rosemary. Soon they were abreast again.

"The lass?" His cousin's eyebrows lifted. "Tell me the whole story, now."

John sighed inwardly. But perhaps it would help him to sort out his thoughts. He told Roy who Abigail was and described her family.

"Ye couldna find a lass at the meetinghouse?"

John frowned. "No." He'd attended several Sabbaths at Mr. Tennent's meetinghouse but had mostly garnered strange looks. Families with daughters of marriageable age had become hesitant to approach him when they'd heard he had come looking for a wife. "Everyone knows how Janet died."

His cousin's expression altered. "So that's how it is." Under the edge of his cap, Roy's curls danced in the breeze. Gusts of wind picked up dust from the street and swirled it around the legs of their horses.

"Aye, that's how it is."

They pulled up at the chandlery and dismounted. John took his time tying up his mount, Abigail's honest face filling his mind. Would she accept him if he proposed?

"But this Boston lass is not afraid?"

He felt his mouth twitch into a smile. "Not yet."

ABIGAIL GAVE the window a final swipe and rinsed the rag in the pail of warm water. She enjoyed her occasional outings to the chandlery. Father wouldn't trust anyone else to clean his office, and the skinny apprentice he'd acquired could barely push a broom. Abigail wondered what he'd do when she left.

She studied the dirty water in the pail. *When? Not if?* Slowly, she'd begun to accept the idea of marriage. At least the possibility. But was it truly what she wanted?

One thing was certain. John was a man, not a boy. Unlike Josiah Mather, whose thoughtlessness shouted selfish immaturity despite his count of years.

Wiping her hands on her apron, she turned and studied the room, searching for more that needed to be set in order. Voices murmured outside the office. A customer.

"I saw her first!" a deep voice barked.

What was going on? Abigail poked her head out of the office. The chandlery was filled with men. She noted her father standing to one side; another man, dressed like a sea captain, stood with his back facing her. Several others crowded around her father's counter, but she couldn't see them clearly.

Then she noticed a woman. Sitting on a giant coil of ship's rope, a pale young woman in ragged, dirty clothing clutched a small child.

"Ten pounds for both."

Abigail jerked in shock. That second voice was John's. She crept out of the office and slipped behind a huge bolt of ship's canvas leaning against the wall.

"I don't want the child. Ten pounds for the woman alone." The angry barking voice.

From her hiding place she could now see John clearly. Rigid lines etched his face.

"Ten gold guineas for both." John's counteroffer.

From behind the canvas, Abigail heard the *clink* of coins slapped on the counter. That was a good offer. Sea captains liked gold. It was international currency.

"Sold." A new, rumbly voice announced the captain's decision.

John had just purchased an indenture—but why? Then she caught a glimpse of the man with the barking voice. Dirty and dressed in buckskin, he was glaring at John, black hair and beard dominating a scowling face. Then he muttered something she couldn't hear.

Pushing aside another man, he stomped out. The door crashed shut.

A hand touched her elbow. The bookkeeper. He helped her to a stool, where she sat, her hands trembling.

"What just happened?" she asked.

"My son saved this young widow from a bad situation."

Studying the woman, she grasped what the ruffian had intended. Underfed and pale from her recent passage across the ocean, the young mother was still very comely. Anyone purchasing her indenture would have full legal control of her for the length of the contract. She'd heard rumors ...

"Her husband died on board ship," she heard the bookkeeper explain. "The captain sold the rest of his contracts yesterday, but the only one with an offer for this young woman wouldna have the money until today. Captain Graves had to start loading his vessel, so he brought her here."

"Is she from Ireland?"

"Aye," he answered quietly. "I'm going to the baker's to fetch a bit more food. Would ye mind helping her? She'd likely find a woman's company comforting after all this."

Abigail nodded.

JOHN READ over the indenture carefully. *Five years.* And he had no idea what the woman could do. Cook, clean, and sew, most likely. Perhaps she'd be a blessing to Abigail.

He signed his name with a flourish, his cousin at his elbow.

"What about our rifles?" Roy asked in an undertone.

John looked him in the eye. "You mean you'd let Sloan take that woman home?"

"Well, no ..."

"Well, then. And we may still have enough money for rifles." John didn't know how much Jake charged for them. In any case, he'd acted according to his conscience. A clear conscience was worth more than gold, his da had once said.

The transaction completed, he lifted his eyes. In front of the young woman, a young lady stood.

Abigail! How much of that had she witnessed? He frowned. He hadn't seen her in the room. He didn't know she ever came here.

John made his way to her side. "Abigail?"

"John?" She turned to face him, her brows raised in a question.

His jaw worked. "I didn't realize you were here."

"I clean for Papa sometimes." She clasped her hands together, then turned and indicated the young woman. "This is Elizabeth Montgomery."

"Pleased to meet ye." John didn't mention that he knew her name from the paper he held in his hands. "I am sorry about the circumstances." Pinched and pale, with dark curls peeping out from underneath a soiled cap, the woman still possessed a certain strength and comeliness—no wonder she'd caught Sloan's eye.

"Fresh bread," his father announced, his voice back to its usual liveliness. For the woman's sake, John guessed.

"And who might ye be?" John asked the child gently, crouching before the boy on the woman's lap.

There was no response. The little boy turned his head to his mother, clinging to her.

"His name is Richard. After his da."

"Abigail, perhaps ye might help me lay out the luncheon," his father suggested.

Soon they were gathered around a rickety table laden with bread, eggs, and cheese. Abigail poured ale for everyone. Elizabeth and her child ate hungrily, but the woman glanced at him often. Sizing him up.

John didn't blame her. Her life and her child's were at his mercy. Then he noticed her gaze darting to Abigail and back to him.

Of course. They had used their given names with each other; the woman could only assume them related or betrothed. In any case, he needed to assure his new servant of his honorable intentions and explain what her new life would be like.

The room darkened as the wind beat upon the window frames. He couldn't linger long. Rain would soon turn the streets into mud, and he had no wish to allow his animals to stand outside unprotected. He watched as Abigail's father lit a lantern and hung it above the counter.

John cleared his throat. "Mrs. Montgomery."

"I dinna mind if ye call me Lizzie."

"Aye, well. I live in the Shenandoah Valley." He doubted if that meant anything to her, but strangely, her eyebrows rose.

"I've heard of it. A nice place, they say."

"A bit rough too. Who mentioned it?" he asked.

"Oh, folks. After the horrible black frost in thirty-nine, word about the colonies was on everyone's lips—even word about this valley. Free land, and fertile."

"Hmph. Well, it isna free, but it is good land." No sense in explaining about bears and painters yet. Bears rarely hurt anyone. And they were good eating. "Robert here is my cousin. He owns the piece next to mine. We call him Roy. For his red hair, of course."

Roy bobbed his head in greeting, mouth full of bread. Wheat flour had to be brought by wagon to the valley; some days they ate little more than corn mush and squirrel stew with turnips. He didn't blame his cousin. Or the little lad, whose eyes had grown round at the sight. Not a crumb would remain.

"Ye have been introduced to Abigail." He wondered how to explain.

"Abigail is my daughter," interjected the chandler, smiling. "Mr. Russell is courting her."

John's shoulders relaxed. Lizzie's gaze remained on him, but the lines around her mouth softened.

"Aye, Mrs. Montgomery. I am sure Abigail will welcome your help in the valley."

Rain assaulted the roof, a sudden rat-tat-tat against the shingles. Somewhere, a shutter banged against a wall.

Lizzie nodded. Tears filled her eyes. She turned to her son and cleaned the crumbs from his face, hiding her own. Clearly she felt safe now.

John turned to Abigail. Her face now reflected the storm outside, eyes narrowed under knitted brows.

Why? Had he said something wrong?

6

... it is faith, only as renouncing our own righteousness, and
relying on that of Christ, provided for the chief of
sinners, by which we are justified.

—Cotton Mather, *Essays To Do Good*, 1710

*A*bigail fastened her stays in the gray light of dawn. After two days and nights, the storm had finally loosened its hold, and she looked forward to sunshine. But the storm seemed to linger in her heart.

The squeal of a child interrupted her thoughts. Ritchie, his mother called him. Abigail's father had volunteered to shelter the servant and her child because of the downpour; their covered wagon was no gentleman's carriage, but the canvas and oilskin above their heads had kept them just as dry on the way home from the ship's chandlery. Mother had looked them over grimly upon their arrival, quickly instructing Gretchen to set up a pallet near the hearth in the keeping room.

Gretchen had brightened considerably. "Abigail," she'd said, "This is a blessing from heaven. An extra pair of hands will lighten the load."

Abigail supposed she was right. And little Richie did make her smile, once he'd lost some of his fear. Already she was thinking of her New England primer. When would he be ready to learn his letters? She guessed him to be her nephew's age. Three, perhaps.

Dressed, she came downstairs. In the kitchen, Mother ladled mush into bowls, which Gretchen then took out to the table, where Father sat reading a copy of the *Gazette*.

"Abigail, help me with the molasses." Mother's voice held a particular intonation that meant she wanted to talk to her.

"Yes, Mother."

They began to pour molasses and maple syrup into pewter cups. "What is troubling you?" She sounded almost solicitous.

After two days, Abigail was bursting to tell someone, and Hannah was simply too far away. "'Tis John." How to explain?

"You disagree with his decision to purchase the woman's contract?"

"That's not it." Her heart beat faster. "'Tis what he said. Afterwards. He spoke as if we were already betrothed. Before everyone."

Mother pursed her lips. They left the kitchen with the condiments and placed them on the table. Abigail saw her mother's eyes flicker toward her father.

"Let's fetch a bit of Gretchen's butter." Advice was coming.

They returned to the kitchen.

"Men take charge, and that is their right. In this case, it was not his right. He probably doesn't even know what he did. Your father has not said anything to me. He clearly did not object."

She faced her daughter. "You must talk to John. Try not to be too hard on him. Men can be blind."

"Yes, Mother," she agreed, her cheeks warming. Well, she'd try.

Returning to the spacious keeping room, they all ate in companionable silence, interrupted only by the happy slurps and smacks of the little lad after discovering the wonders of maple syrup on corn mush. The morning sunlight broke in through the window, laying a bright swath across the table. As they finished, Gretchen began to clear the dishes away.

"Abigail, come with me," her father said.

He set aside his bowl and stood. She couldn't read his expression.

She rose silently and followed him outside to the outbuildings. Like an afterthought, their cramped cowshed stood behind their modest carriage house and stables. He led the way to the entrance.

Blinking, she sought to clear her vision. For two furry heads looked at her from the cowshed instead of one.

"A heifer. Ready-bred. She'll have a calf in the spring." Father cleared his throat with some difficulty. "I wanted to give you a wedding present, and your mother would insist on something useful above all ..." His voice trailed off.

Abigail soon distinguished the two: the family cow, a deep reddish-brown animal with creamy-colored horns, stood on the right. On the left, a slightly smaller version shifted her weight uncertainly. Abigail reached out her hand carefully, close enough for the newcomer to catch her scent. What a generous gift. Now all she needed was a butter churn like Gretchen's.

In order to set up housekeeping in the Shenandoah Valley.

"Thank you, Papa." Abigail's chest tightened. She struggled to make sense of her conflicting feelings. She'd once seen a runaway team of horses crash a carriage into the side of a building. She seemed to be on such an out-of-control carriage, on the road to marriage. "She's wonderful."

What else could she say?

Her father reached forward and rubbed the heifer's face. "What about a name?"

A page from her copybook flashed before her eyes. "Thistle. Thistles grow everywhere." They'd both need to be tough, to live in the wilderness.

He didn't respond, but reached inside his green coat and pulled out a linen bag. "Now don't tell your mother about this." Her father loosened the strings and placed the contents in her hands, a tortoise-shell comb and mirror. "She'd say this was frivolous."

Abigail rubbed the glassy-smooth finish between her fingers. "These are beautiful."

"Swapped a sextant for them. I had too many sextants anyway."

This was nonsense. With all the ships coming in from Ireland, in addition to the normal traffic up the coastline and from Barbados, her father could barely keep some things in stock.

"Thank you. They are beautiful. And I won't tell Mother."

Abigail smiled at her father and slipped the gifts back into the bag. She just needed a little time to think. Was she really ready for this?

And what would she say to John?

In the early light, John stared at the rafters above his head—the familiar loft, his bedroom growing up, seemed to have shrunk—but the oak was fine and solid, comforting even, good for many hard winters still.

He blinked away sleep. His own cabin in the valley needed attention—the new addition he'd started for Susanna could house the servant once completed. Perhaps Mrs. Montgomery could stay with Agnes and Archie for the time being. And what about his daughter? He sighed. Many families in the valley had naught but the one room; they'd manage.

But what about Abigail? She was used to a large, sturdy home with glass windows. When he visited he admired the stone of the walls and the solid oak of the timbers: a solid, well-knit home with few drafts or cold corners. There was even a Quaker-style covering over the front stoop—a practical yet comfortable house. Could she adjust? He hoped so.

He rose from the narrow bed and felt his way down the familiar ladder. Da would have crossed the ferry by now, on his way to his bookkeeping work at the chandlery; the rest of the household was out and about, seeing to stock, mending fences, or weeding.

He pulled on his clothes and sought out breakfast. Surely there was some porridge or old bread left. His sister-in-law wouldn't have forgotten him.

Yes. The pot was hanging from a hook over the banked kitchen hearth, still warm. He shoveled the mush into his mouth, not tasting it. In his mind's eye he saw his cornfields; the stalks had to be knee-high at the very least. The corn was roughly that high here, although to his eye the fields his brother Sam now worked did not seem to bring forth the way the valley fields did. The stalks seemed feeble somehow, and occasionally missing a fellow, like a man with missing teeth. He'd heard that corn could wear out the land, if you planted it in the same field year after year. Perhaps his cornfield could be used for barley or peas next year. And he'd plant corn in his barley field.

In any case, his corn crop pushed him, pressured him. He had to get back by harvest.

John pursed his lips, seeing Abigail's face in his mind's eye; the last time he'd seen her, at the chandlery, her expression had darkened unexpectedly—had she disagreed with his decision to purchase the contract? It had all happened so fast, and he'd left without being able to talk to her. But the weather had cleared. He would go to town today and ask her.

After washing his bowl, he left the house, heading toward the stables. Percy snuffed a greeting as he located her saddle and swung it onto her back. When he cinched it around her, she nosed him from behind. Her warm horsey scent comforted him.

"Ho, girl, can ye help a man with woman troubles?"

Apparently not. John swung up onto the silent mare and headed out to the ferry, alone with his thoughts.

He needed to propose. The corn wouldn't wait forever. But Abigail's scowl that day had troubled him. He couldn't marry a woman who would question his every decision.

Janet. She had spoken her mind but had never fought him. Sometimes she'd been right, and he had changed his course. But she never disagreed in a sassy or contentious way. The memory of her dark eyes clouded his heart for a moment. He shook it away.

Abigail didn't seem contentious. Was she?

John rode into town, breathing deeply of the cooler air swept in by the storm. It wasn't until he caught a whiff of Philadelphia's stench that he made a decision. He'd stop somewhere to pray. As he rode along the muddy track optimistically called Market Street, a deep urgency slowly overcame the vision of knee-high corn. He hadn't sought the Lord in three days.

Remembering George Whitefield's huge meetinghouse, he turned his mare onto Fourth Street.

There. The building had amazed him the first time he'd seen it, a tangible evidence of the unseen influence of the Spirit of God over the land. Folks had wanted a sheltered place to hear Mr. Whitefield preach, and they'd made short work of it, constructing an edifice one hundred feet long. It dwarfed the other structures nearby.

John found a place to tie Percy's reins and tugged at his buckskin jacket, straightening it, as he approached the door.

Dim and empty, the meetinghouse welcomed him.

ABIGAIL EXAMINED HER FINGERNAILS, still black from the garden. Disturbed, she couldn't bear to sew today, not when the beautiful yellow fabric reminded her of John. Instead, she had tackled the weeds, easy to extract now that the soil was soggy.

Gretchen held court in the keeping room next to the spinning wheel, expounding on the virtues of Connecticut wool to her hearers, namely, Lizzie and her son. Richie's interest plainly wandered, but the young widow's eyes were fixed on Gretchen's face.

Seeing them in close proximity, Abigail couldn't help but notice the comparison: the German widow short and wrinkled about the eyes, Lizzie a pale slender reed beside her. And clearly, Gretchen had a purpose. Soon the wheel shuddered into life, Lizzie's hands guiding the wool, the older woman eyeing the emerging yarn. Testing the newcomer. And training her.

Abigail sighed. The whole household was preparing for her wedding. A knock at the door startled her out of her gloomy thoughts.

"Mr. Russell." Her mother's voice at the door.

"Call me John, if ye please, ma'am."

Abigail approached the door and steeled herself. Mother was right. She did need to speak to him.

"Abigail, why don't you show John the garden? Show him your herbs."

Her mother lifted a brow, as if to remind her of their conversation. Abigail nodded and led the way outside.

Stopping by the cowshed, she showed John their latest acquisition. She fumbled with an explanation. "The heifer is a ... gift."

"For you?" John asked. The lines of his face were calm, but a pulse throbbed in his neck.

She looked away. "Yes."

"Ye're upset. Why?"

Abigail led the way behind the house to a rough plank bench next to Mother's straggly rosebush. Here they would be out of sight of the keeping room window. Standing in front of the bench she toyed with her fingertips, keenly aware of the dirt under her nails.

"We're not married and not even betrothed," she sputtered, more harshly than she'd intended.

John blinked several times rapidly. "I ken that." His blue eyes searched her face.

Men can be blind, Mother had said. Abigail decided she would have to explain. "At the ship's chandlery you said Lizzie would be a help to me in the valley."

She took a breath, trying to calm herself, but the anger of the last few days overwhelmed her. "You assumed I was betrothed to you. And you said it publicly."

John sat heavily on the bench and stared at the garden. Then he looked up at her. "I am sorry," he said, swallowing. "Ye are right. I took a liberty that wasna mine to take."

Abigail sat down, facing him.

He leaned over as if studying the ground, his wide square hands resting on his buff-colored leggings. The sunlight glinted red in his dark hair.

"I have sinned against ye." He sat up, and his clear eyes met hers. "Will ye forgive me?"

Her heart melted, and her innards drained of tension, leaving her almost limp. Abigail examined the clean lines of John's face: his strong, smooth jaw, punctuated with a small cleft in the chin; a wide forehead fringed by dark chestnut hair; and the scar cutting its way through one brow.

"Where did you get that scar?" she asked softly.

John looked at his hands. "I am a hasty man."

"What do you mean?"

"Aye, well, it happened when I first came to the valley. With Janet." His voice hitched. His eyes sought their humble garden, where twining vines wound their way up rickety poles. "Someone had brought a keg of whiskey to a cabin raising. After we ate, drink was flowing freely, and a man was there who began to get verra free with his comments about my wife.

"I warned him." John shrugged. "It just made him angry." His right hand opened and closed into a fist. "I hit him. Once, and again. I broke his nose. Then Roy hauled me off and someone else pulled the man away."

"The scar?"

"The other man pulled out his knife."

Abigail gasped. John could have lost his eye. "But weren't you defending your wife?"

He sighed and faced her squarely. "Aye, in a manner of speaking. I should have bid my goodbyes and left. Instead, I gave myself to the rage I felt. I have a temper, Abigail, and ye need to know."

"You don't seem like a fiery-tempered man." She shook her head. "No. You're not wicked like the man at the chandlery."

"Sloan? Aye, I ken ye saw him." He looked at his hands again. "But Abigail, what do the Scriptures say about the human heart?"

"That we have all sinned?"

"Aye. We all have the potential for evil. The Christian walks carefully, for he may fall into wickedness, as King David did." He gave her a lopsided grin. "Maybe I will not give way to my old nature, but it is there, and ye must know it."

Abigail smiled timidly. "I forgive you." She looked away, thinking about her own anger. "I'm sorry too. For my own foolishness. For my temper." She took a breath. "Will you forgive me?"

"Aye. I forgive ye." John's voice was gentle. He studied her face for a few moments and began to blink rapidly. Finally, he produced a pouch and fumbled with it. He loosened the drawstring and a shining object slid into his hand.

"Abigail, will ye marry me?"

She stared at the simple pendant in his hand, a beautiful blue stone with straight, clean lines set in silver. Leaning toward her, he slipped it over her head and kissed her cheek.

"I don't wear jewelry." She clutched at her apron in shock. But she'd known this was coming.

"I ken it would seem a mite frivolous. The stone is a rock I found hunting in the hills. It is part of the land, ye ken. Part of me. Part of my life."

"Oh." Abigail's cheeks throbbed with warmth. With a slight smile, she tucked the pendant inside her shift, knowing her answer to his question. This was a man worth enduring hardship for.

She looked him full in the face. "Yes, John Russell, I'll marry you."

7

It was wonderful to see the Change soon made in the
Manners of our Inhabitants; from being thoughtless or
indifferent about Religion, it seem'd as if all the World
were growing Religious; so that one could not walk thro'
the Town in an Evening without Hearing Psalms sung
in different Families of every Street.

—Benjamin Franklin, *Autobiography*, 1791

July 1744

*A*bigail sat at her small spindly dressing table, tasting the end
of her quill. She spit it out. Nasty habit. She was woolgathering. Carefully, she dipped her pen in her inkwell.

Dearest Hannah, I have the most wonderful News.

She thought over the events of the preceding week, highlighted by the drawing up of the betrothal contract. Lizzie had helped Gretchen produce food for the betrothal ceremony they'd celebrated at the meetinghouse. Her sister would love to come to the wedding, but by the time the letter arrived it would be next to impossible to make the journey in time. In any case, Hannah was close to her confinement.

And they couldn't postpone their vows. John said the corn was growing, and the road was long. Abigail penned a description of John's proposal on the rough paper. She dipped her quill again.

> *Mother is helping me sew a new Sabbath Gown. Father bought beautiful Calicut Cotton for her to use as Hangings and Curtains, but she gave it to me for my Trousseau. We have cut it in the new Style. I hope to wear it as my Wedding Gown.*

Abigail touched one of the pewter earpieces now attached to her spectacles. *That* she needed to describe for her sister.

> *And we went to the Tinker's with Papa. The Man attached pieces of Pewter to my Spectacles that curl over my Ears, and Fix'd the Part on the Nose. You may laugh, but they do not hurt me anymore!*

She concluded the letter and placed it in a packet along with a baby's gown made of scraps of the soft cotton.

Abigail smiled. Maybe, one day soon, she would have her own child.

THE SETTING SUN gilded the Russell farm with soft light. John followed his father and brother outside and surveyed the newcomers, their wagon pulled by two Marsh Tacky ponies. After a day's journey hauling the family's household goods, the animals stood dispirited, heads hanging low.

A young man jumped down from the wagon seat, followed by a little girl. The lad's sister? An older man and woman, along with a younger boy, clustered around them.

"Hallo, there. John Russell, at your service."

"Thomas Kerr, my wife Sophie, and son William." The curve of the man's back spoke of many days' work over an anvil or loom. He gestured toward the younger children. "Tommy and Kitty. Pleased to meet ye and your family. Only you and Roy traveling back?"

"Aye," John said. "And my wife." *Just two more weeks, and I can truly call her that.* The warmth of the thought surprised him.

Soon the ponies were attended to and everyone gathered around the small table for supper. Sam's wife Jenny had simmered a stew all day in her largest iron kettle. Golden wheat biscuits filled the room with their fragrance.

"What are your plans?" John asked the elder Kerr as Jenny ladled stew into wooden trenchers.

"Farming, first." Kerr's rounded shoulders hunched as he ate. "And weaving. I have a loom. Have ye need of a weaver?"

"Oh, aye." John swallowed his stew before continuing. "There's a well-to-do widow with a loom, but she's a wee bit upvalley from us. If ye settle nearby, it'll be a great help. Only a few sheep yet, and very little flax, but every year there's more." He reached for a biscuit. "I'll be hauling a bit of fabric in—some linen cloth. But most settlers are of the ordinary sort, and canna be buying all their dry goods. They'll be happy to spin and bring it to ye."

Finishing his meal he laid out the details of land purchase and settlement to the new family. "It's best if everything be done legal. Some folks just squat on the land, but they're asking for trouble. Once the land is purchased with a valid title, no one can take it away."

"No one?" Sophie, the man's thin wife, had been silent until now. Her plain face squinted at him in challenge.

"No." Gathering his thoughts, John eyed his brother Sam, who was filling his pipe. He turned back to the Kerrs. "The self-styled gentry of Virginia are simple landowners like us. They just have more land and more money. They have no power over us in the valley."

"Aye, well, our service here has been long, but we've worked hard, and the master gave us tools and the loom. But no cash money. We canna buy land." Thomas Kerr scraped the last of his stew off his plate and ladled it into his mouth.

John leaned back in his chair. "No matter. With skills like yours, folks will help ye out. You can work in the fields for hire, learn to shoot and trap game, and ply your trade. I can give ye a few acres in return for a bit of weaving now and again. In time, ye'll have your own land."

Discussions regarding the journey continued until John yawned and stretched with fatigue. He bade them all goodnight and headed for the loft, where he stripped off his clothes and lay down.

His mind was a jumble of last-minute purchases he had to make.

And Abigail's face.

THE CROWDED SHELVES took her breath away. Abigail had been in the apothecary's shop only once before, when her mother was shopping for simples. They hadn't stayed long. Since then she'd eyed it from afar, wistfully.

Gentian. Ipecac. Poppy. Ginger. Many of the labels on the jars were familiar. Some were not. She inhaled, breathing deep of the acrid, woodsy scent of the shop.

John's strong form, smelling comfortably of salve, anchored her. It was easy to feel safe with him. Lizzie, their chaperone for the day, observed the proceedings from behind them—for once, Ritchie had been content to stay at Gretchen's side, so they'd left him home.

"May I help thee?" A man in a dove-gray waistcoat appeared from a dark back room and took his place behind the counter, a canvas apron protecting his neat clothing. Spectacles perched on his crooked, slightly bulbous nose. The apothecary's inquisitive eyes flickered from John to her.

John looked at Abigail and jerked his head. "My betrothed has a list."

"Congratulations." The man's gaze took in John's buckskin jacket. "And where might thee be headed?"

Abigail unfolded her list as she listened to the conversation.

"The Shenandoah Valley. My wife will need a goodly supply of medicinals."

The back of her neck tingled. *My wife.* Surprisingly, she liked the sound of it. "Pray, first I'd like some valerian." Nervously, her fingers rubbed at the paper in her hand.

"Of course." He turned. "Jimmy?"

Soon a lanky lad was packaging the herbs and seeds as she listed them out.

"Lastly, slippery elm, one quarter pound."

"Certainly, and I can do you one better." He motioned to the lad and then leaned on the counter. "The tree is common, and I'm sure you'll see some specimens along the way and possibly near your home."

"Aye, that's true," John said. "There are a few large slippery elm near the settlement."

The man proceeded to describe the tree and method of procuring the bark and gave her tips on using some of the other herbs. "Valerian, now. Measure it carefully. In fact, I have a sheet I give to goodwives." He passed her a printed list of instructions and receipts. "See? There's an instruction for valerian."

"Thank you so much," Abigail said. "I'll write down all you said." This place was botany heaven.

"And she will," John commented. "She has a book."

Abigail's face flushed with mingled pleasure and embarrassment. He was proud of her.

∽

DEEP IN THE CORNFIELD, John chopped at stray weeds with the hoe, his shoulders and back aching with the exercise. The sun's fierce heat penetrated his straw hat, and sweat trickled down his back under his linen shirt. He swung at the base of a deep-rooted weed, breaking open a clod of dirt and savoring the warm, dusty smell of rich loam that emerged. He loved the soil, despite the backbreaking toil involved in tilling it.

Up ahead, his brother Sam worked another row. John stood upright, stretching and rolling his shoulders, and eyed the gourd full of refreshing switchel waiting for him at the end of the row. Taking off his hat, he saw Sam's gaze on him. Then his brother picked his way to his side, using his hoe like a cane to gently push aside the corn.

They stood together without speaking for a moment. In the distance, a bird trilled.

Sam broke the gentle silence. "Ye're sure about this lass?"

John ran his fingers through his sweat-dampened hair and replaced his hat. "I've prayed. I have a peace about the thing. She isna a Presbyterian. They have different customs. But she kens her Catechism."

Sam stared off into the distance. He was a man of few words. What was on his mind?

"Ye say she kens her Catechism. But is Christ the treasure of her heart?"

John blinked. He'd never heard his brother talk quite like this. He shrugged and frowned, studying the clods at his feet.

His brother frowned, as if seeking the right words. "Ye have heard about George Whitefield's visits here."

"Oh, aye. I saw the new meetinghouse too."

"Ye should have been there and heard him preach. I still think on it. In some ways, it was ordinary. Straight gospel preaching. Much like Tennent's. But the crowds ..." His brother's voice cracked with feeling.

John forgot the heat. He'd not heard his taciturn brother so moved.

"Every kind of person attended the open-air meetings. Negro

slaves. Indentured servants. Fancy gentlemen would sit in their carriages nearby, and skinny apprentices perched in the trees. Butchers came with bloody aprons and stood next to ladies in fine muslin."

Sam paused. His eyes brightened with tears. "They would weep. Sometimes only tears, but occasionally sobs would erupt from deep within the crowd."

"Why?" Da had written him, but not with such detail. "Why would the gospel make them cry?"

"Well, ye see, most of these folks considered themselves Christian already. Philadelphia is full of all sorts: Presbyterian, Quakers, Baptists, and even a few Congregationalists, as ye know. And aye, some didna claim any sort of religion. But most did. And they wept because they realized their hope of heaven was false. Again and again, I would hear someone say, 'I was raised in a Christian home. I'm a member. I know my Catechism. I give to the poor. But all that means nothing now. My only hope is in Christ.'"

John fixed his gaze on his brother. "So these folks closed with Christ?"

"Oh aye, many did." His brother's mouth twitched. "So ye see, the weeping wasn't just of sorrow. There were tears of joy as well."

Abigail. Her face came before him. "Are ye wondering about my betrothed?"

"Aye. Is she resting in her own works?" Sam took off his hat and massaged his neck. "Sometimes it's hard to tell. We tend to do it by nature."

"I ken that." John remembered the booklets he'd purchased at the printers'. *George Whitefield.* There was one of his sermons in the stack.

Curious now, he couldn't wait to read it.

ABIGAIL PULLED the needle through the fabric, deciding she liked the tautness of the thread through the tight weave of the yellow cotton.

Most linen had a looser weave that made it well suited for embroi-
dery. But the cotton cloth felt almost like silk in comparison. It would
make a lovely gown.

Her mother sat on her bed across the room, her fingers busy
setting the second sleeve. With the bodice finished, all that remained
was the hem of the skirt. Abigail shifted the fabric of the overskirt in
her hands, feeling its weight. There was a lot to hem, but at least she
felt confident making the simple stitches.

"John will be visiting this afternoon."

"Yes, Mother."

"Only four more days."

Abigail nodded. What was her mother getting at?

Mother set her thread aside and jabbed her needle into the
pincushion. "I've been meaning to speak to you about ... marriage."

That was vague. "You mean about what happens after?" She
hoped she wasn't blushing. With her complexion, it happened all the
time.

Mother took a deep breath and seemed to relax. "Yes." She looked
out the window, then at the floor. Finally she met Abigail's gaze.
"With Hannah it was different." Her brows knit. "There was a longer
courtship. And they had a chance to bundle."

Abigail smiled. Mother had sewed her sister and Amos up in wool
blankets and they'd slept together in Hannah's room. Actually,
there'd been little sleeping. She had hardly slept herself for all the
giggling that had penetrated the walls of her bedchamber. "I
remember that, Mother. I kept wondering, what if they have to use
the chamber pot? They were trapped, all sewed up tight, with that
board between them."

Mother's stolid face cracked into a rare smile. "The secret is no ale
at supper." She paused. "Do you feel rushed? Afraid? Have you ...
held his hand? Kissed?"

Hannah gaped. *Kissed?* Her cheeks warmed. "No, Mother." Once,
she'd stared at his lips and wondered what kissing would be like. But

other times, she thought of his first wife and any warmth in her innards would dissipate.

She had dark hair, was all John had said when she'd asked him about Janet. The shuttered look on his face had discouraged any prying.

"It's an advantage you have."

Had she missed something? "An advantage?"

"Absolutely. You may not have known him long, but he knows how to take care of a wife. In every area." Mother's eyes were on her.

Oh. Abigail looked down. "I see."

"You know the commandments. Obey and reverence your husband. He'll take care of the details. And he'll treat you right. Your papa wouldn't have allowed his suit if he thought otherwise."

Papa? Mother had just used that word. Did she realize it? Biting her lip, Abigail pushed her needle through the fabric once again. "Mother?"

"Yes?"

"I'll write. I don't know how long it takes for letters to come all that way, but you know I'll write."

Were those tears in her mother's eyes?

Of the best Peruvian bark powder'd, one ounce, of Virginia Snake root, and salt of wormwood, each one drachm; mix these well together, and divide them into eight doses ...

—John Theobald, M.D., Intermitting Fever, *Every Man His Own Physician*, 1764

*L*ate afternoon sunlight slanted through the keeping room window, illuminating the room. John was glad the sun didn't land directly on the booklet in his hand; indirect sunlight was usually best for reading. Candlelight flickered. Light from a hearth was even worse. The leaping flames of a fire gave him the headache if he tried to read by it. Sometimes he would simply memorize a single verse of Scripture in the morning and consider it at random moments in the day. It was hard to find good reading light in the valley.

"This is a sermon by George Whitefield. His text is from the prophet Jeremiah."

Sitting at his side on the small settee, Abigail nodded in response. The warmth of her body nudged at his mind, reminding him that they'd be married in only a few short days. Though her mother worked only a few steps away in the kitchen, he was quite conscious of being alone with his betrothed. He forced his mind back to the sermon. If he was to be her husband, he needed to see to all aspects of her welfare, including the welfare of her soul.

"'The Lord our Righteousness' is the text. He unfolds the meaning for us. Here, ye start us out. Read the first bit." He handed her the booklet.

"'Whoever is acquainted with the nature of mankind in general, or the propensity of his own heart in particular, must acknowledge, that self-righteousness is the last idol that is rooted out of the heart: being once born under a covenant of works, it is natural for us all to have recourse to a covenant of works, for our everlasting salvation.'" Abigail frowned. "I know what a covenant is. An agreement. This covenant of works puzzles me."

"D'ye remember Adam? What did the Lord tell him? What commandment did He give him?"

"Not to eat of the fruit of the tree of the knowledge of good and evil."

John stood and stretched. It was too much to ask of a man to sit next to his betrothed on a tiny piece of furniture. "And what happened?"

Abigail regarded him. "He broke that commandment."

"What would have happened if he hadna disobeyed?"

She blinked. "I suppose if they had been obedient they would have continued living in the garden."

"Aye, walking with the Lord every evening." He smiled. Perhaps he was his father's son after all. He didn't mind giving instruction. "So. If they obey, they live in joyful communion. They break the commandment once—only once, mind ye—and they are cast out."

Abigail was all attention. "So that is the covenant of works?"

"Aye. There was more to come under Moses. More laws."

She nodded.

"But only one Person fulfilled the covenant of works. Obeyed God perfectly in every particular."

Abigail frowned slightly and fussed with her cap. "Christ?"

"Aye. The Lord Jesus Christ is the only one Who is righteous. He is the subject of the text: the Lord our Righteousness. So what does Whitefield mean when he says we all have the natural desire to be justified by our works?"

Abigail stood and walked to the window. She turned. "I think we want to be good. To keep the Law. But isn't that right? Isn't that a good thing?"

"Aye, absolutely. But the Law also shows us our sin and drives us to Christ. Let's see what happened to our first parents. Whitefield continues here with an illustration." He found the place in the sermon. "'For, what were the coats that God made to put on our first parents, but types of the application of the merits of righteousness of Jesus Christ to believers' hearts? We are told, that these coats were made of skins of beasts; and, as beasts were not then food for men, we may fairly infer, that those beasts were slain in sacrifice, in commemoration of the great sacrifice, Jesus Christ, thereafter to be offered.'"

Abigail sank down on her stool in the corner. "I knew about those coats of skin. But not what they meant."

"Aye. Adam and Eve were forgiven just as folks today. By the blood and merit of the Lord Jesus Christ, as symbolized in those skins."

Abigail's lips parted as she rubbed the hem of her apron between her fingers. "Do you think I could borrow the sermon?"

"Surely. It's a bit lengthy. I'll leave it so ye might read it at your leisure." He glanced out the window, evaluating the sun's height. He'd never make the ferry before supper.

"John." Abigail's mother stood in the doorway. "Won't you join us for chowder?"

Had she been listening? His mouth slid into a partial smile. "I would like that verra much. Thank ye kindly."

~

ABIGAIL SAT ON HER BED, absently fingering her quilt. It was her last night alone. How would she ever get to sleep? Tomorrow was her wedding day.

The ceremony itself was a simple affair. John had explained to her that many aspects of a Scots Presbyterian wedding were the same: the contract, the civil ceremony with the exchange of promises. "We don't put religious pomp into it," he'd said. "The homily read at the betrothal was similar to what we might do. But even that isna necessary."

It was what happened *after* that made her nervous and excited. Not just the wedding night, but her whole new life afterward. They'd be starting out for the valley right away: tomorrow they'd make the short trek to the Russell farm, eat supper with John's family, and leave the very next morning.

She eyed her polished kidskin Sabbath shoes in the corner. *Mary's shoes.* She'd almost forgotten that the fawn-colored leather boots were originally her oldest sister's. But at fifteen Mary had still been growing, and soon the footwear was passed along to Hannah, and then to her. Her own feet had stayed small enough to fit into them permanently.

Yesterday she'd received a letter from Mary. It was their first contact since she'd left home. Hannah had included a small packet of seeds with her last letter, and smuggled Mary's letter in with the seeds. Abigail understood why. Mother would never have approved. Not after what Mary had done.

She crossed to the desk where the letter lay, along with Whitefield's sermon. She was still trying to digest the sermon, and now this ... she picked up the letter, creased with multiple folds.

Dearest Abigail, you may wonder at this secret Missive. But Hannah gave me the good News of your upcoming Nuptials, and I wish you all the Blessings of it. Many of the Sorrows of my life have been allay'd by the Attentions of a kindly Husband, and such is he, though others may see him as gruff. An even greater Solace I have in my Heavenly Bridegroom, Who loves Sinners. I have one Son and a Girl. If you wish, please send me News through Hannah. All my Love, Mary.

Tears welled in Abigail's eyes. Years before, a young man from Massachusetts, newly arrived in Philadelphia, had courted Mary. He'd disappeared, and soon, so had Mary. Hannah had whispered to her that she'd been with child. Papa had whisked her away and found her a husband in Boston. A sea captain, of all things. Mother, distraught, had wailed and raged for days, making the pronouncement that no contact would ever be made with their errant daughter.

If you wish ... Apparently, Mary didn't know what Abigail would think or do. She scanned the lines again. A kindly husband. Papa had done well for her under the circumstances. Perhaps she would write.

Even if Mother disapproved. But Abigail wouldn't be home anymore, not after tomorrow. What would John think? She hadn't told him about Mary. But was this even the same Mary? Her oldest sister had learned her Catechism with the rest of them, but Abigail would never have imagined her "finding solace" in God.

After replacing the letter, she snuffed out the candle and lay back on the bed, atop the quilt. The warm, close bedroom promised a hot day tomorrow, and Abigail wondered if the rose petals in her wash water would be enough.

She shifted uneasily. Sleep seemed elusive. Staring up into the darkness, she compared Mary's words to the sermon. They were heart-felt words, like Whitefield's. Much of the booklet consisted of logical argument, much like any sermon. But they were forceful arguments, made with great care and even passion. And some of his ideas caught her off guard.

"Were you ever made to abhor yourselves for your actual and original sins, and to loathe your own righteousness ...?" Bits and pieces of Whitefield's words floated to the surface of her mind. *Loathe my own righteousness?* His language might have been Greek for all the sense it made to her.

Yet all his reasoning came from the Scriptures. Abigail was certain of that. The difficult sections of the sermon she'd re-read until she grasped his point. Or at least the meaning of his words. The difficulty wasn't with Whitefield, she realized suddenly.

The difficulty was with *her.*

JOHN'S STOMACH tightened underneath his butternut waistcoat as he thought of Abigail. His fingers felt a bit moist on Percy's reins, and it wasn't just from the warmth of the sticky Philadelphia summer morning. His cravat, a preposterous construction of linen and lace that looked like it belonged on a Parisian aristocrat, choked him. Soon he could be divested of the layers of stiff, overly warm clothing, but he'd never be free from his vows. His very innards seemed to shudder with the seriousness of the day.

His eyes roved over the new construction along Walnut Street as he followed the wagon into town. Roy, resplendent in a borrowed bottle-green coat, clucked at the mules while Da sat next to him on the wagon seat, holding the pony's lead. John studied the contents of the wagon, already partly full of the supplies they would be hauling to the valley; they'd load Abigail's possessions that very day.

The pony's steel-gray coat glistened in the morning light. *Rosemary.* He thought about the day Abigail had accompanied him to purchase—and name—the pony, and an unexpected surge of affection filled him. Yes, she was the one for him. She would never replace Janet, but she'd be a pleasant companion nonetheless.

Roy urged the mules into the final turn. Her street. He'd asked Da the night before about his concerns regarding Abigail's spiritual state.

"She kens her Catechism, Da," he'd said.

His father's eyes had twinkled behind his spectacles. "But ye have a question."

"Aye."

"Let's have it, straight out."

John spread his fingers on the table before them, now cleared of supper dishes. He sighed. "Abigail doesna react to gospel truth the same way as Janet." His throat tightened. Maybe that wasn't the best way to describe it.

Da merely lifted his eyebrows in response.

"I've never heard her speak of her conversion or her love for Christ."

"But ye have been teaching her?"

"Aye, a wee bit. We read through part of a sermon. One of White-field's." John pushed back his chair and stood.

Da blinked at him. "Well, then. She has a profession of faith, she is open to your instruction, and she doesna object to the stink of your salve."

He chuckled despite himself. "Aye."

His father took a long breath and his brows knit briefly. "These are still good questions, son. Ye desire to know if her faith is genuine. Sometimes it's hard to discern." He pushed back his chair and stood. "At this point, obey the Scriptures. Ye are betrothed, and ye are commanded to love your wife. Cherish her. If there is anything lacking, that's God's business. He'll help ye."

Love your wife. Cherish her. Startled, John realized that the wagon had drawn up in front of the house.

They had arrived.

9

But in the main, there has been a great and marvelous work
of conversion and sanctification among the people
here...

—Jonathan Edwards, *A Narrative of Surprising Conversions*, 1736

*A*bigail stepped down the familiar oak steps carefully, conscious of the fullness of her overskirt and Mary's boots on her feet. Gretchen had fixed her hair, braiding and coiling it neatly, placing the new cap of Holland linen just so, and leaving several thick curly strands dangling free in front. Would Mother fuss at the curls?

But in a few moments John would have the say in such matters, and the more she considered it, the more confident she felt that he would treat her kindly. Customs were different among his kin, and she needed to watch and learn. Yes, she did wish to please him.

On the step nearest the bottom, her boot snagged the hem of her skirt, and she sidestepped, pulling the gathered yellow fabric out of the way.

Mary. The footwear reminded her of her sister, and of her words. And Whitefield's. Her gut clenched at the thought that perhaps John would find her wanting. If she couldn't grasp Whitefield's words, if she couldn't measure up ...

There he was, standing in the doorway, his tall form framed by the oak timbers on either side. Frozen in place, he caught sight of her, blue eyes locked on hers, the lines of his face square and strong. Under his cleft chin, lace spilled over a light brown vest that peeped through the lapels of his blue woolen coat.

He took a few steps forward and rolled his shoulder, as if uncomfortable. Roy, his bright copper hair complementing the green of his coat, entered behind him.

Her father welcomed them, and everyone gathered in the keeping room, sitting or standing. A sheet of parchment and a pewter standish lay on the oak table; everything was ready for the magistrate. She found herself on the settee, observing the proceedings in a daze. The aroma of Gretchen's pastries filled the house, but her stomach felt tight. She didn't know if she could eat.

John approached her. "May I sit?"

Abigail nodded and pulled her skirts together, making room for him.

He settled beside her, shoulders stiff. "Are ye well?"

"Oh, yes, quite well. Thank you." He didn't smell of salve today. No, something sweet and musky at the same time. Cinnamon? Yes, cinnamon and another unknown herb.

"Ye look quite well." John cleared his throat. "Your gown is verra pretty."

"Thank you. It's my new Sabbath gown. Mother did most of it ... I am not skillful with the needle." She was babbling.

"Dinna fash yerself. Ye've other talents."

A commotion at the door caused her to straighten. The magistrate? Her stomach tightened. She forced herself to stand.

The faintest pressure at her elbow revealed John's close presence. "Not to worry," he murmured.

Adjusting his wig, the magistrate entered the keeping room, merry eyes flashing. His gaze found Abigail and flickered to John. "The bride and groom?"

She nodded. John's face filled her vision, and her breathing quickened; the rest of the room seemed to fade.

"Witnesses?"

Roy was saying something. And then Gretchen's voice filtered through the haze. *Dear Gretchen.* She'd miss the kindly housekeeper.

John's lips parted slightly, and he slipped a finger under his cravat, as if fighting for air. Then he clasped her hands, communicating sureness, strength—but also tension.

Nervousness moistened her hands. She was glad for her gloves.

The magistrate cleared his throat. "Do you, John Russell, agree to be a loving and faithful husband?"

"Aye. Aye, I do agree."

"Do you, Abigail Williams, agree to be a loving, faithful, and obedient wife?"

"Yes, I agree."

Abigail heard the magistrate speak again, and the tension in John's hands seemed to diminish. He released her and guided her to the table, where the wigged man showed them where to sign.

It was over.

She could breathe again.

Abigail opened the scuffed sea chest her father had given her and studied the compartments under the lid.

"There," Mother pronounced. "I've folded your gown. Let's put your oldest petticoats below and above."

Soon the Sabbath gown—her wedding gown—found its place in the chest. Abigail added a lavender sachet to keep the pests away.

"Thank you, Mother." Her throat swelled up.

Mother blinked away tears and threw her arms around her. "I know I've been hard on you—"

"No, Mother, you just had to be careful lest Papa spoil me."

Her mother's lined face broke into a wistful smile. "There is some truth in that. I have no doubt John will treat you well." She broke away. "I need to help Gretchen load up last minute things."

"Butter won't keep."

"She'll give you a crockful anyway. If she's packed too much, give some to the Russells tonight."

Then she was gone, and Abigail looked around the empty room, her heart aching. She'd folded her quilt and placed it in the cedar chest, leaving her bed bare. Her clothes filled the seaman's chest, but there were a few things she still needed to pack. She looked under the lid again. Where could she put her pewter standish?

Her hand slipped into a leather compartment. There was something inside. A pair of men's gloves. Well-worn and even a bit stained, they wouldn't have been missed by their owner.

There was a knock at the door.

"Come in." She knew it was Papa before she saw him.

"What do you have there?"

His face looked tight, as if he were about to weep. Was it possible? She'd never seen a man shed tears. "Gloves. I found them in one of the compartments under the lid."

Papa's face brightened. "Gloves?"

She handed them over. "They look rather small for a man, don't you think?"

Papa smiled. "I know a sea captain who brings up molasses from Barbados every year. Smaller than you. But feisty. And dangerous, some say." He flipped the gloves over in his paw-like hands. "Hold out your hand."

She complied, and he slipped one of the gloves on.

"It fits! Well, just a little large." She flexed her hand and made a fist.

"Keep these. They'll come in handy." His mouth worked a bit. "I see you laboring in the garden, getting your hands dirty ... your mother doesn't take care of her hands ..."

He was having trouble speaking. "They'll be perfect, Papa. I'll wear them in the garden and anytime I scrub." At least, she would try to remember.

"Let Lizzie scrub. She'll be there to help. Let her help."

"Yes, Papa." She hugged him, and felt a single tremor pass through his body.

"Well," he said, breaking away. "Are you packed?"

"All except for my writing materials."

Soon the last items were stowed. Papa eyed the chest. "I think I'll ask John to carry it to the wagon. Or Roy. That thing is heavy even when empty." He paused. "I'll see if I'm needed downstairs."

He left the room, and Abigail allowed herself a single sob. Then she wiped away the tear that had spilled down her cheek.

JOHN BROUGHT the pony around to the front of the house. He frowned. How much experience did Abigail have with horses? He'd borrowed his sister-in-law's sidesaddle for the trip through town, but most women in the valley who rode did so astride, even the widow McDowell with her fashionable headgear. He imagined riding astride would be much more comfortable for a long trip.

Abigail came out the door. Her eyes lit up when she saw Rosemary. But her face changed when her gaze fell on the saddle.

"D'ye ride much?"

"No. Papa taught me, but there hasn't been much need."

Abigail approached the pony's head and let her catch her scent. She was a natural with animals. This might not be too difficult.

"We will travel slowly. The heifer canna travel fast. Ye'll do fine. And when we get to the farm, we'll switch saddles. Ye'll ride astride."

"Astride?" Her eyebrows shot up.

"Aye, it's common in the country. And truly, I dinna ken how ladies perch on a sidesaddle. It seems terribly uncomfortable to me."

Abigail grinned and he returned her smile. Maybe the rest of the day would go easier. She'd been petrified this morning. And then there was tonight ... His brows twitched. He'd rather not think about tonight. So far, he'd not thought of Janet today. It was as though she'd retreated, having given her blessing. *But still.* His gut twisted suddenly.

"I suppose I'll learn as we travel."

John smiled, his foreboding forgotten. *She'll do. Aye, she'll do.*

～

ABIGAIL ADJUSTED HER STRAW HAT, struggling to keep the hot sun off her face as she swayed in the saddle. *Almost there.* Her muscles were complaining; a spasm had shot through her hip halfway through town. She was glad she wouldn't be riding sidesaddle all the way to the Shenandoah Valley.

It had required two trips to get them all across the ferry. Lizzie and Richie accompanied Roy in the wagon, and then the ferryman had returned to fetch her, John, and John's father.

Now they were less than a mile from the house. On the way, she'd asked about the items in the wagon. Only half of the kegs and crates were hers, if that.

"Supplies for us. Molasses, cider, flour. And dry goods," he'd explained. "Mostly for a man named McClure in the valley. I sell his whiskey—"

"Whiskey?" How such a godly man could deal in spirits was beyond her.

He eyed her carefully. "There isna much cash money in the valley. Or script." He frowned. "So we barter. But if we need things from Lancaster or Philadelphia, or when it comes time to pay taxes and tithes—"

"Tithes?"

"Aye. Here in Pennsylvania ye only give offerings toward the support of your own minister. In Virginia ye must also give to the Anglican Church."

"So you must give double."

"Essentially, yes. But we knew that when we settled there. It's no but a wee hardship after Londonderry, Da says."

She'd let the reference to Londonderry pass, vaguely remembering the dinner discussion in which his father had explained their history. "But the whiskey?"

"It's easy to transport. Ye get more in exchange for whiskey than a like amount of corn or barley. Tavern owners will pay cash money."

"Doesn't that promote drunkenness?"

"Good question." He paused. "Does your father ever drink rum?"

"Oh. Maybe once in a while. Mother doesn't approve."

"Does she approve of ale or cider?"

Abigail caught the drift of his logic. "Yes, we drink ale. Hard cider on occasion."

"Our minister, Mr. Craig, only drinks cider and ale. He won't touch whiskey." John directed his mare around several large mounds of manure in the road.

Abigail nudged her pony the opposite way. Rosemary responded easily to her amateur guidance. Soon they were riding side-by-side again.

"Does he think it wrong?"

"Not exactly. We must be temperate in all things, and some would rather abstain altogether than risk sinning."

"What about you? Do you drink whiskey?"

He grinned. "A wee bit. I keep a jug in the cabin, partly for medicinal use. Ye may want it for your herbs."

Yes. Tinctures. Some herbs were best prepared in alcohol. "Yes, I guess we can keep the whiskey."

John's eyebrows shot up at her pronouncement. "I suppose I am well and truly married."

Abigail remembered feeling heat creep up her cheeks at that

statement. Soon they *would* be well and truly married. She squeezed the reins spasmodically, thinking of her wedding night. Mother had said to trust him.

She glanced at him, sitting tall in the saddle, blue coat straining at the seams. He wasn't a rich man. But he was gentle. She took a deep breath. Yes, she could trust him.

She blinked, roused from her thoughts. Before them stood a rambling house: logs dominated one half, wood siding the other. Wisps of smoke curled into the air from a stone chimney. Outbuildings stood sentinel about the property; the largest structure looked like a barn.

John led the way. Soon they dismounted, and she stretched away the aches in her muscles. Underneath her bodice, her shift felt sticky with sweat.

How would she survive the trip in this heat?

"Jenny likes ye," John said. The worst of the afternoon heat had lifted as evening crept on, and he led Abigail out the door. Glad to be away from the stuffiness of the overcrowded house, he took a deep breath and surveyed the familiar farm. Long streaks of orange and salmon painted the western sky, and a few fireflies blinked in the distance against the tree line. He took her hand gently. They hadn't touched much. Or kissed.

"I like her too. And your brother." She paused. "You haven't said much about your mother."

He hesitated. There wasn't much to say. "She went to her Lord soon after we came here. I was but a lad. She was laid to rest near the edge of our property. I'll show you her grave." He led her toward the tree line.

Abigail walked quietly at his side for a long minute before speaking. "What do you remember of her?"

"Hmph. Hair about my color. Not sure about her eyes. Maybe

gray. They always seemed to change, ye see? She was a good and godly woman, but she also had a bit of temper."

"Like you?"

He smiled. "Aye. When we did something rascally, her eyes would snap fire."

They arrived at the stone marker, and John's heart seemed to seize up for a moment as he studied the humble grave in the dim light. He'd imagined he wouldn't feel grief after all this time.

"You miss her." It was a statement.

"Aye. I canna describe ..."

"I lost a brother. When I was thirteen. Jonathan went to sea and the ship was lost. My heart felt ripped in two. I think of that year as the black year. I couldn't even collect plants."

He turned, surprised. "I am sorry." Impulsively, he drew her into his arms.

Slowly, she slid her arms around him. Then he felt her relax against his chest.

"I'm sorry too. For all you've lost."

He shuddered once and gripped her tighter.

10

But the church... being not large enough to contain a fourth part of the people, we adjourned to the fields, and I preached for an hour-and-a-half from a balcony, to upwards of ten thousand hearers, who were very attentive and much affected.

—George Whitefield, 1739

August 1744

*A*bigail groaned.

"Wake up." John's voice whispered in the darkness.

She rubbed her eyes. No, it wasn't completely dark. A faint pearl-gray light limned the horizon. Every muscle ached, especially her hips and legs. Riding astride *was* easier, but still, ten hours in the saddle left her feeling bruised and beaten. Thankfully, she'd taken Jenny's advice and worn quilted jumps instead of stays on the road.

There was little privacy, and she'd slept in her clothes. Sleeping in stays would have been torture.

"We need to get an early start," John murmured. "It's better to travel in the cool of the day. We'll take a good rest when it gets hot."

She lifted her head from his jacket, which they'd used as a pillow. They both smelled of salve now. And the acrid tang of dried sweat. When would she be able to bathe again? She'd never given it a thought but had always taken wash water for granted. She frowned. Did they bathe in the Shenandoah Valley?

John was at her elbow and helped her stand. "Ye've time to visit the necessary. Coffee's almost ready. Then we'll break camp." He steered her into a small grove of oaks near the stream where they'd stopped. *The stream ... if only ...* Perhaps there'd be opportunities to wash later.

"I'll just be a moment." It was still dark, but shyness overtook her. Their wedding night at the Russells' farm hadn't been disagreeable, just embarrassing. She wished, not for the first time, that she could talk to Hannah face-to-face. She had questions she couldn't imagine writing down on paper. Sleeping next to John on the ground last night had been less intimate, but strange, nonetheless. Strange but not unpleasant—a bit like bundling, she supposed, only on a much firmer bed.

Abigail adjusted her clothing and climbed the bank of the stream, finger-combing her hair. John approached her, his outline visible against the light of the small fire. He handed her a wooden cup full of coffee, and she took it gratefully. After blowing on the steaming liquid, she sipped. *Chicory.* Lizzie had mixed chicory in with the coffee. How much coffee and tea had John purchased? She wished now she'd paid more attention to such things. Several times her mother had impressed upon her the need for household economy in her duties as a wife.

The whimper of a child caught her attention. *Ritchie.* His silhouette revealed tousled locks as he emerged from underneath the wagon, where he and his mother had slept.

"Richie. Come, I'll share with you." She crouched and comforted the sleepy child, holding the cup to his lips. John stood over them for a moment, then turned and walked away.

~

ROSEMARY DIDN'T MOVE while John cinched the saddle, but only turned a sleepy head toward him as if to say, *it's early*. He disliked having to wake Abigail so early, much less subject her to the indignities of sleeping out in the open, but his new wife hadn't complained.

He frowned. She must be sore after riding all day yesterday. Perhaps she could switch with Lizzie and ride on the wagon seat for a time.

Seeing her with Ritchie just now moved him strangely. He knew she'd be good for Susanna, but all at once he'd been swamped by a new thought: they were married now, and she might conceive. Why hadn't he given this thought before? As natural as the four seasons, childbearing followed marriage. His throat worked. Even now, he could be a new father.

Roy approached him. "The Kerrs are ready."

"The mules harnessed?"

"Aye."

"Then let's smother the fire and break camp. We should make the Brandywine well before sundown." John remembered the Kerrs' ponies. "Well, if their ponies dinna collapse."

"Aye. They are hauling too much in that wagon, and the ponies are no' in the best condition."

"We'll keep an eye, Roy. I've an idea. I'll let ye know at midday."

An hour later the sun was well up and cast long shadows before them. John nudged his mare closer to Abigail's pony. "How fare ye?"

She looked up at him, eyes tired under the brim of her straw hat. Her jaw worked for a moment. "I... I wonder if I have blisters."

His jaw dropped. Guilt washed over him. "Would ye swap places with Lizzie on the wagon?"

She nodded. Her shoulders seemed to sag, as if in relief.

"Roy!" John barked instructions, and soon Lizzie held Rosemary's reins, her eyes wide.

"I've never ridden a horse before," she said. "Well, I've taken a few turns with a pony as a young lass ..."

"Ye'll be fine. Rosemary kens her duty. And we'll no' be going fast."

John scratched his hairline and ruminated. He was a bit saddle sore himself. But blisters? Women didn't wear breeches, he realized suddenly. Well, he didn't know for sure what the widow McDowell wore underneath her fancy skirts when she rode.

He blinked as a thought struck him. Now *there* was an idea. But he'd have to wait till darkness fell.

He nudged Percy forward, scouting the road. Rutted and wide, the dusty trail was well traveled and safe as far as Lancaster. After that ... well, the Cumberland wasna truly safe, and though he appreciated the new treaty the governor had made with the Iroquois, it never paid to be careless. He studied the ground. A horse-drawn wagon had passed this way no more than a week past. Other tracks near the side were frozen into dried mud, evidence of travel on a wet day.

John pressed his mare's neck lightly with the reins, and she turned easily, accustomed to his circling. As a result of his backtracking, the poor girl traveled the longest distance of any of the animals; he checked her feet carefully each night. He passed Roy and Abigail in the wagon, Ritchie peeping at him from behind them in the bed. Then he circled the Kerrs' wagon, studying the ponies as they hauled the heavy conveyance.

He frowned. It wasn't yet mid-morning, and both ponies already showed signs of fatigue. Heads down, they moved deliberately. Marsh Tacky ponies were tough creatures, but the wagonload of supplies, people, and the loom was too much for them to haul. John Houston sold good horses in Lancaster, but at this rate, the ponies would never make it there. John longed to examine their fetlocks and cannons.

The animals weren't limping or even favoring their feet, but it was only a matter of time.

"Mr. Kerr." He'd have to speak as graciously as he could. "D'ye ken how old yer ponies are?"

Kerr's thick eyebrows jerked as he glanced at him. "No. I dinna ken how to read their teeth. My master assured me they had plenty of life in them."

"Nae doubt. But they're March Tacky ponies, aye? Wonderful for the mountains. They are surefooted creatures and will carry a full-grown man. But for hauling a fully loaded wagon ye need mules or cart horses."

John felt Kerr's wife's gaze upon him. She was suspicious. She murmured something to her husband.

"Tell ye what. We're coming up on a stream. If ye'll allow it, I'll check their teeth and their fetlocks."

"Fetlocks?"

"Aye. They are ways to tell if they're going to founder. These ponies have great heart. They will pull this wagon till they ruin their feet. Then ye have to shoot them."

Kerr gaped. As he grasped the implications, the reins slackened in his hands. His daughter, perched behind him in the wagon bed, stared up at him, her mouth open. She'd understood too. His wife's mouth was still set in a grim line, but her eyes clouded over.

The ponies halted, heads down. Then Kerr slapped the reins and they threw their shoulders into the harness. The wagon wheels creaked as the heavy load moved forward again, the timbers of the loom standing against the sky like a sail.

Twenty minutes later the caravan pulled up at a shady creek. The trail ran through a wide, shallow spot; on either side, willows and oaks grew in profusion, and cattails extended down the banks. John hastened to lead his own animals to water, then approached the Kerrs.

The first pony had sound feet. But as he knelt before the second and ran his hand down the near fore, he detected a thumping under his fingers. "Mr. Kerr?"

"Aye?" The other man knelt beside him.

"Place your fingers just so."

"I feel something. Like his heartbeat."

"Aye. Now do the same with this animal."

John stood at the pony's head while the other man ran his hands down its foreleg.

"I canna find it."

John rubbed the itchy stubble on his chin. How to explain? "Have ye ever had a cut that swelled and oozed? Or just became red?"

"Aye, my wife had to lance a boil once. I think I ken what ye mean. The other pony's foot is sore?"

He nodded. "Aye, just a wee bit. He's not limping now, but he will be soon."

Thomas Kerr stood up. "What do I do?"

"I have an idea. We'll swap the mules for the ponies. We'll harness my mare and my Connemara to our wagon for now. They won't like it, but we'll all make it to Lancaster that way."

Brows furrowed, Kerr eyed the sturdy mules. "I don't have cash money to pay the difference."

"I know a man in Lancaster who would take the ponies. A few months of good pasture and they'll be worth something."

"I'll speak to my son and my wife. But I dinna think I have a choice."

John intercepted Roy as he led the mules away from the stream. "Roy, I just swapped the mules for the ponies."

"*What?*" His cousin's green eyes flashed. "Those are my mules. How can you swap them?"

Out of the corner of his eye, John saw Abigail's gaze upon them as her bare feet dangled in the stream. "Look." He kept his voice low. "Otherwise one of those ponies will founder by the end of the day. They'll never make it to Lancaster, let alone the valley."

Roy shifted his stance and jerked his chin. "Ye should've asked me first. It wasna right for ye to do."

John's face heated. Anger and guilt tangled in his heart. He turned and watched his wife draw on her stockings as he struggled with his emotions. "Ye're right." He studied the ground. "Of course ye're right." Then the kernel of an idea he'd had emerged as a full-blown thought. "I'll get what I can for these ponies from Houston or someone he knows. Then I'll buy ye a mare. Or two."

Roy's shoulders relaxed. "Or two? We'd need two horses. Can ye afford it?"

An image of a long rifle flashed before his mind. He might not be able to afford one this time. But he had to do right by his cousin. Whatever it took. "Aye, we can afford it. Houston always has good horses, or kens who does. Ye like Clevelands?"

Roy's eyes turned dreamy. "A bay Cleveland mare. And I know who has a stud."

John chuckled. "The widow McDowell.

11

---

*A number of preachers have appeared among us ... The
points on which their preaching mainly turns are those
important ones of man's guilt, corruption, and impo-
tence; supernatural generation by the Spirit of God, and
free justification by faith in the righteousness of Christ;
and the marks of the new birth.*

—William Cooper, 1741

bigail studied the tree near the trail. Was that a slippery elm? She took note of the tree's habit and what she could make out of the leaves—they should be pinnate.

Pinnate? Or was that palmate? A rivulet of sweat ran trickled into her right eye, and she rubbed her face with her sleeve. Glancing down, she saw that her sleeve was grimy, impregnated with the dust of the road. She felt dirty all over.

She focused again on the tree, struggling to ignore the heat that sapped her strength. Step by step she advanced. Slowly, she made her way past the slippery elm—if that's what it was.

She ached all over. And walking in the hot sun was exhausting. But with Rosemary and Percy pulling their wagon, they were all taking turns walking. Convincing the saddle horses to take up their new role had been difficult enough; no one wanted to overload the wagon at present. She checked the pony plodding alongside her, its nose near her shoulder. Glad the animal had been released from its burden of hauling the Kerrs' wagon, she could truly sympathize now.

Abigail searched for another specimen to distract her. Oaks were plentiful, and chestnuts, too; ash and maple were familiar friends, but her gaze roamed the landscape for the unusual. But for some reason, everything began to blur together. All the shrubs and trees looked ordinary now.

"Switchel?" John's strides were easy, his long legs tireless. His face bent toward hers under his straw hat.

"Gladly." Abigail stopped for a moment as she sipped the tangy mixture. Gretchen did not use this much vinegar. Or was that Mother's receipt?

"Have ye the headache?"

"How did you know?" She forced her limbs to move again.

"The heat. Ye're not accustomed to it. But we're almost to the Brandywine."

She blinked. John's face seemed hazy. "The Brandywine?"

"Aye." He placed the gourd of switchel in her hands. "Drink again."

Abigail obeyed, sipping slowly. She turned her eyes to the foliage. "I need to find a tree." But she'd forgotten why.

John was saying something to Roy. She wiped her eyes again. The haze was thicker. Then she was floating, and lying in bed. But a strange bed, with a terrible mattress.

Darkness took her.

SHE WAS DROWNING. Panicking, Abigail thrashed with all her might, trying to reach the surface. Slowly, the blackness ebbed.

She could breathe. Was it a dream? Her head throbbed painfully.

"Look, she's awake. She'll be fine." A woman's voice. Then more murmured words she couldn't make out.

"Abigail?" John's voice. His face loomed over her.

She was wet. Wet all over. "Where am I?" She struggled to sit up, her sodden clothing weighing her down.

"In the Brandywine River," John murmured. "We had a bit of a scare."

Her shoes. Were they ruined? "You put me in the river?" A curtain of willow branches filtered the afternoon sun. No, she hadn't been drowning; she sat in water less than six inches deep. "I thought I was drowning." Her skirt, thoroughly soaked, lay heavy on her legs like lead. But the air felt cool against her hair.

"I poured water on ye." John circled her waist with his arms and helped her to sit on the bank. "Ye were overheated and fainted. We laid ye in the wagon and got here as quick as we could."

She touched her head—both her hat and her cap were missing, and her wet hair was mussed. "Where are we? Besides the river, I mean. I heard someone's voice."

"The Buckmans' farm. That were Mistress Buckman ye heard."

"Wonderful! She's sitting up." A sturdily built woman approached, taking no care for her shoes, which were already streaked with mud. Her face and bare forearms glowed golden brown from the sun.

"Here, Mrs. Russell, I've some buttermilk. It'll be just the thing." She frowned. "You'll be fine. It happens sometimes in the summer. Sometimes because folks wear too many clothes." Her voice turned a bit sharp at the last statement, which seemed to be directed at John.

Abigail sipped at the buttermilk—it was as good and fresh as Gretchen's—and focused on Mrs. Buckman's face. "Thank you," she murmured, relishing the drink and the coolness of her damp clothing. Her thoughts were growing more coherent.

"Too many clothes?" For once, John seemed out of his depth.

"Yes, Mr. Russell. I understand you're but newly married. Did you know your wife was wearing three layers of clothing, and her skirt is wool?"

"Three?"

"Both my linen skirts were soiled, and I could not wear a Sabbath gown." It wasn't John's fault. "Sometimes I wear a wool skirt in the summer."

The farmer's wife turned her attention to her, and her tone was gentler. "But you were inside the house most of the time, is my guess."

"Yes. My family lives in town." Abigail finished the buttermilk. On the opposite bank of the gently flowing river, butterflies danced among purple flowers she didn't recognize. Nearby, nestled among the grass of the bank, waved stalks of proud indigo. Lobelia? Despite her lingering headache, she determined to find the entry in her new book. She couldn't recall the medicinal use of the plant, but she'd stumbled across on one of the pages and remembered the name and description.

"John, why don't you see to your animals." Mrs. Buckman's eyebrows lifted in command, but she wasn't truly a stern woman, Abigail decided.

"Ye'll be fine," he murmured, and stepped up the bank.

"Now, then. No wool when it's hot. We'll get your linen skirts washed right now."

"Yes, ma'am."

"Another thing." Mrs. Buckman eyed her. "No petticoat underneath. Trust me, your chemise is all you need to protect your modesty. Save your stays for your Sabbath gown. Have you jumps instead?"

Abigail nodded and examined the other woman. Loose linen sleeves emerged from underneath a yellow print sleeveless bodice; her skirt was dark blue. An apron completed the ensemble.

"That bodice of yours is too warm as well. Have you a sleeveless one?"

""No, ma'am." Abigail had seen other women dressed like Mrs. Buckman in Philadelphia, but most were servants or ... farmer's wives. "Your sleeves?" She had a sinking feeling that the other woman's loose linen sleeves were not part of a bodice.

"That's my chemise, girl."

Abigail's eyebrows darted up in surprise. Mother would never approve. But Mother didn't have to walk for hours in the August heat. "You do look comfortable."

"I am." She smiled. "Now let's get you settled. My maid will see to your clothes, and your husband has hired our spare cabin for the night."

Abigail looked down. Was she blushing? "Thank you."

JOHN EMPTIED his cup of ale. He nibbled at his bread without appetite. Next to him, her face illumined by the last rays of the sun streaming through the cabin window, Abigail took a bite of cheese. Color had returned to her cheeks. For a long, dreadful quarter hour, she had lain insensate in the wagon, her face strangely pale in the heat. *Thank you, Lord, that we were so close to the Brandywine.*

He clenched a fist. *My fault.* He'd spent all day focused on the ponies and had neglected his wife. He took a breath. He didn't remember having to think about Janet's clothing; if anything, she'd worried more for him than he for her.

"Ye'll freeze out there, John Russell!" she'd exclaimed once, when he'd made ready to check his trap line. Snow was a foot on the ground in some places. "Take this blanket in case ye need to hole up somewhere."

Reluctantly, he'd stashed it in his pack, jealous of the space it took up.

"Tinderbox?"

"Aye, it's here."

"Then be off with ye, and come back to me."

She'd been great with child then—Susanna had been born a scant six weeks later. He sighed. They were different women. Abigail was so young, so naïve.

And she deserved his protection. If his marriage vows meant anything, they meant faithfulness to her person, at the very least.

And he had failed dreadfully. Guilt weighed on him like a heavy cloak.

"Abigail." What to say? "I must beg your forgiveness." The lump in his throat made speech difficult.

She stopped chewing, her eyes quizzical. "You aren't responsible for the heat."

"I took better care for the animals than for ye. I am verra sorry."

"It was ignorance on my part, John. And yours as well—you can't be responsible for understanding women's clothing." She sipped her ale and smiled. "My clothes are washed, and while we were at it, Mrs. Buckman slipped me some soap. I got to bathe a bit."

John attempted a smile. Her cheerfulness shamed him. "Sometimes sins of omission or carelessness can be just as bad as the other kind."

Her gaze was fixed on his face.

He pulled a pair of breeches from his saddlebags on the floor. "For ye."

Abigail's eyes widened. "Breeches?"

"They will help with the soreness. For now." He handed them to her.

She lifted them up. "I can't see how these would fit."

"D'ye have needle and thread?" He indicated the buttons. "Ye can move these over." He guided her hands. "See the back? A bit adjustable."

Twenty minutes later Abigail was pulling them on under her chemise. "Just a bit loose."

"Turn around." Quickly, conscious of her shyness, he tied the gusset. "There. Better?"

She dropped the hem of the chemise back over the breeches. "Yes." She took a few tentative steps about the small cabin. "They feel strange. But thank you. Between you and Mrs. Buckman I feel ready for the rest of the trip." She replaced the needle and thread in her housewife and stowed it. "Where are the others?"

"The Buckmans decided Lizzie should be chaperoned. By the cows." John smiled. "She and Ritchie are in the barn with the heifer. Roy is camping with the Kerrs. The Buckmans dinna run an inn, but they sell milk, ale, cheese, and bread, and provide a safe place to camp for free." He reached for the New Testament in his saddlebag. "Abigail, I've neglected something else."

Her wide blue eyes gazed at him. "Oh?"

Her open countenance helped to settle his roiling emotions. "I thought we'd read through the book of Romans together. As our daily devotion." He flipped through the pages carefully. "Here it is. Chapter one."

Lord, help us both. Help her to learn Your ways. And help me to walk before You as I ought.

12

Brethren, let us depart for God has appointed a new
country for us to dwell in... Let us be free of these
Pharaohs, these rackers of rents and screwers of tithes,
and let us go unto the land of Canaan. We are the
Lord's ain people and he shall divide the ocean
before us.

—James McGregor, Londonderry, 1718

*J*ust a few yards from the trail, Abigail sat beside Lizzie underneath a large sassafras tree. Nearby, in the shade of a chestnut, the Kerrs had just finished their noonday meal; their younger son gamboled among last year's fallen leaves. A single cough floated through the moist, sluggish air. Farther away, John and Roy tended to the animals and inspected the wagon.

Abigail inhaled, enjoying the woodsy blend of decaying leaf litter and tree sap. It was peaceful here with Lizzie's quiet company. Shrubs fought for space under the stately canopy of the trees; in open places, white asters shone against a background of variegated greens and browns.

She'd sketched a sassafras tree once, years ago, back in Philadelphia, but she longed to know more. As Lizzie broke off a piece of Mrs. Buckman's bread to give to Ritchie, Abigail pulled out the treasured botany book. She'd managed to collect some lobelia before they'd left the Brandywine. Perhaps she could add sassafras to her collection of simples as well—she'd heard of its usefulness.

"What's in your book?" Lizzie asked. Loose strands of chestnut curls framed her face. She didn't look like the woman in her father's shop, skinny and pale. Gretchen's cooking had done her good.

"It's for herbs. How to make medicines."

"Och, that's a mighty big book for receipts." Lizzie craned her neck to see as Abigail flipped through the tome, searching for sassafras.

"John gave it to me. He knows I like plants."

"Are ye an herb woman?"

Abigail smiled. "I'd like to be. I don't have a teacher, but my father helped me to learn what I could. And now I have this book."

Sassafras. Here it was. She scooted closer so Lizzie could see the page and traced her finger over the drawing of the tree and its leaves.

"See here, the three-lobed leaves?"

Lizzie's eyes widened. "This book must have cost a lot."

She nodded absently, her gaze skimming the page. The tree had a variety of uses, but the leaves were valuable in a poultice. "See here, Lizzie? The leaves can be used as a poultice. Perhaps we should collect some before we leave."

"Aye, my mother used onions and moss, but I dinna ken where to get moss here. I'll fetch a bag for ye."

As they filled a small canvas bag with leaves, Abigail heard her husband's voice. The horses were harnessed, and he was conferring with Mr. Kerr. Time to leave.

Another cough met her ear. A child's cough. She hoped none of
the children were ill.

"JOHN, WHAT'S AN ENTHUSIAST?" Abigail steeled herself for the few
remaining miles to Lancaster. She'd been careful to drink plenty of
ale and switchel, and refreshed by the noonday break, her mind
seemed to be functioning clearly.

"Enthusiast?" John's dusty face looked puzzled for the briefest
moment. "Oh, ye mean an enthusiast in religion?"

"I've been thinking about Mr. Whitefield's sermon. But isn't he an
enthusiast?" Abigail decided not to mention that she was clueless
about some of what he'd said. Loathing her own righteousness? She
rubbed the leather of the reins between her fingers. If John discovered her ignorance, would he turn away? Despise her? Six months
ago, marriage had been the furthest thing from her mind. Now, his
affection meant everything.

John's eyes shifted left, then right, as he studied his surroundings.
"I've heard your mother criticize them." His gaze slid to her. "An
enthusiast is someone who relies on his experience. He may have
great affections, great stirrings of his feelings, and by these convince
himself that he is accepted by God."

"And this is wrong?"

He nodded. "Your mother is correct. The New England divines
have always understood that to embrace the movements of the
animal spirits as a basis for hope in Christ is not only dangerous, it is
a rejection of the Scriptures as the truth."

Abigail frowned. She had only a vague sense of his meaning. "I've
heard there was great enthusiasm in Northampton, under Mr.
Edwards's preaching. And much emotion is in evidence when George
Whitefield preaches."

John scanned the tree line and shifted his musket as it lay on his
forearm. "But ye read Whitefield's sermon, aye? Was he directing

them to trust in their religious experience, or pointing them to Christ as their only hope?"

"To Christ." It was beginning to make sense.

"Sometimes folk weep when they hear him. But why?"

She wasn't quite sure. "Because they are disturbed in their souls?"

"Aye. They think God accepts them because of their works or their good family name. Then they hear the gospel and suddenly realize their lost condition."

Abigail trembled inside. Was this true of her?

JOHN DIRECTED his steps to the Kerrs' wagon. "Lancaster is just over the rise. There's an ordinary and a smithy, and numerous farms in the area. I'm headed to the Houstons' place first. I suspect ye can find a place nearby to camp."

Kerr nodded his agreement. "I'll follow ye." His younger son sat upright in the wagon, eager to see their destination.

John looked the mules over. The animals' ears drooped, not liking the increased load, but their tails were relaxed. Good—they weren't overburdened. Kerr had been handing off the reins to his wife from time to time and walking alongside. The man was learning.

His mare snuffed as he returned, a rare expression of opinion. Her large brown eyes glared at him as he sidled up to her side, as if blaming him for the unaccustomed harness. Automatically, he checked the animal over, then adjusted his stride to walk alongside Abigail, who was seated on the wagon bench with Roy.

"It's beautiful here." Abigail's eyes roamed the countryside about them.

He nodded. Homesteads sprang into view on either side of the trail, and many of the trees had been harvested for lumber or firewood, revealing a panorama of lush gentle sloping hills, corn fields, and forested glens. "Aye, it's a lovely area. And growing."

They traveled in silence until they reached a tiny side road. John reached for Percy's bridle and helped her make the turn. "The Houston place. I always stay here on my travels. They're godly folk."

"Are they from Ireland too?" Abigail asked, once both wagons had made the turn. Maple and hickory boughs formed a long cool tunnel, branches arching overhead.

"Aye, they're Scots from Ulster." His brow wrinkled. "I believe they came here after my folks did. But John Houston lost no time. He has sturdy sons, and they've helped him clear a good-sized farm. Plenty of good pasture for horses too." He hoped Houston might have a spare Cleveland or two. Or Canadians. He had an eye for sound horseflesh, and he was an honest man. "They've a daughter almost your age, I think."

The trees thinned and parted. Percy nickered, and a chorus of nickers and snorts echoed from a nearby pasture. A bay yearling ran along a split-rail fence, paralleling them, tail waving like a flag, and his compatriots stared with widened nostrils, ears at attention.

Looking ahead, John caught a glimpse of a familiar barn not fifty yards from a rambling frame house. A bit of evening breeze brushed against his cheeks; strands of Abigail's blond hair, loose from the long ride, danced about her neck.

John craned his neck to study the sky. The clouds he'd noticed earlier seemed thicker and darker. At this time of year, a good downpour was welcome, but while traveling, it could be miserable out in the open. He'd see if they could all obtain shelter in Houston's spacious barn.

"Ho, such a one!" John called to a man leading a black horse to the barn. He'd know that heavily muscled frame anywhere. "Hallo!"

John Houston turned. "Hallo! Is that ye, John Russell? Scalawag of the Shenandoah?" The man tied the animal to a post and strode over, his dark hair shot through with more gray than John remembered.

He dismounted. "The very same. And my new wife, Abigail." He introduced Lizzie and the Kerrs.

Houston glanced at the sky. "Normally I'd let ye camp in the south pasture, but d'ye feel that breeze? We can have awful storms in the summer. Hail the size of chestnuts or even larger. I'll be sheltering all my stock tonight, and I'll see if I can find room for all your company too."

"Your corn?"

Houston cocked one eyebrow. "I lost half my crop to hail one year. So I always plant a wee bit more than I think I should."

John helped Abigail down from the pony.

"My son Robert and his wife took over our original cabin." Houston pointed to a log structure. "They'll have room for your maidservant and her son. Margaret will insist on housing you newly-weds, and also the children and Mrs. Kerr. There should be room for the men in the barn." He frowned at the wagons. "John, ye've plenty of oilcloth, I see. What about the Kerrs' belongings? I dinna want to see anything spoilt by rain or hail."

John joined the other men in moving the Kerrs' heavy loom to the barn and securing oilcloth over the rest of their possessions. His own concerns could wait. He turned to Abigail. "Would ye help everyone get settled? I've a mind to help Houston with the stock."

She glanced at the sky. The wind threatened her hat, and she removed it. "Surely."

His heart went out to her. Everything about her new life was strange and challenging, but she hadn't complained.

He wasn't sure he loved her, but he would protect her. With his life.

13

In the year 1740, in the spring before Mr. Whitefield came to
this town, there was a visible alteration: there was more
seriousness and religious conversation, especially
among young people... and it was a very frequent thing
for persons to consult their minister upon the salvation
of their souls ...

—Jonathan Edwards, Northampton, 1743

*A*bigail greeted Mrs. Houston. "May I help you in the kitchen?"

Houston's wife Margaret possessed a kindly, open face, with dark hair loosely pinned under a linen mobcap. A young woman stood nearby, tall and slender with gleaming chestnut hair bound in an open net. A daughter? Younger children darted about.

Stepping up to join Abigail, Sophie Kerr tossed her a sidelong glance.

"No, I'll be fine. Esther will assist me. Ye stay by your husband in the parlor."

Then Margaret addressed Mrs. Kerr. "My maid will help ye get your children settled in the loft."

Abigail's gaze roamed over the inside of the house. Pine and oak timbers stood unmovable against the occasional howl of the wind outside. Why did Mrs. Kerr resent her so? Or did the woman scowl at everyone?

Entering the parlor, she found a stool next to John and sat, glad of the chance to ease her legs. Houston leaned back on a simple horse-hair-covered settee across from them, long limbs outstretched, a pewter tankard in his hand.

John handed her his tankard. "I asked Mr. Houston about stock."

"Aye, young lady." He seemed to be assessing her. "John told me about your ponies. I'll take a better look in the morning. But they seem like decent animals, especially the mare. The gelding is older. And I've some Clevelands ye might be interested in." He leaned forward. "Ten days ago, the Iroquois came to sign the treaty. I told everyone to hide their best stock. With two hundred in gold, I knew the Indians would be in a buying mood. They purchased a lot of ponies, but mostly the older ones. I sold two myself, as well as a few old knives and axes."

"Knives?" John's fingers drummed on his thigh.

The other man's gaze flickered to Abigail and back again. "I ken what ye went through, John Russell, but ye ken as well as I that we need to be neighborly. Or at least keep up the appearance." He chuckled. "Even my daughter Esther sold them a bit of ribbon and such."

Her husband took a deep breath. "I've nae argument with ye there, Houston. What about firearms? Did Deckard sell him anything?"

"Long rifles? Och, no, not on your life. In fact, there's a rumor floating around that he buried his long rifles. I dinna believe it, but I do hear he sold them a few ancient muskets and fowling pieces. Just to be neighborly, mind ye." He took a sip of ale. "Now then. There's a lot of traffic taking the road to the valley. Can ye tell me anything?"

"Land is dear near Philadelphia, and folk keep arriving from Ulster who canna afford those prices."

"I see. I'll let ye in on a secret. Margaret and I have decided to move to the valley as well. My son Robert has already secured title to some land. I just need a buyer for this property and I'll be moving. In the spring, most likely."

John's eyebrows shot up. "Where? Which grant? The best places around Tinkling Spring have already been purchased. And I'm sure ye'd want a fair bit of land."

"A wee bit upvalley from ye, John. Borden's grant. We willna be close neighbors. But my first priority is a meetinghouse and a minister. What can ye tell me?"

"There are several ministers south of the fork. Our own Mr. Craig ministers to two congregations already, Tinkling Spring and one other. I know of one meetinghouse upvalley from us, where ye'll be, but I havena met the minister."

Just then, Margaret Houston entered the room, her face glowing from the heat of the kitchen hearth. Her husband smiled at her. "Let me guess, supper's ready."

She returned the smile, and the room warmed up. "I'll bring ye bowls, and cornbread in a basket. I've a mind to feed all the children and Mr. and Mrs. Kerr at the table. We willna all fit round it."

Returning from the kitchen, she and Esther handed bowls of stew to each one. Then Margaret returned and took a chair near her husband. He cleared his throat and gave thanks for the food, his rumbling voice steady and sure. "Lord our God, Who has brought us through such trials and afflictions, and ever watches over us, please strengthen our hands to serve ye. Thank ye for this our daily provision. In Christ's name, amen."

Abigail's heart constricted. John Houston's simple prayer, like her husband's, was heartfelt. Not dull and dry. But her own prayers were cold, and she was never certain if they were heard. Maybe she wasn't a Christian at all. But she didn't know what to do about that.

IN THE EARLY MORNING DARKNESS, John approached the bedroom window and laid his fingers upon the glass. Behind him, Abigail slept soundly in the featherbed. Margaret had insisted on giving them their own room, and John had pretended to protest. But despite the comfort, he'd awakened suddenly in the middle of the night, his eyes opening to nothingness, the clouds having blocked all light from moon or stars. After lying in the bed for what seemed like an interminable length of time, he arose.

The hail had abated, but rain still pummeled the house, the wind whistling and moaning under the eaves. He finger-combed his hair. The road would be muddy at best. And what of the Susquehanna River? A downpour of this magnitude could render the ferry crossing dangerous. No, they'd not be getting far that day.

But in any case, he needed horses. And perhaps a rifle, if he still had the money. Would a better rifle have made a difference? Could he have saved Janet's life?

Smoke and screams had confused the battlefield, such as it was. In his mind's eye he saw John McDowell bent over the neck of his stallion, urging it to greater speed, grasping his tomahawk. Then he saw a glint of metal through the dim, hazy air, as the man swung the weapon, but smoke and confusion covered the outcome.

From behind him the barking cough of musket fire raged in his ears. Then a dark face appeared out of nowhere, advancing on him. Without thought, he drew his knife and slashed it across the Indian's neck. Hot blood spurted onto his face and clothes, and the brave tumbled to the ground. The shock of seeing the man's sightless eyes above a gaping neck wound stilled him for a moment.

Then John whirled. Was Janet safe inside the Cunninghams' cabin? He'd told her to stay put.

In the dim light of dusk, she stood in the cabin doorway, limned by the light of the hearth inside. *No!* She'd made herself the perfect target. His throat swelled shut, but she probably wouldn't be able to hear him even if he could shout. He peered through the dissipating smoke. Was anyone aiming at her?

He spotted two Indians near the tree line, both with muskets. He kneeled and primed his own weapon. Out of the corner of his eye he saw one of the Cunninghams gallop past; the horse and rider would pass between the Indians and the cabin. One of the Indians swung his firearm to aim at Cunningham—and beyond Cunningham stood his wife! John aimed at the Indian, but the man was over a hundred yards away. *Help, Lord!*

He pulled the trigger. And missed.

Janet's scream tore through the air.

John gasped for breath, his hands trembling. Houston's bedroom took ghostly shape before him in the gray light of early dawn, bringing him back to the present. He felt his way to the washstand and splashed water on his face. Finally his breathing slowed.

He rarely allowed himself to think of the events of that night. Of Janet's agonizing death. He couldn't, for he always blamed himself. Mr. Craig spoke of Providence, and he knew the minister was right. God ordered all events. But still ...

He turned and gazed at Abigail's tousled blond hair on the pillow.

He needed a Deckard rifle.

"Mrs. Houston?" Abigail asked. The kitchen smelled of hickory and pine, the hearth fire banked but still sending small wisps of gray smoke up the chimney. Muted light from a small window illuminated dirty wooden bowls in the washing pan. The rain had diminished to a mere drizzle, and John had excused himself after eating, saying something about a rifle.

"Call me Margaret." Crow's feet framed friendly gray eyes. "How are ye holding up on the road?"

She smiled. "I'm learning." Something in the other woman's countenance invited confidence. She lowered her voice. "I was saddle-sore but John gave me a pair of his breeches."

Margaret smiled broadly. "Och, he's a good man." She paused. "I've got something for ye." She beckoned to Abigail, leading her back to the bedroom, where she opened a chest. Rummaging, she grabbed an item and held it up.

It was furry. Rabbit skin? Abigail wasn't sure.

"It's a muff for little Susanna. It'll keep her hands warm on cold Sabbath mornings. My youngest is nearly grown and canna use it." She bent over the chest again. "I'd forgotten about this." Margaret Houston passed a cloth doll to Abigail.

"Thank you." The doll was well made, with buttons for eyes and a carefully stitched red mouth. "Thank you very much."

"We'll be neighbors soon." Another smile.

"Mrs. Houston?"

"Margaret."

"Margaret." Abigail had a favor to ask, and it made her uncomfortable, especially after such generosity. She swallowed. "Do you have any spirits? Whiskey?"

The other woman's eyebrows shot up. "Well ... aye."

"I gathered some lobelia and ..."

The smile returned. "Ye want to make a tincture."

Abigail nodded, relieved.

A few minutes later, Margaret returned with a jug and a mortar and pestle. "Anyone sick?"

"One of the Kerr children has a cough. I wanted to be ready."

But would Sophie Kerr ever accept help from her?

MORNING MIST VEILED THE LAND. The storm had broken the summer heat, but early moisture presaged afternoon mugginess. John urged Percy to a trot down the Houstons' drive, but the mare champed against her bit, her hooves struggling against the muck, and he slowed her to a walk. By the time he reached Jake Deckard's shop, the mist had lifted, and he caught a glimpse of the sun.

Houston had showed him his stock. A fine Cleveland mare had caught John's attention, priced at five pounds—and it was fair, considering. Only six years old, she stood over sixteen hands, and her muscles rippled under a glossy bay coat. But his friend didn't have an animal he could let go cheaply, and after trading Houston the Marsh Tacky ponies, he'd still owed him three guineas just for the mare.

John dismounted. He needed a rifle and another horse, and he only had six guineas left to spend. He'd kept the remaining seventh coin sewn in his breeches for taxes and tithes. But Deckard's rifle would cost at least five. And the horse?

Staring at the gunsmith's shop, he hesitated. *Lord, give me wisdom.* He'd promised Roy two horses. He had to keep that promise. But who else might sell? Leaving his mare tied in front of Deckard's shop, he walked down the lane, skirting the worst of the mud. He could use a few things while he was in the settlement. A mortise chisel, perhaps. A used one might only cost him two bits. He could craft simple furniture, but for proper chairs or cabinets, he needed more tools. Wasn't there a shop nearby?

Crack! Something slammed against what sounded like a wall. Thuds alternated with guttural shouts and curses.

John hopped to the middle of the street and almost slipped in the slick mud, trying to see what was causing the ruckus. Fifty feet away, a large knobby-kneed horse struggled in harness, nostrils flared. It kicked suddenly, a large hoof landing on the front of the cart it pulled. A man—its owner, presumably—darted to the animal's head and attempted to grab the bridle.

The horse reared, and curses filled the air. The man struck the animal with a whip, and John jerked forward into a jog, heedless of the muck. The horse shrieked and lurched sideways, slipping in the mud, and fell, kicking sporadically.

"Ho! Might I help ye?" John studied the wiry man clutching the whip, careful to stand clear of the horse's head. "Mr. Mifflin, is it?" He'd purchased a few things from the cabinetmaker in the past.

"Yes, my apologies, I don't recall—"

"John Russell, at your service. I've been to your shop before. Horse trouble, aye?" He studied the animal. Its eyes were still wild, but the kicking grew perfunctory. Probably just startled or something.

The cabinetmaker jerked his chin toward the horse. "Silas Sloan sold this worthless piece of horseflesh to me. He seemed sound enough, and the price was right." He unharnessed the animal where it lay, careful to stay out of the reach of its hooves.

John knelt near the gelding's head, murmuring. "See the eye? The filmy color?"

"Yes, I've noticed. Think he's blind on the far side?"

He extended his closed fist for the horse to sniff. The animal's breathing was more regular. "Stay away from the far side, now. Let's see if he'll stand."

Mifflin joined him and soon the horse was upright, front feet splayed, its black coat dull and half covered in mud. John stroked its nose, murmuring to it. The whites of its eyes showed briefly, then the horse subsided, allowing his attention.

"Well, I'll be," Mifflin declared, arms akimbo. "He likes you."

"I think ye must be wary of his blind side, ye ken? He'll startle easy."

But what if a steady mare were harnessed with him, yoked to his far side? John looked over the animal's conformation. The gelding was lean, no doubt underweight, but tall and broad chested. He'd have to see his paces, but Mifflin was probably right about soundness.

The other man looked over the damage to his cart. "I've no use for such a horse."

"How much ye want for him?"

Mifflin's eyebrows shot up. "You're serious?"

"Let me see him move, and I'll make ye an offer." John led the horse up the street at a gentle pace, careful to stay to his near side, watching his feet. Percy pricked up her ears as he approached, and grunted. The gelding swung his ears to her, and soon they stood side-by-side. Then he circled the gelding, bringing it to Percy's other side. Now his blind side was against her.

The animal snorted once, then calmed. *Yes, this will work.*

The cabinetmaker had trailed him but remained a cautious distance away.

John looked at the gelding's teeth. Nine years? Ten? Not very old. "I'll give you a gold guinea for the animal." This could be an answer to his half-formed prayers.

"Russell, that's more than I gave Sloan. I won't take that much." The man scratched at his sandy locks. "Come to the shop. You do a bit of woodworking, as I recall. I think we can make a deal."

John checked the animals before following the cabinetmaker. Silas Sloan's horse. He hoped he wouldn't meet up with the man himself.

14

I had been heaping up my devotions before God, fasting,
praying, &c. pretending, and indeed really thinking
sometimes, that I was aiming at the glory of God;
whereas I never once truly intended it, but only my
own happiness.

—David Brainerd, *The Life and Diary of David Brainerd*, 1749

*A*bigail heard Ritchie before she saw him. Hurriedly, she pinned up her hair and shoved her cap over it, then scrambled to the door. On the Houstons' porch Lizzie sat next to her son, arm around him, while he coughed. The little boy gasped and hacked several times before relaxing.

Abigail crouched next to the other woman. "How long has he been coughing like this?"

"Last night he was coughing some, but it wasna bad. This morning it started again only worse. I took him outside, away from the others."

Lizzie frowned. "But the air is damp." She looked up at Abigail, concern in her dark eyes. "And he's warm." Lizzie stroked her son's curls, which mirrored her own chestnut locks pinned beneath her cap.

Damp air? Was that harmful? Abigail ached, wishing she knew more about such things. "This morning I prepared some lobelia tincture. Let's make hot tea or coffee and add the medicine to it." How bad was the fever? His cheeks did seem just a little flushed. She reached out and felt Richie's forehead. Too warm.

Seeing the lines in Lizzie's face relax, Abigail's shoulders did the same. Perhaps she could help this little boy. "Mrs. Houston has warned me that it's a strong herb, and we should give only a little."

Twenty minutes later Ritchie sat at the Houstons' walnut table, legs swinging as he sipped at a cup of steaming chicory. He grimaced. "What's this?"

"Something to help your cough," his mother soothed.

"It's not that bad." He coughed once and resumed sipping.

Esther stood over the hearth, stirring a thick porridge of peas and barley. "I've an idea, if ye want to try it."

Abigail nodded. Anything that would help.

"We've some honey." She smiled, and opened a crock. With a spoon, she drizzled some into Ritchie's cup and stirred.

"What do ye say?" Lizzie prodded.

"Thank ye kindly." A dimple showed in the boy's cheek.

A swish and a footstep sounded behind her. Abigail turned.

Margaret smiled in the doorway. "I heard coughing."

"I gave him a spoonful of the lobelia in his chicory." She hoped she'd given the right dosage. Reading about such things in a book was one thing...

"Ye realize the flowers are not as strong as seeds. A spoonful willna be too strong." Margaret studied the boy. "What think ye? Catarrh or chin cough?"

Abigail shrugged. "I don't know how to tell the difference."

"Ye canna always tell. But the chin cough is verra bad in babes, and sometimes they make a strange sound when they try to breathe. Like a whoop. But Ritchie is no' a babe, is he now?" She smiled at the boy.

He lifted his chin. "I'll be four ..."

"In December." His mother stroked his hair.

"I heard some coughing from the loft last night. Are the other children sick?" Mrs. Houston crossed the room and glanced at the porridge.

"I heard a bit of coughing on the road. Maybe."

Margaret faced them, straightening her apron. "Good ye have plenty of lobelia. Now, your husband was gracious to give us five pounds of wheat flour. Shall we make it into biscuits for the noon meal?"

A horrible barking cough echoed from somewhere in the house. Abigail darted toward it, and found herself at the foot of a ladder. Margaret appeared at her side.

"The loft." Margaret placed her hands on the ladder. "The Kerr children slept here."

Hitching up her skirt, Abigail followed her up to the sleeping area under the eaves.

Little Kitty Kerr lay in her shift gasping for breath on the bed, alone, her cheeks a furious red.

Where was Mrs. Kerr?

JOHN GAZED around the gunsmith's shop, his eyes adjusting to the light. An apron-clad figure was bent over a workbench. "Hallo, Mr. Deckard?"

"Be right there." The man's rumbling voice still possessed traces of his origins. Was the man Swiss? He couldn't remember.

Fowling pieces competed with pistols and one battered Brown Bess mounted on one wall. Tables lay buried with metal parts, tools, and shot molds. How Deckard could make sense of it all, he didn't know.

Then he spotted the long rifles. Three gleaming beauties adorned the wall near Deckard's workbench, one longer than the others. John spread out his arms to get a sense of the length of the longest. Six feet? In his mind's eye he sighted a buck from a hundred yards, dropping it instantly.

His hands clenched with desire. Then a thought slammed him. *Harness!* He'd need a harness for the horses; the Kerrs' was only suited for ponies.

His shoulders slumped. A decent harness would cost him.

"John Russell, is that you?"

"Aye, on the road back to the valley." He struggled to keep his voice level.

"How can I help you?" The man paused, squinting. "Russell. I remember you. Needing a rifle?"

"Aye. But I dinna ken whether I have the coin. I have a musket in trade."

"Six pounds for one of these." Deckard flung an arm in the general direction of the rifles. "Or five guineas and twelve." He squinted at him again. "Or do you want the price in Spanish dollars?"

John swallowed. He had five guineas but needed a decent harness, which would set him back several dollars at least. "What will ye give me for this?" He held up his weapon, feeling the pulse throb in his neck.

Deckard picked up a pair of spectacles from somewhere on his bench. "Let me see." He grabbed his musket and stood near the window, checking for the maker's mark. He sighted down the barrel. "Looks sound. What can you tell me about it?"

"It's worthless over fifty yards." John took a deep breath, remembering the Indian, who stood just a hundred yards away, but it might as well have been one hundred miles. He curled his fingers into a fist and released them.

"Iron fittings." Deckard mumbled comments while examining the weapon. He looked up. "Not the newest model, but it looks well-cared for. One pound. Or five dollars."

John frowned. He was still a bit short. "I've got four guineas and five."

Deckard studied him and set the musket on a table. "Wait here." He disappeared through a door.

Lord, help. His father's face appeared in his mind's eye. "Remember, John, to be thankful in every situation. Even if your will is not done."

John took a long, steadying breath. *Either way, Father, help me to give thanks.*

Deckard reappeared, carrying a long rifle. He brought it into the light of the window. "Here, Russell, I can give you this. A man brought me this in trade. It had a broken trigger, and the stock is scratched and even gouged."

He eyed the maple stock. One deep scratch ended in a gouge. He shivered inside, knowing what might make that kind of mark. A tomahawk. But if the firearm were sound otherwise ... *Thank you Lord.*

"I replaced the trigger," the man was saying. "I could change out the whole stock, but what's the point?" He shrugged.

"I'll take it." John fingered the wood of the stock. "What happened to the rifle?"

"Something to do with the Indians."

The stock seemed to burn under his hands. Revenge? No, he wouldn't try to take revenge for Janet's death. He glanced at the gouge again. Maybe it was just a picture of his heart.

ABIGAIL HELD Kitty on her lap, smoothing her hair off her hot forehead. Margaret brought a kettle to the table and poured hot chicory into a cup. She added a spoonful of lobelia and mixed in some honey before bringing it to Abigail's side of the table. Across the table Lizzie glanced at the girl with a worried expression as she encouraged Ritchie to sip at his second cup of medicine.

"What's happening?" Sophie Kerr stood in the kitchen doorway, a basket on her arm. Her expression changed from suspicion to alarm as she studied her daughter's face. "What are ye doing?" She bustled in and placed her basket on the table. "Give me my daughter."

Coughing racked the little girl's frame. She slid easily to her mother's lap.

Margaret studied Mrs. Kerr. "We've been giving Ritchie medicine for his cough. We've more if ye like."

"I've my own medicine," Mrs. Kerr barked. "Mr. Kerr took me to the dry goods' merchant."

Roy's copper head appeared. "What's the kerfuffle?"

"Some sick children," Abigail explained. "I gave Ritchie lobelia for his cough, and I fear Kitty has the same illness."

Roy joined Ritchie on the bench, giving his head a tousle. "I'll need ye to help with the new horses."

"Horses?"

"Oh, aye. Ye'll see. It's a surprise."

Margaret bustled about, giving direction to a maidservant and sending a younger daughter out for butter. "We'll have a sickbed made up in the parlor."

Sophie Kerr drew out a small brown bottle from the basket. "I've laudanum. Calms her cough and helps her to rest."

Abigail found her voice. "Perhaps you might save that for evening." The poor girl had slept till almost noon and wasn't any better. And who knew the safe dosage for such a slender child?

"Either way, hot fluid will clear her lungs." Margaret offered her the cup of steaming chicory.

Mrs. Kerr sat rigid on her seat, her gaze landing on Margaret and flickering to Abigail. Her shoulders slumped. "Aye, then. We'll try it your way first."

～

JOHN'S STOMACH GROWLED. He hoped he was in time for the noon meal. Mr. Mifflin followed him on his own mount as Percy pulled the man's cart, her ears twitching, uncertain about the new arrangement. She was not meant to work in harness, of that he was certain.

He clucked at her. "Steady, girl. Almost there." Behind him, tied to the cart, Sloan's horse followed easily. Inside the cart lay a double harness, patched once but fine and strong; his rifle; and a broken spinning wheel. He had plans for that ...

"Roy?" No one was visible outside the Houstons' house or barn. Perhaps everyone was in the house. John released Percy from the harness, placed his purchases in the wagon, and Mifflin was soon off, relaying his greetings to all and sundry.

The gelding nickered to the animals in the pasture as John studied his conformation again. He wasn't much to look at, but hopefully Roy would realize the animal just needed a little meat on his bones. He'd throw in four bits' worth of feed.

He stepped through the doorway, where coughing met his ears. The enticing scent of barley stew and biscuits inflamed his hunger; the kitchen was crowded. But the coughing came from the parlor. He turned that way.

Abigail sat on a stool to one side of the settee, Mrs. Kerr on the other. Propped by pillows, the Kerrs' little daughter reclined on the settee, gingerly sipping a cup of steaming liquid.

Abigail saw him and turned to the other woman. "Mrs. Kerr, I'll leave this here for you." She set a bowl full of water on the stool where she'd been sitting and joined him. "Ritchie and Kitty are sick. Could be the chin cough."

"How bad?"

"I'm not sure. Ritchie's up and about. I'm not sure about little Kitty. They're both taking lobelia, and hot drinks seem to help ease the cough."

John squeezed her hand surreptitiously. "I'm glad ye're along. Do ye think they can travel? I'd like to get to the Susquehanna tonight. It's not far. We can heat water when we camp."

Abigail crossed her arms. "Let's give Kitty an hour. I suppose I could put lobelia in ale or switchel if we need to travel."

"I'm famished. Shall we see if there's any food left?"

An hour later, their host accompanied John and Roy to the barn. Houston ran his fingers along the gelding's cannons and pronounced him fit for the trail. But Roy had eyes only for the mare.

"She's a real beaut." He let her smell his fist. "John, I thank ye."

"Hopefully, ye'll forgive me for the other. I had little funds left."

Roy studied the gelding as John led him from the barn. "Not much to look at."

"He's blind on the far side."

"Blind? Ye bought me a blind horse?"

"He's no good for the saddle, I admit. He startles on that side. But harnessed with the mare on his far side, I think he'll do."

With Houston's assistance, the horses were harnessed to the wagon. Roy jumped on the seat and clucked at them. The loaded wagon jerked forward, its contents rattling as the horses pulled it briskly along; the gelding's eyes flashed once, but the mare paced easily, as if the contraption behind her were of no consequence.

"Gee," his cousin commanded, circling them around. He jumped down and gentled the horses. "Good girl," he murmured. "Good laddie." He looked at John. "Gelding's a bit green to the harness, but the mare's well trained. They'll do. Thank ye, John."

He smiled. "Now ye need names." A cough behind him made him turn.

Lizzie and Richie stood smiling. Roy picked the boy up, and with a meaningful glance at his mother, he led them closer. "Can ye help me with names?"

John crossed his arms. He loved his cousin, but Roy was getting a mite too friendly with his servant.

～

THE GLOW of the fire seemed to warm Abigail's very bones as she gazed into it, sitting with the jug of switchel John had given her. Roy was tending to the horses, giving them a bit of feed, and John stood with Mr. Kerr, looking out over the Susquehanna River.

Her first glimpse of the swollen river in the orange light of sunset had alarmed her. Turgid with rainfall, the muddied water rushed swiftly along, carving out chunks of the bank, and bits of brush and tree limbs floated midstream, like bony hands trying to snatch anyone who dared cross.

When they'd camped, John had assured her that the condition of the river was temporary, only the result of the storm. She could see several other campfires closer to the ferry, other families also waiting for the floodwaters to subside.

Abigail let her shoulders relax. The children seemed to be improving. Ritchie sat nearby, sipping at hot chicory laced with lobelia. Lizzie carried the kettle to the Kerrs' wagon, to give Kitty some of the same. Both had coughed on and off for the duration, but Abigail hadn't heard the same awful gasping sound from the little girl again.

Lizzie was back. "Mrs. Kerr is asking if she should give the laudanum."

Abigail blinked in surprise. "Tell her a small dose is best. Perhaps half of what she gave her before. To help her sleep." It was only good sense—but Sophie was her elder by a decade. Did the woman trust her?

Lizzie nodded and went to the Kerrs' wagon.

John settled beside her and stretched out his legs. "That was a difficult fifteen miles."

She nodded in agreement. Three times the men had had to push one of the wagons out of a miry rut. Thankfully, the ground was firmer here. "When do you expect we will be able to cross?"

John lay back on the ground, heedless of the dirt. "We'll see. It may not take long for the river to calm. I hope to leave in the morning." He pointed at the sky. "See that? The bright star? Sirius."

Abigail spread out their oilcloth and lay next to him. "Yes, it's very bright. What's that other bright one?" The western horizon was still glowing, but stars were beginning to appear, their steady presence a calming counterpoint to the susurrus of the river.

"Hmph. My guess is the planet Jupiter. They wander in the sky, ye see? So unless ye're knowledgeable about that sort of thing, it can be difficult to know where they are."

"I've never looked at the sky much. Not in Philadelphia."

"Aye, out here in the country it's verra beautiful." He paused. "It's too dark to read, and there's not much of a fire. But I've got a bit of the next chapter of Romans memorized. Shall we think on God's Word together?"

"Yes." John was such a faithful husband. She wasn't sure if she had any of the Bible memorized. Maybe a few verses here and there.

"'As it is written, There is none righteous, no, not one.'" He turned on his side to face her. "'There is none that understandeth, there is none that seeketh after God. They are all gone out of the way, they are together become unprofitable; there is none that doeth good, no, not one.'"

"None righteous?" Abigail echoed. Weren't Christians righteous? Didn't the Bible speak of the righteous and the wicked? "I don't understand. I know we're sinners, but ..."

John sat up, ran his fingers through his hair, and shifted to join her on the oilcloth. "Well, then. Adam was righteous."

"Yes."

"What happened?"

They'd spoken of this before. "Adam sinned."

John nodded. "Every person born of Adam is born in his image. In his sinful image. That's part of what original sin means, ye ken?"

She nodded, remembering original sin from her catechism. "But there are places in the Bible that describe the righteous. And we are commanded to be righteous."

"The law is holy, just, and good. But we are none of those things. Only Jesus Christ kept the law perfectly. If we are found in Him, God sees us as holy. It's what Mr. Whitefield meant when he spoke of imputation."

"Yes, I remember imputation. But he said some people spoke against it. He argued quite forcefully of its truth." She'd been surprised how forcefully.

"If ye reject imputation, ye reject salvation."

"Truly?"

"If ye try to merit acceptance with God by your own good works instead, ye are not saved."

Night had settled over them. Abigail removed her cap, loosed her braid, and finger-combed her hair. *None righteous.* Mary had sinned, but she'd never thought of herself that way. Not really.

She'd always been good. *None righteous.* Whitefield's words returned to her mind. *Loathe my own righteousness?* Wait—he didn't mean true righteousness. Her small, inadequate attempts at doing good could never cover the gaping holes of her sin.

What was worse was the creeping realization that she'd ignored God all these years, thinking of herself as righteous, not a sinner like Mary. Thinking of herself as better than other people.

No, she'd never been good. She'd only fooled herself. She was glad for the darkness now. She didn't want John to see her tears.

15

My brethren... plainly and freely tell one another what he
has done for your souls... I know not a better means in
the world to keep hypocrisy out from among you. Phar-
isees and unbelievers will pray, read, and sing psalms;
but none save an Israelite indeed, will endure to have
his heart searched out.

—George Whitefield, *Letter,* 1739

While fastening his leggings, John glanced at Abigail. She looked drawn and pale. He thought he'd heard her sobbing in the night—did she miss her family? That was natural. Would his affection be enough of a consolation? He was taking her to a strange place, to a people with different customs. She reminded him of Ruth, who'd left her kin in Moab to go to Judah. Ruth was a brave lassie. If Abigail were Ruth, that made him Boaz. Well, Boaz had done his duty. He hoped he could be as good a husband.

Dawn had well broken, but they still remained at the side of the river, sipping coffee. The current of the broad Susquehanna had slowed, and the level of the water had decreased by a foot or more. The air was peaceful, disturbed only by a single cough coming from the direction of the Kerrs' camp.

Something caught his eye. "Roy—I think the McCallahans are going to cross."

"Aye, I see them." Roy joined him on the bank, and together they watched the ferryman and his assistant push off from the bank.

A robin chirruped above the sounds of clanking kettles and snuffing animals. John handed his cup to Lizzie, who was securing the pans.

He led Percy to drink at the river's edge and studied the ferry. Midstream, the current tugged at the ungainly craft, but the men knew their job, and though they drifted downstream, the family made it safely to the other side.

John joined his cousin. "Roy, I'll help you harness the horses."

Wisps of smoke spiraled in the air above the Kerrs' smothered fire. They were almost ready to go.

"I dinna trust the gelding." Roy stood at the animal's head, smoothly inserting the bit. "He's calm as a old granny now. But the water—"

"I mind ye. We'll unbuckle the harness once we're onboard, ye ken? Just in case. And we could cover his eyes."

Abigail donated her kerchief for this purpose, and once they led the horses onto the ferry, Roy blindfolded Sloan's horse. The animal snuffed once but remained tractable.

John stood at the mare's head as the boat shoved off. Abigail stood on the bank, her eyes never leaving him as she held the reins of the pony and Percy. Lizzie and Ritchie flanked the heifer.

He offered her a smile. Given the current, he couldn't chance overloading the ferry. They'd need three trips to get them all across.

He murmured to the bay mare, stroking her neck. She stood still, but her ears twitched, and her head jerked up a few times. "Ye got names for them yet?"

"Stormy. The gelding's name is Stormy. Ritchie chose that one, aye? I asked Lizzie about the mare, but she wants to consult with Abigail first." His cousin's mouth jerked. "I think she wants something fancy. Or Latin, maybe."

Lizzie. He needed to speak to Roy about that. He was practically courting her in his familiarity, but how could the girl be free to marry? He hadn't thought it all through when he'd saved the woman from Sloan. True, Da had purchased Archie and Agnes' contracts years before, but they were married at the time. This was different. Lizzie would feel beholden to him, and by extension, Roy.

The mare stiffened under his hand. John grasped her bridle, scanning the river.

There—dead branches projected from the surface of the water, not fifty feet away. The current was sweeping them faster than the boat drifted, which meant the branches were light, not part of a heavy tree. Not a problem. But the mare didn't know that.

She snorted.

"Ho, now, lassie," John murmured. "Roy, keep the gelding covered."

But it was too late. The mare jerked her head, and the gelding, sensing her alarm, panicked. The blindfold slid off, and Roy clung to the bridle as the animal snorted and pawed. Then the gelding caught a glimpse of the branches, and the moving water all about them. His hooves left the deck.

The squeals of the horses mingled with a sudden splash. Mindful of the gelding's hooves, John grabbed the linen kerchief, dangling precariously over the gunwale. One of the ferrymen grabbed the mare's bridle, and John reached for Stormy, now standing crosswise to the mare, with splayed feet, ears flat against his head. He whipped the fabric over the gelding's eyes.

"There, now, there's a good lad." He gently prodded the horse until it stood next to the mare. "Stormy, that's a good name for ye."

Where was Roy?

Then he heard a scream.

ABIGAIL COULDN'T SEE what was happening. Clearly, there was trouble with the horses—the gelding had reared in response to something she didn't notice. The ferry was at least halfway across, and the wagon partially blocked her view of the men. The ferryman and his helper seemed to be assisting John. Wait—where was Roy?

Lizzie screamed.

Abigail's stomach flipped. "What did you see?"

"Roy went overboard." She gasped. "I think the horse hurt him."

Abigail sidestepped closer to the other woman, trying to see. John now had control of the gelding, and one of the ferrymen knelt at one side of the boat. After an interminable pause, Roy's copper head popped into view. His forearms braced against the gunwale and soon he was back on board.

Lizzie's frame was rigid. "I see him. But I think he's hurt. He's just sitting there."

Abigail grabbed her bodice, feeling for the stone pendant lying underneath. How could John help his cousin when he had his hands full with the horse? The ferrymen went back to poling. Was it her imagination, or were they shoving the craft along faster than before?

In any case, the wide river separated them. She wanted to help, and Lizzie was frantic. But the ferry would have to unload the wagon and return for them; not a long trip under normal circumstances, but it seemed like forever now.

Abigail took a deep breath. Surely John knew a bit about what to do for injuries. He was a backwoodsman, after all. She tucked her arm about Lizzie's shoulders. "I'm sure John knows what to do." When had the woman become so attached to Roy?

Mr. Kerr's gruff voice interrupted. "What's the collieshangie about?"

"Roy went overboard—I think it was some trouble with the gelding," Abigail said.

"Seems your man has the animal to rights again. And they're almost across."

"Lizzie thinks Roy might be injured."

"Hmph." He peered at her. "Well, now, my Sophie seems to think ye're a healer." He returned to their wagon.

Abigail wasn't quite sure what to make of his comment. A grudging acceptance? Perhaps they'd thought her worthless before.

Occasionally she'd thought that way herself.

JOHN TUGGED his shirt over his head and squatted. With one motion he drew the tiny dagger in his stocking and slit the shirt near the hem. Replacing the little weapon, he grasped both edges of the cut fabric and tugged. It ripped. In a few moments' time he had several long strips of linen prepared.

Roy sat under the nearest tree, ashen and tight-lipped. Soundlessly he clutched at his left knee, his knuckles white with effort. The calf of his leg had been ripped open almost to the bone.

John hoped the river and the oozing blood had washed the dirt out. He was no healer, but he doubted that horse manure—or anything else on that gelding's hooves—had any medicinal value, despite what some physicians said.

His gaze darted back to the river. Abigail, Lizzie, Ritchie, and the rest of the animals were already on the ferry. Good. Abigail would know what to do. He hoped.

"Hey, Roy." What to say? He'd talk nonsense to an injured horse. "I'll wrap this, now. Abigail will doctor ye." He kept up a soft but steady prattle.

John wrapped the leg, carefully pressing the edges of the gaping wound together. Roy lay down, trembling and moaning, a terrible soft keening sound. After tying the bandage, John placed his rolled-up jacket under his cousin's head. "Rest, now."

Roy's eyelids flickered. His ragged breathing eased slightly, but his body was stiff and still, as if using all his energy to deal with the pain. After a few moments his eyes closed.

John strode to the wagon. Where were Abigail's supplies? Weren't her simples in a canvas bag? Parcels and bags nestled between kegs of molasses and cider. He pulled on a pale strap—yes, her bag, now bulging with what looked like faded leaves. He carried it to Roy, set it down and returned to the riverbank, willing the ferry to hurry.

He caught her gaze now, just twenty feet from shore. The ferrymen poled vigorously, sweat pouring down their bare backs. Then the man in front plunged his pole into the river bottom to slow the craft, but even so, the boat lurched as it met up with the bank. Abigail leaped across the small gap, skirts bouncing. Wordlessly, John grasped her arms and steadied her.

Leaving the others, they went to Roy's side, and Abigail plopped down, heedless of the damp ground. "What happened?"

John explained about Stormy's fright. "Ye see, the river water cleansed the wound." Maybe. "It's deep. I wrapped it, but it needs a bit of sewing up."

"Can you make a fire? And I'll need vinegar."

ABIGAIL'S INNARDS clenched as she examined the wound. She'd never doctored anyone before. John said it needed to be stitched, and he was clearly right. She took a deep breath, a plan forming in her mind. Roy lay pale but silent, looking up as if studying the leaves of the oak tree shading them, his hands curled into tight fists, clenching and unclenching.

Lizzie brought the pail of hot vinegar and squatted on Roy's other side, staring at his face. "Will he be all right?" she whispered.

"As long as the wound doesn't fester. That's what the vinegar is for."

Roy lifted his head, sweat popping out on his forehead. "Vinegar?"

"Dinna fash yerself." John's voice broke in from behind her. "Here, some switchel will do ye good."

John knelt and helped Roy to one elbow so he could drink. His cousin managed a few sips, and John left.

Abigail swished a needle and thread in the warm vinegar, remembering. Mother had always cleaned the house, top to bottom, when sickness threatened. Vinegar was her mainstay. But it hadn't helped Granny Latham, who'd perished with so many others of the smallpox in Boston so long ago. Feeling helpless against such things, Papa had wanted her in the country.

In any case, river water was undrinkable and not sufficient for cleaning out a dirty wound. Washing the gash with vinegar would be painful, but she couldn't think of what else to do. And Roy might develop a fever no matter what she did. "Lizzie, can you make boneset tea?"

The other woman nodded and stepped to the fire. Clean linen for bandages sat on her left. Everything was ready. But this would be excruciating. Where was John?

As if in response to her thoughts, he appeared at her side. "Mrs. Kerr sent ye this." He handed her a small bottle of laudanum.

"Oh, thank God. Give him two spoonfuls." Laudanum took effect quickly. In a few minutes she'd be able to begin.

Abigail glanced about the camp. The Kerrs had hobbled the mules a hundred yards away, in a good patch of grass, their wagon nestled under a large chestnut. Kitty, their daughter, was helping her mother. A single cough punctuated the clink and clank of ordinary camp sounds. She was better. *Thank you, Lord.*

Roy dozed, his mouth slightly open. The pain would wake him. "John, can you be ready to hold him down?"

"Will Kerr is coming to help. He'll hold the leg still as ye work."

A few moments later, William approached. With the lanky lad clutching the leg, and John bracing Roy's shoulders, Abigail poured warm vinegar over the wound.

"Aarrgh!" Roy twisted and trembled.

"Wheesht, lad. The worst is over." John hovered over his cousin, keeping his shoulders on the ground.

"I'll be as quick as I can." Abigail tensed as she drove the needle into the edge of the wound. Thankfully it wasn't bleeding much. She tried to steady her fingers by imagining her mother's hands deftly trussing a turkey, sewing up the skin over the stuffing.

But this was different. Living flesh, muscle and sinew and fat ... she forced herself to continue, her stomach sour. She couldn't vomit, not now.

She sensed Lizzie at her side, holding the bag with the sassafras leaves. A tiny moan escaped the young widow. Roy panted, but made no other sounds.

One last stitch. A bit of vinegar over the closed wound. Her hands seemed to move on their own, wrapping the wound with the leaves as a dressing. Finally she was done.

John helped her to a place under the tree where he'd spread out some oilcloth. "Lie down, Abigail. I'll see that he gets the tea. Ye did fine."

The last thing she remembered was John's hand gently smoothing back her loosened hair.

16

WHEN you find these concurring symptoms, drink 3 or 4
quarts of Whey _as fast as you can, wherein the_ Root _of_
Prickly Pear _has been boil'd. When that has all passed,_
squeeze the Juice _of_ Wild Garlic _into clean sound_
Cider, and drink a moderate Glass of it Night and
Morning, for 6 or 7 days...

—Dr. John Tennent, 1727, Stone in the Kidneys, _Every Man His Own_
Doctor

*J*ohn nudged Percy, and the mare turned. The road had
narrowed, but he was still able to circle around periodically to check on the wagons. They were close to
Shawnee territory here, and the treaty with the Iroquois didn't apply
to them. Perhaps they could camp early enough tonight to hunt;
game was plentiful in these woods.

Lizzie handled the horses well for a novice, her son sitting next to her on the wagon seat. From behind her Roy glared at him, his leg immobilized. Yesterday morning his cousin had demanded to drive the wagon, citing the unreliability of the gelding, but John had insisted. "Ye are two feet from the reins," he'd barked. "And what can Stormy do? Run himself into a tree?"

He'd let his cousin drive tomorrow. In any case, they were coming up on the Cumberland, an area dangerous for a number of reasons, and he needed Roy's eyes and ears—and musket. He could watch best from the wagon bed.

He nudged Percy past Abigail on Rosemary. She glanced at him, slipping him a small smile. She sat tall and sure on her mount, but her expression reflected an elusive uncertainty.

Well, no wonder. She'd collapsed from exhaustion after sewing up Roy two days ago, who'd recovered with alacrity—and no fever. She was a healer, no doubt. But she was young, and the trip was difficult. He resolved to talk to her tonight. Was she troubled about something?

He nodded to Thomas Kerr, now seated on the wagon's seat with his wife, little Kitty in between them. Tommy and William paced behind, serving as sentries; the older lad sported the Kerrs' ancient fowling piece on his shoulder.

"Holler, dinna shoot," John reminded Will. Yesterday he'd given them all basic instruction in dealing with the threats from Indians and assorted ruffians, though he didn't have much faith in the lads' ability to follow it. In the heat of fright or excitement, anything could happen. If the fowling piece did go off, like as not it would just make a big noise, which was as good or better than a shout. However, shooting a peaceful Indian was anything but wise. And peaceful folk were the only kind who showed themselves.

The Indians you didn't see were the dangerous ones. In this country, ambush was the only military tactic practiced.

He made his way up the caravan again. Percy's neck had darkened with sweat. The sun was overhead, and the breeze had fallen; they'd need to stop for the noonday meal soon. Could they reach the spring? Middle Spring meetinghouse couldn't be far. Some good folks there.

With pressure from his knees and thighs he guided Percy ahead of the wagon, desiring to scout the road ahead. The mare's ears flicked to the side of the road.

shweet, shweet, shweet ...

John raised his hand, signaling the others to stop, and slid off the animal in one fluid motion. Percy stood still, unalarmed, as he balanced the rifle across the saddle, aiming at the woods.

A turkey call. It could mean dinner, or it might mean an ambush. *Indians.*

The wagons came to a halt, Stormy whuffing as if impatient at the change in plans.

The calls repeated. The gray birds were so abundant and easy to kill that few mastered the skill of duplicating their calls ... except the Indians. He ground-tied Percy and slipped back to the wagon.

"Roy, is your musket loaded?"

"Aye." His cousin had already adjusted his position in the wagon, eyes trained on the woods. "I'll cover ye."

"Might be dinner. I'll circle around. I've wanted to give this rifle a try."

Roy smiled, his face tight with pain.

John ducked into the shade of oaks and poplars at the side of the road and found a snarl of rhododendron to hide behind. The heavy moist air almost choked him with the familiar scent of leaf mold. Feeling the thud of his own heartbeat in the silence, he waited until he heard the call again. The birds—if they were indeed birds— seemed to be located in a grove of chestnuts. He slipped behind a large tree, bringing his rifle up at the same time, pointing into the grove. The weapon's weight balanced easily in his hands, its maple stock cool to his touch.

Four—no, five—gray shapes scratched in the leaf litter under the trees. Brambles nearby sported berries. They'd be fat.

Reflexively, he lined up a shot and fired. For a long breathless moment, squawks filled the space, and dust and feathers flew. He strode underneath the broad boughs where two turkeys lay dead.

No, one was dead, and the other merely stunned. He drew his skinning knife and dispatched the second with a quick motion. How had he killed two birds? He remembered lining up the shot, trying to maximize his chances by aiming at one bird behind another. Somehow, the single bullet had taken down both. *Thank you, Lord.*

John hefted the birds. Provision, and protection. No Indians today.

ABIGAIL PEEKED at the man across the fire as she helped Lizzie with the turkey. Dark-haired, with an ordinary face above a homespun shirt, the minister seemed a man like anyone else. John Blair and his wife had welcomed them an hour ago and helped them set up camp near the spring. Now he squatted next to John, discussing a book.

Sophie Kerr approached the fire with her crock of Indian corn mush ready for baking; Abigail abhorred the milk-less version of cornbread they sometimes had to gnaw on, but the leftovers would keep for supper and even breakfast. While she helped Sophie wrap bits of the thick batter in leaves and thrust them into the edges of the fire, she listened to the men's conversation. They'd grabbed bits of wood to sit on and sat hunched with their heads together.

"Not everyone would approve, John. In meeting we sing from the Psalter." Blair's voice was as gentle as a smooth stream splashing over hidden rocks, despite his words.

"Och, I ken that fine. But his words are so in keeping with the Scriptures—"

"Ye may be right. Here, this one: 'How sweet and awful is the place, with Christ within the doors ...'"

Both were silent for several moments, poring over a small book.

The minister straightened. "It's as though Samuel Rutherford himself had penned the lines. Watts—that's his name? Yes, Isaac

Watts. He captures the sweetness of the gospel without losing the solid truth underneath."

"But how would ye sing it?"

John Blair rubbed the stubble on his jaw. "Let me see. Ye mind the tunes we use for the Psalter? Well, we can use one of those." His brows contracted for a moment. "Ah. St. Columba, then. That tune will work."

Stomach growling, Abigail prodded the turkey, broiling on a simple spit over the licking flames. Blackened on the outside, still too juicy on the inside. She couldn't let it roast in the embers, as she'd prefer—it would take too long. William Kerr stalked the campsite, his gaze constantly darting to the turkeys as he toted wood and water. The men were undoubtedly hungry.

Perhaps they could start with the cornbread, or journeycake, as John called it. The broiling bird gave off a tantalizing scent—as did the other one, roasting over the Kerrs' fire. She caught her husband's gaze through the smoke.

He nodded and stood. "Mr. Blair, would ye be so kind as to ask the blessing?"

ABIGAIL NIBBLED on her half-eaten turkey leg. It did taste good, even the burnt parts, but her stomach wasn't entirely in the mood. She shifted in the leaf litter under the dogwood tree. Her skirts were dirty and her shift tacky. She plucked a mottled green leaf from the ground and wiped her mouth with it, certain her face was still streaked with grime and turkey grease.

The children bounced about the clearing, the shine of grease around their mouths contrasting with soot and dirt elsewhere. Ritchie's shirt flopped about him, overlarge, but Gretchen had said he'd grow into it. Well, maybe, if it lasted that long. Abigail's eyes spotted a frayed hem and a gaping seam. She needed to mend it.

Tonight, if she had the strength—hopefully they wouldn't travel much farther today.

Kitty stood before her, glancing at her turkey leg. The little girl hadn't coughed all day. That was a blessing.

"Do you think you can help me with this?" Abigail handed her the meat, and the child nodded her thanks before bounding off.

John cleared his throat from his seat nearby, and soon a few uncertain notes lifted into the air, hesitant at first but then gaining in strength. Mr. Blair joined in, his tenor layering neatly with her husband's throaty baritone.

Abigail closed her eyes. The tune was haunting but peaceful.

"Why was I made to hear thy voice, and enter while there's room? When thousands make a wretched choice, and rather starve than come."

She opened her eyes. That was a good question. There should be an answer in the Catechism. Election? Was she not elect? Was that the problem?

"'Twas the same love that spread the feast, that sweetly forced us in; else we had still refused to taste, and perished in our sin."

Love? She blinked. "John? What does the song mean?" She had to know. And she didn't care what anyone thought.

HEARING HIS WIFE'S QUESTION, John faced her. Abigail's face was pale under the golden tan of the summer sun. Soot stained one cheek, and moist, lank strands of blond hair had escaped her cap to fall in tangled disarray about her shoulders. "It's about the sweetness of God's presence. And the wonder of our salvation."

She looked miserable.

Blair squatted next to him. "Aye. What troubles ye?"

John was glad for the minister's presence, and for the gentle, easy cadence of his speech. Abigail's eyes reminded him of a horse just one step away from bolting.

She frowned, her back rigid. "Mr. Whitefield's sermon. He said I was to loathe my own righteousness."

"Aye." Blair eased himself down on the leaf mold and leaned back on one arm. "Do ye ken what he means by that?"

"At first I did not understand. I couldn't see how I was to reject my own righteousness if I was commanded to obey God's precepts." Abigail took a breath and seemed to relax. The minister's easy manner had calmed her a bit.

"Well, now, that is a conundrum." The minister plucked a stem of grass. "Ye said 'at first.' Have ye had any more thoughts on it?" He placed the end of the grass stem between his teeth.

John wanted desperately to take her in his arms, to chase away the strain his wife was clearly under. But what could he do? It wasn't his battle, not in the physical sense. *Oh Lord, help her. Help her to see your grace. Do for her what I cannot.*

"I judged my sister Mary. It was not right."

What? He knew of another sister, the oldest. But what was this all about?

"Did Mary sin?" Blair leaned forward, brown eyes gentle.

Abigail's shoulders slumped. "Yes." Eyes cast downward, she flushed a bit. "Mother said we could not have any contact with her."

"What did you think of Mary?"

"Well, she was the wicked girl, and Hannah and I were good. I realize now I had looked down on her, and later, when I received a letter from her, I saw that my heart was wrong. I had set myself above her. But Mary had found solace from God. To me, when I think of God, I only think of duty. I don't think of solace or comfort or sweetness—like the song says."

John's lips parted as he gazed at his wife. She knew nothing of Christ. Nothing of forgiveness. That day in Philadelphia when he'd voiced his concerns to his father, it had seemed less important. Easily dealt with. But now ...

The minister was speaking. "Mrs. Russell, have ye kept the Commandments?"

Abigail's mouth opened slightly, as if the question was unexpected. "The Ten Commandments?"

"Aye." Blair leaned back on his arm.

A rustle and a clatter caught John's attention. The wagons. Time to be going. But no, they could wait just a wee bit more. He turned and sought Roy's gaze, then signaled to him to give them more time.

"I don't think I've broken any of them."

"When ye roasted the turkey, who were ye trying to please?"

What was he getting at? The first commandment?

Abigail gaped at him. "I don't know. Well, maybe my husband."

"Who are we to serve and worship?"

"God." She bit her lip. "So I can't please my husband?"

"Of course ye can, if by doing so ye have an eye for God's glory." Blair seemed to repress a chuckle, but his kind eyes twinkled. "But give the Commandments a bit of thought. Ye'll see that our best works are shot through with sin. Self-interest and self-worship."

"So I have no righteousness."

"Exactly. The Law of Moses, when rightly used, is a verra handy thing for curing us from self-righteousness. Jesus confronted the Pharisees with the Law, showing them that they were only fooling themselves."

Silence fell, only interrupted by the bray of a mule.

John studied his wife. What was she thinking?

"Then what must I do to be a true Christian?"

17

Dear John: I wish you would see John Harris, at the ferry,
and get him to write to the Governor, to see if he can't
get some guns for us; there's a good wheen of ingns
about here, and I fear they intend to give us a good deal
of troubbel, and may do us a grate dale of harm.

—James Magraw, *Letter,* Falling Spring, 1733

A stray breeze cooled Abigail's neck as she rode Rosemary, the saddle creaking slightly, a now familiar sound. After so many days on the road, the scent of the mare beneath her was no longer strange either. The landscape had slowly changed, with the gently swelling slopes near Lancaster giving way to hills and valleys, tall trees crowding the trail, their shade keeping off the worst of the afternoon heat. But the peacefulness of her surroundings did little to steady her heart.

John sidled up next to her on Percy after having circled the wagons behind them. When they'd left the Blairs, he'd said they were making for Falling Spring, only a few more hours away. At least her hips and thighs no longer burned from the chafing. Considering one's blessings was a good thing, Mother had always said.

The minister's face came to mind. He'd been a blessing, she decided. And yet, her heart felt sliced open. What had he said? That others had asked the same question she had: What must I do to be saved? And the answer was to believe on the Lord Jesus Christ.

Well, she'd thought she believed all along. So what was the problem? It all seemed so elusive, much like the slippery, gooey plant in John Bartram's garden, outside of Philadelphia. Papa had taken her there once when Mother had gone to visit Hannah for her first confinement. Bartram had handed her a tropical plant called an aloe. Good for burns, the man had said, slicing the ugly fat stem and slapping the innards on her forearm.

She glanced at John. He wasn't yet thirty, but the dust settling into the lines of his face made him seem older in the intermittent shafts of sunlight that peppered the trail.

He turned to her, and his lips parted slightly, but his face was unreadable.

"John, could it be I am not elect?"

His eyebrows shot up, the white scar catching her eye. "Not elect?"

"I think I understand about being a sinner better now. And about Christ, what He came to do—that much I've been taught since I was a little child. I don't know what I lack yet."

Her husband seemed tired—well, no wonder. He faced forward and pursed his lips. "Dinna fash yerself about election." He paused, squinting as a beam of sunlight lit up his face. "I'm trying to remember what John Knox said about it. D'ye mind him?"

She frowned. "I think I heard the name once or twice."

"He brought the Reformation to Scotland. He preached the

gospel and the entire country was changed. He said that without these doctrines—predestination and election—men canna be brought to true humility and knowledge of themselves. They'll think they can save themselves."

Abigail took a deep breath, willing away the fatigue of the long day. She struggled to piece it together. "Mr. Blair talked about the Commandments. He wanted me to see my sinfulness."

"Aye, and the doctrine of election amounts to the same thing. Once ye see how truly sinful ye are, how we are all by nature the enemies of God, down to the very core, then we see that only God can save us. He makes the choice, ye ken, because if He didna, none of us would choose Him."

Oh. Abruptly it all became clear. "So I can ask for mercy? God won't reject me because I'm not elect?"

John smiled. The years seemed to fall off and he was young once again. "If you weren't elect ye wouldna seek God. Christ is the Savior of sinners. Are ye a sinner? Then ye qualify."

Abigail clutched the reins, a ray of hope bursting in her mind.

JOHN JERKED his chin and scanned the trail ahead. Deep in conversation, he'd barely noticed the passing brush and trees. Just ahead, a rocky outcrop obscured the path. He held up his hand. "Roy!"

He turned just long enough to see that his cousin had caught his signal. Distracted by Abigail's internal struggles, he'd acquiesced to the young man's badgering, and Roy had eased himself onto the wagon seat to guide the wagon the few miles to Falling Spring and the relative shelter of Magraw's settlement. There were probably two dozen families in the area around the spring and the creek that flowed from it, but it was also Sloan's old stomping ground, and if he'd returned …

He saved that thought for later. The trail curved around the outcropping of limestone just ahead, and he'd check it out before they all proceeded. It was a perfect place for an ambush.

He clucked to Percy, and she flicked her ears about as she trotted smoothly beneath him. The mare detected nothing. When he reached the smooth white stone, he slowed her and raised his tomahawk. For a close encounter it was better than a firearm. A tomahawk couldn't misfire, and it wouldn't announce his presence to all and sundry.

Past the bend, leaves rustled in the late afternoon breeze, speaking their own ancient language. John glanced at Percy's nostrils. No, she didn't smell anything strange. The stink of an Indian's salve could be quite noticeable, even from a dozen feet away. He remembered the smell of the one he'd killed that awful day: bear fat gone rancid, mixed with the copper tang of blood.

He blinked the memory away, and motioned the mare forward a few steps. No, it was safe—as safe as he could determine. *Lord, remember us. Keep us safe from what we cannot see ... and remember Abigail.*

John returned to the caravan and soon they were all past the bend in the road. Abigail seemed to be grasping the truth of the Scriptures, little by little. He'd answered her questions as best he could, but underneath it all, a dark pit of desperation threatened to consume him.

He'd prayed about marriage. He'd really and truly sought God, and even felt a peace about the choice of a wife—and sought counsel from his father. But the past week had brought new doubts. She wasn't a Christian after all, and though today's conversation encouraged him, it was no guarantee. Nothing seemed guaranteed.

Hadn't he suffered enough?

~

"THANK YE KINDLY FOR THE NEWS," John said, shoulders slumping as he kept his seat on Percy, her head dangling in search of grass.

James Magraw nodded, the golden rays of the setting sun illuminating his muscular forearms as he cinched the saddle of his pony.

"I'll see you to the clearing near the stream. It's not far away, and the ground is dry this time of year," the man said. "And I'll look for Indian sign. I havena heard of trouble this past year, but you never can tell."

"Thank ye kindly." Thinking of the night ahead, John felt an unspeakable weariness descend upon him. Despite the presence of the settlers nearby, he'd post a double watch. According to Magraw, Sloan had returned only two days before. John hadn't explained his interest in the man when he'd asked about the ruffian.

Magraw mounted, and soon the wagons were moving again around the foot of the hill where the man had built his cabin. A stand of tall corn came into view, reminding John of his own crop.

"Sloan is unpredictable at best," the settler said, seeming to read his mind. "Do you know the story? What he did when the Shawnee butchered his wife?"

John's stomach clenched with an agony that surprised him. "I— I'd heard something."

"I saw the scalps he brought back. Two Shawnee, and one was clearly a squaw's. Long black hair." Magraw directed his pony ahead of him down a barely discernable track.

John's stomach turned. A woman? Sloan had taken his revenge, then. And managed to escape with his life. "Poisoned by bitterness." The words escaped his lips.

Magraw turned in the saddle. "Yes, you could say that. Unhinged, in truth. I thought of all people you would understand."

The stream came into view, and John drew up alongside the other man. His jaw clenched. "Oh, I understand. I understand I'll be posting a watch tonight." His voice sounded hard to his own ears. He didn't mean to lay any blame on Magraw, but what could he say? Silas Sloan was a menace.

The other man's gaze locked with his for a moment. "God go with you, John Russell," he said in a neutral voice as he turned his pony away.

ABIGAIL STEPPED past the dim form of Will Kerr, his chin dipping low as he sat, keeping watch. Was he sleeping? Everyone was tired, and the clearing was so peaceful, edged on one side by the tiny tinkle of a creek, and fringed elsewhere by trees of every description—a botanist's paradise, surely. She didn't think she'd woken John as she slipped away; she'd never needed to get up at night before on the trail. In Philadelphia she rarely used the chamber pot at night— maybe she'd drunk too much ale at supper.

The moon had already set, but her eyes were adjusted to the darkness, and she could see the faint outline of a giant tree just ahead by the light of the stars. An oak? Once underneath its heavy limbs, the familiar moist, mossy smell of the tree's shelter enveloped her. Insects hummed about her in a friendly fashion as she took care of her needs.

A twig snapped. Had John followed her?

She stood, adjusted her skirts, and turned. Suddenly she was slammed against the tree, its sharp bark digging into her back, a fierce weight pressing against her chest. A hand—someone's hand had pinned her to the trunk. The smell of tobacco and some sort of spirits made her gasp.

"You're Russell's woman." The voice was rough but low, meant only for her ears. "Go along easy now, and no harm will come to you."

She opened her mouth, but couldn't find the breath to scream. Her knees wobbled. Was she going to faint?

The man jerked her deeper into the trees, one of his arms around her back, the other over her mouth. Who was he? She tripped over an unseen root, and he cursed.

Now she recognized the voice. Sloan. The nasty man in the chandlery.

～

"ROY? WHERE'S ABIGAIL?" John shrugged off the clinging shreds of sleep as he realized his wife had left his side. William Kerr's head jerked up suddenly. The lad had nodded off.

"I didna see her." His cousin stood beside him, his musket at the ready. "Perhaps she went to relieve herself under the trees." Roy pointed over Will's head to the woods on that side of their camp.

John strapped on his weapons. "William, watch the camp for us, will ye?" The lad would stay awake now. Time for recriminations later—and perhaps it was nothing.

He searched the tree line, a dark blur in the starlight. No, a call of nature wouldn't take this long. *Abigail.* Where was she?

He approached the trees, thankful for Roy's presence. Not trusting his firearm, he drew his knife from its sheath. Was it Indians? Or Sloan? They halted under the first tree, a large oak. "Abigail?" he called softly. He returned the blade to its place, just in case. In the pitch-black of the woods, he couldn't see to use it safely. He took a few steps into the darkness, the warmth of his cousin discernable at his side.

A thick silence enveloped them. John placed his hand on Roy's shoulder to signal him to stop. They stood there for many long seconds, listening. There was no hum of insects. They'd been disturbed. And a faint scent of something. A man-smell. Tobacco?

If it were Sloan—or for that matter, an Indian—he couldn't risk a light. But he had nose and ears, and only lacked knowledge of the area. He led the way slowly, step by step, deeper into the woods. Should he approach the stream or go uphill? What would Sloan choose?

If the man had Abigail—*oh Lord, let him not harm her*—then he might not make good time. It was his only hope.

Standing silently shoulder-to-shoulder with Roy, he heard a noise. A strangled peep, barely audible above the pulse of his heartbeat in his ears. His cousin touched his hand; he'd heard it too. Downhill, near the stream.

The twisted man had chosen the stream. And that was going to be Silas Sloan's last mistake.

18

What should we have been had God left us to ourselves?
Oh let a sense of this free, distinguishing love
constrain us to obedience: A Christian needs no other
motive.

—George Whitefield, *Letter,* 1739

For several horrific moments, Abigail's mind ceased to function. Her captor half-dragged, half-carried her along, the bear-like strength of his arms preventing any resistance. The stench of his sweat choked her; she could barely breathe above the meaty hand imprisoning her mouth.

Then Sloan stopped. Her heartbeat thudded in her ears. Was he listening for pursuit? Was John following them? But how could he in this darkness?

Sloan jerked her into motion again, with the smooth motion of a hunter, the only sound an occasional soft rustle as her feet slipped on the leaves. They seemed to have changed direction, for now the ground sloped gently downward.

Abigail swallowed. Where was he taking her, and why?

The scene in the chandlery replayed itself in her mind. John had purchased Lizzie's contract—did Sloan think she was Lizzie? Or was he just taking revenge?

Help, Lord! A sense of desperation welled up inside of her. For all she knew, Sloan was a madman. Abigail fought the panic rising up inside her—she needed to think. How could she escape him?

Moving air and a faint light told her they had broken free of the trees. A murmur a few feet away marked a stream. Sloan stopped again and took several deep breaths, each exhalation brushing against her ear. She cringed in revulsion.

He stilled, as if listening. At that moment, his hand over her mouth loosened. Summoning all her strength, Abigail wrenched her jaw free and bit his hand.

With a faint grunt, Sloan jerked his hand back, and she thought he would strike her, but instead his knife appeared, shining faintly in the starlight.

She squealed.

His lips met her ear. "Make another sound, and I'll slit your throat."

She had no choice. *Lord, save me. Save me from this madman—and from everything else. From my sin and confusion.*

A FAINT GLIMMER of starlight just ahead marked the place where the thick canopy of foliage ended over the streambed. John stretched out his hand and touched his cousin. They paused as one man. He hadn't heard a splash; surely Sloan hadn't crossed the stream, at least not yet. He might have gone upstream; it was unlikely he'd venture the other way, closer to camp.

Grabbing Roy's hand, John used simple signs to indicate he

wished him to stay on the bank while John circled upstream. Roy took a single silent step toward the water, showing he understood. They'd hunted together before.

John crept upstream, keeping the faint glimpses of starlight to his right. Spicy tree-scents filled his nostrils as his senses strained in the dark. He passed through the trees easily, guided by smell and faint glimpses of light. The bushes were harder to skirt. He paused at the sharp prick of a bramble. Another two steps, and a low boggy spot yielded beneath his foot. He was very near the water.

He eased up to a smaller tree—a beech?—and looked out toward the susurrus of the stream. A dark shape moved under the stars. Silas Sloan should have kept to the trees where he couldn't be seen. Perhaps he had a horse nearby. It was the only reason the man would expose himself.

"Sloan," he bellowed. "It's me ye want." Could he get the man to attack him? It would be hard for Abigail to escape in these woods, and Sloan might release her for the present, knowing she wouldn't get far. It was risky to attack with her in Sloan's arms.

The dark shape was motionless. A slight glimmer appeared—a knife. "Keep your distance, Russell. I'll cut the woman's throat."

Silas Sloan would not live to see another dawn. John gauged the distance: the man was only ten feet from him. He took one step, then another. Cloaked by the trees, he had the advantage. He could see Sloan, but the other could not see him. Could he get the man to let down his guard?

"Have it your way, Sloan. But I'll set the constable on ye tomorrow. Ye won't get away with stealing my maidservant." John forced his voice to some semblance of normalcy, hoping to fool the other man. Could Sloan be sure, in the darkness, which woman he'd kidnapped?

John took one more step. *Now!* He dashed forward and led with a right hook to what he thought was the man's jaw. A *whump* of breath from Sloan was the only response to the impact. A whimper and splash in the stream revealed Abigail's position as he wrestled with her captor. The man had let her go in order to fight him, and John could only hope she was unscathed.

An unseen fist slammed into his gut and he doubled over, but he gathered his feet under him and sprang upward, slamming his head into the approximate location of Sloan's nose. A sickening crunch vibrated through his forehead, and Sloan staggered back a pace or two.

Then, out of nowhere, fire ran down the side of his face—Sloan's blade. Ducking to avoid the knife, he unsheathed his own dagger and brought his arms up and out, knocking the other man's hands away from his body. Then he launched his whole weight at the other man.

John pinned Sloan to the ground, the end of his knife pointed at Sloan's throat. "This is the day ye meet your Maker," he hissed.

"No it isn't." Roy's voice broke through the red haze.

John gritted his teeth, furious. "What do ye propose we do with him?" He felt like knocking his cousin down for interfering. He kept the knife to Sloan's throat, but the white-hot edge of his rage was ebbing.

"Tie him to a tree. This man is well known. Give him to the magistrate. Could be the governor himself might be interested." Roy fumbled in his pouch. "I've got a bit of something to tie his hands with, at least."

Suddenly, Sloan wriggled underneath him with the furious strength of insanity, flung him aside, and gathered his feet under him. Before John could tackle him, he'd pushed his way past Roy and was heading upstream along the bank. A few moments later, the muffled sound of a horse's snort reached their ears. He was gone.

ABIGAIL SAT gasping on the bank of the stream, trying to calm herself. Sloan was gone. She was wet, but safe; and John—well, he'd come to her rescue, but he'd nearly killed the man. He'd wanted to—she'd heard it in his voice.

What if he had? She wasn't sure she wanted to think about it.

Then John's arms enveloped her and she flinched. His arms relaxed their hold.

"Abigail? Are ye hurt?"

She explored her neck with sluggish fingers. Sloan's blade had nicked her, but she couldn't feel any blood.

"No ... I'm not hurt."

She turned and grasped John's shoulders. "Are you injured?" The violent struggle had lasted only a few moments, but Sloan had a knife.

"Not really. A wee scratch, maybe."

Abigail was dubious. "Where?" John's standards of size were unlikely to match her own. She fumbled in her pocket for a hand-kerchief.

"My face. We'll see to it presently." His voice lowered. "Did he ... hurt you?"

"No." Wasn't that clear? Then she caught the nuance of his question. "Oh, no, he only dragged me to the stream. Kept his hand over my mouth ..." She shuddered anew with the telling of it.

"I heard something—that's how we kent where ye were."

"I bit him." Was that blood on his face? "Here, John, 'tis not clean, but press this on your cheek."

She realized then that Roy was standing next to them. "I'd sit and visit, but with my leg, it's hard to get up again, ye ken?" he said, almost too casually.

Roy—his leg. She hoped he hadn't reinjured it. She took a deep breath. How long had she been sitting here? The wetness creeping up her skirts was uncomfortable, and she shifted, wondering if her legs could support her.

"Let's go," John said, his voice hoarse. He had won the fight, but something about his manner spoke otherwise.

～

"TIME TO ROUSE EVERYONE, RUSSELL?" Kerr's sleepy face stared at the fire, tinder and twigs eagerly burning over stacked hickory and juniper, flames licking and snapping.

John was glad the man hadn't noticed his injury in the darkness. Time enough for explanations later. He glanced at the sky and sniffed the air. The night felt old, but dawn was not imminent just yet. "No, let the children take their rest. Another hour at least."

Drained, he crossed to the fire and sat. Abigail bustled nearby, gathering her things. Would he need to be stitched? Now that the shock of battle was over, his cheek stung fiercely. In the light of the fire, the handkerchief in his hand looked black with his blood.

"I'm ready," she said, her voice pitched only for his ears. "Come closer, and let me see."

She dabbed at his face. *Ouch!* That must be vinegar. He couldn't imagine what Roy had gone through, having the stuff poured into that great gaping wound. But it was healing nicely. He submitted to her ministrations.

Abigail's brows drew together, the lenses of her spectacles reflecting the firelight. "I'll need to stitch it a bit."

His eyebrows rose. "Ye're sure?"

She adjusted one of the pewter earpieces. "If it were your leg or an arm, I could bind it up securely and that might be enough. But I can't bandage your face properly that way. The edges must be held together. Only a few stitches."

"Hmph. Aye, well then." He marveled at her composure. She'd just been abducted by a ruffian, who'd intended—well, nothing good.

The needle bit into his skin. "Argh." How had Roy borne it? He forced himself to remain motionless. Where had Sloan gone? He'd be able to find his horse's prints in the morning. He was a good tracker. And with a good rifle—

No. He wouldn't. The needle bit him again, mirroring the turmoil inside.

What had he almost done?

But Sloan deserved death. He'd attacked his *wife*. And not just with words. Wasn't it his right, as husband, to defend her?

Still, guilt raged in his heart. For a moment he relived the heavy wash of rage that had possessed him like some fell beast. *That* was evil.

The pain of the stitching faded under the burden of his soul.

He hated himself.

Abigail had put away her needle and was now patting his face with a last bit of vinegar. "I'm sorry, John."

What? "Why are ye sorry?"

"I—I left camp. It was my fault."

"No, dinna blame yerself for Sloan. Ye couldna have known." He castigated himself for not warning her. "I should've explained to take someone—to wake me." He took a breath. "It was my fault."

Yes, it was his fault. More than she knew.

Abigail forced her body to relax under the cloak they shared and stared up at the stars. The necessity of seeing to John's injury had kept her from giving into the shock she still felt—the terror of her helplessness, the suddenness of it all. One moment safe, in mortal danger the next. No wonder John had warned her that day in the keeping room that now seemed so far away. Marriage to him would cost her something.

Thank you, Lord. In the midst of the terror, she'd prayed. And He'd answered. A jumble of emotions confused her. Regret, for putting John in danger. The sense of fear—now ebbing, but still at the edge of her mind. Sloan was still out there, somewhere. Would he come for her again? At the same time, a sense of peace and thankfulness undergirded her mind. She'd cried out, and God had preserved her.

Next to her, a faint snore surprised her. Dawn was near, he'd said, but they both were exhausted, and so they'd lain down again to ease their bodies against the demands of the day ahead. Abigail had no notion of sleeping. Perhaps men were different.

Something was troubling John. He was plainly bothered by failing to prevent the attack, but there was something else. While she stitched his face, he'd seemed withdrawn, lost blue eyes staring into the flames of the fire. Was it the pain, perhaps? Or something else?

Guilt slid into her heart. John Russell had come for a godly woman, not a sinner. And her ignorance had put them both in danger.

Is that why he seemed so distant?

19

When I survey the wondrous cross
On which the prince of glory died,
My richest gain I count but loss,
And pour contempt on all my pride.

—Isaac Watts, *Hymns and Spiritual Songs,* 1707

"*R*oy, I'll be needing a word with ye." John pitched his voice low so only the other man would hear as he nudged Percy close to his cousin on the wagon's seat. Ritchie slumped against Roy on the other side of the seat, and Lizzie dozed in the wagon bed, straw hat tilted askew over her face against the midday sun.

"Aye." Roy's green eyes flickered his way, and the exposed muscles of his forearms flexed as he adjusted the reins.

The steel in Roy's face took him aback. His cousin was no longer a stubborn but kindly lad, but a man full-grown. Wasn't last night proof of that?

John glanced back involuntarily to the wagon bed. "Ye canna lead Lizzie along. It isna seemly."

Roy said nothing for a long moment. "I'm no' leading her along. I'm courting her." A muscle in his jaw clenched.

His own brows shot up. "Courting? There's a law against marrying a servant under contract."

"There's a law against ye doing so. She's no' my servant." Roy barked out this last, and Ritchie turned, looking up at Roy, large eyes questioning.

"Ye clot heid," John spat. He drove his heels into his mare's ribs, and she lurched forward into a brisk canter. How could he force his cousin to see reason? His gut tightened with anger.

Percy's ears flicked back as if to ask, *what's the kerfluffle?* The mare's normally smooth motion roughened, and her gleaming chestnut neck arched high, her head canted sideways, mouth chewing on the bit.

He clenched his jaw. Percy was against him too. After several hundred yards of her bone-jarring gait, he slowed the mare and turned back. This was ridiculous. He needed to have a reasoned discussion with Roy—preferably before they reached the Potomac ferry, where all and sundry would witness any disagreement.

He scanned the trees and turned his mount to parallel the wagon once again. Percy snorted once, then calmed.

"Och, I'm sorry Roy." Well, for losing his temper, anyway.

Roy's gaze was upon him. "No, we needed to have this conversation. If there's a way to recompense the expense of the contract, the way will be clear for us to marry." A faint line creased his dusty forehead. "But this isna just about Lizzie, I'm thinking."

John stiffened. He could barely process his cousin's words. Cancel the indenture? That was reasonable, if they could find a way. Ten guineas was a lot of money. "I canna give away her labor for nothing."

"I ken that." Roy's voice was low and tight. "But this is about Sloan."

John ducked as a dogwood branch plucked at him. This section of trail was broader than he'd ever seen it, but still only wide enough for one wagon to pass comfortably at a time.

Sloan. Where was the man? Perhaps it was sheer chance, but he'd killed several Shawnee and lived to tell about it. The ruffian undoubtedly possessed some woodcraft.

His shoulders sagged. "Aye, it's about Sloan. And a lot of other things too."

"No one would blame ye."

John didn't reply. Roy might be a man, but he wasn't married. Or widowed.

No, he couldn't understand.

ABIGAIL CAUGHT a whiff of sharp green pine as she rode Rosemary just ahead of the Kerrs' wagon. Spruce, oak, and longleaf pine cloaked the shoulders of the jumbled hills they passed near, with rhododendron spilling out into the narrow clearings. Sometimes she caught a glimpse of a hazy blue peak to her left.

The breeze curled and changed in direction, wafting an acrid stench to Abigail's nose. She hadn't realized how awful unwashed men could smell. She did consider lanky William Kerr a man, even at sixteen; he did smell like one after days on the trail, and together with his father they overpowered the warm scent of the mules behind her.

Ahead, Percy loped back to the wagon, John's form tall and rigid in the saddle. Too rigid. Perhaps it was common to all men, that they were disinclined to speak of their concerns.

Plainly, John was upset about Sloan's attack. He blamed himself—he'd said as much. Was that the only thing bothering him, or was there more?

She rubbed at the smooth leather of Rosemary's reins in her

hands. The animal was so faithful, she merely needed a nudge in the right direction, figuring out half the navigation herself.

She knew what it was. It was her. Her lack of faith. Last night, a strange hope had filled her—God had delivered her from a terrifying situation, the echoes of which still caused her to jerk and startle now and again. She'd marveled over that strange peace during the aftermath, blended with the shudders of ebbing shock.

But the peace had evaporated with the morning light and a hard realization: she was a liability. When they camped each evening, Lizzie and Sophie Kerr did most of the labor, assisted by the children. Cooking over a campfire took a certain knack, and even Lizzie took to it with a surprising alacrity.

The young widow would be a good help in the valley. A good spinner—Gretchen had made certain of that. And her housekeeper had made Lizzie copy down the best receipts in her sprawling but legible hand. They'd eat.

But what about soap? And candles? Their housekeeper, Gretchen, excelled at soap making, an outdoor task undertaken every winter. After boiling and reducing the filtered wood-ash water, she would add sheep's tallow, carefully rendered and strained just so, then she'd separate the mixture into two batches: one for laundry, set aside in crocks to cool, the other half destined for an old butter churn.

After adding small amounts of oil and herbs, Gretchen would plug the hole of the churn, plop down in the kitchen chair, and rock it back and forth with her foot, and by evening, a sweet-smelling pale soap was ready to pour into tins. Soap for bathing, almost as good as the imported kind.

Gretchen had packed soap of both types as well as candles in a box, which now lay somewhere in the depths of the wagon in front of her. Abigail had no receipt for either. She could learn, she supposed, but at the moment it seemed as though a heavy weight had descended upon her.

John was so kind. But could he bear with a wife who couldn't make soap? She realized it was ridiculous, but still she felt useless. Inferior.

More important questions darted like fireflies in her mind.

Could her husband bear with a woman who didn't have faith?

Percy's nostrils flared at the scent of water. John's gaze flickered to Abigail on Rosemary, riding beside him. After last night, she had to be exhausted, but the hospitality of Mistress Watkins at the ferry should refresh them all.

"Is that the Shenandoah River?" she asked.

So she'd caught the glimmer of the water through the trees. "No, it's the Potomac. The Shenandoah empties into it downstream from here. But once we cross it, we'll be in the valley."

The mare picked up the pace almost imperceptibly, and John gave her leave. Rosemary matched the other animal's stride, the ground springy under the horses' hooves, gently sloping downward to the riverbank.

"Are we almost there?" piped a voice behind them.

Abigail smiled at Ritchie's question. She looked at John. "How far?"

"We've still a good distance to go. Dinna tell the lad, though. Four days, maybe." He took a long breath. "But to me, it's the easiest part of the journey. Fewer trees, a lot of wide-open spaces. Ye'll see."

Soon the rich wet smells of the riverbank enveloped them, and one of the mules brayed its enthusiasm as Will Kerr unharnessed the animals and led them to the river's edge. Before them, a sweet wide expanse of water slid past, reflecting the green of the trees and the blue of the sky in the lazy middle, but swirling white over rocks that emerged shoal-like near the banks.

Thomas Kerr joined him. "That the ferryman over yonder?"

John nodded and pointed. "There's a creek on the other side of the river that's good for washing and drinking, and Mistress Watkins sells ale and cider." He rubbed his jaw, wondering what he looked like. Were the stitches obvious? He needed a shave, but he might have to wait until his cheek healed. "We'll set up camp over there."

Evan Watkins poled the ferry toward them, along with his oldest lad. The man had several sons; John couldn't think of them as anything but children, but there was no disputing the sight of the oldest lad, tall as the man himself. Behind the trees on the opposite bank, smoke curled from the great stone chimney of their log house.

John's shoulders eased. The ferry served as a gateway, a marker welcoming him home.

Home.

When had the Shenandoah Valley become home? During their first year, the place had fought their very existence as he wrestled with wood and stone, soil and frost and heat. But with Janet at his side, he had conquered, carving out a place in the wilderness.

Over the next few years, a thread of satisfaction had grown and swelled in him as the crops flourished—first, small bits of the lowest land, plowed with difficulty, rocks periodically popping through the topsoil; then larger tracts, the fields slowly expanding each year until now he had four acres in corn alone, and no fear of hunger during the snows.

Trap lines had yielded fat rabbits and fierce minks from the beginning; soon thereafter he'd mastered the elusive beaver, and usually acquired several of their skins every year. After Roy joined him, they'd hunted bear. The animals were dangerous and hard to kill, and the safest shot was aimed from a perch in a tree.

Stands of hickory, walnut, and oak yielded wood for building and smoking—pine popped and crackled brightly in the hearth, warming a cold cabin quickly. Cedar on the higher slopes yielded shingles for his cabin, and black birch he tapped for a frothy beverage.

And then a child. Susanna. What a joy it had been when Janet had given him the news. He would never forget the day.

"I've something to tell ye." Her voice but a murmur, Janet's eyes had loomed large in her face.

"What's the matter?"

She smiled. "Ye'll be a father early next year, Lord willing."

His jaw dropped open.

Janet's eyes twinkled. "Close yer mouth, clot heid, or the flies will get in."

He blinked back tears at the memory. His daughter had dark eyes like her mother and a certain feisty spirit that came from ... well, maybe from both of them. It wouldn't be long now—once in the valley, he'd send a letter to his sister. He longed to swing Susanna in his arms and make her laugh.

Now Abigail stood next to him on the ferry, coming home with him, the water of the Potomac sliding beneath them.

But she looked pale, and she hadn't said much all day. Between Sloan and his own failures, it was no wonder.

ABIGAIL LAY on her back beside John in the still darkness. No, it wasn't totally still. Earlier she'd heard a hooting noise—an owl, John had said. And it wasn't totally dark: the warm glow of embers just two yards away comforted her. The kettle nestled alongside the banked fire, ready for morning, and Lizzie snored next to her son nearby.

And the stars. A ghostly band painted the southern night sky with luminosity. What was it called? The Milky Way? She'd never seen it before. In Philadelphia the smoke of countless fires obscured the sky, and for much of the journey, she recalled, clouds had scudded overhead. But the night was clear tonight.

Much as it had been last night. Abigail shivered internally, thinking of Sloan, then relaxed as she became aware of John's warm presence beside her, sleeping. Having drunk her fill at the ferry, where they'd also had the chance to bathe, she'd purposed to drink little at supper. Only one cup of ale. She wasn't going anywhere tonight—even with John.

Tonight he'd read the first part of Romans chapter five, and

Abigail had managed to latch on to the first verse. *Therefore being justified by faith, we have peace with God through our Lord Jesus Christ ...*

Justified by faith. She knew that. Had known it as long as she could remember. But for the first time, she felt hope in the thought—neither the placid acceptance of her youth, nor the troubled worry and guilt Whitefield's words had first brought upon her. For the first time, the Scripture seemed truly important, truly real—and something she wanted to hear.

Did she believe? It almost seemed too good to be true. How could righteousness be a free gift? How could she be made clean so easily, with no effort on her part?

Peace with God. Abigail turned the words over in her mind, clutching at them like a warm quilt, hopeful that someday soon all would be clear. She relaxed.

Then she startled. She'd fallen asleep and woken suddenly. The stars overhead still stood sentinel over their camp; perhaps they'd shifted in their position. Papa had said that mariners used them to navigate. Could they tell time by them too?

John. The warm presence next to her was no longer there.

Where had he gone?

20

Could not but think, as I have often remarked to others,
that much more of true religion consists in deep humil-
ity, brokenness of heart, and an abasing sense of
barrenness and want of grace and holiness than most
who are called Christians imagine.

—David Brainerd, *The Life and Diary of David Brainerd,* 1749

John stumbled over something, a rock perhaps, as he made his way through the buffalo grass toward the trees lining the stream. Recovering, he stood still and took a deep breath, sniffing the air by habit. He caught a hint of chimney smoke; the breeze was slight, but the direction was right. The Quaker cabin he'd glimpsed before they camped was over half a mile away downstream, and he'd not disturb anyone by his wanderings.

By the time he reached the first sycamore, his mind had cleared enough to realize that wandering in the dark was foolish. But he wanted to be alone.

Not even the privacy of his own mind felt private anymore. He'd seen Abigail look at him several times yesterday with a gaze that pierced his soul. She could sense the tenor of his thoughts already, and they'd been married less than two weeks.

Not to mention Roy, who knew his every thought and emotion whether expressed by word, grimace, or even just the way he held the reins. They'd tracked bear together, sweated together, wept together. The man could read his mind.

No, he'd had to get away, only for a little while—away from the others.

John crossed to the next tree, a massive pine. The sharp, clean scent caused him to pause, as if inhaling the aroma might somehow cleanse him on the inside.

He felt dirty.

He stretched out his hands to finger the bark, tracing the wide scales with his fingers. Yes, a longleaf pine—Abigail would want this for her book. Such a strange pattern. All trees had bark that cracked —or even peeled—in ridges or grooves; this one felt more like tiny plates.

And every year the tree would grow, and the bark would break some more, sap rising to heal the wounds. Hence the piney smell— the smell of brokenness. John laid his forehead on the tree, feeling broken himself.

Was this the way of all things under the sun? Grow ... and break?

Oh God ... out of the depths I cry to Thee ...

Maybe he wasn't growing. Maybe it was just sin. The filth of his murderous temper.

Create in me a clean heart, O God ...

He collapsed and found himself kneeling in a thick bed of long pine needles, his shoulders shuddering and heaving. No tears would come, only this shaking and gasping, like an ague that had taken him unawares.

It wasn't just his temper. It wasn't just his anger toward Sloan or Roy.

He was angry with God.

"Roy?" Abigail's heart thudded in her chest.

The man's head popped up, his hand moving to his waist—to his dagger? "Och, it's you." He snorted a bit, as if clearing his mind of sleep. "What is it?" He sat and looked about. "It isna morning yet."

"John. He's gone."

Roy reached for his musket, drew it across his lap, and scanned the camp. "When did he leave?"

"I don't know. I woke up maybe a quarter of an hour ago, and he wasn't here." She'd waited a few minutes before waking Roy, thinking that perhaps John was simply relieving himself.

In the starlight she could make out Roy's form, silhouetted against the pale grasses beyond the camp. He shrugged. "I dinna ken where he went, but he should be back soon."

Abigail's fingers brushed nervously against her mussed hair. How did he know?

"I'll take watch. Ye'll see. A man like John, well, sometimes he needs space to think things through." He got to his feet and stretched. "Not to worry, aye?"

Abigail returned to her bedding across the fire from Lizzie, who cracked an eye open and looked at her, then fell promptly back asleep. She lay down and tried to relax.

Lord, please help John ...

Did God hear her? She wished a good Christian could pray for John, like a minister or deacon. Then God would hear. She wasn't sure if she was a Christian at all.

The stars seemed colder somehow, like icy dots of light, circling far above all earthly cares.

Mary. From out of nowhere she thought of her sister, and her sister's letter. Mary had found solace in God. *Solace.* What did that mean exactly? Studying the pale distant band of the Milky Way, Abigail wondered what it had been like for Mary, facing her sin.

She must have felt horribly ashamed. Abigail's stomach tightened in sympathy. Even if her sister had been tempted, deceived—like Eve —everyone would think evil of her, as if she had planned to transgress God's Law. And even Eve herself, though tricked, had felt ashamed, covering herself with fig leaves along with her guilty husband.

Fig leaves. Covering up with garments of their own manufacture.

Had Mary first tried fig leaves? No, probably not. It wasn't just her mother's condemnation. Or her own. Mary knew the Commandments and would have condemned herself. She'd discovered herself to be a sinner.

What had John said? That Christ came for sinners?

I'm a sinner, too, Lord. Will you help me? Please give me the solace Mary has.

ANGRY? Yes, he was angry. John rose, brushed off the pine needles, and stumbled toward the stream. He couldn't return to camp—and his wife—without settling this matter.

In any other circumstance, he'd be more than pleased to lead a soul to Christ. To speak of the great truths of Scripture.

But now? With his heart barely mended from grief, with the needs of his daughter on his heart, not to mention the responsibility of a homestead and servants.

And Roy, who'd overreached himself with regard to Lizzie. Right now, he needed his cousin to support him, not add another burden to his shoulders.

More tree limbs brushed against his shirt, and branches plucked at his hair. Not far away was the stream—it had a strange name, so he called it the Quakers' stream instead, having met a few of the families settled along its length. He could almost smell the water, sensing the limpid heaviness that surrounded creeks and ponds.

A curtain of hanging willow branches blocked his way. He must be near the water's edge. John slid his hands among the slender boughs and parted them, easing his way forward until the ground softened under his feet.

He was exhausted, but no matter. He kicked off his moccasins.

Lord, give me grace ... I don't know how to pray. Maybe I don't even want to.

Starlight glimmered on the surface of the water, and a peaceful gurgling met his ears. He predicted slimy algae-covered rocks along the edge and stepped carefully as he made his way into the stream.

He was prepared for the cold of the water, but still the icy fingers surprised him, coming to mid-thigh and saturating his breeches instantly. It was August, but the water from the hills never really warmed. He squatted and leaned back, spread his arms, and floated. The aching of his body eased, but the refreshing water couldn't reach his heart. Above him, pinpoints of light pierced the velvet blackness, shining down upon his misery.

He made the stars also.

John blinked and started at the verse that came to his mind. He sat up.

Where wast thou when I laid the foundations of the earth? Declare, if thou hast understanding.

He plunged his head forward into the stream and immersed himself. Then he arose, dripping, water running into his eyes.

And then the tears started.

21

O come and let us worship him,
let us bow down withal,
And on our knees before the Lord
our Maker let us fall.

—The Scottish Psalter, 1650

*A*bigail surveyed her sleeping husband in the gray light of dawn. John's face looked pale and drawn but somehow peaceful, its square lines relaxed in slumber, his mouth bracketed by the faint traces of laugher. The slice in his cheek was healing nicely. There was no angry swelling, only small red dots where the stitches entered the skin along a scabbed pink line perhaps two inches long— maybe the scar would be faint.

His hair, dark as ink in the dim light, lay damp and disordered over the jacket he'd rolled up as a pillow. What had he done? Gone swimming? Well, the stream wasn't far away. Maybe he had.

What pressed so hard upon his heart and soul that he would swim alone at midnight?

Abigail jerked her head up as Lizzie approached with a cup of coffee. At least, she hoped it contained real coffee. "Thanks," she whispered.

Lizzie nodded, eyeing John's form as if wondering when he'd awake.

Abigail shrugged in response. Lizzie left for the fire and grabbed the kettle, continuing her morning routine.

Yes, the cup had coffee in it. She closed her eyes, letting the steam rise into her nose and settle her—settle her heart.

John slept on as morning rose, with golden light replacing gray. The clanking noises from the Kerrs' fire seemed distant; the green of the tall grass around them glinted flaxen in the sun, and birds tittered from the nearby trees.

Abigail stood up, cup in hand, and surveyed the road ahead. The trail had opened up. Aside from the tree line to her left, there was wide-open space ahead of her. To the right, trees dotted the landscape, hiding the far western horizon in a green haze; but straight ahead, the Shenandoah Valley lay broad and flat and free.

"How d'ye like the valley?" John's voice rasped behind her.

She turned. "Oh. You're awake."

He ran his fingers through his unruly hair. "Aye, well, I think so."

"Let me help you. I have a comb. What happened to your binding?"

John grabbed at the back of his neck. "I dinna ken. I took a dip in the stream."

"I thought so." She glanced toward the trees, where Roy was leading the heifer back toward camp. He'd watered the stock, then.

John studied his cousin. "Aye, please, if ye dinna mind. I'd best make myself ready, lest Roy thrash me." He peered at her, almost shyly.

"Sit down." Abigail opened her bag and quickly found her comb. "You have a bit of thread or cord?"

"Aye, I think so. Ouch!"

"You have a lot of hair. When we have a chance, let me wash it for you. Gretchen makes the best soap. I washed Lizzie's hair yesterday." She shortened her strokes, trying to bring order to his damp, greasy locks without hurting him.

"Aye, I mind it. I mean, I didna really see ye washing."

Abigail chuckled. Yes, their bathing spot had been secluded, behind a stand of saplings and willows, as private as anything could be while traveling like this. But John was observant.

She glanced about. John was her husband, but combing his hair —in public—seemed so intimate. He sat quietly, relaxed, unconcerned by the late start they were getting.

"Almost done. Do you have a piece of twine?"

"Aye." He snaked out a long arm and grabbed his bag, the one he kept inside his shirt as they traveled. "Here." Something long and pale dangled from his fingers.

She took it and began to tie his hair back. "What is this?" It wasn't leather or twine.

"Sheep's gut."

"What?" It was smooth in her hands, more slippery than twine.

"Aye—sorry, I dinna have twine. Gut is wonderful for fishing line. And Rob Anderson uses it to string his fiddle."

She gave the pale cord an extra half hitch to secure it and touched his shoulder. "You're not ready to meet the king, but you'll do."

He turned and met her gaze, his blue eyes open and guileless, and the corners of his mouth soft. She was reminded of that moment when he'd asked her to marry him. His Adam's apple bobbed, and then he looked down. Did he mean to say something?

"Why did you take a swim at midnight?" she asked.

"Ho, John!" Roy barked from the wagon. "Horses are ready. Are you?"

~

"AYE, I'LL BE THERE," John said, but his eyes were on his wife.

Abigail's loose tresses shone golden in the morning sun. She hastily scooped them together, and with a twist, had them secured and under her cap.

Was the kettle packed? John didn't see it, but then Lizzie appeared with a cup. He tossed back the warm liquid. Real coffee. "Och, thank ye kindly." He handed it back to her and walked to the horses. After saddling Percy, he looked back at the wagons: the horses and mules were harnessed and ready. Aster, the mare, sniffed the morning breeze, nostrils wide.

John studied the lines of the mare once again. Inspired by the white star on the horse's head, Abigail had named the mare after a flower. He'd informed her that aster meant "star" in Latin, and she'd been thrilled.

He smiled. He never could have imagined a woman being pleased by the bits and pieces of Latin he'd learned. Surely she'd make a good companion regardless of ... other things. But how could he explain the swim?

Returning to his wife's side, he helped her onto her pony. "I'll explain a bit about my swim on the road—I had some things to think about, ye ken?"

She nodded, her face peaceful under the straw hat.

He mounted and edged Percy past Rosemary, desiring to study the road. It was indeed a road, not merely the Indian footpath they'd first traveled half a dozen years before. Ruts gouged it in random places, evidence of a rainy day and wheels sunk several inches in mire. Here and there, old manure crumbled into the dirt. Rarely, a patch of newer leavings gleamed wet and pungent in the warm sun. Even this late in the year, new homesteaders were making their way up the valley, judging by the evidence they left behind.

Another slick mound of horse manure. A rider? Or a wagon with several animals? He bent over Percy's shoulder. Hoof prints, faint— almost undetectable in the soft grass and dirt at the side of the trail. Were they paired?

Yes—another pair of hooves had passed this way on the other side. Two horses, then, pulling a wagon.

Not Sloan—he was on horseback, alone. The man was never far from his thoughts.

But hadn't he settled matters with God? Or rather, hadn't God visited him? Like Job, he had wrestled with his Maker, only to find himself vile and astonished in His Presence.

The peace that had flooded his soul last night filled him once again, like the gold of the morning sun. The same God that made the stars knew where Sloan was. And that same God had sent His Son to take his sin upon Himself.

Even the sin of his own murderous temper. Even the sin of his ungratefulness, his unbelief. All of it. Yes, he would be wary of Sloan —but in some unfathomable way, the burden of it had lifted.

He checked Percy's reins, and in a few moments Rosemary was side by side with his mare.

He studied his wife's profile, her skin soft and glowing despite the sun and rigor of the trail. "Abigail? Ye asked me a question. But first, what d'ye think of the valley?"

"'Tis wonderful." Her eyes searched his face. "But it's not what I expected."

He lifted his brows, urging her to continue.

"I expected more trees. All along the road, there were trees. After Lancaster, the trees and undergrowth became quite thick, like a beautiful garden gone wild. And now ..."

"Aye, all the grass—five feet high in places." He enjoyed seeing the shock on her face. "Some say it's because the Indians have burned it periodically, to keep the buffalo coming back. Buffalo prefer grass, and Indians like to hunt them."

"With arrows?" Abigail's expression indicated doubt. "You said they were huge and difficult to kill."

"They are." How to explain? "My da taught me about the English wars and described the weapons they used in battle. The old English longbow was as tall as a man, and it took a great deal of strength to draw it. A good, strong archer possesses a formidable weapon. Indians use smaller bows, but they are experienced archers and can let loose arrows more quickly than a man can reload a musket."

She gazed at the horizon before them. "Will we see any buffalo?"

"Perhaps." Buffalo could be dangerous if spooked or wounded, and he didn't want to worry her needlessly. "Ye asked me a question too."

Her eyes widened. She seemed hesitant.

"About my swim," he prompted.

She nodded, a tiny frown creasing her forehead.

He didn't know how to explain all the reasons, but he did want to discuss one matter. "I need your advice concerning Lizzie."

Her shoulders seemed to relax. "Lizzie ... and Roy?"

"Aye, ye've guessed it."

"I noticed you had ... a serious conversation with Roy the other day."

He chuckled. "Aye, we had a wee argument." The creaks and groans of harness and wood were far enough behind them; Roy wouldn't hear their conversation. "Roy canna marry her while she's bound to me."

"But that's five years."

"Aye, I dinna like it—I want Roy to be happy." Frustration tinged his voice.

"Is there a way to cancel the indenture? Pay it off somehow?"

His eyes swept the horizon by habit. "Aye, well, I could take the part of Laban. D'ye recall Jacob in the Scriptures? Working all those years for his wives?" He grimaced, and then frowned—he'd forgotten his injury. He put his hand to his face.

"Does it pain you?"

John smiled—or started to. "Only when I smile or make a face." He wiggled his eyebrows. "Now *that* I can do."

Abigail smiled freely then, and her glad expression rejoiced his heart. They rode silently for a few minutes, an easy peace between them.

"Does Roy have anything he can give you in trade?"

"Aye, I dinna want to ask it of him, but it's best. I'll ask him for the mare's first foal—and Lizzie helps you until it's weaned."

She nodded, her open expression seeming to confirm his decision.

"That's settled then. I'll tell the lad at midday."

THE SUN WAS HOT. Abigail removed her straw hat and tucked it under her arm while she unpinned her linen cap. The old-style headgear wasn't loose enough—her sweaty scalp was beginning to itch. She needed the hat, though, with its protective brim.

She thrust the damp cap into her pocket and replaced the hat. The straw hat gave her some sense of modesty, although this morning, while attending to John's hair, she'd neglected her own, letting it hang free like a wanton woman's. Her husband hadn't seemed to mind.

He was circling again, something he did rarely now. They could see for miles in most directions—except for the east, where a line of trees formed a shadowy green border, with a faint bluish haze above and beyond it. Waiting for his return, she rode in the lead on Rosemary, following an interminable dusty track lined by several species of grass.

Gentle yellow grass, three feet high, bent and rippled before the slightest breeze; a harsh green variety, stalks rigid and unyielding, some with seed heads ready to pop, dotted the landscape; and occasionally, large clumps of red-tinged green dwarfed the rest with their great height, tall and thick enough to swallow a man.

Abigail's stomach growled. Where would they stop for the midday meal? John knew the streams and creeks like the back of his hand, and tomorrow, he'd said, they'd be camping on the banks of the Shenandoah River, that line of green to the east. She glanced in the other direction. What were those dark mounds in the distance?

With the barest creak of leather announcing the presence of the mare, John appeared alongside her again. "Switchel?" He offered her the jug.

She took it gratefully, and drank deeply. She hoped her hair wasn't coming unpinned. "Thank you." She handed it back.

"Abigail." John's voice was low and tight; Percy slowed and lifted her head, sensing his mood. "Quietly now, turn Rosemary and get behind the wagon." He lifted his hand, signaling his cousin.

She turned the pony. Roy had stopped the horses, the lines of his face still and serious. Abigail guided Rosemary behind the wagon, next to the heifer, and followed his gaze.

In the yellow-green middle distance, the brown mounds drifted nearer, like ships on the sea. Two large ones were closer than the rest. A bellow rumbled from the ocean of grass.

"Roy, have ye primed your musket?"

John had maneuvered the mare alongside his cousin. Will Kerr's head popped up alongside Percy's near side. Abigail heard only bits and pieces of their conversation.

" ... fowling piece ... tell your da."

John returned to her side. "Stay on Rosemary. Ye'll be safe on her. If she spooks, let her run—keep her to the trail." He jerked his chin down the way they had come.

"What are those animals?"

"Buffalo. The bulls are fighting, aye?" He rubbed his jaw, keeping one eye on the distant brown humps. "Dinna fash." He was clearly worried, despite his words. "They're busy fighting each other—we'll stay put and they willna ken we're here."

Another bellow resounded through the grassy stretches. Louder this time.

John dismounted and helped Lizzie onto the mare. After Lizzie moved off, he whispered to Roy on the wagon seat. Beyond them, the two buffalo were closer, but still indistinguishable as bovines, their legs hidden by the grass. They appeared as great humps like brown rugs maneuvering around each other, dust rising sporadically into the air. Abigail gaped at the surreal image: immense livestock belonging to a Brobdingnag in *Gulliver's Travels*, in a giant-sized meadow.

Mounted on Percy, Lizzie stayed near the wagon bed where Ritchie's head bobbed, the lad clearly wanting to see the show. Will Kerr, now on the wagon seat, had taken the reins of the horses, the Kerrs' fowling piece gleaming in his lap. John stood at his side, speaking, his voice a quiet murmur.

Another bellow met her ears—more like a shriek, loud and frightening. One of the buffaloes lumbered toward them, then slowed, turned, and snorted. The animals continued to maneuver in the tall grass, getting closer and closer to the wagons. One animal seemed to be driven back, and the other pressed his advantage: charging, stopping short, and charging again. There was a sudden grunt and squeal as one charge connected with the flesh of the other, dust swirling about them.

The loser launched into a dead run toward the wagons.

John knelt and lifted his Deckard rifle. Roy moved to the right, keeping low to the ground, musket raised. The shaggy brown monster came into view, legs churning at an incredible rate for so massive a creature. When was John going to fire?

Crack! To her left, the rifle jerked back against John's shoulder. The creature continued its charge, hooves pummeling the ground. Had he missed?

Bang! Wisps of smoke rose from Roy's musket. Both men were frantically reloading as the buffalo drew near; it hesitated, snuffing and pawing, its great head low to the ground, horns small by comparison. It bellowed, its black eyes searching for a target.

Stormy snorted and pawed the ground, and by his side, the black mare, ears flat to her head, backed up against the whiffletree, causing the wagon to jolt and shudder. Lizzie, on Percy, had disappeared, and Rosemary trembled beneath her. The heifer bawled, a loud keening sound, and jerked at her rope.

Rosemary bolted.

22

Why should I start [be startled] at the plough of my Lord,
that maketh deep furrows on my soul? I know he is no
idle husbandman, but purposeth a crop.

—Samuel Rutherford, *Letters*, 1664

*A*ster and Stormy snorted and twitched in fear, but John had no attention to spare for the horses. He'd just stay out of their way if they bolted. He shoved the rod down the barrel of his rifle. The ball was seated, now the powder.

Kneeling, John primed his weapon, his fingers sure, knowing their task. No point in running—buffalo ran as fast as any horse on the racetracks of Williamsburg. But horses respected height and avoided an upright man despite the great disparity in weight. Maybe the crazed bull would slow down if he stood up. He took a steadying breath and rose to his feet.

He aimed the Deckard rifle and paused. If only he had a better angle—straight on, the animal presented a poor target, hard skull and massive shoulder blades blocking the path of any bullet.

The buffalo hesitated, as if choosing which of them to run down. Twenty feet to his right, Roy still fumbled with his powder horn. Even if they got off two more shots, it wouldn't matter. The shaggy brute was so close John could smell the musky stench of its rut. One of them would be trampled.

The heifer bawled.

The buffalo swung in her direction and sniffed the air.

John could now see the thick neck of the creature; finally, a good angle. He pulled the trigger. Without waiting for the result, he threw the weapon down, grabbed his tomahawk and ran forward. Would the animal turn back and charge him?

To his right, from the wagon, came a popping noise—William Kerr had let off the fowling piece. An equine scream followed as Stormy bucked and thrashed in his harness. Facing the wagon and the heifer behind it, the buffalo took an uncertain step forward.

Throwing all his weight behind the motion, John sank his tomahawk into the beast's flesh, just behind the huge jaw. Hot blood spurted out—would this be enough to kill the animal? The great head shook once, and then the animal sank to its knees. Roy stood on the other side, his dagger buried to the hilt in the buffalo's neck.

With a great sigh, the buffalo collapsed on the side of the trail.

WHITE PUFFS SPUN around the blue sky. Abigail blinked slowly, repeatedly, but the sky did not slow its motion.

She opened her mouth to breathe, but nothing happened. Her hands clawed at the grass as she lay helpless for what seemed like a long time, staring at the spinning sky. Finally, a ragged gasp of air entered her lungs.

John—was he hurt? What had happened?

Warm breath brushed her cheek, then softness. "R-rosemary."

The pony nuzzled her gently, its head large in her vision. She needed to sit up—if only everything would stop spinning.

"Abigail!"

Hearing John's voice, relief flooded through her. But the buffalo—was anyone injured? She tried to roll to one side.

"Are ye hurt?" His voice was closer now.

Then she saw him, kneeling next to her, his hands running down her arms, checking her over with the fine touch he used for the fetlocks of a horse—and for her.

"Rosemary stumbled and I fell off. It all happened so quickly." With his help, she managed to sit. The world slowed down. "Where's Lizzie? Was anyone hurt?"

"Everyone is safe. Percy is a canny horse and took Lizzie out of the way without losing her head." He helped her up. "Come."

They led Rosemary the short distance back. Where was the buffalo? Everyone had abandoned the wagons and stood or crouched around something. As they approached, she made out its dark form.

"You killed it?"

John's face was unreadable, motionless except for one twitch of his mouth. "Aye."

"That's good, isn't it?"

His lips parted and his eyebrows quirked as he stood looking at the carcass. "Of course. But it's a gey dangerous thing to hunt buffalo. Ye dinna do it ... with your family around." His hand curled briefly into a fist. Then he met her gaze. "I'm verra, verra thankful the Lord protected us. It was a near thing." He jerked his chin. "Come and see."

Roy crouched near the animal's head. "John, it'll take us both to gut the thing," he said, seeing them.

He was clearly in pain. Had his leg injury reopened? Before she could speculate, John knelt at the tail end of the great creature. A large, glistening brick red wound gaped in the neck, where Roy crouched. The men worked silently and steadily, opening the great belly of the creature. For some reason, there wasn't much smell: only a faint acrid odor that reminded her of a tomcat, overlaid with the copper tang of blood; nothing like the fetid stench of butchers' lane in Philadelphia.

She looked about. Whether or not Roy needed tending, they'd have to wash, surely—they needed hot water. And maybe vinegar. She found Lizzie helping the Kerrs to build a fire.

But where was the closest stream? Her shoulders sagged in helplessness. She joined the other women and followed their lead.

She would be of no help to John in this wilderness. She blinked away tears.

It was dusk before they reached the Henkels' farm. Abigail checked her cap to make sure she looked decent. John had galloped to the Henkels' homestead to get help with the butchering; he'd never leave such a blessing to waste, he'd said. Several gangly lads had returned with a cart, and now they were making their way east along a small stream.

Roy had ripped open some of his stitches, but the wound seemed to be healing well. Abigail had cut the remaining stitches, doused it with vinegar, and bandaged it tightly, with a stern warning to kill no more buffalo for a while.

Rosemary seemed happy to follow Percy, her muzzle sometimes coming close to the other horse's hindquarters. The animals were probably just as tired as they were. Abigail's gaze shifted longingly to the stream. The water swirled and bubbled over rocks in the streambed, murmuring to itself in the softness of the long shadows. They would all need a bit of washing—John was spattered all over with drops of blood.

Ahead, saplings alternated with larger trees against the backdrop of the bluish ridge beyond them. Finally, a stone fence came into view. Past it, a white limestone house gleamed faintly yellow in the last rays of the sun. To the left, a huge barn stood head and shoulders above the house.

"Hallo, the house!"

John's greeting seemed unnecessary, as a number of people poured out of the house like a disturbed anthill. She could see two adults and several children. Her husband edged Percy ahead and greeted them.

He extended his arm toward her. "My wife, Abigail." He turned. "Herr and Frau Henkel." Then he introduced the Kerrs.

Herr Henkel's dark eyes peered at her from a wizened face, illuminated by a broad smile that seemed like it might fracture such a lined visage. Dressed in a strange sort of waistcoat, he might have been of ordinary height but seemed tiny next to his statuesque wife, who towered over him. Where he was dark, she was light, with blond hair peeping out from under a cap and blue eyes framed with crow's feet.

Two young girls stood beside their parents, gawking at the newcomers unashamedly, the older almost as tall as her father. Then all the Henkels seemed to launch into conversation, most of which Abigail could not follow. John had explained that the Henkels were German. Yet once in a while she heard English words.

"Herr Zimmermann, Frau Zimmermann!" The great blond woman was gesturing at them. Zimmermann? Had she mistaken them for someone else?

John leaned closer and spoke in an undertone. "She doesna speak much English. She canna say my name well, so she calls me Zimmermann. It means carpenter in her language."

Carpenter? John had once said he liked to work with wood. They followed Frau Henkel into the house, where she bustled about, serving up bread, cheese, and cider.

Abigail found a corner in their keeping room and sat gratefully on a bench, warm bread in her hand. She took a bite, and saliva filled her mouth—suddenly she was hungry.

The humble house was plastered and whitewashed, as clean as her own home in Philadelphia, with one difference: embroidered linen curtains graced the kitchen window, something her own mother would probably view as "frippery."

So it was possible to keep a clean house in the wilderness. The thought cheered her.

John sat next to her. "Try this cheese." He handed her a small wedge, white and crumbly.

"This is really good."

"Frau Henkel makes it from sheep's milk." He took another bite and swallowed. "I'm hoping to trade most of the carcass for some things. Maybe some cheese as well."

"That would be a blessing. How's Roy? I didn't see him come inside."

John stretched out his long legs. "He's with the lads at the stream. He's got to get the hide scraped and soaked lest it be ruined."

A huge book sat on the top of a small table in the corner. Metal fastenings along the edges of the heavy volume glistened in the glow of the single candle nearby.

"Their Bible." John had followed her gaze. "They're Dunkers, ye ken."

"Dunkers?"

"Aye. I suppose ye could say they're Baptists, hence the name—they dinna baptize babies. They were persecuted in Germany and immigrated here. Most are in Pennsylvania, but a few came to the valley." He finished off his bread.

Dunkers? What would Mother have thought? John didn't seem to mind.

"They're good Christians and good farmers, forbye." He seemed to read her mind. "Now, I need to fetch Roy and the lads their supper." He stood.

Abigail rose. "And then we all need to wash up in the stream."

"Yes, ma'am." His eyes flashed with humor—and something else. She hoped she wasn't blushing.

〜

JOHN OPENED the oak door of the dairy shed and stepped inside. A faint aroma of smoke and soured cream welcomed him. A candle stub perched on the end of a shelf on the far wall, casting shadows on long rows of tawny brown wheels of cheese. The flickering light also revealed an assortment of dishes, implements, and soft folded cheesecloth all segregated and lined up properly along the shelves to his left.

And the candle illumined Abigail's slumbering face, haloed by golden hair, beneath the quiet company of the smoked cheese. The pallet Frau Hankel had made up for them was as cozy and clean as anything he'd seen on the trip, and the slate flagstones underneath were swept and scrubbed. In fact, the Henkels' dairy shed offered better shelter than some of the homes in the valley.

He couldn't help comparing it to his own cabin. He'd laid down oak planking the year after it was built, and Janet had brought her own touches to the place, sweeping, washing, and cleaning, making sure that he and Roy did not lie down at night in their own filth and rise up again on the morrow in the same state, though the strenuous work of certain seasons made filth mighty tempting.

What would Abigail think? His cabin was a solid place, neatly joined and shingled with cedar, but no plaster or whitewash finished the interior. Suddenly he wondered exactly how clean it was inside. Probably not this clean.

"John?"

"I didna mean to trouble ye."

"I was waiting for you but I suppose I dozed off." Abigail rose on one elbow. "Is everyone settled?"

"Oh, aye. Roy is pleased as punch over the buffalo hide. It's well scraped and anchored in the stream for soaking." He lay down on the pallet next to Abigail. It felt wonderful to stretch out after such a day. He'd ache tomorrow after all the labor of butchering. "Perhaps we should give the skin to the Kerrs. That's Roy's idea. For the winter, ye ken."

Abigail was quiet for a few moments. "How cold is the winter? I never thought to ask."

"A wee bit colder than Philadelphia, especially up on the slopes. But it depends. One winter was verra bitter. We had four feet of snow in January, and could barely leave the cabin for almost two weeks. We made a path to the necessary, but the spring was too far—we just scooped up snow and melted it for water." He sighed, thoughtful. "It's why I stack up firewood against the wall of the cabin every autumn— more than I think I could possibly need. And it's why the Kerrs need that skin—for warmth."

Abigail's eyes widened but she said nothing.

How to cheer her? "So ye see, we all find things to do inside the cabin during the winter. I work with wood, and Roy makes things with leather." Janet had spun and knit him stockings, repaired his shirts, and sewed baby things while she was expecting. "Ladies do womanly things."

A smile, finally. "Like sewing?"

"Aye, and spinning, and so forth." He shrugged. "I didna much pay attention," he said sheepishly. "But Janet was always busy."

Abigail's expression softened.

His lips parted in surprise at his own statement. Strangely, there was no stabbing pain of grief, as there used to be when thinking of his first wife. Indeed, for a whole year after her death he didn't speak her name even once. But now, Janet's name only produced a poignant, bittersweet ache that suffused him briefly and then ebbed away.

He was on solid ground at last.

23

Walnut-trees are exceedingly plentiful; this beautiful coffee-brown and hard wood is precious and useful... the greatest ornament of the forests are the beautiful and excellent cedar-trees...

—Gottlieb Mittelberger, *Journey,* 1756

"*A*re we close to the river?" Abigail almost felt embarrassed to ask, as if she were a child waiting impatiently for a tart. They were very near, she knew.

John grinned, a sparkle in his eye. "Oh aye, just beyond the trees."

He sounded happy, and she was glad of it. Even in Philadelphia, while he'd been courting her, she hadn't seen his face light up quite like this.

The road was now edged by occasional saplings: oak mainly, and a few pine. As they traveled farther along, larger trees came into view.

John pointed. "A longleaf pine. Verra interesting bark."

She glimpsed the trunk behind the screen of branches. Instead of cracks or even sheets, the bark was separated into rectangular plates, like a tortoise's shell. Abigail craned her neck. "It's tall. I've never seen such tall pines."

"I thought ye'd like it."

They continued on, the trees getting taller and thicker on either side, and soon the trail entered a green tunnel. Stinging nettle gave way to tree-ears on fallen logs, and the friendly pink of lady's slippers dotted the mottled dark leaf litter. She spotted a willow tree just ahead. *Water.* The faint *shushing* she heard must be the vigorous swirl and rush of the river.

Shafts of sunlight illuminated the trail ahead as the trees thinned again, and soon they were out in the open, the horses behind them snorting with eagerness, smelling water. The sound grew, a soothing rumble.

Then she saw it. The Shenandoah River.

Wide and free, the water was neither stagnant nor threatening, but playful and animated. Rushing gray foam murmured over gray-green stones near the bank where they halted, while in the middle of the river, tiny whitecaps stirred by the wind glittered in the sunlight. Abigail's lips parted.

John pulled up next to her on Percy. "Gey beautiful, such a braw burn." His voice was low and throaty. "I never had much use for poetry as a lad. But out here—"

"Only poetry could describe it."

Their eyes met. Abashed, she looked back out at the water. Something darted down from the sky—a bird, she thought, seeing a final flutter of dark wings—dashed briefly underneath the water, and emerged, gulping down something. A fish?

"What was that?"

"A loon. Fish are plentiful in the river, and some birds dive for them. Some places, in calmer spots, ducks and swans congregate. And geese. Aye, we hunt geese before the winter sets in."

He studied her face, his lips parted slightly, as if wanting to say more. Then he turned Percy around. "Ho, let's camp up yonder. Roy, ye ken the place."

He returned, and in a few minutes they'd all pulled up in a sunny, grassy spot. "Abigail, could ye mind the lamb?"

The Henkels had given them cheese and a yearling ewe lamb from their flourishing flock. Baas and bleats had punctuated the first part of the morning drive after they'd left the farm that morning. Abigail went to the wagon where the animal was tied, gangly limbs folded. The ewe lamb drew its head back and stared at her, then sniffed the air. She reached out a hand and let it smell her, then untied the rope. How would she get it down? It wasn't full grown, but a large animal, nonetheless.

"I'll help ye." Will Kerr strode over. He lifted the animal easily and set it down beside her.

"Thank you."

Will nodded awkwardly and went off to help his mother, who was feeding a small fire. Abigail led the yearling to the river's edge. They'd camped next to a spit, a protrusion of earth and rock that interrupted the rush of the current, creating a pool of gentle water on one side. After several fits and starts, sorting out its gangly legs, the animal scented the water and trotted eagerly to the bank, pulling a little on the rope.

Did sheep need names? Perhaps she ought to think of one. Dandelion? No, too long. Daisy—yes, Daisy was short and sensible.

Lizzie and Sophie seemed to have the dinner well in hand, so Abigail rested on the grass, watching Daisy. Frau Henkel had sent them on their way with some of her cheese, cornbread from breakfast, and choice bits from the carcass. She took a deep breath, enjoying the pleasant smell of the fire. Was Sophie broiling buffalo liver?

The lamb finished drinking and began to nibble at the tender grass near the water's edge. Voices drifted on the breeze.

" ... the end of the year." John's voice.

"But she'll still be your servant," Roy protested. His voice carried clearly.

John said something unintelligible. Abigail decided to lead the lamb upstream, closer to the men.

"It takes many months to wean a colt, ye ken." Roy's voice was hard. "In the meantime, who will do for me?"

Abigail made her way just past the spit, where a willow sapling sprouted graceful boughs. She sat in its shadow, hoping she wouldn't be noticed behind the screen of leaves.

John sighed. "Roy, I dislike playing the part of Laban to ye. I'll consider it settled when the get is foaled. Agreed?"

Roy's response was low, but it sounded like grumbling.

"Ye task me, *mo caraid*. Abigail needs Lizzie's help. Ye canna assume a merchant's daughter from Philadelphia will keep her footing without it. She's accustomed to a servant in the house—"

Roy interrupted, but Abigail lurched to her feet, her eyes burning. She didn't want to hear more.

∽

"Mistress, I think I see pewterwort!" Lizzie seemed excited.

Abigail used the last fragment of cornbread to sop up the meat juices in her trencher. "Pewterwort?" It sounded like a plant. She popped the last piece of cornbread into her mouth. Frau Henkel was a skilled cook. Abigail marveled that the turmoil of her heart hadn't killed her appetite.

"Ye scour with it. There's a great mass of it growing on the bank." Lizzie pointed at the spot where they'd watered the animals.

They walked over, Abigail welcoming the distraction. Perhaps it was listed in the book John had given her.

Along the side of the spit grew green rushes, which on closer inspection possessed tiny stems circling a tough, partially hollow central stem. "You scrub with it?" An intriguing specimen. "I'll get my book."

Grabbing the volume from her satchel, she flipped through the pages. Yes—here it was. *Common horsetail, otherwise known as water horsetail.* A lengthy list of medicinal uses followed. "Thank you, Lizzie. Let's gather some."

Soon they had a supply packed in the wagon, and Sophie joined them as they set to work cleaning the pewter trenchers with some of the extra plants. Then Lizzie took the dishes to dry and pack.

"Have you used horsetail before?" Abigail asked Sophie tentatively.

"Oh, aye. It wasna common, though, where we were." Sophie scrubbed her skillet. "Sometimes we used sand if soap wasna good enough."

"Have you a receipt for soap?"

Nodding, Sophie plunked the skillet and its cover in the clear water of the pool one final time. "The trick is to get the potash filtered and boiled down right. Nasty work." She wiped both the cookware and her hands on her apron and slanted her gaze toward Abigail. "Have ye ever seen it done?"

Abigail didn't know what to make of Sophie's question. The woman had warmed to her, but wouldn't she think her terribly ignorant? Her insides shriveled. "Yes, I watched our housekeeper make it."

"I'll help ye." Sophie's reply was brusque but not unkind.

A shadow fell across the water.

"Abigail?" John stood at her elbow. "Would this spot be a good place to wash hair, d'ye ken?"

"It would be perfect. I'll get the soap." At least this was something she could do.

Sophie accompanied her to the wagon. As Abigail pulled out Gretchen's soap from a crate, a tear escaped one eye and ran down her cheek. Her stomach muscles trembled, but she stifled the threatening sobs. No, she couldn't cry.

"Ye dinna want to do it?" Sophie's question was a mere breath in the air, meant for her ears alone.

"That's not it." Abigail swallowed. "I feel so useless." Why confess to Sophie, of all people? She clutched at the wagon's rough side for support.

"Abigail. He doesna want a servant, aye? He wants a wife."

"But ..." Her throat was tight with unuttered sobs. "A good wife should ..."

"Nonsense." Sophie said. "We'll help ye. Now get along with ye, he needs ye. *I'm* no' going to wash his hair." She perched the cookware on her hip and jerked her chin toward the water.

Abigail found the soap. "Thank you." She wiped her face. The clouds had lifted a little.

Sophie grunted and marched off to the other wagon.

AS THE AFTERNOON AGED, the green haze before them slowly resolved into trees. By the time the shadows fell long against the muhly grass at the edge of the trail, homely cottonwoods stood stiff in the near distance, concealing the water beyond. Despite the heat of the day, John's hair hadn't fully dried beneath his hat; the still, close air weighed on him. The road had thinned to a dusty trail—when had it rained last? A summer shower would be welcome.

A flash of white caught his eye: a goose, probably startled by the sound of their approach, abandoning the water for the safety of the air. He took a deep breath—the North River meant home.

"Let's set up camp, Percy," he said to the mare. She flicked her ears back, then forward, arching her neck. The horse probably knew exactly where they were.

He turned her and guided the others to an open spot, broad and dusty with use, stones and ashes marking old campfires. Dismounting, he spotted a horseshoe and picked it up. Lost by some unknown traveler—maybe Ritchie would like it.

"What is this place?" Abigail asked, as he helped her off her pony. "Have we arrived?"

"Aye, we have." He eyed the nearby trees and brush, looking for firewood. "Just beyond the North River is Augusta County." He grabbed a low-hanging branch of white oak and laid into it with his tomahawk. "We'll have a courthouse soon, if Colonel Lewis has his way."

He dragged the branch back to the clearing and Abigail followed, her apron full of twigs and pine needles. She was learning fast. Again he thought of the cabin. Large, he'd once thought it, and nicer than most, with oak flooring and hand-beveled shelves lining the wall. But it was only one square room—they'd be cramped until the addition was complete.

"That's not the Shenandoah?" Still clutching her apron with its load of kindling, Abigail jerked her chin toward the glint of water past the screen of trees.

John squatted and laid out the wood. "No." He pointed to the place where the rivers joined. "The Shenandoah is formed by several small rivers that come together here. Tomorrow we'll make the crossing." He looked up and smiled.

Abigail began arranging the twigs and bits of litter, and he pulled out his flint. "Who is this Lewis?" she asked.

He struck the flint with his steel, watching sparks rain on a scrap of scorched linen. "He was the first one to settle here. Maybe fifteen years ago." A tiny swirl of smoke rose, and he blew gently. "A braw man, and brave. He attends meeting at Tinkling Spring. Ye'll meet him and his kin, but their property is across the valley from us." He placed leaf litter around the tiny flame.

Finally satisfied that the fire had caught, John stood and motioned toward the blue haze of the nearby peaks. "Our home is at the base of the Blue Ridge, about twenty miles yonder."

"Oh." Abigail's lips parted, her eyes soft with wonder.

He shifted his stance and pointed southwest. "Across the valley from us, there are a number of homesteads and even a wee hamlet with a palisade. That's where Lewis lives."

"Do we have any close neighbors?"

"Oh aye—a number. Roy's cabin is only a furlong away, and then there are the Stuarts, the Robinsons—"

Lizzie rushed up, griddle in hand. "I found wild onion. If ye're willing, I'll scoop out some flour and make bridies from the buffalo meat."

John nodded at her, his stomach rumbling. The small savory pies would be welcome.

THE REMNANTS of the meal were packed away for the morrow. John licked his lips, still relishing the tang of the onion in the pastries. The horses grazed nearby, and the lamb was tied safely to a wagon wheel; farther away, a yellow glow of fire marked the Kerrs' campsite. On the other side of their own fire, Lizzie crawled underneath the wagon to spread out bedding for the night. Roy sat Indian-style near the animals, sipping at a jug. Little Ritchie skipped and bounded between Roy and the wagon, clearly glad to be active after a long day of travel.

A translucent red glow backlit the ridges on the far side of the valley, and a thick crescent moon hung in the sky above the illumination; it would set well before midnight. A flash among the trees caught his eye—then another, and another.

"I do like fireflies," murmured Abigail, as she laid out their bedding. "I suppose I could make birdies—is that what you call them?"

"Bridies. Or pasties, I suppose. Not much difference."

"Yes. It's just a small pie, really, isn't it? I could do that."

He caught the tension in her voice. "Abigail, I didna come to Philadelphia for a cook. Although, if ye've any of Gretchen's receipts, I'll no' fight ye."

She smiled, and the tension in his gut relaxed.

"Can ye read the next bit of Romans? I have a hard time reading by firelight." He passed her the little New Testament. "Only one verse. Romans five, verse nineteen."

Abigail fumbled in her satchel for her spectacles. She put them on and found the place. "'For as by one man's disobedience many were made sinners, so by the obedience of one shall many be made righteous.'"

He laid back and looked at the stars. "Based on the previous verses, what does this mean?"

"He is speaking of Adam previous to this verse, how that by his sin death came upon all men." Her brow furrowed.

"Aye, we've talked about original sin."

"This is interesting."

John's heart lifted at the tone of her voice. She *did* truly sound interested.

"There is a comparison between Adam and Christ here. Just as we became sinners because of Adam, we ..." She hesitated. "We become righteous because of Christ." The firelight danced in the glass of her spectacles.

He sat up slowly, not wanting to break the spell, waiting for her to continue.

"I think this refers to imputation. What Mr. Whitefield preaches."

John swallowed. "Aye, that's what it is. Just as Abraham believed God, and righteousness was imputed to him."

"So I am truly *righteous* because of Christ, even though I sin?"

She sounded as if she'd discovered some great treasure.

"Aye, that's true. Before God ye are clear of guilt."

"What about the Commandments?"

She wasn't arguing, he decided. Only trying to strip away the years of unbelief and misunderstanding, like peeling off the layers of husk from an ear of Indian corn.

"I told ye that I didna come to Philadelphia for a cook."

Her eyebrows shot up. "Yes."

"But my guess is that ye'll try your best to fix me a decent supper."

Abigail's fingers fussed with the hem of her apron. "Yes, I will." Uncertainty had crept back into her voice.

"Can ye accept that if ye burn my supper I'll still love ye?" Hearing his own words, John became very still. Did he truly mean that? Did he love her? It had just popped out of his mouth. "Can ye see that it's the same thing? Ye canna earn my affection. I wouldna want ye to try."

She gazed at him for a long moment. "So God will love me even though I fail Him?"

He nodded. "I took vows when we wed, and I meant them." Yes, he did. He marveled at his confession. "The covenant Christ ratified with His blood is much more sure than that." He took a steadying breath. "Ye'll still want to keep the Commandments, but that's a whole topic in itself. Suffice it to say that the Christian wants to obey God, the way you'll want to fix me a good supper."

He grinned at her, and she smiled—a relaxed, joyful smile.

Just then, a piercing screech tore the air.

24

For coming into the bond of this covenant of grace; it is by faith we take hold of it. This we do when we are thoroughly, clearly convinced of our sin, and misery, and undone state under the covenant of works; and thence betake ourselves to the new covenant...

—John Craig, Farewell Sermon, Tinkling Spring

A woman's scream tore down Abigail's spine. Her whole body jerked, and her spectacles landed in her lap. "Who is that?"

John reached for her. "It's nae but a painter. A great cat—and it's not close, by the sound of it." His voice was low and soft.

Roy, she noticed, stepped around the edge of their campsite, his dark form barely discernible in the fire's ebbing flickers. He paused near the wagon and spoke to Lizzie before moving on to the Kerrs'.

"Roy will let them know there's nothing to fear."

"How big are these cats?" Her heart was still thumping madly.

"I've only caught a glimpse myself, but others say they're about six feet long or so—like a lion, aye? Only without a mane." John stretched out on the oilcloth and motioned for her to lie down.

She replaced her spectacles in her satchel and removed her apron before joining him. "Do they attack people?"

"Usually they avoid people—but there's old Ephraim Preston, who was attacked by one. He fired his musket point-blank, and then used the weapon to block the creature's great teeth as it pounced on him. He was knocked flat, but lived. The painter had died in mid-leap from that musket ball in its chest. After Ephraim wriggled out from underneath the carcass, he skinned the thing. It's huge."

She swallowed. That story didn't help.

"They come out to hunt at dusk and dawn. Their favorite places are streams—they like to take deer as they come down to drink in the early morning. That's when you need to be careful."

Abigail took a deep breath and tried to relax her limbs. "Are there any other animals I need to be wary of? Do buffalo come near the house?"

"Buffalo don't eat folks—you just stay out of their way. What ye saw the other day was the same as a giant billy goat frustrated when another suitor won the day."

She chuckled. She'd seen billy goats butting their owners.

"Bears are the same, mainly." He paused. "Stay out of their way—they'll usually avoid ye. Can ye climb a tree?"

"My brothers could. I suppose I could if I needed to."

"Ye might need to get up a tree if ye stumble upon a mama bear and her cubs. They're gey protective—it's generally the only time a bear will attack. And don't run. Bears are faster."

Abigail had only a vague notion of what a bear looked like, but they had to be large. She'd seen their skins. None of this would help her to sleep—that was sure. But she needed to know. "Anything else?"

"Hmph. Pay attention where ye walk and where ye put your hands, such as pulling out a chunk of firewood. Snakes will find warm hiding places in cold weather. Wolves are becoming scarcer, because of the bounty. Many go wolf hunting for the cash money, to pay their taxes. So I doubt ye'll see any—and they have to be verra hungry to bother a person."

John lay silent for what seemed like a long time. "Janet carried a knife and a primed pistol when she went out foraging. I'd feel better if ye did the same, just in case."

Abigail stared up at the star-studded sky. Wild animals were scarce around Philadelphia. She had few clear memories of Boston, but her Grandfather Latham's wrinkled face appeared before her mind's eye. She'd loved his stories as a child. He hadn't been allowed to speak of the gruesome things that had happened during King Philip's War, but he'd managed to hint at the atrocities inflicted by the Indians on New England families during his youth. In any case, they'd seemed like mere tales, safe as they were beside a warm fire.

He'd also told stories of his own grandparents who'd come across the ocean in the Mayflower, describing those first years of privation and hardship. But she couldn't remember any stories about dangerous animals.

Fatigue pulled at her limbs. Would they sleep on a mattress tomorrow night? It was her last cogent thought before slumber pulled a dark mantle over her mind.

Shadows stalked her dreams. Like smoke, they advanced and retreated, just out of reach. Then a dark form reached out and pulled her in.

Sloan—his hand was clamped against her mouth. Abigail tried to scream. She kicked and thrashed—or tried to, but she couldn't move.

"Abigail, wake up." John's voice murmured in her ear. "A bad dream?"

His arms were about her, and his familiar scent—acrid with sweat, perfumed with pennyroyal—welcomed her to wakefulness. She took a deep breath. Yes, it was only a dream.

"I dreamt about ... about Sloan." She'd hesitated to speak the name. Would John become vengeful?

His body seemed to stiffen slightly. "I'm no' surprised. It was a great shock, what happened to ye." He relaxed against her. "I've had nightmares of my own."

About the death of his first wife? She lay still, not wanting to probe, but curious. Already the darkness of her own dream was fading.

"I've dreamt about Janet. That night—when she died." He swallowed. "In the dreams I reach for my musket and it slips out of my hands. Or, other times, it doesna fire at all. I am helpless to save her."

"What really happened?"

"I did fire, only I missed. The Indian fired—missed his target and hit Janet instead."

She clutched at him. "Oh, John..." She had no words. "I'm so sorry."

His hand smoothed her hair. "The Lord has given me peace. And yet..." He took a deep breath. "And yet, I am a man. God made me to protect my family. Her death was a hard thing to receive from His hand."

He hadn't said anything about Sloan, but that must be a hard thing, too.

JOHN EDGED into the water of the North River as quietly as he could. A single bird chirped on a tree branch nearby, signaling daybreak, but the only light was a pearl glow above the Blue Ridge to his left. He'd left his breeches on the branches of a witch hazel. He didn't have a clean shirt and decided to soap himself and the garment at the same time.

There was no help for the bit of auburn beard he sported, but he wanted to be clean—for Abigail, and for his homecoming.

Finished with the soap, he set the crock on the bank. The glow to the east was strengthening, and the stars were dimming; another bird —a nuthatch, he decided—joined the first, and the limbs of the trees began to solidify in the gray light. As he entered the water again, swirls of mist rose ghost-like from the water's surface.

His factor, Archie, would have something to say about that. Raised a Highlander, he'd grown up with the tales of brownies and wights Presbyterians tended to dismiss. But the man had changed since then. Not that he'd admit it.

It did seem strange, this fog-like phenomenon, but John had seen it before in humid weather. Especially before a storm.

He advanced to the bank and shook his arms to rid himself of excess water. It was no use; his shirt was thoroughly sodden. He stripped it off and wrung it as dry as he could, careful to stay behind a tree lest someone see him in the growing light. Finally he hurried into his clothes. Summer storms could be brief or serious—there was no telling.

The small sounds of a waking campsite greeted him as he poked his way through the trees. Lizzie, as always, had revived the fire, and stood in the semi-darkness fumbling with her hair. A horse snorted, and Roy lifted his head from his bedding on the ground, bits of grass and leaves sticking out of his wavy mass of hair.

Abigail slept on, oblivious. John decided to let her sleep a few more minutes and joined his cousin in leading the animals to the river to drink.

He led Percy and Rosemary to the water. The mare he simply ground-tied, letting her pick her own way the last few feet. He kept hold of the pony, trusting her but knowing, nonetheless, that strange places could startle animals.

Or people, for that matter.

"John." Roy stood a few yards away, his hair a molten fire in the first rays of sunrise. "I apologize. For losing my temper. About Lizzie." His hands held the reins firmly as the gelding drank greedily.

"No, I was too hard on ye."

"Oh, but I goaded ye. Admit it." Roy's brow arched knowingly.

John slid his hand along Rosemary's withers. "Perhaps. But 'to be wise and love exceeds man's might.'"

Both of Roy's eyebrows shot up. "Shakespeare?"

"Aye."

"John, ye're getting fair canny in yer auld age."

They laughed and led the horses away.

STEPPING INTO THE WATER, Rosemary jerked her head up and snorted, as if questioning the wisdom of crossing the river. Ahead, John turned in the saddle and lifted an eyebrow.

Abigail felt a shiver of fear watching Rosemary's ears turn back in apprehension. There was no ferry and the water mid-stream covered Percy's hocks. After several moments, the pony turned her ears forward and followed Percy, perhaps calmed by the other animal's confidence. Soon the whole caravan was across the North River.

Abigail's heart quickened. Augusta County. This was home, John had said. What did his cabin look like? Her first glimpse of Magraw's place had discouraged her—a simple log cabin, weathered and tired. She wasn't quite sure how to feel.

John reined in Percy until they rode side-by-side. "The weather is turning. I told Roy we'd need to pick up the pace."

A strong breeze fought with her hat and ruffled the grasses on the side of the road. "Rain?" Rosemary's ears swiveled, as if listening for something.

"Aye."

Another gust swirled dust into the air. John turned his head to the right and Abigail followed his gaze. A huge mass of towering thunderheads lay above the far ridge to the west, bright against the darkness of the mountains beneath.

Saplings began to edge the trail, and in a few minutes they were deep into a grove of some kind of tree she'd seen before but couldn't name. The bark was white and the leaves unremarkable, except for their long and graceful petioles. Some specimens rose tall for many feet, the lowest branches hanging far above, like a grand cathedral ceiling.

Then the wind gusted through the white wood, and all the leaves began to quake and flutter. Abigail gasped. The air shimmered above her head and to the sides. A horse neighed, and Roy's voice barked some kind of exhortation.

The wind ebbed and rose again; the leaves rustled as they fluttered, and Abigail soaked in the beauty and wonder of the valley.

Thank you, Lord.

The cabin was forgotten.

IT WAS the wind he was hearing. Soughing through the aspens, its strange music comforted him.

But no, there was another sound. John jerked his head. It was coming from behind him—the sound of singing.

"Serve ye Jehovah with gladness, before his presence come with mirth ..."

He slowed the mare and brought her alongside Abigail's mount. "I dinna ken that one."

She smiled. "Psalm one hundred. We sang it often at meeting."

He blinked away a sudden wetness. He'd never heard her sing. "We sing it a little differently: 'All people that on earth do dwell, sing to the Lord with cheerful voice; him serve with joy, his praise forth tell, come ye before him and rejoice.'"

Abigail's lips parted slightly, listening. "I like that tune. And the words ... they are the same, yet better, I think. They glide and flow."

"I should've thought of it sooner, that ye might not ken our psalter. Here's one ye might like—it's from Psalm twenty-three." He launched into the familiar song.

They left the aspen grove riding side-by-side, singing. John scanned the tree-studded grassland by habit, noting a distant column of thin gray smoke to the west. He couldn't remember whose cabin that was, but he could see their cornfield in the distance, the stalks tall and ready for the scythe. Hopefully there'd be no hail.

"Yea, though I walk through death's dark vale, yet will I fear no ill," John sang, hearing Abigail joining in, but also noting the dark clouds creeping up over their heads. Whose homestead were they closest to? They couldn't outrun the storm.

A sudden gust jingled the wagon harness behind them, and a horse whinnied—Stormy, most likely.

Scanning the area once again, John spotted a distant figure striding diagonally across the grass carrying a sack or bundle of some sort. Who was it? The man looked up at the sky and began to lope, not an easy proposition with his burden.

As the man drew closer, John recognized the disheveled blond hair—John Craig, probably out on a pastoral visit.

The man's head turned. Craig had seen the wagons.

"Ho, Mr. Craig! Come and join us." Perhaps he'd give them shelter. His home couldn't be far.

"Mr. Craig?" Abigail asked.

He'd mentioned the name before to her. "Aye, our minister. But he serves two congregations. The other is just west of here."

Craig approached, sack in hand. Turnips, looked like. "John Russell, what a treat." He looked at Abigail, and his face lit up. "Will ye make the introductions?"

"My wife, Abigail Williams Russell."

"I'm verra pleased to meet ye."

Roy motioned him over to the wagon, and Craig hopped onto the seat. Fat raindrops started to fall, dotting the dusty trail ahead.

"It's only a half mile to the cabin from here—I've got someone for ye to meet. Any kin of yours named George? In the Cumberland?"

John didn't remember any relations there. Da would know. "No, I dinna ken any George Russell."

"Hmph. Well, I married his daughter Isabella."

"I'd heard rumors about a possible wedding." He grinned in

delight, flinching as the action hurt his cheek. He'd almost forgotten the injury as it was healing so well.

"What happened to your face?"

The man was too observant. "Long story. Perhaps next to a fire, aye?"

The fat sprinkles thickened, and the animals were agreeable to quickening the pace. In a few minutes John spotted the minister's cabin, smoke curling from the stone chimney. A thatched roof topped the log sides, and a lean-to adjoined the main structure. As they drew closer, another structure appeared. Had Craig built a barn? Extra logs lay on the ground near the lean-to. Apparently the prospect of marriage had caused the man to spend time on his property.

"Working on your cabin?"

"Aye, the lean-to will be a proper room soon enough. Eventually I'll shingle the roof."

"With my cedar, I hope."

Craig grinned his thanks.

Not all the animals could fit into the shelter the minister had built for his horse and goat, but the pony, lamb, and heifer were lodged dry and safe, with the horses and mules standing just outside the large open shed, their heads protected by the overhang.

John carried his saddlebags into the house, thinking of the materials he'd purchased for Mr. Craig. The minister's young wife greeted them.

"How do. Come inside." Mrs. Craig stepped back to let them in.

Her hair—what he could see of it under her matron's cap—was dark, and her eyes were too. Janet's coloring—but it wasn't Janet's face, and the reminder drifted away. "Thank ye kindly. I apologize. We are a crowd."

John scanned the room. While the cabin was still in many ways a bachelor's quarters, the space seemed almost crowded with the addition of a settle and a proper chair with beautifully crafted legs. In the corner stood a small mahogany table that seemed to glow from within.

"I've more places for folks to sit, now that I'm a married man." Craig's arm indicated the furniture.

The minister made the Kerrs welcome, and soon they were perched on stools, all except Will, who sat slouched against the wall, his lanky legs folded up. Isabella Craig and Lizzie had vanished, probably to the lean-to, which served as a kitchen. John found Ritchie next to Abigail on the settle. A rumble of thunder sounded outside, and the thatch above thrummed with the strong steady patter of rain. He was thankful to have found shelter.

John Craig pulled the chair closer to the settle and motioned to him to sit. "Give me the news."

John fumbled with the straps on his saddlebags. "First, tell me about that table. Handsome wood."

"Ye've noticed? Well ye would—it's a wedding gift from the widow McDowell. No, make that Mistress Borden."

"Borden?"

"Aye, surely ye kent she meant to remarry. And the man, rich as he is, wouldna need all her furniture. That's what she claimed, anyway. Took pity on me, I suppose." He chuckled.

John smiled, careful not to grin too widely lest he pull on his injury. How would he explain Sloan? "I brought back sermons from Philadelphia." He handed the materials to Mr. Craig. "Mrs. Russell, would ye have the sermon we were reading together?"

Abigail jerked slightly, not being accustomed to her new public name. "Yes, in my satchel."

Mr. Craig looked up with approbation in his eyes. "I see ye are leading your family well, but then I expected that of ye."

John passed George Whitefield's sermon to the minister.

He cocked one bushy blond eyebrow. "I dinna ken about this man." He looked up, his blue eyes piercing. "Ye ken what they say. That he's an enthusiast. Worse even than Mr. Tennent."

"I dinna ken ye objected to Gilbert Tennent." John's innards tightened.

What was this?

25

*For I am verily persuaded the generality of preachers talk of
an unknown and unfelt Christ; and the reason why
congregations have been so dead is, because they have
had dead men preaching to them.*

—George Whitefield, sermon, *Works*, 1771

*A*bigail tensed at the look on John's face. Was there gong to be a disagreement?

The thrumming of rain against the roof grew louder. Sophie deposited a sleepy Kitty into her husband's lap and left through the open door to the lean-to kitchen. Little Tommy fidgeted on his seat, but both Will and his father sat still, eyes on the minister's face.

"I read Tennent's sermons, aye. And some of Whitefield's. But have ye wondered if he's adding to the biblical requirements for ministers, thinking they must have some sort of experience?" John

Craig's knobby shoulders pressed against his shirt as he leaned forward.

"No, I dinna think that's what he means. I believe he means only that a man must be a Christian himself to preach to others."

The minister snorted. "To be sure. But all this talk of experience... I dinna like it."

"I used to wonder about that. About experiences." Abigail shocked herself. Women didn't generally join into men's theological discussions.

"How so?" Mr. Craig studied her, his voice gentle.

"My mother objects to the enthusiasts, and I asked my husband about it." She glanced at John, and his soft expression encouraged her. "He said that Mother is right, that the movement of the animal spirits alone is no evidence for having peace with God." She took a deep breath. "But then he asked me what Mr. Whitefield preached about our grounds for hope."

"What does Whitefield say?" Mr. Craig's eyes flickered to John's and back again.

"He speaks of Christ as our basis for hope." Her throat seemed to close up. "I didn't understand some parts at first." She rolled the hem of her apron between her fingers. "But my husband helped me."

"What parts were confusing?" Mr. Craig probed.

A sudden crash of thunder and the braying of a mule interrupted them. John stiffened, but relaxed again. He'd been worried about hail, she knew.

As the echoes died, Abigail gathered her thoughts. "He said that we were to loathe our own righteousness, but my parents taught me to keep the Commandments. I didn't understand."

The minister leaned back in his chair and folded his arms against his chest. "Ho, now, John—how did you explain that? Ye must ken that Whitefield is charged with antinomianism."

"By frivolous folk who twist the Scriptures."

"Bold words. Explain."

Abigail sensed the battle here was between friends. As if in response to her thoughts, John slanted her a friendly glance. *Dinna fash,* his eyes seemed to say.

"Whitefield merely states that we canna depend on our works to save us. Our best righteousness is as filthy rags before God. He decries those who preach license."

"Well said. But ye canna deny that others do encourage all sorts of excesses in the wake of his preaching."

"Then your problem is with them, not with Whitefield." John pulled out Jonathan Edward's book he'd purchased in Franklin's shop. "Mr. Edwards addresses some of these matters in here. I read it before I left Philadelphia, and he seems sensible enough."

"Well, then." Craig examined the volume with a critical eye. "*The Distinguishing Marks of a Work of the Spirit of God.* I'll read it." Then his eyes focused on Abigail. "And do ye now understand what Whitefield meant by loathing your own righteousness? Does it mean ye can act as ye please?"

She smiled, thinking of John's explanation involving her cooking. "John said that I should try to please him as a wife—"

Mr. Craig lifted one bushy brow.

"—But that he would love me even if I burnt his supper." She swallowed. "And in the same way I should please God by keeping His Commandments, knowing that I am accepted in Christ even if I fail in my duty."

The man chuckled and looked at John. "Ye'll make a decent theologian yet."

"John, let me help ye with the animals." Mr. Craig's voice was low, even a bit strained.

John stepped out of the overly warm, bustling cabin into the misty drizzle. Across the fields patches of sunlight broke out here and there, bright against the wet leaves of saplings and yellow-green grass. The air was still humid but fresh and alive. They'd be able to leave soon.

They circled to the shed, where Stormy leaned into Aster's side, as if to shove her into the shelter as far as they could get. Percy jerked up her head in welcome, and shook all over, flinging water in all directions.

"Ho, girl. Glad to see ye too." The flying drops had missed him, but he was already damp. No matter.

"I need to speak with ye privately," Mr. Craig said.

"Aye." John wiped Percy down with a handful of dry straw. "Is it Captain Patton?"

Craig grunted. "Well, yea and no. Patton and his kin havena changed their ways, and ye've seen it."

It was true. Some of the major landowners constantly bickered with the minister. "Lewis has stood by ye."

Craig wiped down the neck and withers of a mule. "Lewis is a good man, but by himself he canna help much. Patton and his sister want to rule the kirk, and enough of the congregation follow them, not seeing the problem."

"Hmph." John pulled on Percy's cinch strap, and walked the mare aside. "Mr. Craig, I will pray."

"I need that first of all." The minister led Rosemary out of the shelter. The sun broke through the clouds and shone on her gray coat.

"But there's more ye want of me." That much was obvious.

"This irascible bunch may reject me as pastor. Either way, I need another elder."

"What?" John stilled, his arm across Aster's broad back. "I have no training—"

"Ye've some schooling. But more than that, ye are a steady, godly man."

"No, I'm not."

~

THE ROAD HAD DWINDLED to a mere track through the grass, but Abigail kept her eye out for large ruts or holes to avoid. She didn't want Rosemary to pull up lame, even this close to home.

Home? She hadn't even seen the homestead, so she couldn't call it home, exactly. But perhaps she could, if she thought of it as John's. Philadelphia was no longer home, not really. John was "home." No matter what the cabin looked like.

She glanced at him as he rode by her side. He'd been quiet and thoughtful since they'd left the Craigs'. "Tell me more about Archie and Agnes." She needed to know, in any case, and perhaps if he were troubled about something else …

John's blue eyes widened, as if startled out of a reverie. "Och, aye, the Mays. Archie and Agnes May—did I tell ye they are Highlanders? Well, Archie was. Agnes was a Presbyterian Campbell from Edinburgh—and Campbells are Highlanders, but they dinna see eye-to-eye with some of the other clans, or so Da says."

Perhaps she had asked the wrong question. It sounded complex.

John smiled. "Seeing as we're no' going to study Scottish history, let me just say that Archie is Catholic. Or was."

"Was?"

"Well, now." He paused as they guided their horses over a small stream gurgling happily across the path. "He comes to meeting with us. Claims to believe what Mr. Craig preaches. The only Catholic belief he holds to seems to be the Christ Mass."

Abigail remembered a sermon about the ungodly celebration. "Does a priest come?"

"No, I dinna mean a literal mass. Only a day to acknowledge Christ's birth. And eat roast goose." He shrugged. "Many Anglicans follow the custom as well. In any case, I pay it nae mind. If Archie renounces his own good works as a basis of salvation, then I dinna care if he paints himself purple."

She chuckled. "You said Mrs. May is a Presbyterian."

"Aye, and she was raised that way. So it's verra interesting that he married her in the first place—and him of the clan MacDonald, who have nae dealings with the Campbells."

Abigail frowned. "MacDonald?"

"Aye, the Mays are part of the clan." He waved a hand in dismissal. "We have our own squabbles in the valley, but thankfully, most of those are no' worth mentioning."

She peered ahead. When would they arrive? Her stomach tightened in anticipation.

John pointed to the right. "Those are the Andersons' fields. He's growing wheat. Seems to do well in this place."

She could barely make out the fields, but spotted a faint gray spiral of smoke above a distant chimney. "I think I see them."

They rode silently side-by-side for several minutes, the warm sun piercing through the clouds to her right. Abigail tried to see past the trees. Just a few more miles.

"John Craig wants me to be an elder." John's face was shadowed.

That sounded serious. Perhaps this was what was troubling him. "Is an elder a pastor?"

"Not necessarily." His shoulders seemed to slump. "But it is a position of leadership, of responsibility."

And you don't want the position? she wanted to ask. In the middle distance, she caught a glimpse of shining water, one of the Shenandoah's tributaries, its sinuous length partially hidden by a screen of reeds and trees. A waterfowl's nasal *honk* carried on the breeze.

"I told him about Sloan."

Abigail straightened. Sparks tore along her spine. She took a deep breath and turned to him. "I don't understand."

Only a faint twitch of the corner of his mouth relieved the hard lines of his face. "Oh, Abigail." He clenched the reins fiercely, his forearms ridged where they emerged from rolled sleeves. "Dinna ye see? I canna be an elder, not with my temper." He swallowed, Percy fidgeting underneath him. "I nearly killed Silas Sloan. I would have—"

"But Roy stopped you."

"Aye, but what of that? I am a hasty man."

What could she say? Then a story from childhood popped into her mind.

"Do you remember the story of David and Abigail?"

John quirked an eyebrow. "Aye."

"David was angry at Nabal and would have taken vengeance on him," Abigail said. She knew the particulars of this story by heart, connected as it was with her own namesake.

"And Nabal's wife Abigail stopped David from wrongdoing." One side of his mouth lifted into a half-smile. "I ken the story. David was a bloody man, as I recall. He wasna allowed to build the temple for that reason."

"But wasn't David called a man after God's own heart?"

John's eyes widened. A grin slowly spread across his face. "Aye, well, I guess he was at that."

JOHN INHALED DEEPLY. A gentle, familiar peace settled upon his soul. If nothing else, Abigail would be a good companion to him. *Thank you, Lord.*

He spotted a familiar hemlock. "Look, Abigail." He pointed left. "Beyond those tulip trees is the meetinghouse. We call it Tinkling Spring because of a spring in the rocks just above. It makes a wee sound, like a tinkle."

Abigail's gaze took in the landscape. "It's lovely with the blue mountain rising behind it."

He glanced up. "My cabin is on a lower slope of the Blue Ridge. We're almost there."

He couldn't wait to be home. And he'd need to send word to his sister to fetch Susanna back. Sudden emotion roiled his gut. He missed his daughter. But he was glad, too. Abigail was a gentle soul, not like some of the women in the valley, hardened by toil or loss. She'd treat a stepdaughter well.

Percy lengthened her stride slightly, ears forward. "Ho, girl!" He turned slightly. "She knows she's home. See yon stone wall? That's a boundary of my property."

He reined Percy in at the crumbling masonry and they waited for the wagons to catch up.

Abigail examined the structure. "Did you build this?"

"No, it was already here—it's verra old. See how the mortar is weathered and crumbling?" Farther along, the wall vanished into the grass, tumbled stones marking its former extent.

"Who built it?"

"I dinna ken." He shrugged. "Indians? I dinna imagine Indians building walls, but their pottery and such is buried all over the valley. I have a stack of it, collected each spring when I plow." He motioned to the grassy area beyond. "This place serves as my hayfield. If ye look through the chestnuts there, ye can see my cornfield."

Abigail seemed tired but alert, her eyes roving over the property. Glancing back, he spotted the wagons.

"I have a place for the Kerrs, a bit of land and a good site for a cabin. Follow Roy up the slope to the cabin, and I'll join ye as soon as they are settled," John said.

Would his humble home be enough for the daughter of a prosperous merchant?

26

I to the hills lift mine eyes,
from whence doth come mine aid.
My safety cometh from the Lord,
who heav'n and earth hath made

—Psalm 121:1,2 *The Scottish Psalter*, 1650

The cabin was both larger and smaller than Abigail had imagined. Larger, because it seemed to grow out of a rocky outcropping behind it, and to one side a low stonewall of sorts extended; John had said something about an addition, and perhaps this was the foundation. Smaller, because as she opened the door, there was only the one room beyond, and conscious of Lizzie and Ritchie behind her, she wondered: would they all share the single space?

Abigail stepped into the cabin, keeping the heavy oak door wide open for light.

Wood of every hue greeted her. Golden planks lay beneath her feet, their sheen broken by three months of dust. A dark, smooth ridgepole was crossed above by strong, straight rafters. But the dark logs forming the walls were covered here and there with something lighter in color. She took another step.

Gray skins, no bigger than a sheep's, adorned the sides of the cabin. One specimen, larger and lighter in color than the others, lay on the floor next to a broad, low bed that was itself covered in a buffalo skin.

"Look at all those wolf skins," Lizzie blurted.

"Let me see!" Ritchie piped. He darted to the skin on the floor. "Are there lots of wolves here?" Fear edged the excitement in his voice.

"I suspect there canna be many left if Mr. Russell killed all these," Lizzie said.

Abigail knelt at the fireplace. She traced the slick smoothness of the slate hearthstone, a single gray slab that reminded her of learning to cipher in childhood. The walls of the hearth were white stone, carefully mortared; very different from the old wall at the boundary. John's handiwork, strong with straight lines.

"Shall I start the fire?" Lizzie asked. "I saw firewood against the side—I'll grab some pine." She stepped outside.

"Everything to rights?" Roy was back from tending to the animals. "I'll help ye get your things into the cabin."

As they unloaded crates and kegs, Abigail searched for places to store her things. A glimpse of polished wood caught her eye just above her head. All four corners of the cabin sported triangular shelves. She smiled. These must also be John's handiwork.

Several longer shelves were fastened to one wall, one above another, like a bookcase. Some held kitchen utensils. A large bowl perched at eye level: was that a kneading bowl? It seemed too beautiful for such a common use. Below it, several books stood at attention, held upright by large and unusual stones. And next to these a larger book, laid flat. A Bible, well-worn about the edges. What were the other books?

John Bunyan was a familiar name. But she'd never heard of Samuel Rutherford. She glimpsed another book about farming. In any case, she'd have a place to put her new book on medicinals—and the primer. Oh, and *Robinson Crusoe.* Yes, there was room here.

Where could she put her cedar chest? The end of the bed would be ideal ... but what was this? Between the bed and the far wall nestled a gleaming walnut cradle. Abigail knelt and caressed the wood, smooth and curved beneath her fingers.

Zimmermann ... the carpenter. Yes, John was a carpenter. This was beautiful. Inside, a thick blanket nestled, the soft ecru of undyed wool.

Susanna's? Abigail blinked rapidly, realizing who'd knitted this blanket—and in all likelihood, had spun the wool, judging from the spinning wheel in the other corner of the room.

Suddenly she felt like an intruder.

DRYING SWEAT CAUSED John's shirt to stick to his skin as he directed Percy the final few yards to the cabin. And he'd just bathed. Well, no matter. Abigail seemed used to his grime, and even the harsh exigencies of travel hadn't grieved her overmuch. Only spiritual matters had troubled her, and now he had more hope than ever before of her condition before God. Would she confess Christ? Some folks waited months before making a formal confession, confused or fearing to make a mistake; others took the matter more lightly, claiming their baptism and knowledge of sound doctrine as sufficient for membership in the kirk. But some knew the exact day of their regeneration.

As a youth John had alternated between guilt and self-justification. He'd struggled with his sin until one day, in his father's cornfield, he'd finally come to a place where he decided he must settle it.

While the sun mounted to its zenith, he'd fought the weeds—and the holy demands of God. Then as the gold of late afternoon edged the field, he saw the cross, where the demands of Justice were satisfied—perfectly and entirely and forever.

He dropped the hoe, fell to his knees, and wept. *It is finished.*

It was both a beginning and an ending—and yet, he still struggled with sin. But not without hope.

"Johnny! My lad!"

Dismounting, John peered through the trees lining the path to the Mays'.

Agnes Mays came into view, her skirts kirtled in her hands.

ABIGAIL STARTLED at the voice through the trees, a woman's voice. She stepped out of the cabin and turned toward the sound.

John dismounted Percy as a thin woman, skirts hiked well above her feet to allow movement, loped toward them, shouting a greeting as she came.

Loping wasn't the exact word. No, she was limping. No, not that exactly—Agnes, if that were she—was scuttling along at a rapid pace, as if her bones were not quite knit together correctly. And yet, judging from the volume of sound emanating from her slender frame, she was hale and hearty enough.

Hair tucked into a cap, the woman's face was lined with age, but sparkling blue eyes enlivened her appearance. "Mr. Russell, welcome home, and ye as well, young Russell." She jerked her chin at Roy.

Somehow even this formal address sounded motherly.

"Agnes, meet my wife, Abigail."

"I'm that pleased to meet ye."

"Likewise." Abigail clutched at her apron. Thankfully John continued the introductions.

The woman beamed at Ritchie. "Och, ye've done well," Agnes said. "Ye've brought back a playmate for Susanna."

The woman's voice was even stranger than Mr. Craig's. They all possessed the same lilt and burr, but Abigail had to listen carefully to understand her words. Did she sound as strange to the other woman?

John was now explaining that she'd come from Boston originally.

"Boston? What's the town like?" Agnes made it sound like the moon.

What could she say about the dingy place? Her main memories were smells—salt and fish. And food—lots of chowder and dark molasses bread. "Fishing," she said. "It's a good-sized place, right on a harbor. The ships go out for cod—and whales, too." She decided not to mention how dangerous it all was, or that Papa had lost a ship of which he was part owner, prompting a move to Philadelphia, where a chandlery seemed to offer a safer income.

And then, a different ship had foundered at sea. Jonathan's. No, the gray sea was treacherous, and Boston a hard memory.

"Fishing?" Agnes appeared to latch on to this information. "Edinburgh is a fishing town, too. Plenty of trade of all kinds. Even papermaking." Her eyes seemed far away. "Aye, always a number of ships in the harbor."

Then her eyes focused on Abigail's face. "I ken ye're far from home." Her gaze slanted to John. "I'll make sure this lout willna neglect ye. Come ben—we'll need to get supper on for the menfolk."

John grinned at her. "Aye, go—the rest of us will finish unloading."

THE MAYS' cabin was not much bigger than Papa's cowshed, but infinitely more inviting, nestled as it was between a large chestnut and a conifer of some kind. In front of the door, a lone gray chicken patrolled, its beady eyes alert for bugs.

"That's Petunia," Agnes said. "We've several good layers. Lily gives me an egg every day without fail, but Rose is a sluggard. So I let her set on a clutch of eggs. I'll have a few pullets to give ye soon."

"You name them after flowers?"

"Well, then, it's better than a name ye'd give folks. Some laugh that I name chickens at all."

"I'm not criticizing. I named the new mare Aster. I...I like plants."

"Herbs and such?"

Abigail nodded.

"I dinna have much of that sort in my kailyard. Cabbages, onions —speaking of which, I need some neeps for the pot. Come." Agnes took her by the arm. "How did Mr. Russell end up with a maidservant?"

Abigail told her the story, minimizing Sloan's awful interest, but the other woman seemed to understand anyway.

"That's my Johnny. Looking out for folks."

They reached a jumbled mélange of greenery bordered by uncertain fencing.

"Follow me—my Arch sets snares for the rabbits. Not that the traps would hurt ye, they're twine, mainly. The pesky creatures still get to my cabbages on occasion, but we eat a good amount of rabbit stew, so I call it more than even."

Abigail stepped carefully along diffident rows. "What is this plant?" Dotted with immature berries, a tangle of small bushes swallowed up half the garden.

"Madder. Ye'll not mind it?"

"I think I do. 'Tis a dye, isn't it?" How fascinating. "Do you dye your own wool and flax?" Following Agnes's lead, she stooped to pull a few turnips out of the crumbly soil.

"I hope to soon. Madder takes several years to grow, because ye harvest the roots, ye ken? Mr. Russell promised me a bit of alum from Philadelphia for the dyeing. And I can sell any I dinna use over the Gap." Agnes stooped and added an onion to the dirty lumps in her apron.

Abigail had only a vague notion of geography. "The Gap ... east, you mean?" She followed Agnes to the cabin.

"Aye. Wagons take goods to the James River, and from thence to Richmond and Williamsburg. When we first settled here, the only goods we could sell were skins and such. But that's been changing." Agnes paused at the cabin door, her eyes darkening. "Are ye afraid? Ye mind how Mr. Russell's wife died?"

"Yes." Abigail stared at the turnips in her apron. "I mean, I know how she died." How could she explain her feelings when she didn't understand them herself? "I don't know if I'm afraid. Maybe I am. I wonder what people will think of me."

That sounded foolish.

But Agnes's eyes were twinkling. "Och, never mind what folks think. There are always a few bad apples in every place—folks ye canna please." The other woman studied her face. "Ye'll do just fine. Let's add these to the pot."

Agnes added a chunk of pine to the hearth, above which simmered a kettle of savory-smelling soup or stew. Abigail peered at the brown mixture. What was in it?

Agnes glanced at her. "Barley brose with rabbit. And peas. Even with no meat, it'll fill your man. And we usually have some meat. John is a good hunter, and the other men put out trap lines."

Abigail sliced turnips to add to the stew while Agnes stirred in handfuls of cornmeal. Already she felt a peaceful kinship with this woman, much as she had with Gretchen.

"Ho, Aggie!" A bellowed sounded from outside.

"That'll be Mr. May," Agnes said.

Abigail stepped to the door. A rawboned man strode up the path, dressed like John above the waist. Below the waist, red fabric fluttered with each stride. What was he wearing?

A petticoat?

27

Adam, our father and our head,
Transgressed, and justice doomed us dead;
The fiery law speaks all despair:
There's no reprieve nor pardon there.

—Isaac Watts, *Hymns and Spiritual Songs,* 1707

The last rays of the setting sun shone through the cabin's open door, reflecting off the brass fittings of the sea chest and warming the wood of the floor. His wife kneeled in front of the chest, her hands buried in her belongings.

"Why do Catholic men wear skirts?" Abigail asked.

John gaped at his wife. She awaited his answer, her cheeks pink.

"Catholic ... oh, ye mean Archie?" John chuckled at the thought of Archibald May, owner of a ten-pound claymore, described as wearing a skirt. The chuckles turned to great, gasping guffaws.

Abigail's eyes widened.

"No, I'm no' laughing at ye. It's Arch …" He sat on the bed, recovering. When had he last laughed out loud? "I hope ye didna ask him why he was wearing a skirt." No wonder she'd stared at the man during supper.

She shook her head, smiling.

"It's called a kilt. Most days Arch wears breeches, but on the Sabbath, or when he goes out trading, he dresses more formally."

"The colors are quite striking."

"Aye, that's the MacDonald clan tartan. And it's naught to do with religion. The Highland clans weave them, to tell folks where they come from."

Abigail stood and shook out a long piece of linen. "Like a flag?"

"Aye, something like."

She spread the linen over the narrow board he'd purposed for a table, but removed it. The tablecloth—if that's what it was—overwhelmed the tiny furniture.

He swallowed. She didn't seem disappointed in the cabin, exactly. But he couldn't help the tightness in his chest. "Abigail, your father gave me a few items. Something about too many sextants."

Her eyebrows shot up, and she grinned. "That does sound like Papa. What'd he give you?"

His innards relaxed a little. "Perhaps ye could tell me. It's a bolt of some kind of fabric, but I dinna recognize the type. Is it for trading or for us?" He pulled out the wrapped rectangle from the corner and laid it on the bed.

Abigail pulled off the cover. "Linen diaper." She frowned, touching the soft ale-colored weave. "Mother uses it for towels." She paused. "It can also be used for…" Her lips parted. Was she blushing?

"Towels are useful." John groped for words. He couldn't remember what Janet had used for towels. Probably rags.

Abigail looked up at him, cheeks flushed. "They are also for babies."

It struck him then. "Clouts, ye mean." He pushed the bolt aside and sat. "Well, now." He couldn't help but grin. "It could be. I mean, we might need them soon."

Abigail looked away, her expression unreadable for a moment. Her gaze returned to his face. "Yes, I suppose we'll be ready."

John's eyebrows drew together. They'd never spoken of more children, only Susanna. He changed the subject. "What did Gretchen pack in that crate?" Items from home might cheer her.

Abigail uncovered the crude box and he scooted closer.

"Candles." She peered inside a burlap bag. "Sheep's tallow—oh, here's a couple of beeswax ones." She passed them to him for inspection. He heard a tiny gasp. "Oh, look—a bayberry candle." She drew out a wide red candle and handed it to him.

"I've seen these in the dry goods shop in Philadelphia. Expensive." He hefted the waxy pillar and sniffed at it. Even unlit, the scent was pleasant.

"We used to make them in Boston where the bushes were more plentiful. Mother must've hoarded some." She dived back into the crate as if searching for treasure.

Crocks of foodstuffs and herbs followed. A bag of nutmeg and a grater. Small packets of seeds. And several sheets of paper, crowded with tiny handwriting.

Abigail gasped, reading. A tear rolled down her cheek.

"What is it?" Bad news from home? No, that was impossible. They'd left with all these items onboard.

"Gretchen's receipt for soap."

Two days later, John slipped out of the cabin at dawn and headed for the spring as he did each morning, to water the animals and haul a few buckets back for the house. He'd been careful not to wake his wife. Abigail had a lovely bloom in her cheeks, but she seemed tired. And no wonder—a long trip and a new home would tire anyone. Both Lizzie and Agnes were helpful, turning out stew, bridies, and cornbread for them all, including the Kerrs, and pouring New England maple syrup on, well, everything. Abigail hovered during these preparations, chopping vegetables while learning the finer points of how to cook rabbit and squirrel.

The door creaked as he slipped into the cabin with the water, trying not to slosh. He almost succeeded. John set the buckets down near the hearth and stared at the floor in the dim early light. Several fat blotches darkened the dust of the oak planks.

He looked more closely. Lumps of hardened mud disguised the grain of the wood near the door. He studied his shoes, crusty with filth.

What would Abigail's mother say? He winced at the thought. He visualized the entranceway of the family's home in Philadelphia. Right inside their doorway, a large woven mat—probably hemp—caught much of the dirt of their shoes, and a boot scraper stood at the ready. The wood floor beyond fairly gleamed; they must have swept it daily.

He glanced at the broom leaning against the cabin's far wall and cringed. He'd seen Abigail using it, but to little effect. It was no more than a bundle of sticks. He could do better.

Well, then. He needed to mark a cedar tree and show Abigail the best berry patches, and look for materials for a broom. And he had rope—could he create a mat?

"WHEN DO THE CHESTNUTS RIPEN?" Abigail asked, excited about their first venture upslope.

"Around the time of the first frost," John said, slinging his rifle over his shoulder.

After a late breakfast of porridge, John had invited her to his favorite haunts—and to mark a tree. Abigail stashed her botany book and a pencil in her satchel on her way out the door.

She followed him out to the small barn, a shed really, constructed against a rocky outcrop, where they saddled the horses. After mounting, John directed Percy to a nearly invisible track. Without any urging, Rosemary kept pace, her footing sure. The forest thickened as they ascended the slope, and everywhere Abigail looked there was something new. New plants for her book.

After a quarter hour of riding, an open patch of grass opened up before them, and they tethered the horses.

"John," she whispered. "Look. This tree is huge." Many chestnuts were quite large, but this specimen dwarfed the others in the grove. She spread out her arms, but the trunk was wider.

"Oh, aye. Beautiful," he said, craning his neck to gaze at the canopy. "Better yet, this grove produces bushels of nuts every fall." He jerked his chin. "Let me show you the berries."

She followed John, uncertain if they were still following a path, pushing her way past branches and brambles and stepping over rotting logs. She spotted wood ears and puffballs as they ascended, passing oaks and poplars and skirting large masses of rhododendron.

After about a quarter hour of climbing, her lungs burned and her legs grew heavy.

John turned and studied her. "Shall we rest?" He handed her a jug, and they sipped cider for a few minutes. "It's no' far."

He pointed out a couple of trees in the middle distance. "Black birch—part of my farm, if I do say so."

Her fatigue fell away, and once they gained the trees, Abigail reached for her copybook. She traced the bark. She'd not seen a birch quite like this.

"I drain the sap from several of the largest every year, much as ye do for maple syrup. It makes a fine ale of sorts." John broke off several twigs and handed one to her. "Peel the bark."

It wasn't difficult. Then John thrust his twig in his mouth, and she did the same.

"Chew it," he instructed. "A fine substitute for tooth powder."

Mint and licorice flooded her mouth. This was definitely going into the book.

After gathering a small supply of birch twigs, they continued the ascent. Another few minutes brought them to cane thickets filling the sunny gaps between soaring pines—those were raspberries, John explained, and farther on, he pointed out blueberries.

She knelt at a blueberry bush. The berries were fully formed. It wouldn't be long.

"Don't move, Abigail."

She froze, hearing the quiet intensity of his voice.

"Dinna fash, it's a bear."

Dinna fash? She was terrified. But John had his rifle. She stayed where she was, unable to see where he was looking, her heart pounding.

"Get up verra slowly. He's moving away."

On her feet, she turned and followed John's gaze. In the distance she caught a flash of black fur before the animal disappeared behind the trees. Her husband stood silently, immobile, hands ready on his weapon.

"This is good news." His voice was still pitched very low.

Hands clammy, she discovered her blue pendant hanging free and replaced it inside her bodice.

"I wanted to kill a bear this autumn, but didn't know of any this close. And he's no' as big as some." His shoulders eased, and he smiled. "Roy will be glad of the skin, and it's good meat."

She frowned. How could it be safe to pick berries? "But the berries—"

"We'll let the animal eat some of them first. It sweetens the meat. Then we'll kill it, and ye'll take the rest."

Abigail's mouth parted. This was truly a new world.

JOHN DARTED a glance back at Stormy, the gelding's lead rope wound around his forearm. So far the animal had followed Percy sedately as they picked their way down the path.

"Just the same, dinna get any ideas," he said.

"I'll be good, dinna fash," Ritchie said from his perch on the saddle in front of him.

He chuckled at the lad. "I was speaking to Stormy, ye ken. I dinna trouble myself about ye. Still have the horseshoe? The blacksmith will likely give ye a copper ha'penny for it."

"Right here!" Ritchie held up the item in question.

John hoped the gelding would cooperate with the smith who doubled as a farrier. Both animals need their hooves trimmed and checked—he would do it himself in a pinch, but a horse's feet were its life.

The morning had been productive, and he'd enjoyed seeing the forest of the Blue Ridge through Abigail's eyes, showing her the treasures of his hidden larder. She'd never seen hemlock trees, and the cedar had startled her. His mouth twitched, thinking of her eyes as he'd pointed out the giant tree he planned to harvest.

Abigail had traced the red fibrous bark in awe. "'Tis so tall. So ... magnificent." She stepped back, trying to comprehend the scale of the branches, craning her neck to see the crown. "I've seen cedars before, but not so large."

"Sometimes ye see it as a scrubby bush, especially down in the valley."

"I have an entry in my book, but I've never seen such an extraordinary specimen." Her gaze roamed over the cedar. She smiled. "'Tis truly grand."

He laid his own hand on the bark then. "On occasion I regret taking trees, especially ones so magnificent." How tall was it? He couldn't tell, but the width of the trunk would make for hard work.

They'd made plans to return after the bear hunt. Abigail would accompany him and fill her baskets with berries while he cut down the tree.

What a wonderful woman. She'd not panicked at the sight of the bear.

John gave Percy her head as he and Ritchie approached Lewis's palisade, loath to relinquish his woolgathering, loving the memory of Abigail's hand reaching for the blue quartz pendant that had escaped her bodice as she stood and looked after the lumbering animal.

The blue quartz. The red cedar. His home and his heart, all part of her now.

28

---

one morning all of a Suding there came a messanger & said
mr whitefield is to preach at middletown at 10 o'clock. i
was in the field, dropt my tool & run home and throu
my house and bad my wife to get ready quick & run to
the pastire for my hors with all my might fearing i
would be too late to hear him...

—Nathan Cole, quoted in *George Whitefield*, 1990

*A*bigail woke and reached for the quilt. John was gone, and without his body heat, the crisp early morning air cut through her chemise. They'd been in the valley only four days, but August was waning, and John had explained that while the valley was quite warm all summer, the flanks of the mountain felt winter first.

Was John haying or helping build the Kerrs' cabin today? No, it was the Sabbath. In the haze of waking, she'd forgotten.

She sat up, and her stomach rebelled. Surprised, she lunged for the chamber pot under the foot of the bed.

Abigail was still heaving, the unpleasant bite of vomit in her mouth, when the door creaked open. She cringed, hating that John should see her so.

And then he was beside her, with washbasin and a length of the linen diaper she'd cut for towels.

"I don't know what ails me," she said, after the worst had passed. "A little peppermint and ginger tea should set me to rights." She'd seen peppermint sprawling wild over half of Janet's old herb garden, along with a few stalks of leggy basil.

"I'll fetch the peppermint." John didn't sound alarmed.

Truly, she was feeling better already. She filled the teakettle, placed it over the hearth, and thought about breakfast. No time for porridge. Perhaps leftover cornbread would do.

John returned with the peppermint. "Feeling better?"

"Yes. 'Tis strange. I don't feel ill."

"Janet was the same." He paused and sat beside her on the bed. "When she discovered she was with child."

A wash of heat flooded her. She was a week late—that had never happened before. Could it be? She'd never discussed particulars with her mother.

"Dinna worry, aye? Mrs. McClure is a fine midwife."

She met his blue gaze. "Oh, John. I think you're going to be a father." She wrapped her arms around him, and he stroked her back gently.

The teakettle whistled.

ABIGAIL WAS glad for John's remade breeches underneath her clothing. She still felt mildly ridiculous, riding astride in her Sabbath gown, but they couldn't all fit in the wagon, and it was too far to walk. Perhaps one day they'd be able to purchase a sidesaddle.

"Mr. Craig normally walks to the meetinghouse, but he's married now. I dinna think he'll make his wife do the same," mused John as they crossed the little stream below the cabin. Abigail had been overjoyed to discover its source, a spring fifty yards from the little house, spouting clear cool water that trickled over smooth dark stones to form a little pool beneath. The overflow birthed a cheerful stream that wound its way down the slope. They had plenty of water—and a place for milk, John had explained. He'd always wanted a milk goat or cow, and the heifer was a blessing. Lord willing, once the animal calved, they'd have a supply of their own.

God bless Papa. Her father had known what they'd need.

Abigail peered through the screen of apple saplings that formed a nascent orchard. The Kerrs' cabin was just beyond—or what they'd managed to build so far. There—a dark structure came into view. The roof was light in color.

"We've nailed oilcloth over the ridgepole for a roof," John said. "We'll need to take some wood to Stuart's sawpit for proper rafters. William is a fair hand with building. The lad will be a blessing to his parents."

What about the other children? "Perhaps I could teach Kitty and Tommy to read as well as Susanna."

John turned and smiled. "Aye. When the cold weather sets in and the nuts and berries are collected, there will be less for the little ones to do. And your instruction will be welcome, I'm sure. Even the poorest folk in the valley want their children to read and write."

"Is there much slate in the hills?" she asked, thinking of the hearthstone.

"Och, aye. I'll take you with me this week." His eyes twinkled. "There's also a lot of limestone in the valley. We could find something suitable for writing utensils, most likely."

Abigail forgot her lingering nausea. Slate and chalk. Would Sophie accept her help? Probably—but it surprised her that others might as well.

In Boston and Philadelphia, reading was taught as a means of learning the Scriptures, but there were always some who learned poorly, or not at all. She doubted if the chimney sweep who visited their home in Philadelphia once a year knew how to read or even write his own name. She hadn't known what to expect here in the valley, but she'd imagined that the effort just to survive in the wilderness would crowd out other things.

For some reason she'd thought of John as an exception. Maybe he wasn't.

Once past their property, the vista opened up, grassland and cornfields punctuated with stands of poplar, oak, and cottonwood. In the distance, Abigail glimpsed the South River, glimmering pewter under the cloudy sky.

As they approached the meetinghouse, she became conscious of her ankles, bare beneath her hiked skirts as she straddled Rosemary. And she hoped her garment wasn't too fine. Neither Agnes nor Lizzie had anything so nice as her yellow print Calicut gown, with extravagant gathers at her hips, and John had explained that many of the folks here were poor, some simply working on others' land, as the Kerrs would be doing.

A mule brayed up ahead. Abigail spotted wagons and animals clustered under the trees near a long building made of logs. And people gathering—some walking, whole families together, carrying bundles and baskets. Their own dinner was packed in Roy's wagon.

Her stomach clenched. Would these people accept her?

JOHN SCANNED THE HORIZON, innards tightening at the thought of yesterday's discovery. Spending the Lord's Day at the meetinghouse was normally a peaceful outing—well, if Captain Patton and his sister minded themselves. He generally avoided Mistress Preston and her sharp tongue.

But the horseshoe had changed everything. Silas Sloan was here. At least, the smith had identified the maker's mark on the shoe: the smith at Middle Spring had made it, he'd said, and not long ago. It must be Sloan, unless someone else from Magraw's settlement had made the trek upvalley this month. But wouldn't James Magraw have mentioned it?

As they drew near to the meetinghouse, he glanced at Abigail, who was tugging at her skirts as if to lengthen them. She was a pretty picture on Rosemary, the pony's coat gleaming like burnished steel under the drape of her beautiful yellow gown. And her hat sported a blue ribbon that matched the print of the fabric—and her eyes.

"Over here," he said, directing her to a tulip tree. He helped her dismount in its shade, suddenly conscious once again of his impending fatherhood. His chest ached with pride and protectiveness, and he patted his coat, reassured at the lumps underneath. He'd left his rifle in Roy's wagon and armed himself with a pistol in addition to his customary knife. Surely Sloan wouldn't trouble them here, but John went nowhere unprepared.

Oh no. Mistress Preston stood near the door of the meetinghouse, chatting with another woman, both of them decked out in their customary silk Sabbath gowns. Abigail would have to run the gauntlet today. Perhaps he could ease her way. How, he didn't know.

"Good day to ye, Mr. Russell." Mistress Preston opened a painted fan and ostentatiously waved it before her face. "And who might this be?"

"My wife, Abigail Williams Russell." He turned and nodded to Abigail. "May I present Mrs. John Preston."

"I am pleased to meet you." Abigail bobbed in a curtsey.

The fan fluttered. "Charmed." The woman's eyes darted to his face. "And your dear daughter? I hope she hasna forgotten ye yet."

"My sister will return with Susanna shortly." John tried to keep his fists from clenching. The woman was infuriating.

"I cannot wait to meet my stepdaughter." Abigail's voice soothed him.

"Your speech is ... interesting," Mistress Preston said. Her tone made Abigail sound mentally incompetent.

Perhaps the woman had never met anyone from Boston, but in any case, he was not going to stand by and allow her to insult his wife.

"Mrs. Russell," Sophie Kerr appeared at Abigail's side. "I'm that glad for the remedy you gave my Kitty. I'd be grateful if ye'd see clear to write down the receipt for me."

"Of course I will," Abigail replied. "Pray excuse me, Mistress Preston, 'twas kind of you to make my acquaintance." Sophie led her away.

Some of the tension left John's shoulders. He followed his wife into the building. Thank God for the weaver's wife.

ABIGAIL FORGOT the insulting woman's words when the singing started. Mr. Craig would sing a line of a Psalm in his gruff, lilting voice, and the rest of the congregation would repeat it. There were no Psalters to be seen, and in any case, the lighting was dim. The minister's face glowed in the light of the open door at the side of the building, but the other door was far to the back, and the windows along the sides were very small and set high.

They sat near the front, and the swell of song from behind surprised her. In Philadelphia, their meetinghouse was equally large, but not quite as well attended, and the singing had been anemic compared to this.

John's baritone rumbled in the air beside her. Somewhere behind them, a man with a croaking voice bellowed out an approximation of the tune, but his cracklings were largely smoothed over by the massed voices filling the close, dim place.

"We take our text this morning from Romans the third chapter," Mr. Craig said, standing at a minister's desk that looked slapped together. Certainly John had not fashioned it, Abigail decided, thinking of the walnut cradle.

"'That every mouth may be stopped.' Verse nineteen contains a concluding statement, a general thesis, concerning all that the Apostle Paul had written previously in the opening chapters of this epistle."

Abigail straightened. Despite the man's ordinary appearance and strange accent, he sounded like a true preacher, a man with education.

He continued with his introduction. " ... especially as it appears in the doctrine of justification by faith alone. And the more clearly to evince this doctrine, and show the reason of it, the apostle, in the first place, establishes the point, that no flesh living can be justified by the deeds of the law."

She was glad he'd chosen Romans. Her heart swelled with gratefulness toward the man at her side, who had patiently taught her in the bits of time they had on the road.

Point by point, Mr. Craig retraced the wickedness of the Gentiles and the condemnation of the Jews in the beginning of chapter three. "God is just in condemning all men, Jew and Gentile alike. No man has a case before the righteous bar of heaven. He canna plead his own good deeds."

Abigail was only faintly conscious of the hard bench she sat upon. The sunlight no longer shone on Mr. Craig's face—it must be getting toward the dinner hour. But the sermon didn't seem overly long, somehow.

He was speaking now of the justice of God in the damnation of sinners. "'The judgments of the Lord are true and righteous altogether.' Job justified God in his worst suffering while Abraham used it in divine argument: 'Shall not the Judge of all the earth do right?'"

Her stomach grumbled. But truly, in one sense she felt as if she'd already eaten.

A final song concluded the morning service, and Abigail stood, stretching her limbs. Suddenly she was aware of an acute need to use the necessary. She whispered to John, and he guided her gently out the door, nodding to several men on his way.

Several hickory and tulip trees shaded the crude outbuilding below the meetinghouse. Beyond the trees a dark-haired man walked briskly away. Had he attended the morning service?

He seemed familiar—but no, it couldn't be Sloan. Why would a man like that listen to preaching?

She glanced at John. Had he noticed the man? But no—his eyes were on her.

29

Bears, Young or Old, if Fat, is much esteem'd by many Men,
that the Flesh is almost comparable to Hog's or Swine's
Flesh...We have store of Rabbits... *and* Squirrels *also,*
which are very good Meat.

—John Norris, *Profitable Advice,* 1712

September 1744

*A*bigail forced her hands to keep moving as she twisted the mortar in the pestle. Lavender buds weren't all that hard to grind, but after days of husking corn, her hands were raw, and she sported a blister on one thumb. But she couldn't very well have worn gloves.

Papa wouldn't like to see her hands now. But Arch May had shot several fat geese, and armed with a crock full of warm grease, she was ready to make a large batch of salve. How good it would feel on her hands. Just a little more lavender ...

A knock sounded at the cabin door. "Abigail?"

A welcome voice. "Come on in, Mrs. McClure."

The woman bustled inside, a basket over one arm. "How many times must I tell ye to call me Maggie?"

"Have a seat, Maggie." There was one more stool, and the bed, her quilt folded neatly at the foot.

The plump woman sat on the bed and rummaged in the basket. "I brought ye marigold flowers." She peered at the pestle in Abigail's lap and raised a brow.

"Lavender. I've comfrey too."

Maggie McClure grinned. "Oh, wonderful. Ye dinna ken how glad I am to have ye here. I'm just an ordinary midwife and folks barely listen to me as it is. And now ye're here—with your book."

"Are the flowers dried?" The book said calendula was good for salves.

"Aye. They'd need only a few turns to powder them fine." She frowned. "Let me finish that. Your hands are chapped."

Abigail emptied the lavender and comfrey into the crock of grease and handed the mortar and pestle over to the midwife. "Thank you."

Maggie quickly ground the flowers and dumped them into the grease. "Can we use this right away?"

"I suppose it might be more potent after a few days. That's how other preparations work."

"Och, ye're likely right. But let's put some on ye now. Canna hurt."

The midwife gently examined Abigail's hands and scooped a little of the cloudy grease onto her palms. "Rub it in a little."

Abigail's shoulders slumped in relief. It was so good to be cared for. "Take a cupful home. Better yet—there's a small wooden crock with a lid on the shelf."

"Your Mr. Russell is right canny with wood."

Abigail smiled, thinking of the Kerrs, who'd been refusing help—and the buffalo skin, now supple and smooth, thanks to Roy. John had solved that problem by asking for one of the mules in trade, telling Mr. Kerr that he'd only need one animal for spring plowing.

And John had thrown in barley, turnips, and seed as part of the exchange, as well as freshly sawn planks for the roof. Yes, he was canny in a lot of ways. And kind.

Then she frowned, worried. "He's out hunting with Roy. He told me he'd likely be gone one night, perhaps two. Lizzie and Ritchie stayed the night here."

"Let me guess. They're hunting bear." Maggie poured a little of the warm salve into the container. "It's no' like hunting deer. There aren't so many bears, and they tend to ramble. Then, once they kill it, the beast is verra large. So it can take them days. Dinna fash—John is experienced." She placed the lid on securely and looked up with a twinkle in her eye. "Have ye heard about the wedding ceilidh?"

"Wedding kay ..." Abigail struggled to form the word.

"Ceilidh. It's a gathering, a dance. The Andersons are offering their big barn, and their oldest son Rob plays the fiddle."

"Who is to be married?" What was this? She'd thought Presbyterian customs were similar to her own.

"It's no' but a celebration after the fact. We've had several marriages this year, including your own. Now that the corn is in, folks are looking for a chance to gather, visit, and dance."

A dance? Mother would certainly not approve.

But Abigail couldn't help looking forward to it, nonetheless.

AFTER THE MORNING'S salve making, Abigail eyed the dirty crocks. She pulled on a glove before grabbing a bucket and heading out the door for the spring. Hopefully John would return by sunset.

The path, the merest track in the leaf litter beneath several large oaks, welcomed her. A single walnut tree, its limbs studded with green globes, marked the turn, beyond which lay the little bubbling spring. The walnuts were almost ripe, but John said they needed to fall first. Abigail inhaled the musty air beneath the dark branches, savoring the woodsy scent. She rounded the bend.

She smelled the man at the same time she saw him, lying on his back, one arm in the spring. He smelled like John after a long day on the trail—and worse.

But it wasn't John. Her heart thudded wildly as she took in the man's bare chest, dark as a copper halfpenny. Below the waist he wore leggings like John's, although in the place of breeches he wore some kind of long leather flap secured at the waist. A single feather adorned greasy black hair.

A twig snapped as she took a cautious step forward. *An Indian.*

She set the bucket down and advanced slowly. He didn't seem to be awake. The small pool was murky around his arm. Was the man bleeding?

He moaned and his eyelids flickered.

Bucket forgotten, she dashed back up the path. She needed Lizzie. And bandages.

THE MAYS' cabin was empty. Abigail scanned the property. Where was everyone? She'd heard Agnes talking about the chestnuts ripening. Perhaps she'd taken Lizzie and Ritchie up to the chestnut grove.

She gulped. John had left her a knife and a pistol. But the man was hurt—and not all Indians were dangerous, surely. She'd seen peaceful Delawares in the streets of Philadelphia. She scurried back to their cabin, mentally categorizing her medicinals. Boneset for fever, yarrow for wound packing.

And vinegar ...

What? The Indian was sitting against the front of the cabin, legs sprawled out before him, one hand gripping the opposite arm. He must have followed her.

Abigail slowed. The man's dark eyes turned toward her, his gaze unreadable. She eased her way toward the door, studying his arm. Blood, old and new, layered the exposed skin of the limb. Even his leggings were splattered with dark spots.

The injury would need to be cleaned. But first she'd have to gain his trust.

"I'll return in a moment," she said, unsure if he could understand. Perhaps just the sound of her voice would be helpful.

Abigail slipped inside and noticed the remains of her dinner—cornbread. She slipped it in a basket and snatched the jug of cider from the narrow table. Then she opened the door again, feeling a chill run up her spine.

She could have simply bolted the door and waited for John. But her feet seemed to move of their own accord. She approached the Indian and set down the basket of food and the cider, the man's dark gaze following her every move.

She dashed back inside and grabbed the bag of herbs. Bandages—some of that linen diaper would do. And vinegar.

She wrestled the keg of vinegar out the door, along with several small cups. One she filled with cider and placed to the man's lips. He sipped slowly at first, then more eagerly.

Was his gaze merely stoic, or was he in that much pain?

Abigail filled a cup with vinegar and cut a piece of linen to use as a rag. "I'm terribly sorry, but this will hurt." Would he understand? Would it anger him?

Watching his face, she gently but insistently pried his fingers away to see the wound. She felt his gaze on her as she dipped the rag in the vinegar and began to clean the dried blood around the edges of what looked like a rather small injury.

He didn't move, though he must be hurting. The arm was swollen and warm, but she saw no pus. Perhaps it would heal without much fever. Fresh blood appeared at the center of the wound, then she spotted a drip coming from behind his arm.

There were two wounds, one before and one behind.

Someone had shot this man.

WITH ONE HAND on his mare's bridle, John glimpsed the cabin beyond the screen of familiar oaks. A flash of indigo blue revealed Abigail's presence. His heart thumped with glad anticipation.

Percy's nostrils flared and she jerked her head. Instantly his other hand slid to his side for his knife. Earlier his mare had grumbled at the task of dragging home two hundredweight of bear meat, but he knew her moods. This was different.

"Ho, girl," he breathed. He took a cautious half step to his right and peered through the foliage.

Someone sat propped against the cabin, legs clad in leather. Dark hair. *Sloan?* Surely not. He clucked softly to Percy and led her slowly forward.

Abigail moved slightly, and John caught a glimpse of the man's face and chest.

An Indian. He froze. Was his rifle loaded?

He took a deep breath. *Help, Lord.* He had to be calm—he had to think.

As they approached the cabin, he heard Abigail saying something, but he couldn't make out what—she didn't sound upset or frightened. She was winding a wide swath of white around the man's upper arm. Was he injured?

Percy nickered, and the Indian startled. John tightened his grip on the mare's bridle with one hand, the other hand gripping the hilt of his knife.

"Ho, the house," he called. Would the man understand that his intentions were peaceful? Janet had died through misadventure, and he didn't want to start another accidental battle.

The Indian fled up the slope, his gait halting and weak, but he soon disappeared into the woods. Was he Shawnee?

"Abigail?" He ran.

"John?" She turned, and her smile was like a morning sunrise.

She was in his arms. "Did he harm ye?" She was perfectly well, he could see that, but he couldn't help asking.

"No, I am well. Someone shot him." Abigail described the wound and her treatment.

John sighed, the thudding in his chest subsiding. Percy nosed at him and blew in his ear, impatient to be rid of the bear meat behind her. "Help me get this in the smoking shed." He glanced at the woods. Unless the man had friends, there should be no danger. But would his friends abandon him? No. He must be alone.

Abigail eyed the meat on the travois. "How big was this bear?"

"Young, barely full grown, but fat. I'd say almost four hundred pounds dressed. Roy took the rest of the carcass, including the skin." It had taken three shots to bring it down, which was about what he'd expected. "Did this Indian say anything?" Many of them knew a few words of English or French.

"No. When I found him he'd swooned at the spring. Then he woke up." She frowned.

"Did he seem to want your help?" Unlikely. Indians were as proud as Scotsmen, if not worse.

"He did not refuse it, but then, he wasn't in very good shape. I gave him cider and I think it helped." She looked at him. "I wanted to give him tea for fever, but he ran away."

John chuckled at her disappointment. He felt Abigail's questioning gaze upon him, but he couldn't help his reaction. After the shock of finding an Indian at his doorstep, the relief of finding her safe made him almost delirious. "I dinna suppose it's as funny as all that, but I'm just glad ye're well."

But as they hung the bear meat in the shed, he sobered, thinking of the man.

Who'd shot him? And why?

30

In Adam's fall
We sinned all

—*The New England Primer,* 1727

The loveliness of the day eased Abigail's nervousness. She even forgot the purple blueberry stains on her hands as she gazed into the valley from her perch atop Rosemary. The sun shone golden and glorious in the western sky, poised to descend below the tall ridges across the valley. The air was fresh and warm, smelling faintly of wood smoke from distant fires; she'd brought her cloak for the return trip as the ceilidh would last until well after dark.

Lizzie and Ritchie had accompanied them that morning to the berry patches while Agnes stayed behind to begin turning the previous day's harvest into preserves. Abigail had washed her hands, but the berry stain was stubborn; John had persuaded her to don her

Sabbath gown for the dance anyway, saying that as they were guests of honor, they must look the part.

"They willna notice your hands," he'd said.

"But I don't know how to dance. I'll just sit somewhere and watch."

"To be sure." His eyes twinkled.

She'd given in on the condition that he wear his blue coat, and he'd rolled his eyes but grinned at her.

She followed John riding Percy down the path. His best shirt billowed bright in the breeze, the coat in question slung across his lap. Roy's wagon creaked behind them, along with the murmur of conversation: Agnes's pointed comments, Archie's chuckles, and Ritchie's inquiry: "Ma, what's a kay dee?"

Abigail rubbed at the leather of the reins. Not everyone at the meetinghouse was friendly, and folks were coming from as far as twenty miles away to the wedding frolic celebrating the Craigs' and the Bordens' marriages as well as their own.

Why would Mr. Craig attend a dance, even in his honor? He certainly preached against sin. In fact, sometimes she felt like the lowest of all creatures listening to his sermons, as though none were more sinful than she. Peace—that strange peace and comfort—came and went as she struggled with her doubts.

She drew up alongside John when they reached the crumbling stone wall. A strange bird cried out far in the distance, piercing but sweet, a long haunting cry that finally warbled into nothingness.

"What was that?"

"Rob Anderson's fiddle," John said. "Have ye never heard a fiddle—a violin?"

Abigail pursed her lips. She'd heard a pianoforte before. The Logans in Philadelphia owned one, and their daughter played. "No."

"'Is it not strange that sheep's guts could hail souls out of men's bodies?'"

Abigail lifted an eyebrow. "You're quoting someone. And what do sheep's guts have to do with music?"

"The strings of a fiddle are made of gut." John smiled. His chestnut hair, tied back in a gleaming queue, glinted fire in the afternoon sun. "Shakespeare said that."

"Mother said Shakespeare was highly improper." Even Papa hadn't given her plays. Another wail of the fiddle soared into the air. Now she could distinguish it as a tune.

"Och, she was likely right. Books are like men. Even the best of men have spotty garments. And there are few books—or men—that come anywhere close to what we have in the Scriptures." He shrugged. "Shakespeare was my rebellion as a lad. Kept it under my mattress. When Da found out, he sighed, but said I could have done worse."

She smiled. It sounded like something the bookkeeper would have said.

They passed a stand of cottonwoods and came to several open fields. On her left, corn stubble protruded from a sea of broad green leaves: pumpkins had been planted Indian-style with the corn, and orange globes peeked out shyly from their covering. On her right, bare soil lay tilled and ready for planting. Zigzag fencing made of crudely chopped lumber flanked the path to a large structure.

The bray of a mule competed briefly with the fiddle. A few oaks shaded a confusion of animals and wagons up ahead, and soon their own horses were secured near an open patch of grass. Roy drew up Stormy and Aster to a halt behind them, the gelding shaking his head and worrying the bit. The animal had filled out since his days on the road and become unused to labor, a situation that would change in the spring, according to Roy, who planned to break him to the plow.

"The Andersons are good farmers. See yon field?" John pointed back at the plowed earth. "That's for rye—it grows in cool weather. He plants wheat there in the spring, but ships it over the Gap to sell. We don't have a proper gristmill." He pulled on his coat and checked his stock.

"How do you grind the Indian corn?" Abigail asked. She followed him to the open barn, careful to keep her hem above the muck. Near the entrance, straw had been strewn over the ground. That would help.

"Colonel Lewis has a mill of sorts. Two large stones—an animal turns the topmost. He keeps a mule for this purpose, but he charges you next to nothing if you bring your own. Ye can grind it by hand, but we bring ours to Lewis."

They entered the musty shade of the barn. Large bundles of hay alternated with kegs and boxes along the sides for seating. Several women were perched on a nearby bale, visiting. Above, braided and tied to the rafters to dry, hung rows of corn like the teeth of a saw. In the back, a lanky young man with a fiddle ran a bow along a single string, listened, adjusted something at the top of the instrument, then ran the bow again, this time against two strings at once.

The harmony riveted her. If a glowing sunset could be heard, it would sound like that.

The fiddler began to play. Slow and sweet and lilting, the music pierced the air, seeming to float above all other sound.

John sidled up to her. "That's an old Scottish tune we use in meeting."

Yes, it was familiar. "You sang something with the minister at a place with a spring—"

"Middle Spring. Aye, we did. We both knew the tune, so we used it for a new hymn."

She fell silent, absorbing the song. Perhaps this frolic wasn't as wicked as she thought.

"Mr. John Russell, greetings to ye, and congratulations." A woman's voice, lilting and confident.

Abigail spun. A woman wearing a feathered hat rode high on a massive black stallion.

"Ho, Mistress Borden." John took Abigail's arm and they approached her. "Congratulations are due to ye as well, I hear."

The flaxen-haired woman flung a colorful green cloak back over her shoulder, and a man helped her down from the huge horse. "Mr. Russell, have ye met my new husband, Mr. Borden?"

The men exchanged nods. "Aye, we've spoken a time or two," John said.

Mr. Borden was supposed to be rich, but his puce coat was ordinary. His buttons and shoe buckles were pewter, not silver. And his features were unremarkable, his chin difficult to discern atop a fleshy neck. "Congratulations," the man said, his brown eyes flickering from John to her. He proceeded to nod over Abigail's hand like a Williamsburg gentleman.

"And to ye as well. Welcome to our neck of the woods," John said. He turned to Abigail. "It's the better part of a day's ride from Borden's grant."

"La, nonsense, John." The tall woman took Abigail's arm in her own as if they were old friends. "Mr. Borden owns a fine hunter, and my Dobbie laughs at the distance."

"Dobbie?" Abigail asked. The name seemed so ordinary for such an extraordinary horse.

"Dionysius is his real name." She smiled, her gray-green eyes twinkling. "He would surely get an inflated view of himself if he should hear it." She steered Abigail inside. "I'm parched. Is there ale? Or cider?"

"Yes, and there's even a bowl of punch, though I have no idea what is in it."

"Aye, well, I'll wager someone slips whiskey in it before the night is out, minister or no."

Abigail poured two cups of cider. "Your cloak is very beautiful. It reminds me of our factor's kilt, only his is red."

Mrs. Borden chuckled. "Ye're a sharp lass. He's Clan MacDonald. My grandsire was the eighth Earl of Argyll in Scotland, the chief of Clan Campbell." She grabbed the edge of her cloak and swung it closer. "Green and blue, the Campbell colors."

Abigail reminded herself that this vivacious woman was the

former Widow McDowell, who'd lost her husband when John had lost his wife. "I'm sorry for your loss, Mrs. Borden."

"Call me Lena. My name is Magdalena, but Lena is more every-day-like." Her expression grew thoughtful. "Aye, I lost a husband. Several did. Some remarried, and a few left the valley. Your Mr. Russell—I confess we were all curious to see who'd he'd bring back from Philadelphia."

Abigail warmed to this unusual woman. "He wore a tomahawk when he came courting."

Lena chortled. "Och, I like that. Showing ye his true colors!" She sobered. "Have any of the folks here treated ye ill?"

Abigail blinked, not knowing how to answer the question. "There may be a few folks who treat everyone ill." Had she said too much?

"Aye, and does a certain one use a painted fan?"

Abigail almost wept. She'd made another friend. "Yes," she said, shrugging slightly.

"Never ye mind this Mistress Fan. She's just blowing air." Lena looked about at the growing crowd. The fiddler was playing some-thing lively now. "Come with me. Mr. Borden sent to Williamsburg for a few things, including almonds. Ye canna have a wedding cele-bration without favors for the guests. We can pass them out."

They turned and made their way to the sunny entrance.

"Aha! A Campbell!" exclaimed a familiar gruff voice. Arch May stood square in the entrance, a slightly faded crimson plaid draped over his shoulder, secured with a brooch. At his waist fluttered his customary kilt—and a sword.

Lena swirled her green cloak theatrically. "Yon MacDonald— have ye business with the laird's daughter?"

WATCHING his factor strut before the crowd, John leaned on the barn's doorframe and chuckled. Mrs. Borden stepped up and faced Arch, displaying the colors of Clan Campbell with theatrical flair. The woman had a sense of humor a mile wide.

Arch lifted his chin and raised his voice. "I have business with the laird of Campbell—on the field at Sherriffmuir."

Arch May's father had died at the battle of Sherriffmuir, the bloody conflict that set Campbell against MacDonald. How could he joke about it?

No, it wasn't entirely a joke. Suddenly the red tartan seemed more a sad memorial than a challenge. A memory of things lost and gone.

Mrs. Borden curtseyed deeply. "Aye, well, since the laird is gone to his long home, will ye do me the honor of a dance?"

The crowd whistled and cheered, and Arch's hoary brows lifted in approbation. "Of a surety, lass, of a surety." He made a great show of unbuckling his claymore and leaning it against the wall of the barn. He led her back inside, where two lines formed for the first reel.

Abigail moved to John's side, watching closely as the lines of dancers shuffled up and back, then broke to swing their partners.

"Everyone knows the steps?" she asked.

He smiled. She'd never seen dancing of any sort, he supposed, and probably thought it sinful. "Aye, most do. I'm no' much of a dancer myself."

Her face looked slightly flushed. "Roy and Lizzie seem to be having a good time."

"Aye." His cousin swung Lizzie then returned to his place in the set. "Hungry?"

They stepped outside, where the aroma of roast pork awakened his belly. He guided Abigail to a couple of crude tables composed of boards over sawhorses. "Colonel Lewis donated a huge boar." The sun was sinking below the far ridge, and the air cooled abruptly. "Let's find a place by the fire."

The pork was delicious—and greasy. John wiped his hands on a slice of bread and reached for the bridie on his trencher. Abigail leaned over her food, undoubtedly trying to eat neatly.

"Russell, may I congratulate you." Colonel Lewis joined him on the other side. The fire had died down, flaring up as drips of hog fat fell from the remnants of the carcass.

"I thank ye. And for the pork. That were generous of ye."

Lewis frowned, his grizzled beard silver in the firelight. "One less troublemaker. I don't know why I raise pigs sometimes."

From the door of the barn John spotted Mr. Craig and his wife coming their way. He finished his bridie and stood. Perhaps he could speak with Lewis privately if the Craigs joined Abigail at the fire.

Isabella Craig greeted Abigail and they began to converse.

"Lewis," John said. "I've a question for ye." He jerked his chin toward the nearby oaks, and they slipped a few paces into the shadows.

"What's on your mind?"

"Have ye heard of a man named Silas Sloan? From Magraw's settlement?" John described Sloan's appearance.

Lewis pursed his lips. "There's a new hired man on the McKees' place that fits the description." He lifted one shoulder. "Is he dangerous? Or just a drunkard?"

John told him about the chandlery incident, and everything since, including Magraw's story of the scalps.

"You still itching to kill this feller?" There was steel in the casual question.

Colonel Lewis was sympathetic, but he was also the closest thing they had to a magistrate in the valley until an election was held. John had to be careful with his answer. "I wanted to kill him."

"Yes, you said your cousin stopped you."

"I want to do the right thing before God, but I canna let him harm my family."

Lewis regarded him. "I can't ask for a better answer. I'll find out this hired man's name and do what I can. D'you think the Shawnee are after him?"

"Could be." John described the Indian Abigail had treated.

The older man put his hands on his hips. "That could be a problem. You saw only one Indian?"

John nodded.

"Good. We don't need another massacre."

John had nothing to say to that. For a single moment in time, the smoke of the fire pit became the smoke of the muskets that awful evening. Then he blinked the image away.

Colonel Lewis's gaze rested on Abigail, sitting in the light of the fire. "Congratulations are in order, and I mean it, John Russell. I wouldn't have thought a Philadelphia girl would have that much gumption. Doctoring an Indian."

John nodded, warmth rising in his chest.

"Oh, and Russell—my son took the wagon over Rockfish Gap last week. So your sister should have your letter by now."

"Thank ye kindly." He frowned. His daughter would return soon.

But could he keep her safe with Sloan around?

31

How sweet and awful is the place
With Christ within the doors
While everlasting love displays
The sweetness of her stores

—Isaac Watts, *Hymns and Spiritual Songs,* 1707

October 1744

*A*bigail lay motionless under the warm buffalo skin for several moments, blinking away sleep from her eyes. She sat up, and with the smooth motion of habit, leaned over and plucked the chamber pot out from underneath the bed. They employed two chamber pots now—one for her, this well-glazed but unadorned brown piece of earthenware, and another green one for, well, ordinary uses.

She sat staring at the gleaming brown surface, smelling the sharp note of pine and hearing a fat pop from the hearth; John must've added a chunk of wood and stirred the embers while she slept. A wave of nausea rose but subsided.

Abigail eased out of bed and set the teakettle on, the smooth planking cold under her bare feet. *Coffee.* Today was the Sabbath, and real coffee or tea was a weekly treat. The soup kettle was full of water —John's doing—so she added oats, swung it over the fire, and added a piece of oak to the hearth. Usually breakfast consisted of barley brose or cornmeal mush—or leftovers of any kind—but on this day oat porridge did sound appealing.

Maybe she wouldn't suffer much longer. Maggie McClure said most ladies felt better about the time their bellies started swelling.

She placed a hand over her stomach. No, it was still flat. But it wouldn't be flat much longer. She approached the window, wondering when John would return from his morning chores. Like she often did, Abigail flipped up the wolf skin window cover over the wooden bar nailed just above, about the right size and shape for a curtain rod, once she made true curtains. For now, a wolf skin served the purpose and kept out the chill.

Cold early morning air slammed into her face and cut through the thin linen of her chemise. Abigail flipped the skin back down and fastened it. The cabin could be aired out later in the day, she decided.

She returned to the fire and jabbed it with the poker, then added coffee to the teakettle. John said that Susanna would be arriving soon, perhaps in a week or two. Did the little girl need clothing? Abigail's sewing basket overflowed with linsey-woolsey, already sized and cut for a shirt for John. Agnes had promised to help with the cuffs, and for once Abigail was looking forward to a sewing lesson. There was enough leftover material for a shirt for Ritchie, too. Did Susanna need a chemise?

But surely clothing was less important than other things. Susanna was a girl who'd lost her mother. In Philadelphia such problems had seemed far away. Abigail had stashed her New England Primer in her sea chest, not thinking of much beyond teaching the little girl to read, but now her heart rate quickened, pondering the situation. Would Susanna view her as an intruder?

She stirred the porridge. Cold air swirled around her ankles. Had she not properly secured the skin over the window?

"Good morning." John stood in the doorway, his face slightly flushed with both exertion and the chill of the air. He latched the door.

Lost in her thoughts, she hadn't heard him open it.

John made scraping motions with his feet over a mat of some sort —a mat she didn't recognize. Had he placed it there this morning?

"I wove this out of some rope I had." He stared at her helplessly, in the manner of a boy seeking approval.

Abigail stepped nearer and studied the tangle of brown hemp. He'd braided the strands and sewn them together somehow. But the clumsy mat would serve its purpose.

"I dinna want to spoil your clean floor." John lifted one of her hands and studied it. "Ye work too hard cleaning it."

It was true. Even with the sturdy new broom he'd fashioned for her, the cabin was hard to keep clean, and she hadn't wanted to mention the dirt and mud he continually tracked in. Her chest swelled with thankfulness.

"This is so thoughtful, John." Her throat tightened. She blinked— why would she cry over a mat?

John guided her to the bed where they sat. He must have snagged her jar of salve at some point, because he was now applying it to her hands. Her hands weren't *that* bad—no, not really.

Abigail sniffed and finally found her voice again. "Could we make one for Roy and Lizzie?"

John clasped her greasy hands between his own larger ones. "Oh, aye, let's—for their wedding. And a broom." His eyes stole back to the mat at the door. "I think with your help the next one will be prettier."

She smiled. "I like the first one, John. I always will."

THE SERMON WAS AN ORDINARY ONE; at least, it started out that way. Mr. Craig opened his heavy Bible and flipped to a passage. "John the third chapter," he began. On the front pew Mrs. Preston opened her fan.

Abigail recognized the story of Nicodemus coming to Jesus by night. He was a Pharisee, that much she remembered.

"Ye ken, Nicodemus was an important man. A learned man. He came by night because the other Pharisees would not approve. Now, the Pharisees believed the same way many believe today: that a man is saved by obedience to the Law of Moses. To the Commandments."

Abigail sat up straighter.

"Jesus explained that a man is saved by faith, not works, by reminding Nicodemus of the story of the fiery serpents in the wilderness. Moses made a brazen serpent for the bitten Israelites to look at, and if they did, they lived. All they had to do was look. Look and live."

Look and live. Was it that simple?

"There were no other conditions. Moses didna say, 'Only those who have tried their best,' or, 'Only those who also give an offering.' No, just look and live."

Mr. Craig cleared his throat and looked over the congregation. "Nicodemus went home. He didna respond to Jesus' words right away. Perhaps he had to mull it over some. Perhaps he was afraid of what the other Pharisees would think if he followed Jesus and confessed Him as the Messiah.

"Here is what we do know: later, he helped Joseph of Arimathea take down the body of Jesus from the cross. He helped prepare the body for burial. For a Jew, touching a dead body made the person unclean for a time. And it was Passover. He was stepping away from the other Jewish leaders, stepping away from Passover, and publicly identifying with Christ, no matter what the cost."

Abigail was stunned. She'd never heard this part of the story before. In her mind, Pharisees were hypocrites, somehow incurably bad. But this man—a hypocrite?—had embraced Christ. She could too.

She blinked back tears. Behind her, she heard a sniffle. She wasn't the only one affected.

The whole meetinghouse seemed unnaturally still, and it seemed as if the whole room glowed with a light she couldn't see.

Then, far behind her, a man bellowed incoherently and broke down in sobs.

JOHN SOAKED IN THE SERMON. He remembered Nicodemus but had forgotten his presence at the cross. Mr. Craig was a blessing.

At his side his wife seemed attentive as usual. She always seemed to welcome the Word of God, whether it came from him or from the minister. It was a good sign.

Abigail raised her handkerchief to her face. Mrs. Preston fluttered her fan unconcernedly in front of him, but he heard muffled sniffles from behind—was it the lad, William? He didn't know how much gospel preaching the Kerrs had been under before now.

His own heart felt tender. The self-accusations he'd carried around began to dissolve in a bittersweet awareness of God's forgiveness through Christ. Why didn't he always stand in awe of the great work of Christ in redemption? But he was a man, forgetful. Thank God for His goodness in drawing him back to Himself, time and time again. He surely didn't deserve it. He blinked back tears.

Someone groaned and bellowed from the back. A man he didn't know—no, he recognized the rough timbre of the voice, even disguised as it was by sobbing.

Silas Sloan.

John stiffened but remained still. His eyes flickered up to the minister's face—what did he make of it? Mr. Craig was alert, but calm, finishing his sermon with a final exhortation.

Abigail seemed unconcerned as well. Perhaps she hadn't recognized the voice. John didn't move, not wanting to disturb the service, but he moved his hand to his side. The bulge of his loaded pistol under his coat reassured him, but he'd rely on his knife if he needed to act quickly. The firearm wasn't primed.

Why would a man like Silas Sloan attend meeting? He'd have thought the man past redemption. His pulse raced and throbbed.

"Let us pray," Mr. Craig instructed.

John bowed his head slightly but did not close his eyes. When the prayer ended he turned around in his seat.

Sloan was gone.

JOHN TOOK the trencher of bear stew from Abigail, but his focus was on Mr. Craig's face across from him. Why a visit in the middle of the week?

"Thank ye kindly," the minister said to Abigail as she sat on her accustomed stool. "This smells delicious." He led them in asking a blessing for the midday meal.

"I only wish your wife could have accompanied you," Abigail said. "'Tis a treat to have folks come to visit." A few blond strands dangled from his wife's hairline, having escaped the pins.

"Isabella is at the Robinsons' place. It seemed a good time to bring a basket."

Abigail nodded at the minister in agreement.

John fought a smile. He knew better than to mention child-bearing in mixed company, but everyone could see that Mrs. Robinson would have another bairn soon.

"John." Craig took a large bite of stew and chewed thoughtfully, his brows arching. "A man named Silas Sloan came to see me."

John swallowed and his gut constricted. He put his spoon back in the trencher.

"I see ye ken the name."

"I do."

Mr. Craig sighed. "Sloan's broken up by the sermons he's been hearing."

"I heard him cry out at the meeting last Lord's Day."

Abigail's face had gone white. "That was him?"

John's shoulders slumped. Should he have said something? "I didn't want to upset ye."

Mr. Craig waved his hand in dismissal. "Dinna fash—I dinna think the man's a danger. Not at this point." He took another bite and swallowed. "I believe he's been converted. Or at least, under thorough conviction of sin."

"Explain." His own voice sounded harsh, but could it be true?

"Sloan told me a bit of his history, especially those parts involving the both of you."

"He told ye that he attacked my wife?" John's hand clenched.

"Aye, he did. He's been attending the meetings—in secret, sometimes only listening outside the windows. Something drew him, he said, even though his sins appeared blacker and blacker each Sabbath. He had no hope. Not to mention, the Shawnee were on his trail. He'd been attacked once, shot the man, and escaped, but suspected it was only a matter of time before they caught up to him again."

That explained the wounded Indian. John idly stirred the stew with his spoon. "Did he explain why they were after him?"

Mr. Craig nodded. "Sloan broke down in telling the tale. He took the lives of two innocent people in seeking revenge for the death of his wife."

A sudden realization shook him. He'd almost done the same. Not that Sloan was innocent, but wasn't innocence relative? Who was he, a sinner, to take vengeance on another sinner?

He looked up. Abigail was studying him, her face a picture of concern. Did she know what he was thinking? After all they'd been through, he wouldn't doubt it.

"Well then, Mr. Craig, why come to me with all this?"

"I believe Silas Sloan has repented, John Russell. He kens that he's wronged ye, and wants to make things right as much as he can. He wants to meet with ye."

32

With Christ our Lord, we share our part
In the affections of His heart,
Nor shall our souls be thence removed
Till He forgets His first Beloved.

—Isaac Watts, *Hymns and Spiritual Songs,* 1707

"*A*bigail?" A muffled voice accompanied the knock on the cabin door.

Maggie McClure? Abigail stood and smoothed her apron.

John wolfed down the last of his cornbread. It was a wonder he'd eaten at all, considering. Abigail had forced her own breakfast down her throat, trying not to picture his meeting with Silas Sloan at midday. Of course she couldn't come. But then, what could she do in any case? And if what Mr. Craig said was correct, they wouldn't come to blows.

John set his cup down. "Are ye expecting Mrs. McClure?"

Abigail shook her head as she stepped to the door and unfastened the latch.

"Abigail." Maggie's warm presence filled the doorway, blocking most of the brisk morning air. "I'm on my way to the Robinsons." Her gaze flickered to John, then back again. "It's her time." A furrow deepened between her brows.

Abigail frowned. "You want me to come?" She had no experience with midwifery.

"I can use another pair of hands. And ye're close neighbors, forbye."

She was right. Anne Robinson had several little ones—more than several. Would this be her sixth child? If nothing else, she could help mind the children. Abigail turned to John.

He nodded, the blue of his eyes a fathomless sea behind a glass wall. "I'll get the horses and ride down with ye. I'll sit with Rob until it's time for my errand."

My errand. Her heart lurched.

"Thank ye, Mr. Russell." Maggie lowered her voice, speaking in Abigail's ear. "Men are useless during childbirth. Dinna ken what to do with themselves. They need minding just like the bairns."

Abigail's chuckle died in her throat as she watched John leave for the barn. She took down her herb satchel, full of new additions she'd found in the valley. Distracted, she picked through the linen bags within. She really had no idea what a midwife would need. *Or what John would need if …*

Maggie nodded in approval. "I've got my own mix of herbs for tea. I add nettle for strength, fennel for milk, and yarrow for the bleeding."

Yarrow. Yes, she had plenty of that. It was plentiful here, and she'd gathered quite a bit before the first frost had wilted even the hardiest asters. It was good for wounds … but no, she needed to focus on the Robinsons. Maybe Lizzie could come. "Maggie? I'll go to the Mays' cabin and see if Agnes can help us with dinner—and Lizzie may be of help too."

"Aye, good thinking. And Lizzie's little lad can play with the children."

THE ROBINSONS' cabin lacked John's guiding hand—Abigail could see that at once. Here and there, tiny chinks let in cool air, and the crude chimney drew poorly. A veil of smoke made her sneeze when she walked over the threshold.

Pursing her lips, Maggie McClure stood at the bedside, hands on her stout hips. "Abigail, we'll open the window for now. I want to build up that fire and heat some water."

Abigail studied the woman on the bed. Her dark hair snaked damp about her face, dark eyes staring off at something unseen. Anne Robinson was thin, her face pale under a summer's golden brown. One corded forearm curled around her huge midsection.

"Ma'am," Lizzie broke in. "Mr. Russell showed me a fire pit—I'll stoke a fire and boil water out here."

"Good—we can keep the window closed." Maggie shooed the children out to play. "A woman needs her privacy."

In a matter of minutes, the teakettle was on the hearth, its glowing coals sufficient for the purpose, and *thunks* resonated outside as the men took turns chopping wood for the fire pit. Mrs. McClure sat next to her charge, and Abigail opened her bag.

A big wad of linen diaper sat on top. After doctoring the Indian, she'd determined that the fabric was well suited for bandages and stashed some in her swelling satchel. She snipped off several lengths for toweling and dampened a piece.

Abigail sat on the side of the bed and wiped the woman's forehead gently, smoothing back the dark locks that had strayed from her long braid.

"I canna do it again, Maggie," Mrs. Robinson hissed, her voice raspy with strain. She twisted on the ratty quilt beneath her.

"Fiddlesticks, Anne. Everyone says that. Take a deep breath, now."

Maggie's voice was light and cheerful, but her smile failed to reach her eyes. "The babe will be here soon."

Under her damp shift, Mrs. Robinson's belly was enormous. Abigail had seen women in Philadelphia wearing outsized skirts in a vain attempt to conceal a growing child. But she'd never seen a woman so swollen.

The tittering voices of playing children filtered through the chinks in the cabin, a strange counterpoint to Mrs. Robinson's groans. Abigail placed a hand over her own belly. Was childbirth always this bad?

She rinsed out the cloth and resumed ministering to the woman.

"Get away!" Mrs. Robinson barked.

Abigail retreated.

"Never mind," Maggie murmured. "She's crankit. They all are." She met Abigail's gaze. "Get me the hot water now. It willna be long."

She grabbed the bucket. Did Maggie want her there? Or need her? By the time Abigail had hauled in two steaming buckets she knew the answer. Mrs. McClure was worried.

Women spoke darkly of confinement sometimes. But some women gave birth to more than twelve children. What was Maggie worried about?

The regular *thunk* of the wood axe outside had ceased by the time Maggie urged her charge to a reclining position. "Abigail, put your arm around her shoulders and hold her hands if she wants ye to."

Maggie crouched at the foot of the bed, and the furrows in the midwife's forehead caused Abigail's stomach to churn.

"Anne, that's a good lass now. Give us a push." Maggie's cheery voice was edged with command. One arm curved around Mrs. Robinson's belly as if assisting the effort.

Mrs. Robinson howled and grabbed at Abigail's hands so hard it seemed as her finger bones would snap. "Canna do it," she wailed.

Then the pains left, and the woman sagged against Abigail, her dark head canted to the side.

Abigail's arms went numb as the pains came and went, the dim cabin echoing with painful cries. When would the agony end? *Lord, help her. Preserve her—and the child.*

"One more, girl! One hard push!" There was a note of triumph in Maggie's voice.

Mrs. Robinson whimpered. Her limbs slackened.

"A beautiful boy!" The midwife lifted her brows, signaling Abigail to come.

The thin mewling cry of a newborn caused Abigail's heart to lurch in gladness. She took the baby and wiped him down as Maggie tied the cord and cut it. Finally the infant was safe and warm in a blanket.

"D'ye have any more of that cloth?" Maggie asked.

Abigail passed her some of the linen while holding the baby in one arm. "Do I give her the babe?"

Maggie shook her head. "She's exhausted. And we're not done."

Abigail gaped.

"I think there's another coming."

Throat dry, Abigail placed the infant in a basket, his periodic whimpers mixing with his mother's, and returned to her place at the head of the bed.

"Push, Anne. I ken ye can hear me." Cords in Maggie's neck stood out as if she were the one in agony. "Push, lass!" There was a desperate note in her voice Abigail hadn't heard before.

Mrs. Robinson heaved, her entire body stiff with effort. She wrenched Abigail's arms until stars flashed in her vision.

"Good lass—ye've done it!" Sweat ran down Maggie's face. "A little girl."

Tears welled in Abigail's eyes. A second little cry rose beside the first. Soon the twin babies were snuggled side by side in the basket, and they quieted, as if relieved to be together again.

Mrs. Robinson lay insensate.

"Abigail, I need more towels. Or rags. Anything." Maggie's eyes widened with fear.

Bringing the rags, Abigail saw a spreading pool of blood at the foot of the bed. "Is that to be expected?"

"Some, aye. Not this much."

The midwife adjusted her position and kneaded the woman's belly like dough—only harder. Mrs. Robinson flinched once but made no protest.

Blood—bleeding. She knew what to do for bleeding. "Maggie, I have plenty of yarrow."

"Aye, I ken, in the tea—no time for that."

"I have an idea."

JOHN DISMOUNTED, the smooth leather of Percy's reins sliding through his clammy hands. He realized he'd chosen the lee side of the animal, away from the other man, with the horse between them. But this was not a battle. He took a deep breath. *Help, Lord.*

Silas Sloan stood quietly at the edge of the Tinkling Springs graveyard, hands hanging empty at his sides. Sloan's horse was ground-tied under a nearby maple, its leaves flashing blood red.

John led Percy toward the other animal. "Good day to ye." His words felt sharp as steel in his mouth.

Sloan's dark eyes followed him. He smelled the same as before—even bears didn't smell this rank. The only thing worse than a man who never bathed was a skunk. But there was something about Sloan's demeanor that was different.

He wasn't scowling.

John's innards relaxed a notch. "Mr. Craig said ye wanted to meet me."

Sloan nodded. "You have aught against me, as the Good Book says." His Adam's apple bobbed and he shifted his stance. "I will give you what you ask." He hesitated. "The Shawnee want my life. I don't know what to give you."

How could Sloan make it right? Abigail's nightmares were the least of it. John clenched his fists and forced himself to relax them. He wished for the minister's presence.

John scanned the graveyard and the meetinghouse beyond then jerked his chin. "Let's water the horses at the spring." He needed time to think.

Percy nuzzled him gently as he led her to the water. The sun, warm on his back, chased away the autumn chill. The horses slobbered into the water companionably. Somewhere, a chickadee twittered.

The beauty of the day mocked him.

Sloan was asking him to extract payment. *An eye for an eye.* He was asking him to serve as judge and executioner. The Shawnee had no qualms about doing just that.

He'd had no qualms either that day on the stream bank.

"I would've killed ye, ye ken." He picked up the tin cup from its place on a rock next to the gurgling, tinkling water. "Here."

Sloan nodded and took the cup. "Yes—and I would have gone straight to hell." He filled the cup but sat on a stone clutching it. "I deserved to perish," he choked out, and one great tear rolled down his cheek, disappearing into the blackness of his beard.

John's throat seized up. A man stealer—a kidnapper—deserved death according to the Law of Moses. But the mercy of God through Christ had covered his own sins and wretchedness. How could he ask for naked justice?

A verse of Scripture dropped into his heart.

33

No condemnation now I dread;
Jesus and all in him is mine!
Alive in Him, my living Head,
and clothed in righteousness divine!

—Charles Wesley, *A Collection of Hymns,* 1814

*J*ohn slackened the reins and let Percy have her way. But instead of trying to head for the cabin, the mare picked her way toward the Robinsons' home, her gait smooth and sure. Was she reading his mind? More likely, the horse had decided Abigail was a part of him and winged her way back to his wife's location, like a swan to her nesting place.

Peace flooded his heart. He knew he'd made the right decision when he'd seen the look on Sloan's face.

A curl of wood smoke topped the cottonwoods ahead, marking the Robinsons' property. Had the babe been born yet? Sometimes babies took a long time to appear—his own daughter had. The memory of Susanna's birth rushed into his mind, fresh as if it were yesterday.

Janet had labored all night, her face tense but uncomplaining. Incredibly, she'd swept the cabin by the light of a candle and stirred up cornbread to bake in the hearth, stopping her work now and again as the pains hit her.

He'd hovered, wanting her to rest, but she'd only shrugged. "I canna sleep anyway."

Just as the ghostly gray light of wintry dawn seeped in the window, a gush of water drenched her skirts.

"Time for Maggie," Janet said. She looked at him but her focus was elsewhere.

He fled in search of the midwife.

Maggie McClure chased him off to the Mays' cabin, and Arch took him in hand, pulling him along his factor's trap lines, half covered in snow, until he couldn't feel his feet.

When the afternoon sun dimmed behind the clouds, he thawed himself at the Mays' hearth. Barely eating, he moved about in a fog until finally Maggie appeared at the door.

"It's a girl." The midwife's tired face had beamed.

Susanna. Was his baby girl almost five years old now? It hardly seemed possible. And she'd be returning any day. His heart ached with joy at the thought.

The Robinsons' cabin came within view. The fire in the pit had died down, and the children were out of sight. He frowned, surveying the structure. Before the snows, the Robinsons needed to repair the cabin and plug the chinks. He could check the faulty chimney and see what he could do. And the Kerr lads—and even Ritchie—could help with the chinking.

He slid off Percy. "Hallo, the house!"

Abigail stumbled out the door, her hair tumbled down from its normal neat coils. Was something wrong? A sudden chill coursed through him. Women could die in childbirth. Abigail was—

"John?" Abigail's apron was damp and spotted.

He gathered her in his arms. "Is the babe—?"

She smiled. "Twins."

His shoulders slumped in relief. Everything must be fine, then. He led her to a crude bench and eased her down. She looked exhausted, and dark streaks of blood marked one arm. "Is Mrs. Robinson well?"

She nodded, frowning. "Maggie says twin births are hard on a woman. Dangerous. She's still very weak."

Mrs. McClure emerged from the cabin, mopping her face with a rag. She spotted him. "Thank ye, Mr. Russell, for your wife." She sank down beside them. "Did she tell ye it was twins?" At his nod, she continued. "Abigail saved her life, most likely."

What?

"Yarrow stops bleeding," Abigail said simply.

Maggie snorted. "But I'd have never thought to—"

Abigail cleared her throat.

John chuckled, guessing the reason for the interruption. He'd married a discreet New England lass after all. But canny, too. "What do ye need, Mrs. McClure? Agnes has a big kettle of something on the hearth. I'll send some with Roy and Lizzie."

"Thank ye kindly. I'm starved. And there's all the young'uns to feed too."

God bless Mrs. McClure.

"John?" Abigail asked, a slight tremor in her voice.

They'd spoken little on the way back to the cabin, but he'd felt her gaze on him. "I saw Sloan. Dinna fash, it went well." He'd explain more once he saw to the animals.

He wiped down the horses, went to Roy's cabin to arrange for the transport of the meal, and returned to find Abigail clean and neat as a pin. Savory smells filled the cabin.

"Agnes ladled some stew out for us and forbade me to help."

A pot hung from the hook over the fire. "Smells good." His mouth twitched. "Dinna tell her but I like yours better."

"But I've been copying her!"

"But ye put in wee bits of this and that. Herbs and such."

Abigail's eyebrow lifted and she smiled. It was good to see after the drama of the morning. After his own drama.

She poured them both some ale, which he took gratefully.

"I spoke to Sloan." He took a swallow of the ale. "He wanted to make things right but wasna sure how."

Abigail rubbed the hem of her apron between her fingers.

He met her gaze. "I didna ken what to do, what to tell him." He set aside the tankard, his insides clogged with emotion.

"You didn't want revenge?" she guessed.

He nodded. "I couldna ... not after what Christ has done for me."

"I know."

"Ye do?"

"When Mr. Craig preached about Nicodemus..."

He leaned forward. "The Pharisee?"

She nodded, her eyes glistening with unshed tears. "I thought, if God would forgive him, then He would receive me."

John scooted his stool next to hers and wrapped his arms around her. "Aye, we serve a good God." His heart seemed to swell and he blinked away a tear. Abigail had found safety, not just in his feeble arms, but in the arms of the Beloved.

"Do you think Christ has received Sloan too?" she asked.

John found it hard to speak. "Aye, he seems a different man." He released her and held her hands. "I couldna ask an eye for an eye. That's in the Bible, ye ken, but that's for the magistrate, not the believer."

Abigail wiped her eyes. "So what did you tell him?"

"The Bible says to turn the other cheek, and that I will do. I will forgive him from my heart." John winced. The memory of the stream bank could still bring back a rush of rage, but the heat of his anger had subsided. "But I kent that his conscience needed relief. And restitution is right at all times."

"But he didn't steal. How could he restore?"

"There is a verse in the Old Testament about a young man who…" His face warmed. "Let's just say he does what he ought not to do with a young lady. He must either marry her or pay her father the bride price."

Abigail's lips parted as she grasped the context. "But Sloan never…"

"The penalty for man-stealing is death."

Her eyes widened. "John. You chose a lesser penalty." She turned and looked into the hearth, the fire now a feeble flicker. "So he will pay you money?"

"He doesna have much, so I will take it in labor."

"Around here?" She seemed unsettled at this.

"Aye, but perhaps he can also help other folks get their cabins ready for winter."

Her face cleared. "The Robinsons?"

He grinned. "Aye."

ABIGAIL SWALLOWED, her throat strangely dry. Her neck felt hot—but then, the meetinghouse had warmed with the crush of bodies during the morning sermon.

Mr. Craig had closed the service, and his piercing gray gaze was now on her.

"I've examined Mrs. John Russell and determined that she qualifies for membership in the kirk. She will be permitted to partake of Communion this afternoon."

The examination at the Craigs' cabin had been pointed, but brief, followed by a teary-eyed hug from Isabella.

"We've been praying for ye," the dark-eyed woman had said.

"You could tell I wasn't a true Christian?"

"Not by your actions, no. But by your words. We could see that ye were under great conviction. Ye kent the truth but had trouble believing it." Isabella pursed her lips. "I need to tell ye something. A true believer can fall back into doubt. Lose his assurance, though he is safe in Christ still. Sometimes because of sin, sometimes for other reasons."

"What should I do if that happens?"

"Look to Christ. Dinna look at your doubts or failures. His work is finished for all time, and He ever lives to make intercession for us." She turned her eyes to the men. "And speak to your husband. He'll help ye."

Abigail blinked back the memory as John's hand slid over hers.

Mr. Craig was still speaking. "I have also examined Silas Sloan and recommend him for membership."

Rustling and murmurs met this announcement. Mrs. Preston's fan fluttered at twice its normal rate.

"I've heard unsavory things about this man." Captain Patton, Mrs. Preston's brother, sat in the front. Abigail could finally keep the names straight. The two large landowners, John Lewis and James Patton, were always at loggerheads according to John.

"I've heard unsavory things about a current member of our assembly." Mr. Craig stared unflinchingly at Patton.

Someone gasped.

"Any man or woman desiring membership must show evidence of repentance and faith," the minister said. "I am convinced Mr. Sloan possesses this evidence. Any further questions about either new member will be directed to myself." His eyes swept the room. "We can speak over the noon meal."

"Ye overstep yourself, Craig." Patton shot to his feet, his dark hair and huge size reminding Abigail of a certain sea captain who'd come to the chandlery occasionally. She'd thought of him as a pirate, and scurried into her father's office at the sight of him.

Mr. Craig didn't raise his voice, but every corner of the meetinghouse could hear his reply. "Christ is King of the kirk, and ye'd do well to remember that."

The tension in the room alarmed Abigail. Next to her, John seemed taut, rigid, his feet drawn up under him as if to spring.

"Patton, I'm hungry," drawled Colonel Lewis from the back. "Can this wait?"

The room seemed to heave a collective sigh, and in moments the congregation spilled out the door into the fall sunshine. Abigail made her way to the wagon, where they'd packed their dinner and ale. Lizzie, Sophie, and Agnes soon joined her.

But under the huge oak where Roy had hobbled the horses two unfamiliar mules grazed. Next to the mules stood several people.

And a little girl.

34

Pity the nations, O our God,
constrain the earth to come;
send Thy victorious Word abroad
and bring the strangers home.

—Isaac Watts, *Hymns and Spiritual Songs,* 1707

*S*usanna was taller, John was almost sure of it. Her dark hair was pulled back like an older girl's, bound in a net and fastened with a red ribbon over the top of her head. She was certainly dressed more neatly than he'd ever been able to accomplish— between the headgear and the matching short red cloak, her appearance revealed the influence of his sister. His daughter's warm brown eyes searched the crowd.

He strode toward her, heart aching at the thought that he'd neglected his daughter for so many months after Janet's death. Left her to dress and behave as she would. His sister, Sarah, had helped in various ways, as had Agnes, but still, he'd been absent from his own child in heart and soul.

"Da!" She'd spotted him.

Then he kneeled, eager to embrace her, but hesitating in his guilt. "Susanna," he croaked.

"We're late for meeting," she said, grinning and bouncing from foot to foot. Then her smile faded. "I'm sorry, Da." Her eyes searched his face; she'd probably spotted the lone tear that had escaped his eyes.

"No, my sweet rose. Folks weep for happiness sometimes." He blinked and sniffed.

Then her arms were around his neck. "I haven't lost the wee stone ye gave me." She released him and fumbled under her cloak. "Cousin Willie made me a locket to put it in." She drew out a tiny container made of walnut burl and finished to a high shine. "He had help from his da but he did *most* of it himself." Her eyebrows rose to emphasize this point.

John slid open the trinket. The clasp was ingenious. Willie's father had done most of the work, that was sure. Her little rose-colored stone, smooth from years in the streambed where he'd found it, peeped from within. "What a fine locket. Willie must be a canny lad."

A shadow fell next to them on the grass. "Hello, Johnny."

John looked up. "Sarah." He scrambled awkwardly to his feet. "Did ye fare well on the journey?" They'd arrived at a strange time— and he saw mules but no wagon. His sister seemed well enough, dressed for meeting with her hair bound up under her best straw hat, but where had they spent the night?

"An axle broke, and we camped last night in Rockfish Gap. Rode the mules down this morning."

"An axle?" John glanced at his brother-in-law, James, who stood near his wife, dark hair ruffling in the breeze. "We can help ye after dinner. I'm sure Agnes packed enough food for everyone."

"Thank ye kindly." James's hazel eyes seemed to smile, but he was looking elsewhere.

Abigail.

"Who's that lady, Da?"

ABIGAIL DREW NEARER, hoping to get a better view without calling attention to herself. Susanna had dark hair, much like John's—bound quite neatly in a finely knitted snood of the type Abigail had seen on young ladies in the valley—and dark eyes, unlike her father's. Her mother must have had brown eyes. Abigail swallowed past a lump in her throat. She felt like an intruder. *Help, Lord.*

Susanna sported a tiny cleft in her chin just like her father, and something about her mouth reminded her of John, but the rest of her face might have been her mother's. And she seemed tall. Kitty Kerr was a year older, but not quite as big.

Susanna put her arms around John's neck as he crouched in front of his daughter, and Abigail's stomach tumbled. She took a step closer, trying to see his face. It gladdened her to see his joy in their reunion, though at the same time a tiny edge of doubt crept in. How would the little girl react to her?

Behind Susanna stood a man and woman—she must be his sister; she did resemble John around the eyes, blue and snapping with life and wry humor. Her auburn hair was a shade in between John's and Roy's, quite comely, tucked under a straw bergère-style hat.

The man stood slightly behind her and to the side. His sleeves were rolled up, revealing knotted forearms folded across his chest. Deep sun lines framed his eyes—kindly eyes, despite his no-nonsense stance.

The man looked her way.

Susanna's gaze also shifted to her. "Who's that lady, Da?"

John turned, and his gaze sought hers for a moment. "That's Mrs. Russell." He stepped closer and took her hand in his.

Her heart thudded in her chest. "Susanna. Such a pretty name."

"Are you my new ma? Aunt Sarah says I'm getting a new ma." Her brow furrowed. "I think ye look like an angel."

Abigail exhaled, not realizing she'd been holding her breath.

"Why d'ye say that?" John asked.

"Angels have golden hair. I saw it in a book. And since Ma's in heaven, she'd have to send a new ma from heaven."

Abigail knelt and removed her hat. "Here, touch my hair. 'Tis ordinary hair."

Susanna took a step closer but did not touch her. "So ye're no' an angel?"

"No," John said. "But God did send her." He glanced at Abigail, eyes twinkling.

The little girl looked to her father and back, and an expression of wonder grew on her features. "She *is* my new ma. Because ye have that same look on your face, Da. Ye look at her like ye looked at Ma."

JOHN WAS STUPEFIED. An angel in a book? What book was that? But the question melted before her last pronouncement.

Ye look at her like ye looked at Ma.

He met Abigail's gaze. She seemed equally at sea. He smiled at his wife, shyly, as if it were their wedding day. He'd felt his affections for her growing day by day, first on the road, then here in the valley, as they faced each challenge together. And when the Lord had given her new life in Christ, why his joy had known no bounds.

But he knew no one could replace Janet in his heart. Well, maybe Abigail hadn't. Maybe Abigail had her own place—and it was certainly a good place, a large place. His chest tightened.

"Aye, Susanna, she is your new ma." A thought struck him. "But what shall ye call her? We canna say 'new ma', do ye ken?"

"How about, 'Mother'?" Abigail's voice sounded husky. "'Tis what I call my own mother."

"Why do ye talk strangely?" his daughter asked.

It was a rude question, but an honest one. "Your new mother was born in Boston, a city on the ocean with many ships."

Susanna's face lit up. "Is that close to London?"

John glanced at Sarah and quirked an eyebrow.

"We stopped on the trip back with an order Peter Jefferson had placed with the Bashams," his sister said. "A curio cabinet. His wife Jane hails from London, or thereabouts."

He picked up his daughter. "Well, my rose, ye are seeing the great wide world. And your new mother shall teach ye all sorts of things. Now then, is anyone hungry?"

JOHN HAD a hard time keeping his mind on the adult conversation. Susanna had kept to herself for most of the meal, shy of the other children, but now she was playing some sort of game that involved holding hands with the others and singing or chanting some verses. Ritchie, Kitty, and one of the Robinson children linked hands with Susanna and spun around in the circle yet again.

"John? Are ye attending?" James asked.

"Och, forgive me."

"I ken ye are glad to see your daughter. We enjoyed having her."

James and Sarah had no children of their own yet, and there was nothing he could say to ease that. "Roy will help ye, then, with the wagon, and we'll see ye tomorrow?"

"Aye. Ye'll like to see my cargo." James's eyes twinkled. "I managed to lay my hands on plans for a sawmill."

"How?" John knew their habits. The Bashams went to Williamsburg only once a year or so.

"Peter Jefferson—ye'll have heard of the man? He lives only a day's ride from here. He's a surveyor, and he's got a good hand. Drew me a fair copy of plans he had in his own library." James cast his eyes on the wooded hillside behind the meetinghouse. "Put some cedar in my wagon and I'll see about some gears for the mill. I'm sure they're available in Williamsburg."

This was wonderful news. Sawing a log using a two-man sawpit was backbreaking work. And slow. "I thank ye—thank ye kindly." John grasped his brother-in-law's hand warmly. They'd construct the simple mill right on their property, next to the stream. *Thank you, Lord.*

"John Russell?"

His brother-in-law's gaze shifted. They both turned.

"Mr. McKee. How may I help ye?" John asked. The slight scowl on the man's lined face unsettled him.

"Silas Sloan. There's rumors about him."

James's gaze met his own, eyebrow lifting in acknowledgement. He moved off and joined his wife.

"Aye." John took a deep breath and faced the man. McKee wasn't a particular friend of Patton—but if Sloan's run-in with the Shawnee were known, or even suspected, he would become *persona non grata*, regardless of the source of the information.

"I have nae complaints about his work. Nae complaints at all." McKee studied the dirt at his feet. "But ye ken, I canna have the Shawnee coming to my door." He looked up, his gaze fixed on John.

"So why are ye telling me this?" John's jaw clenched. He had exactly the same concerns.

"I say, he has nae place in our community." When he continued, his voice was low, pitched only for John's ears. "I ken ye support Mr. Craig. I have nae problem with it, ye ken. But ye're a practical-minded man. Ye ken we maun defend ourselves. I've seen your new rifle and I ken what it means. If we receive Sloan into the kirk ..." He shrugged, as if the rest did not need to be explained.

And no, it really didn't. He stood alone before McKee, the breeze gusting in his ears. How to answer this question?

His father's words came to his mind: *duty is the foundation of all good choices.*

Did he have a duty here? Yes, he did.

"I understand ye fine, McKee. But Sloan has a debt to pay. He owes me something, and until that is settled, we'll have no talk of running anyone off."

He'd just taken the man under his protection. But the Shawnee were after him. His innards seized up at the thought. *Abigail ... Susanna.*

McKee huffed.

"Dinna mind it, McKee. My rifle will be loaded."

35

And I add this Part here, to hint to whoever shall read it,
that whenever they come to a true Sense of things, they
will find Deliverance from Sin a much greater Blessing,
than Deliverance from Affliction.

—Daniel Defoe, *Robinson Crusoe*, 1719

December 1744

𝒶 cold tendril of wintry air from the open window snaked
over Abigail's neck as she sat sewing with Susanna seated
next to her. Lizzie perched on a stool on the other side of the hearth.
At least their feet and legs were warm this close to the glowing logs.
The temperature had plummeted after James and Sarah had
returned to their home east of the Gap, and the oaks had lost their
leaves. Still, sewing required good light, and enduring a bit of chill
was worth it.

Abigail drew another stitch through the hem of the curtain.

"Here, Susanna. You make two stitches, and then I will make several more." The leftover remnants of the yellow Calicut cotton would look beautiful—and cheerful—on the window.

"But Mother, your stitches are so much better."

Mother. It was the first time the little girl had addressed her so, and the corner of her mouth twitched into a smile. "You do quite well for your first try. My stitches were very poor when I was small." Her mother had given her tongue-lashings for her errors, tongue-lashings that in retrospect weren't all that harsh. What would Mother say to making curtains out of this expensive fabric? A waste? No, she'd probably make the excuse that in such a wilderness something beautiful was necessary for a woman's sanity.

Susanna handed the yellow rectangle back to her. "How is this?" Her brows lifted uncertainly.

Two large, jagged stitches sprawled along the fold. "Just a bit big. Here, watch how I do it." As Abigail demonstrated, tiny taps in her belly distracted her. "Oh!"

"What is it, Mother?"

Abigail had felt flutters before, unsure if what she guessed were true. "Lizzie, I think someone is trying to get my attention."

"What do ye mean?" Lizzie paused over her mending.

Abigail's cheeks warmed as she slid a hand over her gently swollen abdomen. "Little taps in my belly."

Lizzie grinned. "Susanna, your wee brother or sister wants to join the conversation."

The little girl's mouth formed a wide "O" as she looked at Abigail.

"You will be a big sister soon. In the spring." The nausea had subsided, just as Maggie had predicted. The flutters and kicks filled her with joy.

"I'll tell Ritchie and Kitty. Will we have twins? Like the Robinsons?" Susanna squirmed on her seat.

Abigail hoped not. "Probably just the one baby." Her heart warmed to see Susanna enthused.

Lizzie continued to smile as she bent over a shirt—Roy's?—on her stool. She was always smiling, her cheeks rosy—generally from the cold, but the wedding was only two weeks away. Even a widow could blush—and Abigail was glad of it. Though John rarely spoke of Janet, she'd sensed her death had left a great and gaping wound in his soul, taking many months to ease, and likewise Lizzie's own expression had occasionally turned melancholy in Philadelphia. But now Lizzie was all blushing happiness.

Abigail rose to stir the kettle over the hearth. Silas Sloan had brought down a fat yearling buck, and John had rejoiced, saying it would be prime eating. A large chunk of the haunch was stewing in the kettle, along with onions, turnips, barley, and a bit of thyme; the fragrant mixture simmered almost to the brim, enough for all the men. They'd been working in the sawpit for days, and returned for meals famished and filthy.

Abigail opened the lid over the cornbread, and a toasty smell made her mouth water. Almost done.

She moved to the window. Still no sign of the men.

JOHN'S SHOULDERS ACHED. Underneath his buckskin jacket, his sweat was drying, mixed with the filth of the sawpit, and embedding yet another layer of grime in his linen shirt. But this morning had been their last foray into the sawpit, and Abigail would be able to wash it. He envisioned the hogshead he'd obtained for bathing from the cooper. He had no objection to a good soak. After three days of hard work they all stank.

"Thank ye, Roy." He glanced at his cousin on the wagon seat next to him. "But next time wear gloves, ye ken?" Roy had been transporting the finished planks—first to the Kerrs' cabin, then to his own.

Roy sucked at his palm briefly while holding the reins with his other hand. "I'll get Lizzie to pull out this splinter. And thank ye for the offer of Sloan's labor. Not that I like the man, but with his help I'll get the new field cleared that much faster."

John studied Sloan's form, a dark figure far up the path before them. The man was built like an ox and no stranger to labor. The Kerrs were already nailing in their new oak rafters, and by the end of the day he'd have his own pile of boards ready for roofing the new addition. But he could do that himself. Best to let Sloan help Roy for a time.

He supposed he'd forgiven the man, but from time to time a tickle of uncertainty would nag at him. It was one thing to forgive, and another to trust. As they'd gone first to the Robinsons' and then to the Stuarts', helping them to weatherproof their homes, he'd kept his eye on the dark man the way he would a skittish horse.

But Silas Sloan had shown himself trustworthy over the past few weeks, silent for the most part, and willing to throw his weight into the harness. By the time John had decided to haul some oak logs down to the sawpit, he'd been able to trust him to a point—at least able to face him from the other end of a sharp double-handled saw.

Sloan disappeared in the trees ahead. The wagon jolted over a rut, and the boards in the wagon bed clattered. John's belly contracted in hunger. What was Abigail cooking for their midday meal?

As the horses pulled the wagon up the slope leading to their cabin, and nearly naked trees thickened on either side of the trail, doubt still niggled at John's mind. It wasn't just about Sloan—the man was rapidly proving himself—but it was everyone else. As for the Shawnee, they hadn't returned in over a month. John's rifle was always loaded, but it always would be. Danger was a constant here. His own fear of reprisal from the Indians was ebbing, but there would always be a dark cloud over Sloan in the minds of many.

But if the man wasn't accepted here, where could he go? Into the western mountains? Itinerant traders brought pelts and salt to the valley—if he went southwest, he could trade in this way with the Cherokee. Or Sloan could follow the Indian pathways south to the Carolinas, and settle in an area far from the Shawnee.

A woman screamed.

John grabbed his rifle and leaped off the wagon. Was that Abigail?

"I'll be right there," Roy barked, slapping the reins against the rumps of the horses, urging them to speed.

Branches lashed John's face as he cut through the trees, his feet finding the fastest possible way home.

ABIGAIL OPENED the door to a familiar face. "Agnes—are you joining us for dinner?"

"Oh, I might bring a bit home, if ye've extra. I've got bread on the hearth, and I started a fire for laundry. Some shirts will need some extra boiling if I'm any judge." Crows' feet danced around her eyes.

"Can I come?" Susanna asked.

Ladling a generous portion of stew into a skillet, Agnes looked at Abigail, and she smiled her permission. "Of course you may."

Susanna grabbed her doll from the walnut cradle and bounded toward the door.

"I'll come and fill the laundry pot for ye," Lizzie offered, and Agnes nodded her thanks as she took Susanna's hand.

Laundry was backbreaking work. First building the fire, then hauling water to fill the pot, then bending over the hot soapy water and beating the clothes with a paddle. Rinsing and hanging the clothes to dry took more time and energy. "Lizzie, I'll join you later— I'll bring the hogshead for rinsing, along with as many of John's clothes as he will spare," Abigail said.

Lizzie paused in the doorway. "What about Mr. Sloan?" She placed her fingers over her nose, pantomiming a nasty smell.

Abigail smiled. "We'll see. I'll offer. It's a big laundry pot."

She closed the door after Lizzie, but when she crossed to the hearth she caught a glimpse of buckskin outside the window. The men were here.

Abigail returned to the door and opened it. Sloan stood, his back to her, near the chopping block, where the wood axe perched half-buried. John and Roy couldn't be far behind with the wagon.

Ale—she needed to open a cask. Fingering her necklace, she looked toward the barn. Perhaps Sloan could retrieve a cask from the barn for her.

"Get back!" Sloan shouted without glancing back, his voice startling in its intensity.

Before she could react, the man staggered and fell backward. Twenty paces beyond, an Indian stood next to a barren oak, bow raised, his dark figure seemingly carved from the tree itself.

She heard screaming and realized it was her own voice.

Silas Sloan lay on the ground with two arrows in his chest. Pools of crimson welled around the shafts—she needed her satchel, and quickly.

But her eyes were fixed helplessly on the Indian. He seemed familiar.

With deer-like swiftness he approached with the bow on his shoulder and a knife in his hand. Would she now die, as Janet had, at the hands of a savage?

Peace flooded her. Her heart thumped madly—how could she be peaceful and fearful at the same time? But inexplicably, she was.

Abigail stood frozen as he grabbed her necklace. Yes, it was the same man—the Indian she'd bandaged. He stared into her eyes for a heartbeat, and then lowered the knife and jerked at the pendant. It came off in his hand, and he loped away.

THERE—AN Indian—near the cabin. John raised his rifle and sighted along its length. But the copper-skinned man, naked from the waist up, was bounding away.

He had time for one shot. The range was too great for a musket, but Jake Deckard's rifle was accurate. He wouldn't miss this time.

John's hand slackened. He couldn't shoot a man in the back, not even an Indian.

He ran toward the cabin. "Abigail!" His throat thickened and choked off further speech.

Sloan lay prone near the chopping block. Abigail erupted from the cabin, herb satchel under her arm, cheeks pale.

"Abigail—"

"An Indian." She was on her knees next to Sloan.

John knelt on his other side. Was he still alive? Yes—his eyes were open and his lips jerked and trembled, as if trying to speak. Two arrows, Shawnee by the looks of them, protruded from his chest near one shoulder. Blood welled around each one, but that wouldn't kill the man. What mattered was how deep the damage went. "Shush, Sloan. Abigail can help ye." His eyes narrowed as he studied the arrows. They needed to come out. But if they did ...

"John, I need vinegar, and a bowl."

He jumped to retrieve the items, judging that his skinning knife was sharp enough for the task at hand. He'd never extracted an arrow himself, but the night Janet had died he'd watched as an arrow was excised from a man's leg. Sometimes the arrows were poisoned—but he couldn't think of that now.

How was it done? Sometimes, when the arrowhead plunged deep into the flesh, it was best to pull it out the other side. Abigail clipped away the man's shirt with her scissors and wiped the area clean with vinegar, the sour smell clashing with the metallic tang of blood and the acrid stench of the man's sweat. His stomach roiled.

No, the wound wasn't that deep—or rather, Sloan's chest was thick with muscle. In any case, behind the arrows the shoulder blade blocked the way. They would have to be extracted from above. "Abigail, I'll need to cut the arrowheads out." He drew out his knife and dipped it in the bowl of vinegar. He'd do it straightway.

"Sloan, this will hurt a wee bit, but I'll be quick about it."

The man met his gaze, his expression strangely peaceful. "I'll be leaving soon."

The chill of the air felt clean against John's cheek, and the bare branches of the oaks stood sentinel around the quiet clearing, calming him somehow. He blinked at Sloan's statement. "We'll speak of that later." He sliced quickly around the first arrow. Blood flooded up around his blade—a bad sign. Abigail wiped it away, but the bright red fluid kept bubbling up. He probed with the tip of his knife —not enough, he must go deeper.

Sloan's body jerked slightly as he cut again. There—he could feel it. John grabbed the arrowhead and yanked it out. The crimson of his blood gushed from the incision and flowed down the man's side to the leaves.

"No!" Abigail exclaimed as she sprinkled some kind of herb over the wound and then pressed on it with a wad of linen. The linen turned red. She grabbed more of the herb.

Sloan groaned.

"Here—I'll press while ye add the herb."

"I'll be leaving." Sloan's voice was weak. A small bubble of blood appeared at the corner of his mouth. "Thank you...for your kindness." He coughed, a mere gurgle.

John raised his knife to take out the second arrow. If anything it was deeper and lower down on the man's chest. The Shawnee had shot him at close range. He had to try. Blood welled around his blade as he pierced through skin and muscle.

Sloan jerked once as John wrestled out the second arrowhead. Abigail was silent, her bloody hands mounding dried green flakes over the oozing wound. Then John pressed linen over it with enough force to make the man grunt.

Sloan's eyelids fluttered shut. They were losing him.

Red continued to seep through every scrap of toweling. A brown leaf fluttered down, spiraling slowly, and finally landed next to John's knee. The breeze stilled.

Sloan opened his eyes. Looking past them, his face lit up in recognition, and his lips curved into a gentle smile. He took one more breath, and his body relaxed as if in sleep.

Silas Sloan was gone.

JOHN TOOK a deep breath of the cold air, lifting his face to the sun. For late December, it was a mild day—and an auspicious one for Roy and Lizzie, who'd just said their vows in the meetinghouse.

"Da, where is Ritchie's ma?" Susanna's form was draped in an old cloak of Janet's cut down to size, her hands enclosed in a rabbit-skin muff.

"They're still inside. They had to sign a paper."

"Is that how ye married Mother? Ye signed a paper?"

He nodded. "A verra important paper."

John led Susanna to the little cemetery behind the meetinghouse. The men had started building a low stone wall around the area; Mr. Craig had said nothing, but John knew it meant the congregation would never move to a more central location, much to the minister's chagrin.

"It's of no account," he'd said to Mr. Craig after one morning service. "Ye canna mind it. There are more important things to give yourself to than the question of a building."

"It's not the building, John Russell, and it never has been." The minster had lowered his voice. "I need ye as elder. I may not last, ye ken. They may pressure me out and I need someone I can trust to hold the fort, at least until another man is found."

John stared at the ground. "I'll pray on it."

Mr. Craig had smiled. "It's all I can ask."

John led Susanna to the wall and lifted her onto it, then sat next to her. He mused over the recent conversation—him, an elder?

Whatsoever thy hand findeth to do, do it with all thy might.

He'd wielded axe and adze and plane with all his might. He'd married a wife and grown to cherish her—duty first, then joy following, in everything the Lord had brought his way. He wasn't seeking a church office, but it had come to him. Who was he to refuse? And perhaps in the doing of it, he would find grace and strength and even joy.

Yes—he'd tell Mr. Craig yes.

A wren disputed with the winter, its piercing call comforting in its familiarity. Few birds were that vocal in cold weather.

In season, out of season.

A peace descended on his soul.

"Da, what's that next to Ma?" Susanna pointed at her mother's grave.

"Let's go look." He lifted her down.

Agnes had kept Susanna away from Sloan's body and the subsequent burial. John's shoulders seemed to ache with the memory of that long afternoon as he, Roy, and Arch had dug the grave. Mr. Craig had said a few words, and they had rejoiced that Sloan had found peace with God, but it was a private affair. In fact, Mrs. Preston would no doubt have something nasty to say about Sloan being buried here at all. Little had been said publicly.

"See that mound of dirt? That's where we buried Mr. Sloan. I told ye he died and went to heaven."

"Will he see Ma?"

"Well, to be absent from the body is to be present with the Lord. But other believers are there too, and I expect there's plenty of time to get acquainted."

"Mother's necklace!"

Something glinted on top of the fresh grave. Something small and blue. In two steps he'd closed the gap—yes, Abigail's necklace. But she'd said the Shawnee had taken it.

And yet here it was.

He straightened and turned about, studying the landscape carefully. He forced himself to relax. He doubted the Indian were still here, and unlikely that he meant further harm; he'd taken his revenge against Sloan but had spared Abigail. "Here, Susanna, ye take it and give it to her—she'll be that glad to have it."

"I suppose she dropped it."

John said nothing. They hadn't told her the whole story, just that Sloan had died. She hadn't seen much of the man in any case. He wasn't quite sure what to make of the return of the pendant—a peace offering?

That, and perhaps something more. Yes, he was sure of it now. The Indian was saying the blood debt was settled.

He heard voices and turned. Roy and Lizzie were leaving the meetinghouse, smiling and chattering away. Ritchie darted out the door and bounded over the grass toward Susanna. Abigail followed, wearing her Sabbath gown, pretty as a picture.

His feet closed the distance between them. "I've something for ye."

She looked up expectantly.

The necklace could wait. "This." He untied her straw hat and removed it, and his other hand snaked around her waist. Mr. Craig and his wife had emerged from the meetinghouse, but he didn't care.

John Russell kissed his wife.

EPILOGUE

There is as much in our Lord's pantry as will satisfy all his bairns, and as much wine in his cellar as will quench all their thirst.

—Samuel Rutherford, *Letters*, 1664

May 1745

Abigail shifted on the chair. She was uncomfortable, huge as a ship at the docks. And now her back ached. In fact, it had ached all night, come to think of it.

She picked up her quill. She'd been writing to Hannah all winter, a paragraph at a time, and now that wagons were traveling both north and east, she could send out her missives. The chair—Hannah would like to know about that.

"John fashioned a Lathe out of a broken Spinning Wheel. A Lathe spins a Piece of Wood rapidly so it can be trimmed and smoothed into a cylindrical Shape, such as the Leg of a Chair. He managed to build one Chair before Spring Plowing. He also has plans for a Sawmill. Not a Large one, as you may be thinking, but a small Device over a Stream."

She'd already written about Sloan, and Susanna's return. The dark-haired girl was happy and even mischievous.

"Over the Winter Susanna learned her Letters and part of the Shorter Catechism, which in Susanna's words, is not Short. We also began reading the Adventures of Robinson Crusoe, a Christian Man who is Shipwrecked. Susanna and Ritchie sometimes slip away to play Shipwreck, and she comes Home covered in Filth. John laughs to see her happy. I am glad that she accepts me. John says that I am the Reason she has become Cheerful. In any case, I am Glad."

On the other hand, maybe Susanna was happy because John was. His face lit up with joy now and again as he glanced at them in the fire lit evenings.

Abigail chewed on the end of the quill and shifted again. What had she done to strain her back? Perhaps it was the bucket of water she'd taken to Rosemary yesterday. The pony was due to foal any time now, and she had taken to checking on the animal during the day. Their cow had greeted them one morning with a wet new companion nuzzling her flank, and perhaps Rosemary would likewise have no trouble, but nevertheless, Abigail fussed over her.

She rubbed her back. Her letter to her parents had been cheerful, omitting any mention of Sloan. Rather, she'd described the building of the new courthouse. If her parents thought civilization was coming to the valley, they might worry less.

And she'd written a brief letter to her sister Mary. She'd sketched out her circumstances and summarized her spiritual journey. It was strange, now that she looked back on it, how simple the gospel seemed. Yet during the weeks of struggle and doubt it had appeared anything but. It was as if she'd been fighting to enter through a doorway that was already standing wide open.

John said the Bible was full of paradoxes like that.

Abigail set down the quill, restless. Perhaps if she walked around her back pain would ease. John didn't want her exerting herself, but she had to get up. She pushed open the door and breathed in the fresh odors of spring: freshly tilled earth and honeysuckle, overlaid with the warm scent of manure.

A giant band tightened around her belly. A gush of warm fluid followed, and Abigail stared down helplessly.

She stood frozen in the doorway, looking for John. Where was he? The lower field? She couldn't remember what he'd said he was doing today.

Well, she needed to wipe this up in any case. She reached for the towel they used for bathing. Every motion seemed awkward and incredibly difficult.

"Abigail?" Lizzie stood in the doorway. "What—"

"I need John—and Maggie McClure." The band tightened again.

Lizzie's mouth gaped open for a moment as she stared. "Aye, I see —here, ye set yourself down. Dinna fash now, I'll fetch the midwife."

John—she needed John. Each time her belly tightened, it hurt worse. Strangely, she wasn't afraid. Six weeks previously, John put the mule into harness to plow the ground for barley. The mule had flattened its ears and even bared its teeth, but at John's reprimand it had thrown its weight into the traces.

Like the mule, she wouldn't fight the heavy plow—she'd just bear with it. She took a slow breath and looked about.

The mess. She could at least finish cleaning while she waited. And there was a bucket here with enough water to clean the floor; well, not the whole floor, just this small area. She kneeled down.

Her stomach tightened again and she stared at the oak planking before her eyes. She remained on hands and knees, staring at the patterns in the wood. The tension eased and she wiped the floor. Then the pain returned. Slowly she made progress.

After what seemed like an interminable length of time, the door creaked.

"Abigail! What are ye doing on the floor?" John's arms were around her.

"I was...cleaning." The pain returned.

"Your skirt...it's wet."

Clearly Lizzie had dashed off to find Maggie first. "Lizzie went... for the midwife."

"I see."

He helped her onto the bed and Abigail remembered her mother's voice, telling her that John would know what to do. Yes, he knew what this was.

The room seemed to fade each time the pain returned. John had put something at the head of the bed for her to lean against, and now he was putting a cup in her hand.

"Just a wee bit of cider," he said.

She took a few sips and thrust it back. "Oh!" She exclaimed, as a surprisingly hard pain took her. Mrs. Robinson's travail came to mind, and for the first time, fear edged her cloudy thoughts. "John, read to me."

He moved away but soon returned to her side with his Bible.

Where was Maggie? How could she bear with this any longer? *Help, Lord.*

"Fear thou not; for I am with thee: be not dismayed; for I am thy God," John read.

Fear thou not ... for I am with thee.

Abigail held on to the words for dear life. The baby was coming.

"Susanna, let's stop by the stream and look for rocks on the way back." John took his daughter's hand. He wanted to get back to his wife but wondered how Susanna would react to the new baby. Thankfully Maggie McClure had arrived at the cabin before the babe. When Abigail had told him to put water on to heat, he'd become alarmed. Then the midwife had arrived, shooed him out the door, and twenty minutes later he'd heard a mewling cry.

As they stepped along the path joining the Mays' cabin to their own, John scanned the trees for danger; he didn't expect the Shawnee back, but even so, it was habit, a habit he wasn't going to relinquish.

The foliage was joyful with the lighter hues of new growth variegated with the darker greens of older leaves. Susanna skipped playfully, dislodging old leaves along the way. They stepped off the path to the stream.

The water slipped and flashed and gurgled between banks of mossy stone and mud, flanked by fresh reeds and tiny flowers. Abigail would know some of the names of the plants, he suspected, but all he knew was that they signaled springtime and new life.

"I found one!" In her excitement, Susanna had stepped into the stream, moccasins and all. She scooped up her prize and showed it to him. A green stone, smoothed by the water, but still generally angular in its shape, shone in his daughter's palm.

"That's a wonderful prize!"

"It's for the baby."

John smiled. "Aye, well. I'll have to carve it a wee box."

"Or a locket—or a necklace, like Mother's."

"If it's a girl."

"But Da, why won't ye tell me?"

"Come, lass, and see for yourself."

They found the path and walked to the cabin, Susanna's legs churning rapidly in her haste. John opened the door.

Maggie McClure sat on a stool near the bed but quickly moved aside as she saw them enter.

Abigail's face still looked pale, but she was smiling. In her arms she held a bundle. "Come meet your baby brother, Susanna."

Susanna's jaw dropped.

John led her to the bedside. "His name is Jonathan."

"Jonathan?" She tilted her head to peer at the newborn's face. "He's so *small!*"

John chuckled. "Ye may call him Jonnie then. And boys love rocks."

"I love rocks too," Abigail said. "Blue ones especially." Eyes on him, she felt for her pendant.

Susanna frowned. "Da, dinna cry. All is well."

"Oh, I ken that." He fought for control of his voice. "I ken that well."

Thank you for reading *The Shenandoah Road*. If you enjoyed it, please post a review—reviews are a writer's lifeblood. And share with your friends! To contact me or check out other titles, see my website.

For an excerpt from the sequel, *The Heart of Courage*, keep turning!

What's Real?

Whenever I read historical fiction, I often wonder what is real and what is made up. In my case, I did take a bit of a liberty with the actual route my characters took. I think it would have been shorter to go through (present-day) Gettysburg than to send them where I did, but it seemed like a nice idea to visit the folks in Middle Spring—and Falling Spring, the villain's home. The Great Wagon Road had a couple of side paths, so they could have gone the way they did.

The buffalo? Yes, they really did roam as far east as the Shenandoah, but not for much longer. Some types of trees disappeared as well: there are no more long leaf pines in the area. There are a few old gemstone mines in the region; we might think of an amethyst as a second-rate stone today, but in the 18th century it was very valuable.

As for their speech, I can't say that Abigail's is authentic. I wrote for modern readers and didn't stress overprecision. However, the New England accent, referred to in the book, has its origin in the area of England from which many of the original immigrants came. The famous Boston accent is very old!

It is a mystery as to how the Scots from Ulster (the "Scots-Irish") spoke, but there are clues. They would have lost their Gaelic by this time (Lowlanders in Scotland weren't speaking it either), but they undoubtedly spoke a version of English called "Scots," packed with unique idioms. I included some of these in the dialogue. Words such as "malarkey" and "smidgen" are Scots and endure today as part of American rural slang.

Here's a glossary of the terms I used, either Scots (s) or Scots Gaelic (g):

Bridie (s): a small meat pie

Caraid (g): kinsman or friend

Ceilidh (g): a social event, usually involving music and dance

Clot heid (s): idiot

Collieshangie (s): squabble

Come ben (s): literally "come in the kitchen," it is a term of welcome

Gey (s): considerable, a lot

Kerfluffle (s): commotion

Maun (s): must

Wheesht (s): shush, be quiet

Who's Real?

My fictional characters all have surnames (and given names) that are appropriate for the time period and the region or background (Scots-Irish vs. New Englander). But many of the characters are real people, and this led to one rather strange conversation between John Russell (fictional) and John Craig (real) about the latter's wife. It was only after I'd created the character John Russell that I discovered that Isabella Craig was a Russell! Well, of course John didn't know of a connection (an easy solution). One problem I did have with this real/pretend interface was creating a persona for the real characters. I put words in the mouths of historical people, and I was as careful as I could be to be true to the historical record. Apologies in advance if I made your ancestor look bad!

Here's a list of the historical characters, either mentioned or brought to life:

James Logan: Philadelphia statesman with a huge library.

Jonathan Edwards: Pastor of a congregation in Northampton, Connecticut, he is well known today for his theological writings, sermons, and analysis of phenomena occurring at the time of the Great Awakening.

Gilbert Tennent: Presbyterian pastor who supported the Great Awakening, which divided Presbyterians; Tennent labored to heal the breaches. His father William began a school to train ministers called the "Log College."

Benjamin Franklin: Philadelphia printer and inventor acquainted with George Whitefield.

David Hall: a business connection of Franklin's from London.

George Whitefield: a young Anglican minister close to John and Charles Wesley who preached in the fields when denied access to a pulpit. Unlike the Wesleys, he made numerous preaching trips to the colonies. These men are regarded as the founders of the Methodist denomination.

Mr. Gutens: There really was a goldsmith by that name but I don't know more.

Thomas Fitzwater: Owner of a quarry, an ancestor of mine.

John and Margaret Houston: Sam Houston's great-grandparents. They may never have lived in Lancaster, but it is certain that they moved to the Shenandoah Valley by 1745. Unlike many of the immigrants from Ulster, they were prosperous and arrived in the colonies with a good amount of gold.

Jacob Deckard: Famous for his long rifle, also known as the "Pennsylvania long rifle." Later editions, carried into Kentucky, were known as the "Kentucky long rifle."

James Magraw: Early settler in the present-day Shippensburg area.

Evan Watkins: Owner of Watkins' ferry on the Potomac.

John Blair: Pastor at the Middle Spring meetinghouse.

John and Isabella Craig: Alternated his time between two congregations until the one at Tinkling Spring kicked him out. He owned land near Lewis's but I moved him for the purpose of the story.

James Patton: Sea captain, land agent, and businessman, Patton was known as a man who could get things done. He was also known as a rogue by those who did business with him.

Elizabeth Patton Preston: James Patton's sister and wife of John Preston. There seems to have been a feud between John Craig and this family, mainly about the location of the Tinkling Spring meetinghouse, which ended up on the Prestons' land. Craig vowed never to taste the water of the spring. One wonders why, and I had to fill in the gaps for the purposes of the story.

John Lewis: First settler in the Augusta County area. Built a palisade in the present location of Staunton, Virginia.

Magdalena (Woods) McDowell Borden: Eventually this remarkable woman would marry a third time after Benjamin Borden died. She was known for beauty, intelligence, and wit, as well as a black stallion and a green cloak. She was the granddaughter of the Earl of Argyll, Laird of the Campbells, so I guessed that her famous green cloak was the blue-and-green Campbell tartan. Green was an ordinary color in those days and wouldn't have been notable.

The Bashams: a real family in the Virginia piedmont (my ancestors), who, according to oral family history, descended from an Edinburgh cabinetmaker.

Peter Jefferson: Surveyor who lived in the piedmont region, not far from where his son Thomas would build Monticello.

ACKNOWLEDGMENTS

Many thanks to my beta-readers and others who gave me feedback along the way: Gail Kittleson, Tisha Martin, John ("Jack") Cunningham—no relation to the valley Cunninghams, so far as we can tell—Cathryn Swallia, my horse expert, who has the scars to prove it, and the members of my ACFW Scribes group, especially Laura Hilton and Linda Strawn. All of these writers have helped me in various ways to learn the craft.

Special thanks to David Jack, expert on Scots English, translator of several of George MacDonald's stories. Who knew there was a difference between no and nae?

Kudos to Douglas Bond for writing excellent Christian historical fiction, showing me that it could be done. He also looked at some chapters and gave me helpful suggestions.

Thanks to Jodi White, for taking the time to give her input, and for all the members of Community Baptist Church for their support of my writing and enthusiasm when each book appears.

But mostly I thank my husband, Geary, who has been a supporter of my writing from the get-go. Writing takes a great deal of effort over the long haul, and I needed to know this was truly something I should be doing.

Grace to you, and peace, from sunny South Texas.

Soli deo gloria.

Red Hawk crouched under the shelter of a tall oak and studied the ground. The damp leaf litter was disturbed. He lifted himself slowly, breathing deeply, trying to get a sense of wind direction, which sometimes changed at a moment's notice on the higher slopes.

The breeze brushed his cheek like a kiss. *Good.* The buck he followed couldn't smell him. Just yesterday he'd scrubbed himself in the stream to make doubly sure; he had no clue how white men managed to hunt. Everyone said they smelled like skunks.

Red Hawk followed the trail up the slope where oak and maple gave way to pine and hemlock. Ahead he glimpsed a break in the trees near the top of the ridge. Had the animal descended into the next valley?

Sweat trickled down his neck. Yesterday's rain had done little to cut the summer heat, but at least the ground was damp, and he might find more sign.

There. The beautiful double print of a deer in a muddy spot. A good-sized buck, by the size of the depression, and the animal was moving slowly.

Heart quickening, he grasped his bow and removed two arrows from his quiver. The smell of juniper and cedar sharpened his mind as he skirted the clearing and negotiated a rocky outcrop.

The damp ground past the rocks revealed a partial print. Yes, he was on the right path. The buck was descending now, probably looking for the lush foraging available downslope.

He paused and scanned the landscape. The trees, the soil, even the rocks called to him, sang their own song, echoes from the hand of the Creator Himself. Red Hawk loved hunting, even though in the instant when the deer gave its life, its liquid eye dulling in death, he felt remorse and pain. His prayer to the spirit of the animal was always earnest. Laughing Wolf merely mumbled the words when he brought down a deer. Laughing Wolf seemed to enjoy killing for its own sake.

Something moved. Red Hawk tightened his grip on his bow and took a cautious step forward. The breeze had turned, but not enough to betray him.

A black-tipped ear flipped forward, then back, and a great rack of antlers appeared in the midst of the foliage ahead.

There wasn't much cover, just a single red spruce to his left. A laurel thicket rolled away to his right. Head low, he chose his steps carefully as he approached the thicket, his moccasins pressing soundlessly into the moist ground.

Suddenly the buck stiffened, his head in the air. Red Hawk drew and released two arrows, one after another, but even as they left his bow, he knew he'd missed. The deer's flashing rump disappeared up the slope to his left.

The animal hadn't fled from him. He'd made no sound. Had something else alarmed it? He stilled and took a slow breath. The birds began to chirp again, no longer threatened by his presence. Perhaps there was a bear nearby.

He flexed his hand around the bow, loving the feel of the smooth ash; his new weapon had enough draw strength to take down a bear, Father said. He ached for the chance. Would today be the day?

Red Hawk stepped around the thicket and made his way cautiously downslope. The smell of fire stopped him. Peering out from behind a chestnut tree, he saw the thin wisps of smoke above the foliage. There were men in the valley. But who? Shawnee or white men? He didn't know of any from his own village who had come this way today, but you never knew. Could be a trader.

Or not. Stomach prickling, he circled the tree and looked for a place where he might observe in secret. The elders would want to know about white men.

The thick green foliage to his right suggested a stream. He wriggled into the lush wet stillness, stepping on ferns and slick beds of moss until he found the soft narrow trickle at its heart. Hidden from view, he descended until he heard voices and the clank of a metal object. He left the tiny channel and took refuge behind a large beech. Were there dogs? He slid around the tree.

A mule and three horses drank from the stream below. A kettle perched above a campfire. A large silver-bearded man entered Red Hawk's field of view and attended the fire. Red Hawk sidestepped to a place behind a hawthorn patch and found a better view.

There didn't seem to be any dogs. He heard voices again, and now he could see the speakers. Nearest him stood a young man with hair the color of the sun; he held an object with one hand, and with the other he grasped a tiny stick. A vague sense of familiarity brushed Red Hawk's mind as he watched the man turn a leaf-like part of the object. A trader might have the sticks and leaves; perhaps that's where he'd seen them before. Then Hair-Like-The-Sun put the leaves in his bag and motioned to the other men. Silver Beard, a massive man, stood watching as the others busied themselves.

One of the horses, a fine chestnut with a wide blaze, raised its head. Red Hawk shrank within himself. Horses could smell. Then it turned slightly and dipped its head again. He exhaled.

A rope clanked as two men struggled to draw it out.

Chains. So these were the chains he'd heard his father mention. He settled himself to watch and listen.